TARGET AMERICA

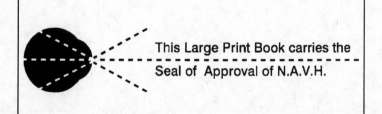

This Large Print Book carries the
Seal of Approval of N.A.V.H.

A SNIPER ELITE NOVEL

TARGET AMERICA

SCOTT MCEWEN
WITH THOMAS KOLONIAR

THORNDIKE PRESS
A part of Gale, Cengage Learning

GALE
CENGAGE Learning·

Farmington Hills, Mich • San Francisco • New York • Waterville, Maine
Meriden, Conn • Mason, Ohio • Chicago

GALE
CENGAGE Learning®

LIBRARY OF CONGRESS CATALOGING-IN-PUBLICATION DATA

McEwen, Scott.
    Target America : a Sniper Elite novel / by Scott McEwen with Thomas Koloniar. — Large print edition.
        pages ; cm. — (Thorndike Press large print thriller)
    ISBN 978-1-4104-7259-5 (hardcover) — ISBN 1-4104-7259-0 (hardcover)
    1. Snipers— Fiction. 2. United States. Navy. SEALs— Fiction. 3. Undercover operations— Fiction. 4. Terrorism— Prevention— Fiction. 5. Large type books. I. Koloniar, Thomas. II. Title.
PS3613.M4355T37 2014b
813'.6— dc23   2014026579

Published in 2014 by arrangement with Touchstone, a division of Simon & Schuster, Inc.

Printed in Mexico
1 2 3 4 5 6 7 18 17 16 15 14

This book is dedicated to the warriors of the SEAL Teams that are always in the fight, even when dealt serious injuries and overwhelming odds. The fictional accounts are based on actual Black Ops missions.

— *Scott McEwen*

This book is dedicated to the memory of Tyrone Snowden (Ty) Woods and Glen Anthony Doherty. Former Navy SEALs killed in Benghazi, Libya, on September 12, 2012. In the proud and storied tradition of the Navy SEALs they took the fight to an overwhelming number of the enemy in order to save dozens of American lives. They did not have to go, they went anyway. We will not forget your heroic acts, gentlemen, nor will we let others.

Bravo Zulu!

— *Scott McEwen*

PROLOGUE

US NAVAL STATION GUANTANAMO BAY
It was mid-June, and it was hot. Naeem Wardak could not remember ever having been so hot, nor could he remember ever having been more miserable. He was a prisoner of war in the detention camp at Guantanamo Bay, where he had been held since his capture in the Waigal Valley of Afghanistan the previous fall. He had been charged as a war criminal for the rape of an American female POW, and since his capture at the hands of SEAL Team VI, he'd been interrogated dozens of times by the CIA, grilled extensively on his knowledge of Taliban activities in Afghanistan and elsewhere in the Middle East.

Not being nearly as tough as he'd believed himself to be, Naeem had broken early in the softening-up process, unable to bear the strain of sleep deprivation and constant dehydration. Giving up hope of ever being found worthy in the eyes of Allah, he told the CIA men all they wanted to know, pathetically grateful for every hour of sleep he was permitted in exchange for the truth, for every cold bottle of orange soda, every meager meal. Toward the end, even the smallest of mercies had made him weep like a child in gratitude. Only after the interrogations ceased for good did his shame at last begin to catch up to him. Ultimately, he lost the will even to pray for forgiveness, certain that Allah had turned his back on him. And why shouldn't he turn his back? Naeem had failed in every aspect of the jihad.

With the blistering sun at its apex, he sat on his haunches, sagging back against the chain-link fence of his six-by-six outdoor "recreation" pen, watching the Chechen prisoner lie on his back in the rec pen across from his. The Chechen was a young Caucasian man from the Caucasus Mountains, where he'd been raised a Salafi Muslim to join the RSMB (Riyad us-Saliheyn Martyrs' Brigade) at the age of twenty. The Salafi movement was virtually one and the same as the Wahhabi movement, of which Naeem was a member, and under either name, it was a highly puritanical belief system that proposed violent jihad against anyone outside of Islam.

Neither prisoner much liked or trusted the other, but they were both bored beyond belief, and since both happened to speak the North Mesopotamian Arabic dialect, they often passed the outdoor rec hours with meaningless small talk.

Alik Zakayev, the Chechen, turned his head with a smirk at Naeem. "Eh, have you heard the news?"

Naeem scratched at his thick black beard. "What news?" he replied sullenly.

"That American lawyer secured my release."

Naeem wished he could kick the Chechen in the face, knowing that he himself would undoubtedly rot in American captivity unless he found the courage to take matters into his own hands. "And how did he do that?"

"There's no proof I had anything to do with those bombings in Boston," Zakayev said. "The pig Russians falsely accused me and turned me over to the CIA because of my ties to the RSMB." He turned his head away again, draping an arm over his eyes to shield them from the sun and slipping his other hand into his orange trousers to scratch his crotch. "The Russians are pigs. I'm lucky the Americans have softer laws."

Naeem eyed him balefully. "When do you leave?"

Zakayev took a moment to smell his fingers, and then scratched at his belly. "The lawyer said four or five days."

"Where will you go?"

"Wherever they take me . . . probably back to Chechnya."

Naeem's misery seemed to have no limit. Every time a prisoner was released, it was like another wall was thrown up around him. "And what will you do then? Return to the coal mines?"

"Never to the fucking mines." Zakayev sat up against the fence, pulling his knees to his chest and wrapping his arms around them. "But it's true, I'm a dead man in Chechnya. I will have to leave there as soon as I arrive, or the pig Russians will have me done in."

"Then where will you go?"

Zakayev darkened, his blue eyes narrowing. "Why do you want to know these things, eh? So you can whisper them to your CIA friends?"

Naeem knew that Zakayev and the other prisoners distrusted him for having broken so easily, but he no longer possessed the energy even to feel ashamed. Instead, he shifted his gaze far beyond Zakayev's pen to

12

stare out over the sterile expanse of the base. It was now or never. Somewhere out there was a world beyond this living hell, a world he might get to see again if his courage held. He slipped a small, jagged piece of steel from the waistband of his trousers. It wasn't much larger than a half-dollar coin, but it was big enough for the job he had in mind. He'd found it in the corner of his rec pen three days before, after an earthmover had been used to demolish a nearby guard shack earlier that same day. The broken piece of metal had popped off a steel truss and dropped into the rec area unnoticed.

He had since taken time to file the jagged point to a needle-like sharpness against the floor of his cell during the night. Now he sat thumbing the point in silence while Zakayev watched. The nearest Marine sentry stood some fifty feet away in the shade of an outbuilding, with his carbine slung.

"What are you going to do with that?" the Chechen asked, not yet grasping that Naeem was looking to take his own life.

Naeem ignored him, putting the point against the side of his neck and drawing a deep breath.

"Do it!" Zakayev hissed, his eyes dancing

as he glanced furtively at the Marine. "He's not watching!"

Naeem pressed the point deep into the flesh over his carotid artery and jerked it across. A bright red spurt of blood arced from his neck, followed by another and another.

"Yes!" Zakayev hissed triumphantly, slapping his leg. "Yes!"

Naeem stood up and began to run in place, the blood spurting with more force.

The Marine glanced their way, but at first he didn't react to what he thought was just an exercising prisoner. A few moments later, he realized there was blood spurting from the prisoner's neck and shouted for a corpsman as he sprinted toward the rec pen.

Naeem grew dizzy and collapsed to the floor of the pen. His head thudded on the concrete, and he lay staring up at the bright sun, feeling it burning his retinas until all the world was blackness.

1

Alik Zakayev's palms would not stop sweating no matter how often he wiped them on his jeans. Being belowground again was putting him on edge. It reminded him of the Taldinsky coal mine in Siberia, where he had barely survived a cave-in ten years earlier, spending four days buried alive with six other men before rescue workers finally dug them out, all of them raving, half out of their minds with delirium and dehydration. He still had nightmares about it.

The smuggling tunnel he was in ran one hundred feet beneath the US-Mexico border between New Mexico and Chihuahua State. It was over three thousand feet long, six feet high, and five feet wide, complete with a concrete floor, incandescent lighting, ventilation ducts, and a drainage system to pump out any gathering groundwater. Of

15

the fifty-five migrant workers pressed into service by the deadly Castañeda cartel to work belowground for weeks on end, eleven of them had died during the five-month construction, and the rest were murdered upon completion to ensure its secrecy. The passage had been in service for almost fifteen months now, and so far more than one million pounds of marijuana had been smuggled through it into the United States.

The tunnel was accessed on the Mexican side of the border from inside an industrial warehouse, but its genius lay in the exit point on the American side: it opened up into the space of an exposed corral where cattle were regularly loaded onto semi–tractor trailers for transport to a processing plant sixty miles to the north. On loading days, special trailers with trap doors in their bottoms would park over the tunnel's opening, and the fifty-pound bales of marijuana would be loaded from below into modified forward compartments while the cattle embarked at the rear. After the cattle were off-loaded at the plant some ninety minutes later, the marijuana would be dispersed into waiting employee vehicles.

Zakayev had been all too correct about being a marked man in his home country. Upon his release from Guantanamo Bay, he'd flown on a direct route to the capital city of Grozny in the Chechen Republic. Chechen officials took him briefly into custody for routine questioning. After his release, he went immediately to his brother's house, where he learned that a black van had been parked across the street the entire night before with the engine running. This confirmed the worst. His next contact was with the Riyad us-Saliheyn Martyrs' Brigade, which took him under its protection that same evening. Within a week, he was spirited out of Chechnya to Germany. There he received an intrepid assignment. Three weeks later, he arrived in Mexico posing as a tourist on a German passport obtained in Bad Tölz from a master Chechen forger working as a printer in the state of Bavaria.

Zakayev's American attorney had been correct to assert that Zakayev was not involved in the Boston bombings. He had never even heard of the Tsarnaev brothers before their faces were plastered all over the television. However, this did not mean he wasn't part of the jihad, and no one knew this better than the Russian SVR (foreign intelligence service). Six months after the Boston attacks in April 2013, Russian police had snagged Zakayev in Moscow, where he'd been in the midst of pulling reconnaissance for a planned attack on the city's subway system.

Though the SVR had been unable to produce any actual evidence against him, it knew that he was a member of the RSMB, and so the agency concluded rapidly Zakayev could not have arrived in Moscow with any good intentions. Within forty-eight hours, they had revoked his visa, trumped up an ambiguous story about an alleged relationship with the Tsarnaev brothers, and promptly turned him over to the CIA as a gesture of interservice cooperation. Zakayev's subsequent five-month stint in Guantanamo Bay had not only steeled his resolve to continue with the jihad but also served to switch the focal point of his disdain from the Russian Federation to the United States.

Now he was deep below the border between Mexico and the US, only weeks away from striking the single greatest blow against Western democracy the world had ever seen. *In sha Allah!* God willing! It was a good time to be a Muslim, a proud time, a proud time to be a part of the jihad. Where Osama bin Laden had broken a cricket bat across the shins of the pig Uncle Sam, Zakayev and his RSMB compatriots were poised to bring him right to his knees, and the Western world would never again be the same.

The Riyad us-Saliheyn Martyrs' Brigade had been established in 1999 by a Chechen terrorist named Shamil Basayev, and though the brigade had briefly faded after his death in 2006, it suddenly reappeared in 2010, carrying out a series of suicide bombings in the Caucasus. By 2013, the RSMB had shifted much of its focus from Russia to the West in order to garner financial support from its Al Qaeda allies.

Zakayev was the only Salafi in the tunnel tonight; the only Chechen. There were five Mexican Castañeda cartel members with him helping to move a seventy-five-pound bomb through the tunnel on a four-wheeled dolly cart. The Castañedas were blissfully unaware of what type of bomb they were helping to move, assuming that it was a conventional bomb similar to those used in the Boston attacks. They had no idea that it was a stolen Russian RA-115 "suitcase" nuke with a two-kiloton yield. If they had known this, they would have quickly killed the Chechen and taken the device for themselves, regardless of the money that Zakayev's people had paid them for their help.

One of the Castañedas spoke English. His

name was Javier, and he had been working the tunnel since its completion. "We are exactly under the border now," he said, "a little more than halfway across."

"Good," Zakayev said pensively, increasingly eager to be out of the dimly lit tomb.

Javier's four helpers swore at the dolly as they wrestled to keep it rolling along. The awkward contraption did not have proper rubber wheels, and the large metal casters seemed to lock up every few feet, stymied by the tiny pebbles that fell constantly from the tunnel walls.

Javier kicked the corner of the dolly to get it rolling again and grinned at Zakayev. "Do you know the other Chechen we took across last week?"

Zakayev took his eyes from the bomb and stared at Javier in the shadowy light of the tunnel. "What other Chechen?"

The Mexican pointed at Zakayev's face. "A blue-eye like you. He arrived with a green case like this one. We had a better cart last week with better wheels, but someone up above took it away." He shrugged. "Who knows why? In Mexico, things come up missing all the time."

"Did this other man give a name?" Zakayev asked.

Javier wiped a bead of sweat from his

brow. "No, he didn't speak much at all. He was very serious all the time. A man of about fifty."

Zakayev knew at once who this other man had to be. "Kashkin," he muttered, scratching his groin, where a nagging fungal infection continued to plague him. The fact he had not been informed that Kashkin had already crossed into the US with the other RA-115 — both weapons purchased from a retired KGB agent — did not surprise him. Kashkin was a consummate loner and professional, and now that Zakayev knew he was involved, he realized that this entire mission was probably the old man's brainchild.

The tunnel lights dimmed and went out, throwing the passage into pitch blackness for three long seconds before they came back on again.

"Is that normal?" Zakayev asked, feeling a cold sweat break out across his back.

All five Castañedas stood watching warily up and down the tunnel.

"No," Javier said, whispering orders to his men in Spanish: *"Armas arriba!"* "Guns up!"

The four men quickly unshouldered their AK-47s, two of them facing northward, two facing back the way they'd come.

"What is it?" Zakayev whispered. "Why

did the lights go out?"

"I don't know." Javier drew a pistol from the holster on his hip and stood chewing the inside of his cheek, his obsidian eyes showing like black glass as he stared ahead up the tunnel. "It could be *gringos* to the north, *federales* to the south — or both — or nothing at all. We have to wait and see."

Zakayev got to his knees beside the bomb, threw back the tarp, and unlocked the lid on the footlocker-sized green aluminum box, pulling out a trigger mechanism attached to the RA-115 by what looked like an old-fashioned telephone cord. He flipped a switch on the side of the mechanism and depressed the trigger grip with all four fingers, holding it like a pistol against his leg. The green light on the side of the mechanism beeped once and then turned to red.

Seeing this, the four men with AK-47s bridled uneasily, jabbering away at Javier in hushed Spanish.

"What is that?" Javier asked, his eyes even more wary.

"A dead-man switch," Zakayev replied. "If I am killed, the bomb will detonate."

"Turn it off!" Javier ordered at once.

"No," the Chechen said quietly, locking eyes with the Mexican, his gaze set, ignoring the four AK-47s now trained on him from just a few feet away. "I will not be taken alive, and this bomb will not be captured. So for now, it's as you say — we have to wait and see. If this is nothing, I will deactivate the switch, and we will continue the operation."

But Zakayev knew it was not nothing, and he began to pray silently to Allah, his ears tuned to the gathering silence.

2

NEW MEXICO,
South of Deming, on the Border

Dressed in their assault gear, Federal Agent Christopher Hitch and a dozen other ICE agents (US Immigration and Customs Enforcement) stood in the dark over the tunnel on the US side of the border. Twelve men had been all that Hitch could muster on short notice after a Mexican informant had tipped him off about the tunnel, saying that a special shipment of some kind was coming across at midnight. He would have preferred double the manpower, but the limited window had given him less than an hour to put together a tactical crew. The local sheriff had arrived with a couple of young deputies, but local law enforcement wasn't good for much more than securing the scene.

The sheriff hitched his trousers up over his ample belly and stood with the heel of his hand resting on the pearl-handled butt of his revolver. "I advise you to wait, Agent Hicks."

"The name's *Hitch*."

"My mistake." The sheriff spat a gooey wad of tobacco juice onto the ground. "My advice is to get the authorities across the border in Chihuahua to secure the other end of this poop shoot before you fellas even think about goin' down there. My daddy was a tunnel rat in Cu Chi back in '68. He told some pretty gory tales about what can happen to a man down there in the dirty dark."

Hitch was unimpressed. "Yeah, well, this isn't Vietnam, Sheriff, and I'm not giving the Mexican police a chance to warn these guys." He turned to his men. "Lock and load. I'll be the first man down." He primed his MP5 and switched on the flashlight mounted within the fore stock.

"Now, let's think about this a minute," the sheriff cautioned. "You people don't even have night vision, for Jesus's sake! Why don't we just hide out up here and wait 'til the buggers come up? My God, man, you people could be walkin' into an ambush down there!"

Hitch was beginning to wonder if the sheriff might be on Antonio Castañeda's payroll. There were rumors the drug lord had made him a lucrative offer through an intermediary. "I'll be counting on you to look after things up here, Sheriff. You can handle that much, I assume?"

The sheriff nodded. "Oh, we can handle it, but if you men get into trouble down there, you're on your own, and I mean it. My boys aren't trained for this kinda thing, and I'm too damn fat to be dangling myself over a bottomless pit in the middle of the night."

"No one's asking you to do anything above your pay grade, Sheriff."

Nettled, the sheriff turned to his deputies, shaking his head and gesturing. "Let's stand over here outta the way, men. We don't wanna knock nobody down the mine shaft."

Hitch mounted the ladder, descending with the other ICE agents lining up to follow after him. "Keep six feet between each man."

Standing well back from the mouth of the shaft, one of the sheriff's deputies shifted his weight uncomfortably. "How deep would you say that thing is, Sheriff?"

"Gotta be a hundred feet or more," the sheriff said. "I aimed my Streamlight straight down and couldn't hardly see the bottom."

The deputy let out a low whistle. "You wouldn't get me down there, not unless you dropped a grenade down it first."

The sheriff frowned. "That would kindly spoil the surprise there, Jeff."

The second deputy stood biting his thumbnail, looking around nervously. He'd been on the Castañeda payroll for the better part of eight months now, and he was more than a little worried that the tunnel's discovery could lead to him being ratted out by any captured Mexicans. "Um, Sheriff, do you care if I smoke?"

"No, Landry," the sheriff said sardonically. "Why don't ya build yourself a nice big bonfire yonder; let every drug smuggler in Mexico know we're out here. Hey, you wanna use the flare gun in my trunk — or do ya think that might be a little obvious?"

Landry cringed, realizing the sheriff must already be suspicious of him. "I asked first, didn't I?"

"That, ya did, son. That, ya did."

Agent Hitch was mindful of his footing as he descended the ladder, but the rungs were slippery against the hard rubber of his Vibram boot soles. Twice his foot slipped off, forcing him to grab onto the rung with the crook of his arm. The bulk of his gear made the going awkward, and he hoped the men

27

above were having less trouble. Anyone who fell would take every man below him all the way to the bottom.

After what felt like an eternity, he saw a dim light below, and his heart began to race. If the lights were on down there, someone was using the tunnel. He whispered up a warning about the light and continued down. Hitch arrived at the bottom a minute later and stepped from the ladder onto terra firma: a concrete landing with space enough to stack large quantities of product off to the side. A pile of nylon straps and cargo hooks told him that the smugglers were using a winch to pull the drugs to the surface.

Looking south, the tunnel curved slightly to the east, reducing visibility to about eighty feet. An incandescent lightbulb burned every twenty feet or so, screwed into sockets attached to a long wire that must have been strung the length of the passage. Within two minutes, the rest of the ICE agents were on the ground and gathered tightly together at the foot of the ladder.

One of the men bumped into a shoddy fuse panel on the wall, and sparks flew, throwing the tunnel into blackness. A few seconds later, the lights came back on by themselves.

"What the fuck did you do?" Hitch hissed.

"Nothing," the agent answered. "I barely touched the damn thing. There's no room to move down here."

Hitch knew they might have just screwed the pooch, but there was nothing to do now but press on. "Okay . . . shit." He gripped the MP5. "I've got point. Gutierrez, you're on my six. Be ready to give orders in Spanish when we run into these people. No one fires unless we're fired upon. Look sharp now! Let's go."

They moved out single file down the tunnel.

Up above, the sheriff was leaning against the fender of his cruiser with his arms folded when a semi–tractor trailer came rumbling down the dirt road, gearing down and slowing near the entrance to the property. He stood up straight. "I'd say this is an odd hour for a cattle hauler to show up." He spit another wad of tobacco juice. "Particularly when there ain't no cattle here to haul."

Deputy Landry recognized the yellow rig at once, knowing the driver to be one of Castañeda's men. "I'll see what he's up to." He set off at a fast trot.

"Hey, wait here!" the sheriff called, un-snapping the strap on his holster.

But Landry kept going.

The sheriff looked at Jeff. "Remind me to hunt us up a replacement for his stupid ass. That boy's dumber'n shit."

Jeff grunted, knowing that Landry was on the take, but not wanting to be the one to tell.

Seventy yards away, Landry was waving his arms to stop the rig as it pulled in. He jogged around to the driver's side, recognizing the driver and grabbing the handhold to haul himself up onto the running board. "You gotta get the hell outta here, amigo. ICE is down there in the tunnel right now! Somebody called the feds and ratted the whole thing out."

The Castañeda man looked around wildly. Spotting the cruisers and ICE vehicles parked on the far side of the corral for the first time, he grabbed a Tec-9 machine pistol from his lap and sprayed Landry point-blank with a twelve-round burst of 9 mm fire.

Landry flew off the running board, landing flat on his back with his neck and face blown apart. The Castañeda jammed the rig into gear and floored the accelerator, aiming for the cruiser where the sheriff and Deputy Jeff stood gaping.

"Holy Christ!" The sheriff jerked a .357

from its holster, emptying all six rounds at the oncoming tractor trailer. Four of the bullets struck the windshield on the driver's side, but the rig kept coming.

Jeff drew his 9 mm Beretta and stood firing at the grill of the truck, while the sheriff skirted to the other side of the cruiser, dumping the empty shells from the cylinder as he moved. Jeff jumped aside as the rig zoomed between them and plowed into the cruiser, bashing it easily aside to roar on toward the ICE vehicles.

The sheriff snatched a speed loader from his belt to reload the .357 with six Federal hollow-points, running after the rig as fast as his squat little legs could carry him.

Jeff chased along after the cab on the passenger side, firing the last three rounds from the magazine into the front right tire. The rig crashed into the parked ICE vehicles and came to a halt. Jeff was fumbling to insert a fresh mag into the Beretta when the Castañeda bailed out on the passenger side, landing in the dirt before him to level the Tec-9 on Jeff's belly, his eyes appearing flat and reptilian in the dim light.

Jeff froze, the fresh mag jammed into the butt of his pistol with the bullets facing backward. "Don't shoot me!"

The Mexican cut him down and dashed

toward the rear of the trailer.

The sheriff was running up the driver's side toward the cab when he heard the burst of fire that blasted Jeff's guts open. He jerked to a stop, pivoted on his heel, and waited to see where the Mexican would show his face. Spitting tobacco juice, he called out, *"Donde estás, cabrón?"* Where are you, asshole?

The Castañeda sprang out from behind the trailer, and both men fired at the same time. The sheriff's hollow-point round struck the Castañeda right between the eyes to blow out the back of his skull, and the Castañeda's four-round burst struck the sheriff in the belly, dropping him to his knees.

"Goddamn!" the old man groaned in agony. "What I get for not wearin' a vest."

He didn't have a portable radio on him, and the cruiser was fifty yards away, which may as well have been fifty miles. He was in too much pain to move, bleeding out fast. He swiped at the blood pooling in his shirt and looked at his hand. Even in the night, he could see the blood was very dark, realizing he'd been hit in the liver.

"Must be why it hurts so damn bad." He rolled onto his back, tossing the .357 aside. "I shoulda taken Castañeda up on

32

that offer," he muttered. "I coulda been in Tahiti."

3

DOWN IN THE TUNNEL

Zakayev and the Castañedas hunkered near the walls on either side of the passageway, bracing for an attack.

Javier ordered his men onto their bellies and covered them with a tarp. "Let them come as close as possible before you fire." He knew that because of the crazy Chechen with his finger on the bomb, they would have to kill every cop coming against them in order to escape with their lives.

Zakayev gripped the dead-man switch, keeping a wary eye on the Mexicans. He wasn't worried about the RA-115 taking damage in a firefight. It was of Russian manufacture, awkward looking and ugly but built to take a genuine beating.

Flashlight beams came dancing down the walls from the north.

Agent Hitch spotted what appeared to be a

lump of cargo on the floor near the wall 150 feet down the tunnel. He held up a fist to halt the column.

"Looks like they took off and left their shit." He moved out again, determined to catch the smugglers before they made it back to the other side. It didn't matter to Hitch how far down the tunnel they caught them, just so they grabbed them before stepping out of the tunnel on the Mexican side. Let their lawyers try to prove they'd been bagged south of the border.

As they drew within fifty feet of the lump in the floor, Hitch made out the muzzles of the AK-47s sticking from beneath the edge of the tarp, stopping in his tracks.

Javier shouted, *"Fuego!"* and the AK-47s opened up with a deafening roar.

Hitch was struck in the face, arms, and torso, dead before he hit the concrete. Gutierrez and another agent went down at the same time, exposing three more agents to enemy fire. These three were also cut down before ever firing a shot. The seven remaining ICE men hit the deck and opened up with their MP5s.

The two groups blasted away at one another with automatic fire at 50 feet, nearly point-blank range for any automatic weapon.

The Castañedas' ammo was old and corrosive, a mark manufactured in Korea during the midseventies, so the tunnel quickly filled with an acrid smoke, obscuring everyone's vision. To make matters worse, a number of lightbulbs were shattered by ricocheting spall.

When the guns finally fell silent, there were only four men still left alive on each side.

Zakayev remained hunched behind the RA-115, with a death grip on the trigger mechanism.

"Deja de disparar!" Agent Gutierrez screamed. "Cease fire!"

"Regrésate!" Javier shouted from where he lay on his belly. "Go back!" He was amazed to still be alive and didn't want to risk another hideous exchange of gunfire.

"We're going back!" Gutierrez said. "Just give us a chance to pick up our wounded."

"I give you one minute," Javier shouted. "Then we fire again!"

"Cálmate," Gutierrez said easily. *"Cálmate, amigo."* Calm down. He couldn't see much through the smoke but could hear the Castañedas switching out their magazines over the ringing in his ears. There was nothing to be served by continuing the battle. Besides, he was pretty sure he was bleeding

36

to death, hit in the brachial artery of his right arm.

"We're throwing away our weapons!" he called. "Just give us time to get the fuck out of here! *De acuerdo?*" Agreed?

"Okay. *De acuerdo,*" Javier replied, satisfied the fighting was over and the Americans were leaving.

Gutierrez told his men to throw away their weapons and struggled to his feet, bleeding profusely from the right arm. "I'm gonna need help," he said to the others.

The ladder was more than twelve hundred feet back the way they'd come.

"Motha'fucker," muttered the only unwounded ICE man, stepping over the bodies of their dead compatriots to slip Gutierrez's good arm over his shoulders. "We just got our asses handed to us."

"Hitch was an idiot," Gutierrez grumbled, glancing back at the body.

"Goddamn glory hound," added one of the others in disgust.

Gutierrez saw one of the agents still gripping a pistol. "Put that weapon down!" he ordered. "You trying to get us killed?"

The agent dropped the weapon as if it had suddenly burned his hand.

"This fight is over — *we lost*! Now let's get outta here while we still can."

■ ■ ■ ■

Javier remained crouched near the wall, bleeding from a shoulder wound. All things considered, he didn't feel too bad about the firefight. He had just led a battle against the supposedly unbeatable Americans, and he had driven them back with their tails tucked. Now all he had to do was get the crazy Chechen to put away the bomb's detonator so he could shoot him in the head. He waited five minutes after the gringos were out of sight, and then ordered his men to their feet. He walked up to Zakayev and stood looking down at him, where he remained hunched behind the bomb.

"It's safe now," he said harshly. "You can put the detonator away."

Zakayev didn't reply — didn't even move.

"Did you hear what I said?" Javier nudged him with the muzzle of the pistol. "It's time to go. Put the detonator away!"

The Chechen keeled over on his side, a single bullet hole in the center of his forehead. The dead-man switch clattered against the concrete.

Before Javier could even blink, the RA-115 suitcase nuke detonated with a force of nearly two kilotons, vaporizing the Castañedas and the ICE agents — who were just arriving at the foot of the ladder — within a single microsecond. A microsecond later the surrounding rock was vaporized, the temperature at the center of the explosion reaching millions of degrees Fahrenheit. A few milliseconds after that, the earth and rock covering the explosion were heaving upward, compelled by a giant bubble of high-pressure gas and steam as the heat and expanding shock wave melted or vaporized still more rock, creating a molten cavity within the bubble. This expansion continued on for another few tenths of a second until the pressure within the bubble began to equalize with that of the outside atmosphere. Then, when it could no longer sustain the rate of the expansion, the bubble collapsed back in on itself, leaving a giant subsidence crater more three hundred feet wide and sixty feet deep.

The tiny Mexican border town of Puerto Palomas was devastated by the shock wave that traveled through the alluvial plain to knock out all power not only there but also to the city of Deming. Ground tremors were felt as far away as Roswell, New Mexico. And forty miles north of the blast, the US Geological Seismographic Station at Cookes Peak registered a seismic event of 5.1 on the Richter scale.

Though most of the blast's radiation had been contained by the encapsulating earth and rock, the open shafts at both ends of the tunnel had allowed twin jets of fallout to blast ten thousand feet into the sky, resulting in a deadly cloud of radioactive dust and debris that was soon drifting eastward toward El Paso, Texas.

4

WASHINGTON, DC,
The White House

"You still haven't told me what the hell it was," the president of the United States said to the director of Homeland Security. "Was it a meteor? An atom bomb? *What?* Why is it taking so much time to get information?"

DHS director Merrill Radcliff was on the hot seat. They were standing in the hall outside the Oval Office flanked by numerous representatives from nearly all US security branches. The Joint Chiefs were there, the FBI, CIA, NSA, DOD — and of course, the White House chief of staff, the ever-present Tim Hagen, a distasteful young fellow whom Radcliff couldn't stand.

He drew a breath and held out his hands. "We just don't know yet, Mr. President. It's a very isolated, very remote area, and it's taking time to get resources into —"

The president cut him off. "Are you telling me you people still haven't learned a damn thing from the Sandy and Katrina debacles — that you're *still* not ready to react when something happens?" The question was very obviously not rhetorical.

"Mr. President, we've learned a great deal from those disasters, but it takes time to get resources in place, to get things organized. We can't just —"

"You're relieved," the president said, shocking everyone present and turning to Hagen. "Get the deputy director of DHS into position to take over for Mr. Radcliff." He then looked to the chairman of the Joint Chiefs, General William J. Couture, who was just stepping from the Oval Office, cellular phone in hand. "General Couture, the military will be in charge of handling this crisis from here on — effective immediately. Now, what do you need from me?"

The jagged scar on the left side of Couture's face made him a fierce and daunting presence, but he exuded an undeniable confidence. "Mr. President, I've already ordered a swift reaction team of army NBC specialists prepped and ready." NBC stood for Nuclear, Chemical, and Biological. "They're standing by at Fort Bliss in El Paso awaiting orders to move into the impact area and begin taking readings. All I need is your clearance, sir."

"Get 'em in there," the president said. "If we've been attacked, we need to know now, not a few days from now."

"I'm afraid there's more, Mr. President."

The president's brow furrowed. "Go ahead."

"I've just been on the phone with General Cruz at Fort Bliss. All indications there are that this was a *nuclear* event, Mr. President, not seismic and definitely not meteorological. Radiation levels at the base are on the rise, and General Cruz has ordered the base to activate the nuclear defense protocols. I'm requesting permission to order every base in Texas to do the same, sir."

Feeling suddenly sick to his stomach, the president found himself glad to have taken Tim Hagen's advice urging him to appoint Couture as chairman of the Joint Chiefs. Without Couture's company in this moment, he would have felt completely rudderless. "Order every base in the country to do the same, General."

"If I may offer a word of caution?" the general said.

"Of course."

"I don't believe a national activation will be necessary at this time, sir. We should definitely put all bases on alert, but to activate the nuclear defense protocols at a national level would almost certainly cause widespread panic among the civilian population."

"But where there's one bomb, General," Tim Hagen interjected, "surely, there could be another."

Couture seemed not to have heard, his eyes fixed on the president. "Does the order stand, Mr. President?"

The president considered Couture's assessment of the situation and found the reasoning sound. "No, General. I think you're probably right. For now, we'll allow the situation to develop — isn't that how you people in the military like to put it?"

The general smiled. "Yes, sir."

"Very well then," the president said, looking at Hagen. "Make sure the deputy director of DHS alerts the city of El Paso about the radiation levels, so their emergency personnel can take appropriate action." He cast a disgusted glance at the humiliated Radcliff. "It's apparently going to be some time before DHS and FEMA can get in there to help them."

Hagen was busy marking something on the electronic notepad that never seemed to be out of his possession. "I'll make the call right away, Mr. President."

"Now, gentlemen," the president said to all, opening the door to the Oval Office, "I need to see the directors of the FBI, CIA, and the NSA. I want to make sure everyone's on the same page moving forward. After you, gentlemen."

The three directors filed past the president into the Oval Office, and everyone else moved off down the corridor — everyone but Couture, Hagen, and a pair of Secret Service agents.

After Hagen finished writing, he slipped the stylus into the side of the notepad and turned to reach for the knob on the Oval Office door.

To his nearly infinite disbelief, the towering Couture reached out and grabbed him by the necktie, shoving him up against the wall, his merciless gray eyes boring into him.

"If you ever contradict me again, I'll break your goddamn neck! Do you understand me?"

Hagen felt his feet coming off the floor, panic sweeping through him as he looked at the Secret Service agents, who merely stood watching as if made of stone. This was the first time in Hagen's life that another human being had laid a hand on him in anger, and it was the most unnerving sensation he had ever experienced. "Yes, sir," he croaked,

45

feeling his bladder threatening to let go.

Couture released him and set off down the hall with a curt nod to the Secret Service men, both of whom nodded back.

Hagen stood straightening his suit, taking the time to regain his composure and to make sure that he hadn't wet himself. "Thanks a lot for the help," he said to the lead Secret Service man.

The agent stared back at him, expressionless. "Help with what, Mr. Hagen?"

5

MOROCCO, CASABLANCA,
Rick's Café

Gil Shannon sat at a table in Rick's Café drinking a cup of coffee. This was not the same Rick's Café from the 1942 film classic *Casablanca*. The movie had not even been shot in Morocco. However, the café was modeled after the café from the Humphrey Bogart film, and since its doors had opened in 2004, it had become one of the city's main tourist attractions.

The largest city in Morocco, Casablanca proper was home to three and a half million people, catering to many different corporations from all over the world and boasting the largest artificial port in North Africa. It was a modern city that had kept in touch with its cultural past, but it was not without political and religious turmoil. Since 2003, at least seventeen suicide bombers had blown themselves up there, killing more than thirty-five people and injuring well over a hundred. Most of the bombers were known to have been linked with Al Qaeda.

Gil was waiting for a Russian contact named Sergei Zhilov. A former member of the Russian Vysotniki (Rangers), Zhilov was now a freelance operator who prowled the African continent from Casablanca to Mombasa, Kenya, in search of mercenary work. The CIA had employed him shortly after the 2012 attack on the American diplomatic mission in Benghazi, Libya, to help root out Islamic terrorists in North Africa — specifically terrorists linked to a group called Al Qaeda in the Arabian Peninsula (AQAP), an extremist organization operating predominantly out of Yemen, though it had originally formed in Saudi Arabia in direct resistance to the al-Saud monarchy (the Saudi royal family). AQAP was known to be the primary force behind the attack on the American mission in Benghazi, during which two former US Navy SEALs, Glen Doherty and Tyrone Woods, had been killed on a rooftop by mortar fire while helping defend American diplomatic personnel.

Gil had come to Casablanca at the behest of SAD (Special Activities Division of the CIA) director Robert Pope to hunt down and kill two AQAP operatives known to be hiding within the city. Though Gil had never known Doherty or Woods, he was a fellow Navy SEAL, and he had taken their deaths personally. So when Bob Pope had offered to bring him out of retirement and put him back into the game for the purpose of eliminating AQAP insurgents, he had been unable to turn down the offer.

Gil's wife, Marie, had not taken his decision to go back in very well. In fact, she'd more or less kicked him out of the house because of it. She told him he could either turn down Pope's offer or find another place to live, because she could not go back to worrying about him 24/7 whenever he was not at home.

Gil was sickened by the thought of separation, but he just wasn't ready to give up the life of an operator, so he had kissed her and left the house, with tears welling in his eyes.

The CIA had not been permitted its own in-house operators since the Cold War, so at Pope's "suggestion," Gil was hired by a PMC (private military company) called Obsidian Optio Inc. Obsidian held security contracts with the CIA all over the world, and this made it easy for Gil to move around without drawing attention. Another benefit to being officially employed in the private sector was that he was well paid, even though he did virtually no work for Obsidian itself. In 1989 the United Nations Mercenary Convention strictly forbid governments from contracting of mercenaries; however, countries sidestepped this technicality by never referring to the mercenaries they hired as mercenaries. They were "security specialists."

Sergei Zhilov entered the café dressed in khaki trousers and a maroon T-shirt. He was a big man, with reddish hair and green eyes, knotted muscles in his neck, shoulders, and arms, and he was sweating like he'd just come from a dead lift competition.

Gil raised a hand to get his attention, and he came to sit at the table.

"Can I get you a cup of coffee?" Gil had blue eyes and sandy blond hair that he kept cut high and tight in military fashion.

Zhilov shook his head. "That I don't drink," he remarked in a gravelly voice, resting his arms on the table, the veins in his forearms bulging like power cords beneath the skin. "Bad for digestion."

"More for me then." Gil took a drink of his coffee and set down the cup. It was a fine white coffee cup bearing the inscription "Rick's Café." "So have you found them?"

Zhilov nodded. "They've rented a house near the old Medina." The Medina was the old Arab quarter of the city, full of markets and tourists anxious to haggle with the vendors. "They must have problems with money," Zhilov added. "The place is a toilet."

"You're sure it's them, though, you've seen them?"

Zhilov nodded again, signaling to a waiter for a glass of water by tipping his big hand toward his mouth. "They come and go without worry. They buy food and eat in the street like there is no danger. They're watchful, but they feel secure. I can see."

"Are they armed?"

"I think yes." Zhilov wiped the sweat from his face with his hand. "They wear jackets, and it's too hot for that, so I think yes."

"How did you find them?"

Zhilov shrugged. "I ask the Jews. The Jews know everything in this city."

Gil narrowed his gaze. "What Jews?"

Zhilov thumbed casually over his shoulder, as if the people in question might be standing in the doorway behind him. "Those goddamn guys with Mohave."

LX Mohave was another American-owned PMC, one that focused primarily on intelligence and cryptographic technologies, and the company was known to hire former Israeli Mossad agents.

Gil's eyes narrowed. "You were talking with Mohave about my mission?"

"No," Zhilov said irritably. "Why would I talk to them about you? They don't care about you. I was talking to them about these goddamn guys you wanted me to find." He snatched the glass of water from the waiter's hand as he arrived, gulping it down. "Another," he said, shoving the glass back into his hand and waving him away.

"Hey, Sergei," Gil said, "I need to know if Mohave knows about my mission here. It's extremely important."

Zhilov leaned into the table, meeting Gil's gaze. "Listen to me, you goddamn guy. Mohave doesn't give a tough shit about your mission, okay? You got it? I don't tell them nothing. These goddamn guys over there, they owe me favors, so I ask them. And I tell you these goddamn Jews, they know everything around here. Don't ask me how they know, because I don't care, and I don't ask. All I care is that they know. See? That's why your goddamn CIA, they hire *me* and not some other goddamn guy. They know I know who knows the shit. See what I say?"

Gil chuckled and sat back. "Yeah, I see what you say. Can you show me where they live, these goddamn guys?"

"You bet," Zhilov said. "But first we eat. I

know good place. Then we wait for dark. These goddamn guys over there, they're watchful right now. They see your face, they gonna run because you look like what you are. Me, I look nothing like what I am. See? I can go anywhere in the daylight, but you, you goddamn guy . . ." He shook his head. "You look like a Yankee killer. They see you, they run. So you trust me. I know Casablanca. I know how to get you close to these goddamn guys. But first we eat."

Gil sat watching him across the table. "You fought in Chechnya, right?"

Zhilov rolled his eyes and shook his head. "Don't ask me about Chechnya, Yankee. I don't want to remember. Those goddamn guys with the Martyrs' Brigade . . ." He shook his head again. "Salafi fanatics, they make these goddamn guys you're hunting look like girl who suck penis for a living." He laughed. "That I tell you for free, you goddamn Yankee. Now, you ready to eat yet or what?"

Gil smiled and stood up from the table. "I got a feelin' I'm gonna regret it, but yeah, I'm ready."

Zhilov got to his feet. "Come on. I show you good place for last meal." He clapped Gil on the back, laughing uproariously as if it were the funniest thing he had ever heard.

53

Gil smiled without humor, watching the Russian guardedly. "I'm glad we never had to fight you people."

Zhilov laughed some more. "Me too! You goddamn Yankees still think you playing cowboys and Indians!"

6

MOROCCO, CASABLANCA,
The Old Medina

Abdu Bashwar was a thirty-two-year-old soldier of Allah, and though he had yet to personally kill another human being, he had participated in the attack on the CIA annex in Benghazi as a spotter for the mortar team that bombarded the building. His compatriot Cesar Koutry was a twenty-nine-year-old deserter from the Saudi Arabian army who had spent the last seven years of his life designing bomb vests and other explosive devices for AQAP insurgents.

Koutry's dream was the total overthrow of the al-Saud monarchy — which was greatly supported by the United States — and to one day return to a Saudi Arabia governed solely by Sharia law. In Koutry's world, Saudi Arabian oil would be sold only to other Muslim nations, and the profits would belong to the people — not to any so-called royal family.

They had arrived in Casablanca the month before with orders to begin preparations for a renewed insurgency in Morocco. With the recent influx of international businesses, Western influence was growing, and as a result, Morocco was beginning to experience a slight resurgence in both Christianity and Judaism. Though Islam was the official legal religion, the Moroccan constitution did allow for freedom of belief — so long as non-Muslims did not attempt to convert Muslims to their own religions. To do so was considered a crime, but most Christian and Jewish missionaries ignored the law.

AQAP had decided that it was again time to make Westerners less comfortable in Casablanca. The last significant terrorist attack there had taken place in 2007, when two brothers blew themselves up in front of the American Consulate. Things had been comparatively quiet since then, with the brief exception of the Arab Spring protests that took place during 2011 and 2012.

Koutry sat in a beat-up chair surfing through the channels on the television until at last he yawned and tossed aside the remote. "There's nothing to watch."

Bashwar sat at the table behind him eating a late supper. "There has to be a soccer game."

"I'm sick of soccer." Koutry glanced over his shoulder. "Where is Izaan? The little turd is late."

"He's always late," Bashwar answered through a mouthful of couscous. "This isn't new."

"I think we need a new contact. That kid is a little stupid for this kind of work."

"He's all we've got right now. I've already asked for another."

The door burst open, and sixteen-year-old Izaan barged into the room, causing both men to nearly jump out of their skins. "The big man with red hair!" Izaan blurted. "He's parked on the street in a black van. He has an American commando with him."

Koutry jumped up from the chair, looking at Bashwar. "I told you that fat Russian was trouble!"

Bashwar gulped down a glass of water and wiped his mouth with the back of his hand; then he took a Czech-made pistol from beneath his shirt and got up from the table. "How do you know it's an American commando?"

Izaan shrugged. "He looks like one to me."

"Did they follow you here?"

"No, Bashwar. They were already parked

there when I came down the street."

Bashwar thumbed back the hammer on the CZ-75. "Why didn't you keep walking instead of letting them see you come in here?"

Izaan became frightened. "What have I done wrong? I only wanted to warn you."

Koutry stepped over and took the teenager by the arm, patting him down to find a cellular in his back pocket and tossing it to Bashwar. "You could have *called* to warn us."

"I didn't think of it. I'm sorry."

Bashwar stood thumbing through the call list on Izaan's phone, checking his messages and phone book for anything suspicious. After a moment, he looked up and said, "Kill him."

Izaan tried to jerk his arm free, but Koutry was too fast. He grabbed the kid around the head and gave his neck a vicious twist, breaking his spinal cord with a crunch and letting the body fall to the floor with the forehead thudding against the tile.

"What did you find?" Koutry asked, putting out his hand for the phone.

Bashwar tucked the phone into his pocket. "I didn't find anything, but this house is obviously compromised, and there's no way to be sure that fool wasn't working for the enemy."

Koutry grew angry. "You had me kill a boy for no reason?"

Bashwar shrugged. "Who else knows we're in Casablanca? No one. But still there's a Russian mercenary parked down the street — *with an American commando.*" He pointed at the body. "How else could that imbecile know he was an American commando? You said yourself he was too stupid for this kind of work."

Koutry straightened his shirt and stepped over the body, pointing his finger into Bashwar's face. "Next time, you do your own killing."

Bashwar pointed the CZ-75 into Koutry's face with the intention of making some kind of tough guy remark, but Koutry grabbed the weapon from his hand, knocking him backward over the chair and pointing the pistol at him.

"Hear me well," Koutry said quietly. "Until you've learned how to kill a man, you had better never point a gun at me again."

Bashwar nodded slowly, slightly concerned that Koutry might actually shoot him.

Koutry let down the hammer and tossed the weapon onto the table. "Now we have to deal with the fat Russian and his friend. I think I'll send them both to the moon."

7

MOROCCO, CASABLANCA,
The Old Medina

To Gil, the old Medina district looked like something out of a Jason Bourne movie, with its narrow streets and old houses built on top of one another, and all of them looking exactly alike to his eye. They were old stucco homes, most of them constructed around the turn of the twentieth century, before the French arrived to take the country under its "protection." The street vendors had packed away their wares for the night, and the cobblestone alleys were relatively empty, save for a few parked cars and empty vendor carts.

"A guy could get lost in the neighborhood."

Zhilov chuckled. "If you get lost in Casablanca, just walk toward the sea until you hit the coastal road. The sea is very big. Not even a Yankee can miss it."

Gil checked the side-view mirror, but all he could see was a wall. "I don't think there's a straight road in this entire district."

"This is the Anfa," Zhilov said. "The original part of the city, before the French took over and tried to make the city look like Paris."

A teenager rounded the corner and seemed to check himself for a moment before continuing forward, stopping halfway down the short block and going into the house they were watching.

"Do you know that kid?"

Zhilov shook his head. "I never see him before."

"He seemed to know you."

Zhilov gripped the wheel, adjusting himself in the seat that was too small for him. "I cannot disagree."

Gil muttered an obscenity. "The op is blown. He'll tell the hajis we're out here and put 'em on alert. We should clear."

The Russian shook his head, his good humor gone now. "If we leave, they disappear. Then it takes weeks to find them again. I think to wait is good idea. When they come out, you shoot them, and I take you back to hotel for the rest of my money."

Gil drew the suppressed USP .45 from inside his jacket. "And suppose they come out blasting with automatic weapons."

Zhilov reached beneath his seat for a micro Uzi submachine pistol. "Suppose they do?" he said in his gravelly voice.

Gil glanced around, feeling boxed in by the limited field of vision due to the curvy nature of the alley. There were almost no positions of cover. He knew they should clear the scene; that the situation was borderline untenable. But he also knew that Zhilov was right: Bashwar and Koutry would disappear to another safe house and would be ten times harder to reacquire.

The Russian took a suppressor from under the seat and attached it to the muzzle of the Uzi. "We going in to get these goddamn guys or what?"

Gil shook his head. "We'll let the situation develop." He glanced into the back of the van, which was crammed full of rolled-up carpets. "What is all that shit back there, anyway?"

Zhilov shrugged. "Rugs rolled up. I steal the van from rug vendor other side of city."

Gil gave him a wry grin. "Weren't exactly planning a fast getaway, were you?"

"Listen, you goddamn guy. You want to unload the shit? You are my guest."

"*Be* my guest. We say *be* my guest."

Zhilov looked out the window at the

house. "You say your way, Yankee. I say mine. I just want to kill these goddamn guys and get my money."

A few minutes later, a black van with its headlights off pulled past them, stopping near the house three doors up on the left. The back doors opened, and a man stepped out holding a suppressed MP5 submachine gun. There were three more men in the back.

Gil sat back in the seat. "What the fuck is *this* happy horseshit?"

Zhilov sat back as well, though it scarcely made a difference in his case because of his bulk. "It's those goddamn Jews I tell you about."

"Mohave? What the fuck are they doing here?"

Zhilov looked at him. "To kill Arab terrorist, maybe?"

Gil got ready to dismount the vehicle in case shit started flying in their direction. The boys with LX Mohave were well known for shooting first and never bothering to ask any questions. A softball-sized glob of what looked like modeling clay landed on the roof of the Mohave van with a heavy thud and stuck in place. Gil knew instantly that it was a wad of C4 plastic explosive molded around a timer-detonator, having seen the

64

same kind of bomb used in Indonesia a few years earlier during a rooftop attack on a diplomatic convoy.

"Sticky bomb — get down!"

He and Zhilov squashed themselves as low as they could as the Mohave men rushed to dismount the doomed vehicle. The bomb detonated with a blinding white flash, catching the driver and one of the gunners inside, flattening the van and throwing the dismounting gunners through the air. The concussion spider-webbed the windshield of the carpet van and echoed through the alleyway.

Like a giant bird dropping, a second glob of C4 landed in the street unseen among the stunned Mohave men struggling to pick themselves up. It detonated in another thunderclap of blinding light, and all three men disintegrated.

Gil jumped out of the carpet van as a third glob of C4 landed on the roof. Zhilov remained in the driver's seat, knocked unconscious by the concussion of the second blast. Gil rolled beneath the van, expelling the air from his lungs and covering his ears. The bomb exploded, and the load of carpet absorbed much of the pressure wave, but the chassis of the van was thrust violently downward on its leaf springs, and

Gil's head was briefly sandwiched between the exhaust pipe and the street. It felt like a mule kick to the head, and his internal combat systems were knocked off-line.

8

MOROCCO, CASABLANCA,
The Old Medina

As his head cleared slowly from the effects of the explosion, Gil opened his eyes to see two pairs of feet hurrying past the burning Mohave van. When they paused to grab a pair of MP5s, he knew they had to be Bashwar and Koutry fleeing the scene. He groped around for his .45, finding it beneath him, and began to drag himself from beneath the burning carpet van.

He saw the two disappearing down the alleyway in the dark beyond the flames and forced himself to his feet, hearing the distant wail of European-style high-low sirens. Still shaken, he tucked the .45 inside his jacket and hobbled after them, keeping close to the wall and using the doorways to keep under cover as he shadowed them through the alleyways of the Anfa.

People emerged from their homes but no

one moved toward the glow of the flames. Gil could feel their accusatory glances as he passed, but he kept his face hidden as best he could. When the fuel tank of the carpet van erupted behind him, everyone ducked back inside, slamming their doors in fear. He lost sight of Bashwar and Koutry at the end of the alley as they ran across the Boulevard Mohamed El Hansali toward the Café Al Jazeera. His balance returning, he darted across the boulevard after them. He caught sight of the two again as they dashed past the café and down the street into a park dotted with trees. So far nothing about their movements gave Gil reason to believe they were aware of their tail. They didn't even look back as they hurried to put distance between them and the scene of the crime.

He crouched behind a car and watched through the windows as they stashed the MP5s up in a tree and hurried off toward a slightly crowded area to the north. Gil tailed them up another street, where they ducked inside the Casablanca youth hostel. He checked his watch and decided to give them an hour to get settled before going in after them. Walking back in the direction he'd come, he heard the sirens of fire trucks racing down Boulevard Hansali.

Getting blown up in the street was not

Gil's idea of how to efficiently execute a mission. He found a table at a street-side café with a television on the counter and ordered a mutton sandwich. He was still eating ten minutes later when the BBC reported there had been a possible nuclear *event* in the southern United States. It went on to report that both US and British military forces were now on alert all around the world.

He took a satellite phone from his jacket and called Pope.

Pope answered after a number of rings. "Typhoon?"

"Yeah," Gil said. "Hey, I'm watching the BBC. What the hell's going on back home?"

"We don't know yet," Pope said. "But if I had to guess, I'd say there's been a premature nuclear detonation on or near the Mexican border.

"How did it go with our AQAP friends?" he asked.

"Not good," Gil answered. "Those jackasses over at Mohave showed up and queered the deal. They tried to cut in on our action and got themselves blown up — the Russian too. I'm still tracking the targets and should be mission complete within a couple of hours. Who's responsible for the nuke? Any idea?"

"None. But I want you back here as soon as this op concludes."

"Roger that."

"Are you compromised?"

"I don't think so," Gil said. "A few locals may have seen my face, but it's dark, so there shouldn't be anything to worry about it. I'll fly out ASAP."

"Are you injured?"

"Mildly concussed, but nothing I can't handle."

"You've definitely dealt with worse," Pope remarked. "What happened to the Russian?"

"They were dropping monkey bombs on us from the roof, and he got smashed."

"You'd better fly out on your Canadian passport," Pope advised. "You can cross at Niagara Falls. I'll have a woman there waiting to bring you over."

"I can bring myself over."

"Okay. Let me know when our AQAP friends are out of the picture."

"Roger that. Typhoon out." Gil put the phone away.

He sat pretending to watch the television for another hour, keeping one eye on the street, and then got up and returned to the youth hostel. He walked through the doorway into an open courtyard, finding the office on the far side behind a sliding glass window. There a bald, unpleasant-looking fellow in his fifties sat watching a soccer game on a tiny television set. When he glanced up to see Gil standing on the other side of the window, his eyes grew wide, and he grabbed for a pistol beneath his shirt.

Gil jerked the suppressed USP .45 and shot him through the glass. The window shattered, and the man pitched over in the chair, landing on the tile floor with his brains blown out the other side of his head.

Gil looked around to make sure no one had seen and put the weapon away. He hadn't counted on the hostel being a safe house. Stepping around the corner and into the office, he switched off the television and squatted down, using the man's jacket from the back of the chair to wrap up his head, tying it tight with the sleeves to keep what was left of his gray matter from oozing out onto the floor. Then he carried the body across the hall and dumped it in the janitor's closet.

Within a few minutes, he'd swept the broken glass into a dust bin and mopped up most of the gore. The crime scene was by no means spic and span, but with the light turned off, it would easily pass the cursory inspection of a late-night traveler standing outside the window. He took the ledger and a copy of the floor map into the dining room, where he wouldn't likely be bothered by anyone looking for the dead man. There were seventy-two beds in the hostel, and just as Gil suspected, there was no record of two males having checked in within the last couple of hours.

He sat studying the map, checking off the occupied beds against the guest ledger. Thirty-three of the beds were occupied, with roughly a fifty-fifty split between males and females, the hostel providing separate dorm rooms for men and women. There were a number of two-bed rooms set apart from the dorms, normally reserved for married couples, and Gil guessed that Bashwar and Koutry would be in one of those.

He put the ledger back on the manager's desk and made his way up the stairs with his hand inside his jacket. At the landing atop the stairs, he oriented himself with the map and made a right down the hall, deciding to check the most isolated room first. Halfway down the hall, he came to a rusty chain stretched across the corridor where he was supposed to make a left. A battered tin sign hanging from the chain read No Admittance, in Arabic, English, French, and Spanish. Light shown beneath the door at the end of the short hallway.

Gil drew the USP and stepped carefully over the chain. A washstand stood against the wall, and a black daypack sat on the floor beneath it. He knelt low in the shadowy light to spot the monofilament line running across the corridor from inside the pack to a rusty screw set knee high in the opposite wall. He knew better than to mess with a booby trap unnecessarily, but he didn't want his line of retreat obstructed in the event things went bad and he needed to egress in a hurry. Besides, this chintzy black-bag affair looked more to him like a Columbine High cum wannabe warrior booby trap than a device rigged with anything as sensitive or complex as a mercury switch.

So he pulled the bag gently from beneath the washstand to release the tension from the monofilament line. Then he checked to be sure that there was no second line attached to the bag before sliding it across and up against the opposite wall, where both bag and trip line would be clear of his path. He stepped to the door and put his hand on the doorknob, listening for movement or conversation from within the room. Hearing nothing, he turned the knob and stepped smoothly inside with the pistol before him.

Koutry looked up in complete shock from where he lay in bed. Gil shot him dead center between the eyes, blowing blood, brains, and bone fragments all over the white pillowcase.

Bashwar was not in the room. This meant he had either stepped out of the hostel while Gil was eating or had gone to take a shower. Koutry had obviously not been expecting him to return so soon. Gil checked the map and moved out down the hall toward the bathrooms.

The showers were empty, but in the next room he saw a pair of feet beneath one of the stall doors in the lavatory, easily recognizing the same Nike basketball sneakers he had seen from beneath the van. A towel and a bar of soap sat waiting on the sink. Gil put five quick rounds through the stall door. The only sound was that of the pistol cycling the rounds and the 230-grain bullets striking the tiled wall after they passed through Bashwar's body.

Bashwar toppled off the toilet and his feet sprawled out beneath the door.

Gil kicked the door in to see the young man's face jammed between the commode and the wall, his eyes open, face frozen in shock, with his gun hand still gripping the CZ-75.

"That's for Benghazi, cocksucker." He pulled the door closed.

On his way down the stairs, he met a group of Australian tourists on their way up and pretended to stifle a yawn, covering his face with his hand.

"Hey, mate?" one of them called after him. "Have you seen the manager?"

"No," Gil said without looking back.

A half mile from the hostel along Boulevard des Almohades, directly in front of a pier lined with Moroccan naval vessels, he ditched the USP down a sewer drain and hailed a cab for the airport. It was time to get home and find out what the hell was going on.

9

DETROIT

Though one would not have necessarily guessed it by his present line of work, Daniel Crosswhite was a Medal of Honor recipient and a former Delta Force operator who had survived many deadly incursions behind enemy lines. He had been discharged from the army six months prior due to a fractured hip and pelvis sustained in his last combat jump. He could still run and fight, just not well enough by Special Forces standards, and so the army had asked him to resign his commission.

There were other factors involved, of course, primarily the fact that Crosswhite had led an unauthorized rescue mission in Afghanistan to rescue a female helicopter pilot named Sandra Brux. The mission had been a failure and had very nearly resulted in the deaths of two of the men in his command. Even though Crosswhite had gone on to help successfully rescue Brux a couple of weeks later, winning himself the Medal of Honor in the process, this had only caused his superiors to resent his presence in Delta Force all the more.

Crosswhite now drew a small disability pension from the Veterans Administration, but that barely paid the bills, and he was not the type to sit around waiting on what he considered to be a handout, especially when so many other veterans were receiving no assistance whatsoever. So he had sought out a former Navy SEAL named Brett Tuckerman to help him with a little enterprise he had dreamed up one night while watching the local news in his hometown of New York City.

Tuckerman was a true wild card: a gunfighter and gambling addict who couldn't pass a poker game if he was chained to a D8 Cat going in the opposite direction. His friends within the Special Ops community all called him Conman, a nickname he had come by honestly. He and Crosswhite had first met during the unauthorized rescue mission into the Waigal Valley, and Tuckerman too had eventually paid the price for his involvement in the ill-fated mission by being kicked out of DEVGRU (also known as SEAL Team VI) a few months later — as had every other SEAL involved in the same op.

After that, Tuckerman had lost all interest in serving in the United States Navy, returning home to Las Vegas to take up the game of poker full-time. He spent the next five months snorting coke and chasing women up and down the Strip. When Crosswhite finally caught up to him, he'd been face-down in his own vomit in a Bellagio hotel room that wasn't even registered in his name.

Tuckerman and Crosswhite now sat staring out the back window of a beat-up dog grooming van in Detroit, watching the house of a methamphetamine dealer named Terrance Booker. A decked-out yellow Hummer pulled up in front of the house, and two men got out, each with a bulging black backpack slung over his shoulder. He glanced at his watch, shaking his head in dismay. "Exactly zero three-thirty hours. How are these motherfuckers so punctual? They're fuckin' criminals."

"So are we," Crosswhite said, shrugging into his body armor. "They got our goddamn money with 'em?"

"They do." Tuckerman wasn't a large fellow — only five foot six, 145 pounds — but at twenty-nine, he still carried most of his muscle from his days in the SEALs.

Crosswhite was taller, a few years older, handsome with dark hair and a devil-may-care smile. "Remember," he said, "this motherfucker's been down twice for child molestation, so if he puts up any fight at all, don't hesitate to waste his ass."

They were dressed for combat pretty much the same as when they'd operated with Special Forces, only instead of camouflage, they were dressed all in black with *FBI* stenciled on their body armor front and back. They carried no identification, and they always wore leather tactical gloves. They'd made a pact with each other on the first day: if either man was ever wounded badly enough that he needed a hospital, the other would put a bullet through his head.

Neither wanted to end up in prison.

The adrenaline rush they experienced in their new line of work was as important to them as the cash, most of which they blew in Vegas anyhow. For them, life outside of Special Ops just moved too slowly, and they scarcely knew how to function among regular people with no concept of the things they had done and seen during their time in combat.

"I find myself unable to adjust," Crosswhite had said dryly, by way of explanation, on the morning he'd first pitched his idea to Tuckerman.

"Yeah, well look at me," Tuckerman had replied, gesturing at his vomit-stained shirt, the two of them sitting in a buffet breakfast joint on the northern end of the Vegas Strip. "I'm not exactly the poster child for assimilation."

They waited until the men in the Hummer came back out and drove off before dismounting the van and moving quickly into the shadows alongside the house. The night vision monoculars attached to their IBH helmets allowed them to see everything with perfect clarity. The two moved stealthily around to the back of the house, where they would use a double length of commercial detonating cord to blow the reinforced steel door off its hinges. Their main armament were suppressed M4s, with suppressed .45 caliber Sig Sauer pistols for backup, all of it equipped with laser sighting. They hadn't yet acquired fragmentation grenades, but their load-out did consist of six flash-bangs apiece. The body armor was of Special Forces quality and would stop an AK-47 round point-blank. They were not loaded out for speed or agility. They were loaded out for hard-hitting, break-your-fucking-head-open combat, and they were prepared to do whatever it took to get what they came for.

To their way of the thinking, the drug dealers they took down — and had so far twice ended up killing — were no different from any other enemy they'd ever encountered in combat. In many cases, they were probably worse. Take Terrance Booker, for example, a twice-convicted child molester and meth dealer. How many lives had this joker helped destroy during his thirty-five years on the planet? The figure likely stretched into the thousands.

Tuckerman opened the storm door, and Crosswhite duct taped the det cord across the hinges, lighting the fused end of the blasting cap and ducking back around the corner of the house, each man wearing earplugs, goggles, and a black balaclava to cover his face.

Ten seconds later, the det cord exploded with a sharp blast, and Crosswhite jumped out to kick the door into the house, where it fell with a crash against the kitchen floor. A woman started screaming immediately from the living room, and Crosswhite shouted "FBI!" at the top of his voice as they bounded inside.

"FBI!" Tuckerman echoed as they moved into the living room. Two men sat looking stunned on the couch in front of the television. "FBI! Everybody down on the fucking floor — now!"

Crosswhite shoved the woman into a chair and told her to shut the fuck up as the two men threw themselves onto the floor with their hands over the backs of their heads.

Neither one of them was Terrance Booker.

"Where the fuck is Booker?" demanded Crosswhite.

"Upstairs, man," said one of the men on the floor. "He upstairs."

Tuckerman kept them covered while Crosswhite moved toward the stairs on the far side of the living room. Four shots rang out, and Crosswhite felt the bullets pelt against the back of his armor. He spun around, cutting loose with the M4 and spraying twenty rounds of 5.56 mm straight down the hallway through the bathroom door just as it was slamming shut. He charged down the hall and kicked the door open to see a bloody Terrance Booker sprawled backward over the edge of the bathtub.

He bounded back into the living room. "All clear back there," he said. "Booker's dead. Punish those cocksuckers for lying!"

Tuckerman put a round through each of their knees, and they both howled in agony, crippled for life. The woman began to scream again, one of the men apparently being her boyfriend, and Tuckerman busted her in the face with the stock of the M4, sprawling her out cold on the floor.

"You ain't no fuckin' FBI, motha'fucker!" the boyfriend bellowed, gripping his knee with blood gushing through his fingers.

Tuckerman delivered him a kick to the face and signaled for Crosswhite to move up the stairs.

The black backpacks were sitting in plain sight on the bed in the master bedroom. Crosswhite took a moment to check them out, making sure they were full of money, as their informant had told them they would be. He was slinging them over his shoulder and turning for the door when the sound of someone coughing stopped him. The cough had come from the closet and sounded like that of a child. He opened the door, and a young black girl sat on a pillow looking up at him. She could not have been more than nine or ten years old, her big brown eyes wide and hopeful. From the looks of things, she had been living in the closet for some time.

"Can I go home now?" she asked.

Crosswhite knelt down and lifted her up. "You bet you can," he said, carrying her into the hall. "Coming down!" he shouted.

"Clear!" Tuckerman answered.

Crosswhite made the landing and stood at the bottom of the stairs with the girl in one arm and the backpacks of cash in the other. "What's wrong with this picture?" he said. "She's been living in a goddamn closet."

"Are these people your family?" Tuckerman asked the child, pointing at the men on the floor.

The little girl, too scared to speak, just shook her head no. "Get 'er out of here," Tuckerman said. "I'm right behind you." Ninety seconds later, he climbed in on the passenger side of the van. "Hit it."

Crosswhite shifted into drive and pulled away from the curb. He wasn't surprised that the neighbors were all still inside their homes. This wasn't the part of town where people came out to gawk when the feds showed up blowing holes in the walls; that was a good way of getting caught in a cross-fire that had nothing to do with you.

"Are we solid back there?" he asked a couple of minutes down the road.

Tuckerman took a moment to pull off his balaclava. "I made it look like a gangland hit." He looked into the back, where the little girl was sitting on the floor, resting against the backpacks full of money. "I'm sorry it's not more comfortable back there, sweetheart. Where do you live?"

"Chicago," she said.

Tuckerman slugged the door panel, wishing he could kill the little girl's abductors again.

"Take it easy," Crosswhite said quietly. "Do we have any accounts in Chicago that need servicing?"

"Yeah. There's a guy on the South Side who can put something together for us."

Crosswhite turned the corner as a police cruiser passed them going in the opposite direction without any lights flashing. "And still nobody's called it in," he said, watching the cop in the side-view mirror. "I think I might actually miss this town. It's been good to us."

"Too good," Tuckerman said, pointing a thumb toward the back. "This here is definitely a sign that it's time to go."

"Roger that," Crosswhite replied. "I was just thinking the same thing. Chi-Town's a good place to expand our business."

10

LAS VEGAS

Born in Novosibirsk, Russia, in 1962, Nikolai Kashkin was not pure Chechen. His mother had moved from Chechnya in the months before his birth to marry his father, who was a soldier in the Soviet Army. Raised to follow in his father's footsteps, Nikolai served as a lieutenant in his father's armored battalion late in the Afghan War.

Their service together was not lengthy. His father was killed in action in the Panjshir Valley during the same battle in which Kashkin himself was taken prisoner along with seventeen other Soviet tankers. His fellow prisoners were summarily executed by Tajik fighters, but because Kashkin was half Muslim, an officer, and the son of a Russian colonel, he was spared until the Mujahedeen warlord Ahmad Shah Massoud could determine his value as a potential hostage. It was during his time as a prisoner of the Mujahedeen in the Afghan village of Bazarak that he first came to truly appreciate his Muslim heritage.

To that point in his life, in keeping with the policies of the Supreme Soviet, his father had forbidden Kashkin to practice any religion at all, while at the same time insisting that Kashkin's mother keep her own religion private. Kashkin's father was rarely home during his childhood, however, so his mother had been able to teach him about Islam in secret. Though Kashkin did not grow up a devout Muslim by any stretch of the imagination, he did reach adulthood with an intimate understanding of the Islamic faith, and it was this understanding of his mother's faith that had saved his life in the Panjshir Valley.

During his meeting with Ahmad Massoud, the warlord spoke with Kashkin about his childhood, questioning him at length about the teachings he had received from his mother. By the end of their discussion, Massoud decided that the young Russian lieutenant was merely a misguided Muslim who had never been given the opportunity to properly allow Allah to come into his life. He then assigned to him a mentor named Orzu Karimov, and over the next eleven months, Karimov taught Kashkin how to walk the enlightened path of Muhammad.

When the fighting finally ended, and the Soviets agreed to leave Afghanistan in 1989, Kashkin was released to return home as a brother Muslim. Shortly thereafter, he and his mother relocated to Grozny, Chechnya, and it was there that Kashkin was exposed to the radical Salafi movement for the first time. Though he had not remained particularly loyal to the Russian army after the fall of the Soviet Union, nor had he bore it any ill will. It was not until his mother was killed by Russian artillery fire during the First Chechen War in the mid-1990s that he first took up the sword against the Russian Federation and, ultimately, all of Western democracy.

Kashkin was now sitting in front of the television in his Las Vegas hotel room watching CNN's coverage of a so-far-unexplained explosion in southern New Mexico. As the hours passed, word got out that Texas's Fort Bliss was on a nuclear alert status, and it was reported that a large-scale evacuation was taking place in the city of El Paso, where radiation levels were said to be on the rise. Ciudad Juárez, directly across the border from El Paso, was being evacuated as well, with the population there streaming south, deeper into Mexico. Fortunately, the land east of both cities was largely barren and sparsely populated.

There were no aerial shots provided of ground zero because a strict no-fly zone had been imposed by both governments, which were said to be working closely together in an effort to determine exactly what had happened. By two in the morning Vegas time, the talking heads on all major US news networks were blabbing a hundred words a minute, spouting all the possible worst-case scenarios, and managing to drive the national anxiety level off the charts with half the nation still asleep. A tired Wolf Blitzer of CNN eventually appeared in the wee hours to report that people all across the country were calling friends and relatives in the greatest call volume seen since September 11, 2001.

Kashkin had no way of knowing exactly what had occurred down on the Mexican border, but he was pleased to have chosen Zakayev to carry the second bomb, realizing that Zakayev must have been forced to make a choice between capture and detonation. The fact there had been limited immediate loss of life was a disappointment to Kashkin, but the news wasn't all bad.

The New York Stock Exchange had announced that it would remain closed for at least the next thirty-six hours, and damaging the Western economy was at least as important as taking Western lives. Westerners were like flies on a manure pile — you couldn't possibly hope to kill them all. What you *could* do was devastate their already struggling, interdependent capitalistic economies on both sides of the Atlantic. You could frighten their greedy, corporate-owned governments into imposing more and more restrictions upon their beloved freedoms.

Nuclear terror was the number one way to accomplish this.

Kashkin's ultimate goal was far more ambitious than taking lives. He wanted to push the United States to the breaking point of its depraved society, steadily applying more and more pressure until Americans were finally killing one another in the streets, burning their own cities to the ground in protest over ever-increasing austerity measures. He did not expect to live to see the end results of his work any more than bin Laden had expected to, but the attacks of September 11, 2001, had taught Kashkin a very important lesson in the war with the West. Bin Laden's strategy had exposed not only how fragile America's economy truly was but also, even more importantly, it had exposed the fact that, as went the US economy, so went the economies of the rest of the Western world.

This was the key to defeating them.

Final victory was at last within sight, within the collective reach of the arm of Islam, and all for the cost of a few million wicked American dollars won at a Las Vegas poker table, passed on to a dying old KGB agent wanting to live out his last few months in the South Pacific being pampered by exotic women.

Kashkin switched off the television as the sun was beginning to dawn in the east, opening the drapes to a bright new day. He ran his fingers through a head of gray hair and drew a deep breath to alleviate the tension in his chest over his heart, gazing out at the Luxor pyramid, the Sphinx, and the obelisk, shaking his head with antipathy. What decadence, what an obscenity. The United States had just been attacked with a nuclear weapon, and this city of vice and greed continued to function as though nothing had happened. He felt it fitting that the money he'd used to purchase both RA-115s from Daniel Mulinkov had been won right across the street in the Luxor casino.

He'd been friends with Mulinkov since the Afghan War, and Kashkin had long suspected the KGB man to be in possession of a Cold War suitcase nuke, but Mulinkov had always denied it. "There's no such thing, Nikolai," he would say, waving his hand. "There never was."

Then came the day five months ago when Mulinkov had arrived unexpectedly at Kashkin's home in Grozny, the whites of his eyes just beginning to yellow, the cancer in his pancreas having spread to his liver. He admitted to being in possession of not just one but two RA-115s, confiding in Kashkin that it had been his responsibility to retrieve them from East Berlin in the final days of the Soviet Union. Very few people in the Soviet government had been privy to the bombs' existence in those days, so when Mulinkov's direct superior died of a heart attack while making love to his mistress, there had been no one left alive who knew that Mulinkov was in possession of the weapons. It was in this manner that a pair of two-kiloton nuclear bombs had simply ceased to be.

Kashkin's cellular phone beeped on the nightstand. He picked it up. "Hello?" he said in English.

"What went wrong?" asked a voice in English with an Arabic accent. "Did one of your stupid couriers make a mistake?"

Kashkin looked at himself in the mirror, his pale blue eyes smiling back at him. "There have been no mistakes, Faisal. Everything is fine."

"So then you people won't be bothering me for more money?"

"I don't think so," Kashkin lied. "Everything is going according to plan."

"That's it then," the caller replied. "I'm out. Leave me alone."

The caller hung up without another word, and Kashkin tossed the phone onto the bed.

He was packing his bag a short time later when there came a knock at the door.

It was his nephew Bworz, another blue-eyed Caucasian from the Caucasus. "What happened?" was the first thing he said after closing the door behind him.

Kashkin shrugged, going back to packing his bag. He had important business up in Montana. A request had been made by his AQAP allies living in Windsor, Canada, two brothers named Akram and Haroun al-Rashid. He had met the fundamentalist Wahhabi brothers through his contacts in the Riyad us-Saliheyn Martyrs' Brigade, and they had arranged for the funding he needed to purchase the RA-115s, asking only a simple quid pro quo in return . . . to kill an American hero at his own game . . .

on his own soil.

"Obviously something went wrong," he said. "There's no point to worry about it. What's important is that Zakayev did his duty. The bomb did not fall into enemy hands. Your men are protecting the other weapon?"

"Yes," Bworz said. "We rented the house on the corner . . . the one you suggested. It's extremely close to the target."

"Good." Kashkin flipped the suitcase closed and buckled it. "I'll meet you there as soon as I'm finished in Montana, and we'll work out the details of our escape."

Bworz stood staring at him. "I don't like the idea of you going after Shannon by yourself. He's dangerous . . . as dangerous as any the Americans have."

"I can travel more easily alone." Kashkin handed him a small blue laptop from the dresser. It was one of two, the only difference between them being the color. "There's no need for the red one now that the second bomb has been lost."

"There's no need for this one either," Bworz said, tucking the blue laptop under his arm. "We've studied the target area in great detail. My men know it by heart."

"Then be sure to destroy the hard drive before you get rid of it."

"I will," Bworz promised. "Have you purchased a rifle for the hit?"

"I found one yesterday at a local gun show," Kashkin replied. "I had to pay the vendor quadruple his asking price because I'm not a citizen, but it's a good rifle. The Germans killed many Russians with it during the Great War."

"A Mauser," Bworz muttered. "Shannon will have something much better."

Kashkin hefted the suitcase from the bed to the floor. "The man will never even know I am there. Now take that down to the car for me. I have to pray."

11

MEXICO,
Jalisco, Puerto Vallarta

Antonio Castañeda was thirty-seven years old and a former member of the Mexican Special Forces. Trained by American Green Berets in the midnineties, he knew a great deal about military operations and the Mexican Army that hunted him. He also knew a thing or two about explosives, and you didn't need to be Alberto Einstein to know the explosion in Puerto Paloma the night before had been a hell of a lot bigger than anything a footlocker full of C4 could've produced. This meant he'd been lied to by the Chechen dogs who had paid to use his tunnel, and he was more than a little sore in the ass about it.

To look at him, however, you would not have guessed he had anything at all unpleasant on his mind. Castañeda was sitting on a white leather sofa in his villa on the west coast of Mexico, sipping tequila and scratching his German shepherd between the ears while a beautiful Mexican woman with long black hair stood behind him massaging his shoulders. He was not a particularly handsome man. His face was heavily pockmarked, and his dark eyes bulged slightly in their sockets. He had recently finished eating dinner with a thirty-four-year-old Chechen member of the RSMB named Marko Dudaev, and they were now relaxing in the living room.

There was a young lady massaging Dudaev as well. She was the other woman's younger sister, and they looked very much alike.

"Her name is Tanya," Castañeda said across the thick white marble coffee table. "I'm sorry she doesn't speak any English."

Dudaev smiled up at her, his blue eyes glassy from the tequila he was not yet accustomed to drinking. He had never tasted alcohol or smoked marijuana before coming to Mexico, as it was forbidden within Islam, but, as with any religion, some Muslims were more easily led astray than others. "I'm sure we'll manage," he said with a playful wink at Tanya, his own English heavily accented. "They say love is an international language."

Castañeda chortled. "Allow me to thank you for the deposit that was made to the account yesterday." He was referring to a bank account in the Cayman Islands. "Your people are very punctual when it comes to payment."

"We try hard to be," Dudaev said, still gazing up at Tanya, who could not have been a day over nineteen. "It is important to be punctual in business."

Tanya smiled down at him as she stood kneading the knotted muscles in his neck and shoulders, her touch strong and deft.

"It is, *sí,*" Castañeda said with a nod, taking a sip from his tequila. "Honesty is important as well, would you not agree?"

"Of course," Dudaev remarked, obviously enchanted by the young lady with the silky black hair. He took a stiff belt from his own glass, marveling at the feel of being drunk. It was as though he were floating on a cloud without a single care in the world.

"Bueno," Castañeda said, setting his glass down on the table as he remarked casually to Tanya, *"Prepárate, corazón."*

Tanya gave him a knowing wink as he sat back to extend his arms across the back of the sofa. He told the shepherd to go outside, and it trotted out the open door toward the pool, where a number of other women and a half dozen security personnel lounged around. As the dog slipped out, one of the security men got up to close the sliding glass door.

Then Castañeda clapped his hands, rubbing the palms together. "Yes, I agree that honesty is a very important part of business. So, amigo, why didn't you tell me your people were smuggling nuclear weapons into *los Estados Unidos*? Why did you lie and tell me the bombs were made from C4?"

Dudaev straightened up in the recliner, Tanya's hands still working his shoulders. Castañeda's people had been talking about the detonation in Spanish all day, but Dudaev hadn't understood a word of it. Castañeda had ordered him kept in the dark until there could be some kind of confirmation by his people in the North. Now that Castañeda had received the necessary verification, it was time to get to the bottom of things, time to try to determine whether there was a way to extricate himself from the deadly trap the Chechens had put him in.

"I don't know what you mean," Dudaev said, his expression marked by a trace of fear. "I don't know about nuclear weapons."

Castañeda smiled, saying to the girl,

"Ahora, corazón." Now, sweetheart.

Tanya ran the fingers of one hand through Dudaev's short-cropped hair while reaching nonchalantly into the small of her back to produce a pearl-handled straight razor, and then gracefully slipping the blade beneath his chin and jerking back his head to expose the jugular vein.

Dudaev let out a sharp, startled cry, grabbing the arms of the leather recliner, his entire body going ramrod stiff.

"Keep still now," Castañeda said to him quietly, signaling for the woman behind him to come around the sofa. "Lorena is going to make an exposition."

"Don Antonio," Dudaev said. "Please. This isn't necessary. We can —"

Tanya pressed the razor into his flesh to shut him up, increasing her grip on the turf of his hair. He gasped, increasing his own grip on the arms of the recliner.

The other woman, Lorena, also held a straight razor. She knelt with it between Dudaev's legs and began to carefully cut away the crotch of his khaki trousers. Dudaev shivered, a cold sweat breaking out across his chest as she worked the blade with a surgical dexterity, first cutting away the heavy material of his trousers, and then the thin white cotton of his boxer briefs to fully expose his uncircumcised penis and scrotum without so much as nicking him. Both organs were an unbecoming reddish-purple, shrunken to their minimum as if Dudaev had just come from the pool.

Lorena tossed the swatches of cloth aside and sat back on her haunches, awaiting Castañeda's instructions.

Castañeda smiled, sitting forward to take up his drink again. "Do I have your attention now, Señor Dudaev?" he asked in a friendly voice.

"Yes, Don Antonio," croaked the terrified Chechen.

Tanya lessened her grip, though only slightly, so he could speak a bit more clearly.

"Gracias," he muttered, swallowing hard.

Castañeda took a sip from the glass, setting it aside once more. "It is important for you to listen very carefully now. There is no time for games. You will tell me what you know about the bombs your people have smuggled into the United States. If not, Lorena will cut out your *heuvos* one by one, and Tanya will feed them to you." He stood up from the sofa, stepping around the marble table, adjusting the tuck of his black silk shirt as he stood frowning over the shuddering Dudaev.

He put his hands into his pockets, and his

overall presence took on an unmistakably menacing air. *"Pendejo!"* he hissed venomously. "Because of you and your lying friends, I will be hunted to the end of the world! I will be labeled a nuclear terrorist! My government will partner with the gringos, and together they will hunt me down like a rabid dog! Do you understand me? There will be no place on earth for me to hide!"

"Yes, Don Antonio, I understand you very well . . . but . . . but, please, I know nothing about nuclear weapons. I can't imagine what makes you think we have lied to you!"

Castañeda smirked in disgust, turning to lift his drink. *"Comienza, Lorena."* Begin.

Lorena took a firm grip on the Chechen's scrotum, and Tanya pulled back hard on his head, keeping the razor tight against his jugular. Dudaev gasped in pain and then screamed aloud as Lorena sliced out one of his testicles. He reflexively grabbed his groin, but when Tanya depressed the razor hard enough to bite into the flesh of his throat, his bloody hands shot back to the arms of the recliner, his legs quaking uncontrollably as he began to sob. Blood gushed from the incision in his scrotum, running down the front of the recliner to pool on the tile.

Castañeda finished the tequila and tossed aside the glass, which shattered on the floor. Then he snatched the bloody orb from Lorena's outstretched hand, savagely jamming it down Dudaev's throat.

"I know you are lying to me!" he shouted into the gagging man's face. "The fucking bomb went off, you stinking *cabrón*! It destroyed an entire town!" He pulled his hand from Dudaev's throat, wiping it off on the Chechen's white guayabera shirt, and then watched on, grim faced, as the strangling man finally managed to choke down the testicle.

Dudaev sat coughing, suppressing the urge to vomit. "Please!" he begged, his voice trembling. "I don't know anything. I'm only a legate — an ambassador!"

Castañeda stood with his hands on his hips, shaking his head. "I don't know what more to tell you, amigo. You only have one *huevo* left. After that, Lorena will cut out your eyes. And after that . . ." He sighed and held out his hands in exasperation. "After that, I fear life will become very unpleasant for you."

Lorena took a bloody grip on his scrotum once more.

"Stop!" Dudaev shouted, gnashing his teeth in agony and self-loathing, knowing he deserved this fate for having strayed from the path; for having spent the last month living in sin. "I will tell you," he sobbed shamefully. "Please, just no more cutting — for the love of Allah!"

"Okay then, amigo," Castañeda said softly, patting the Chechen on the shoulder. "No more cutting, I promise. Now tell me what you know."

After Dudaev spilled his guts about the two Russian-made RA-115s, Castañeda signaled Tanya to cut his throat. He would use the information when the time was right. When he needed to save himself, he would contact the CIA.

12

LANGLEY

Robert Pope, director of SAD, the Special Activities Division of the CIA, arrived at the office of the CIA director, George Shroyer. The director and his deputy, Cletus Webb, were expecting him.

"Good morning," he said, taking a seat in front of Shroyer's desk. Pope, a tall man in his midsixties with bright blue eyes and a head of thick white hair, was regarded as somewhat eccentric by his CIA counterparts.

"Good morning." Shroyer was a hawk-faced individual with a bony nose and peering green eyes. He wouldn't have dared let on, but he'd been extremely relieved when Pope had requested an immediate meeting. On a personal level, he didn't care for Pope; he was a little bit afraid of him. But he knew that Pope was probably the most gifted member of the US intelligence community, and if he was asking for a meeting less than twenty-four hours after a nuclear bomb had been detonated on American soil — which was what the army had determined to be the case — there was a good chance he had something important to share.

The president had gone surprisingly easy on Shroyer and the directors of the NSA and FBI during their closed meeting in the Oval Office. All three had expected him to ream their asses good for having been caught completely unaware by what was now being called the "New Mexico Event," particularly with the presidential election only a couple of months away, but the president was leading in the polls by a margin of greater than 20 percent, and his opponent was seen as weak on foreign policy and even weaker on national defense. The president had crushed him during the first televised debate, and the sad truth was that a terrorist attack on the United States would probably only serve to lock up his reelection. Conspiracy theorists were already lighting up the web, accusing the president of having staged the New Mexico Event for that very reason.

If Pope were able to provide Shroyer with something actionable that he could take to the White House, that would put the CIA far out in front of both the FBI and the NSA, which hadn't been able to provide any intel at all.

"What can we do for you, Bob?" Shroyer asked, concealing the eager anxiety rising in his gut.

Pope offered a small flash drive over the desk. "There's a WMA file on there I think you gentlemen should find interesting."

Shroyer clicked the audio file, and the three of them sat listening to the phone conversation between Kashkin and the man with the Arabic accent. When the exchange ended, Shroyer sat gazing quietly at Webb.

Webb understood that he was expected to speak first so that Shroyer would be less likely to end up looking ignorant in front of Pope. "What did we just hear, Bob? Who are they?"

"The Arabic voice was Muhammad Faisal," Pope replied. "He's a very minor member of the House of Saud who became a naturalized American citizen last year." The House of Saud was the Saudi royal family that ruled Saudi Arabia and promoted Salafi Islam. The family was composed of roughly fifteen thousand members, though most of the wealth and power resided with an elite two thousand.

"A member of the Saudi royal family."

Shroyer took off his glasses to rub the bridge of his nose. "Okay. So who's the other guy?"

"We don't know yet," Pope said. "We're working to pin down the accent now. It could be Russian, but it's more probably Chechen."

"When was this recorded?" Webb asked.

"About seven this morning, Las Vegas time, and both men were within half a mile of the Luxor casino during the conversation — not more than a quarter mile apart. I believe that's significant."

Shroyer stole a suspicious glance at Webb. "Bob, electronic eavesdropping isn't in your job description — as I seem to recall you pointing out not too long ago. CIA doesn't even have jurisdiction within the US."

"That's never stopped us before," Pope said matter-of-factly.

Webb cleared his throat, hoping to avert a blowup on Shroyer's part. "How long have you been spying on Faisal, Bob?"

Pope blinked once. "Since he applied for American citizenship."

"On your own authority?" Shroyer blurted.

"On a hunch, George."

Shroyer held his temples for a long moment and then looked up. "All right, let's get past that. What exactly is this telephone conversation supposed to mean?"

"I think they were talking about the New Mexico Event."

"It sounded to me like they could've been talking about anything."

"But they were talking about the explosion," Pope said confidently. "The Chechen said, 'Everything is going according to plan.' It has to be related. The timing of this conversation is too close . . . too cryptic."

Shroyer was still stuck on the fact Pope had so blatantly overstepped his authority and jurisdiction, jeopardizing the CIA director's own position. At least now he had all he needed to get rid of the enigmatic pain in the ass once and for all. But did he dare? There were rumors about Pope having secret files on various people within the agency and elsewhere in DC. And if the son of a bitch had time enough to spy on apparent nobodies like Muhammad Faisal, who the hell else was he busy using government time to spy on?

"I would hardly call this evidence of any kind," he said.

"There's another file on the flash drive," Pope replied.

Shroyer opened a photo file. The first photo was of an Arabic man dressed in a blue Western-style suit with an open collar. He was in his midthirties, with dark features and a closely trimmed beard.

"That's Faisal," Pope said. "In the next photo, you'll see him eating breakfast with a Salafi fundamentalist named Alik Zakayev two weeks ago at an inn in the Bavarian Alps. Zakayev is Chechen — a known member of the Riyad us-Saliheyn Martyrs' Brigade."

Webb sat forward in his chair to see the photo better. "Zakayev . . . the same guy the Russians turned over to us in connection with the Boston bombings?"

Pope nodded. "Yes, as a matter of fact, but he had nothing to do with Boston. That's why he was released from Guantanamo back in June."

Shroyer shot a look at Webb. "Why wasn't I made aware of that?"

The deputy director shrugged. "It's news to me as well."

"Given their unlikely location in that photo," Pope went on, "combined with the fact they're both Salafi Muslims, I think we should seriously consider —"

"Wait a second," Shroyer said, holding up his hand. "Isn't the Saudi family Wahhabi?"

"Salafi and Wahhabi are one in the same," Pope answered. "The only difference is in what they call themselves. Some Salafi find the term *Wahhabi* offensive, but that's a regional issue, nothing to do with a difference in beliefs." He pushed his glasses up onto his nose. "As I was saying, we need to consider the facts at hand. Faisal was breaking bread with a known member of the RSMB a month ago. And this morning he was talking on the phone — within eight hours of a nuclear blast — to a man who is also very likely a Chechen about something that *went wrong.*" He shook his head. "This is not coincidence. They were talking about the New Mexico Event. Also, Faisal is a known high-stakes gambler, and we know that Islamic terrorists have used Vegas casinos to raise funds in the past. I believe he's a fund-raiser hiding in plain sight, using his familial status as a cover."

"Are you saying the Chechens and the Arabs are working together?" Webb asked.

"We've seen it before."

"Do you have any actual evidence?" Shroyer asked. "You know damn well we can't accuse a member of the House of Saud without hard evidence, no matter how minor a member he may be."

"I don't have any yet, but I know how to get it."

"How's that?" Shroyer was more than

moderately disappointed by Pope's supposed intel. "We bring him in," Pope said. "Sweat him for information."

Shroyer stole an exasperated glance at Webb. "Bob, the man is not only a member of the Saudi royal family, but you just said yourself that he's an American citizen now. We don't *sweat* American citizens for intelligence."

"Oh? Since when?"

Shroyer's face reddened.

"Forget I said that," Pope said with a wave of a hand. "Being a US citizen strips Faisal of whatever protection his Saudi familial status may have afforded him."

"That's what *you* think," Shroyer said. "He'll lawyer up so damn fast —"

"I didn't say to arrest him," Pope said. "I said to bring him in — to snatch him. He's well looked after by his own security people, but a team of spec ops professionals could handle the grab easily enough."

"What team of spec ops professionals?" Webb asked.

"ST6-B."

"That does it!" Shroyer snapped, pulling the flash drive from the laptop and tossing it across the desk at Pope. "I don't want to hear any more of this. SEAL Team Six Black was disbanded nine months ago — as you damn well know! — and you're suggesting that we operate completely outside the rules to kidnap an American citizen directly related to the most important family in the Middle East — a family very deeply invested in the American economy."

Pope remained placid. "I'm not suggesting we use active-duty DEVGRU personnel. There are plenty of former operatives working in the private sector that we could call upon."

Again, Shroyer looked at Webb. "Can you believe your fucking ears?"

Webb demurred for a moment, taking time to consider his response. "I'm sorry, Bob, but you've overstepped this time."

Pope slipped the flash drive into his jacket pocket. "I don't see how that's even vaguely relevant. A nuclear bomb has just been detonated on American soil. Wall Street has been shut down for the first time since 9/11. And people are already beginning to hoard food and fuel. How long do you intend to let this threat go on? I've just given you actionable intelligence."

"Whether it's actionable or not," Shroyer said, "is wide open to debate. Not to mention it was illegally obtained, which jeopardizes the integrity of this entire agency!"

Unapologetic, Pope removed his glasses,

staring hard at the director. "Contrary to popular belief, George, the time to start bending the rules comes *before* the enemy gets a second bomb into play, not after, because by then it will be too late."

Shroyer sat back, folding his arms across his chest. "Well, Bob, if you think I'm strolling into the Oval Office with this ridiculous audio file and suggesting to the president that he okay a black operation on American soil, then you've lost your marbles." He rocked forward, putting his hands on the desktop and throwing caution to the wind. "In fact, I'm going to recommend that you be asked for your resignation. I'm sorry, but your shenanigans have gone far enough."

13

MEXICO, CHIHUAHUA

Twenty-eight-year-old Mariana Mederos was a second-generation Mexican American working as a field agent for the CIA in the city of Chihuahua, the capital of Chihuahua State. She was five foot nine, with a runner's physique, brown hair, and brown eyes. She'd been two hundred miles south of the border during the New Mexico Event. Awake at zero hour chatting with a contact over the internet, she heard the incongruous roll of distant thunder and felt the tremor in the earth a short time later. Her satellite phone rang soon afterward with a call from the Mexico station chief wanting to know if she could supply any intel as to what the hell had just happened. No one else within the agency was as close to ground zero, and there hadn't been even the slightest jot of intelligence to indicate that a nuke had been in play.

Since those early hours after the explosion, life had moved pretty fast for Mariana, even if only in the communicative sense. Much of her work was done over the computer from the privacy of her apartment, where she kept in contact with her network of informants — common citizens on the CIA payroll. It didn't cost a great deal to keep the information flowing in the drug-ravaged state, with its struggling economy. As little as a thousand pesos a week (less than one hundred dollars) could be enough. The majority of the intel she collected was passed on to the DEA and the ICE, to be used in the war on drugs — a "war" that she believed the United States had been fighting with at least one hand behind its back, especially when she considered how much of the information she passed up the chain that was never acted upon.

After the New Mexico Event, however, the nature of her job took on a whole new aspect with an unprecedented sense of urgency. Suddenly she was the CIA's go-to gal on the ground in the middle of a hot zone, and within only a few hours, she found herself entrusted with resources and information that were customarily reserved for personnel well above her pay grade. The "company" was coming to Chihuahua, and it would be her responsibility to establish arriving operatives in and around the city, introducing them to the appropriate contacts or state officials.

The Mexican government had given its tacit approval for this, but only at the intelligence level. The Policía Federal Ministerial, Mexico's equivalent of the CIA, was agreeing to a limited influx of American intelligence personnel for one reason and one reason only: nuclear weapons scared the living hell out of everyone, and when it came to such a threat, it didn't much matter whether or not you liked or trusted the CIA, because its people were the ones you unquestionably wanted on your team upon confirmation that the lunatic fringe had gotten their hands on the bomb.

This morning Mariana had agreed to meet with a contact in La Catedral de Chihuahua, a large, ornate Catholic church in the Plaza de Armas. This would be her first face-to-face with the contact Carolina Rodríguez, a woman from the northern part of the state who had sent her an email claiming to have detailed information about the explosion. She had asked that Mariana bring one thousand American dollars, apologizing for the size of the request, though promising that Mariana would find the information well worth it.

Seated at the back of the cathedral, pretending to be lost in prayer, Mariana considered the amount of Carolina's demand, knowing that a thousand dollars was a great deal of money to the woman who supported three daughters by cleaning houses for less than ninety dollars a week. Mariana guessed the information she was bringing would either be worth a great deal more than a thousand dollars or nothing at all, and she was leaning toward the latter, but this was the kind of lead that had eventually killed Bin Laden in 2011.

There were only twenty or thirty people in the cathedral this morning, scattered among the pews, some sitting and some on their knees, all of them lost in their own thoughts. A man in a black suit and dark sunglasses entered the pew behind her and sat down just off her right shoulder. She could feel him looking at her, realizing he'd probably sat there to stare, something not uncommon in her experience. Since he was too close for her to have a private conversation anyway, she decided to move.

"What's wrong?" the man said in Spanish as she stood up to leave. "Am I not good enough to pray with?"

She looked at him, and he removed the glasses, his bulbous eyes unmistakable.

Fear surged in her veins. She cast a panicked look around, seeing that one of Castañeda's men covered every exit.

"Please," Castañeda said. "Sit. We have much to talk about, you and I."

Having little choice, Mariana retook her seat. "What have you done with Señora Rodríguez?"

Castañeda smiled, placing a hand upon his breast. "I am Señora Rodríguez," he said pleasantly, "and I remain at your service."

Mariana felt like the biggest idiot of all time. One of her most reliable informants over the last nine months had been Castañeda himself, the very man whose movement she'd been attempting to track. He'd been leading her on a wild goose chase, feeding her intel that, while reliable, always led the DEA to only small shipments of drugs — never the coveted mother lode, and never anywhere close to Castañeda.

He saw the angry look on her face and chortled. "Don't look that way," he said, switching to English to reduce their chances of being understood by anyone coming close. "I've given you nothing but truthful information since we began our correspondence. You should be grateful."

Mariana was remembering that she'd been put into contact with Señora Rodriguez through a man named Sergio, whom she had not heard from in some time. "And Sergio?" she asked quietly.

"Oh, I'm afraid Sergio is quite dead," Castañeda said. "It's interesting, don't you think, that the DEA chose to act on only about a third of the information I sent to you? Why do you believe that is?"

Mariana felt her face grow hot. "Why are we having this meeting, Señor Castañeda?"

"I've already told you. I have information about the nuclear device that was detonated in Puerto Paloma."

She stared at him, wondering how seriously to take what he was saying. He was known to toy with his victims before killing them. She put her arm over the back of the pew, turning to look at him more directly in an attempt to appear confident. "In that case, I'm listening."

He became very serious, and she saw genuine concern on his face. "First, I'm going to need certain guarantees."

She almost didn't believe her eyes or her ears. Castañeda wasn't just concerned, he was afraid of something, and he was coming to the CIA for help — coming to *her,* the woman who'd been hunting him all across the state of Chihuahua. "Guarantees? You're the leader of a drug cartel, and your people have done horrible things on both sides of the border. I'm not sure what kinds of guarantees you think anyone would be willing to give you."

He sat forward, resting his elbows on his knees and keeping his voice low. "Listen to me. I am prepared to tell you precisely what kind of device was detonated, exactly how many kilotons, who made it, who detonated it, and exactly where he was when he detonated it . . . but not without guarantees."

Mariana was hard pressed to conceal the excitement that began to simmer in her blood. She suddenly saw herself halfway to having her own office in Langley, the white Range Rover she'd been dreaming about, a house in Georgetown, out of the field and into the upper echelon — all for the price of a few guarantees. "What guarantees?" she asked, trying to appear doubtful.

"I had nothing to do with the bomb," he said. "I'm a business man, not a terrorist." She made a *pssh* sound at that. "I don't want to be blamed for this explosion just because it happened in my territory in one of my tunnels. Do you understand?"

Did that slip about the tunnel? she wondered. *Or was he throwing me a bone?*

"Okay," she said, "I don't see a problem with that. If you didn't do it, you didn't do it."

He looked at her, his half-lidded eyes taking on a menacing air for the first time. "What I am telling you is that I do not want to be hunted."

"Excuse me, but you're a drug lord; you're already hunted. Nobody on either side of the Rio Grande is going to just forget about you."

"No," he said, shaking his head. "I am not hunted the way you think I am hunted. I have friends who protect me: friends among the army and the police who warn me not to be in certain places when it is dangerous for me to be there. Do you understand?"

She drew a breath and sighed. "Of course. This is Mexico, after all."

"So," he continued, "these friends, these people who protect me, would be forced to turn their backs on me if I were labeled a nuclear terrorist. Some of them might even find it advantageous to betray certain of my secrets, which would undoubtedly lead to my capture. Is this making sense to you? Are you located high enough in your agency to guarantee that I will not be associated with this bomb; that I will not be labeled a nuclear terrorist?"

"I don't know," she said. "Most of what you're offering sounds to me like information we'd uncover on our own in due course."

He sat back, extending his arms across the back of the pew. "Has your army isolated the isotopes yet? If they have, then you know it was a uranium bomb and not plutonium . . . and in time you will discover that it was probably enriched at the Soviet enrichment facility in the Urals."

For Castañeda to know this level of detail meant the rest of his information might be reliable, because she herself had only been made privy to the isotope results a few hours earlier, and as yet there had been no public disclosure. If he was correct about the bomb being made with *Russian* uranium — which the army would not be able to determine right away — that was absolutely going to set a cat among the pigeons. Castañeda had already given her enough intel to ensure her superiors' ongoing confidence — provided she was able to get out of the cathedral alive — but she really wanted that office in Langley, so she began to angle. "What I can guarantee is this," she said. "I'll do everything I can to make sure you're not blamed or associated with the bomb. It wouldn't be advantageous for my government to blame the wrong person anyhow."

"In other words, you have the authority to guarantee me nothing."

"Look," she said, "nobody would in a situation like this. Clearances have to be obtained. You were military. You know how it works."

He leaned forward again, very close to her this time because there were people passing behind them. "What kinds of guarantees would your government have given for information that could have prevented 9/11?"

"What's that supposed to mean?"

He sat back and smiled. "Use your imagination."

"The bomb already went off."

"Did it?" he asked, the smile lingering as he got to his feet. "You can contact me at the usual email address if and when you are able to make the necessary guarantees."

"Wait!" she said, experiencing a burst of inspiration. "If you really do have the kind of information that you've just implied, then . . . for a little extra, I can give you the guarantees you're looking for."

He sat back down. "Extra? What extra?"

"In exchange for being left alone — which

is what you're really asking for here, let's be honest — you're going to have to cool it with the violence on both sides of the border. Stop killing cops and civilians. Stick to battling your rival cartels. If you'll make me that guarantee now, then I'm sure I can get the guarantees you're asking for."

He stared at her, a dubious frown creasing his face.

"Think about it," she said. "If you offer this . . . oh, I don't know, call it a *cease-fire;* cartels have offered that kind of treaty before — that would motivate my government to not only grant the guarantees you want, but to keep their word. And that should matter to you, Tony, because a guarantee isn't any good unless there's an incentive to stand behind it."

Castañeda didn't like to be called Tony, and he was sure she knew it. He sat looking at her, thinking that he'd like to fuck her; that she was very lucky he needed her help. Because under normal circumstances, a CIA operative as pretty as this one would have looked very good to him down on all fours with a leash around her neck.

"Chechenos," he said. "The bombs were smuggled into Mexico by stinking, lying Chechen dogs."

14

General William Couture stalked into a heavily guarded conference room at the Pentagon dressed in his starched universal camouflage ACU, flanked by his aide-de-camp, an equally towering army major who looked as though he'd been chiseled from a block of granite and who wore a .45 caliber Glock 21 pistol slung beneath each arm. Rumor had it that he carried two weapons so he could toss one to the general in the event there was ever a need to defend themselves. Couture stood at the head of a long mahogany table lined with generals and admirals from all branches of the United States military. All seven of the Joint Chiefs were present, as were several other uniformed service chiefs.

Couture's expression was stern, his merciless gaze set firmly.

"Gentlemen," he said in a sonorous voice, "the secretary of defense has ordered us to Fast Pace." This was the code phrase for DEFCON 2. "The president is aboard Air Force One, and the vice president has already been taken to a hardened location belowground. In addition, the United States Congress is being evacuated from the District of Columbia as we speak. Each member of Congress will return to his or her home state, where they will remain until we are back to at least DEFCON 4." DEFCON 5, code named Fade Out, was the most relaxed of the defense conditions.

Most of what Couture had just announced, the Joint Chiefs already knew. What they did not know was *why* the defense condition had been escalated again. The moment the army had verified a nuclear explosion in southern New Mexico, the US military had been ordered to DEFCON 3, but the last time the US had stood at DEFCON 2 was during the three-week Yom Kippur War of 1973, when Egypt and Syria launched surprise attacks against Israel, only to be driven back into their own countries before a cease-fire was reached. DEFCON 2 was the last stage before nuclear war, and no one seated at the table had yet heard anything to merit an escalation of this magnitude.

"Within the hour," Couture continued, "everyone in this room — myself included — will be airlifted to Edwards Air Force Base, where a command center is being prepared. All submarine captains are being alerted that a nuclear strike on the District of Columbia may be imminent." Couture shifted his gaze to a pair of navy admirals. "These vessels are not — repeat, *not* — to assume Cocked Pistol status without a direct order from the president aboard Air Force One, where he will remain for the foreseeable future." Cocked Pistol was the code name for DEFCON 1: clearance to use nuclear force.

"In addition, the Russian Federation and the Republic of China have been put on notice. There has been no provocative language, but the president has made it to clear to both nations that the United States will remain poised to defend itself *with full military capacity* in the event that Washington, DC, is destroyed."

By now the Joint Chiefs were exchanging pensive glances.

Couture pulled out his chair, taking a seat and lacing his fingers on the tabletop. "Now, here is the reason we are at Fast Pace, gentlemen: there is an active two-kiloton

RA-115 loose within the United States, and we have no idea where it is."

"Jesus," muttered a buzz-cut Marine Corps general, clicking a pen and rocking back in his seat. "So they're real."

"What's an RA-115?" asked the Coast Guard admiral seated next to him. "Never heard of it."

"Until now," the Marine said, "nothing more than a rumor — a Cold War legend."

"It's a Russian suitcase nuke," Couture explained. "We're pressing the Russians to provide us the necessary intel, but so far they're vacillating. Regardless, CIA has determined — to within what they consider a ninety-five-percent certainty — that the New Mexico Event was the result of a be-lowground detonation of one of *two* of these damn things. From what CIA has pieced together, it looks like Chechen insurgents paid one of the Mexican cartels to let them cross through a tunnel under the border. The reason for the president's immediate departure is that one of these Chechens is reported to have brought the other device into the country seventeen days ago."

"Good God!" said the pallid-looking vice chairman, General John Pickett. "With a seventeen-day head start, it could be any-where." He had arrived at the Pentagon only

129

a half hour earlier, having been in hospital for the last three days with an intestinal virus he'd picked up during a recent visit to Pakistan.

"What went wrong with the other bomb, General?" asked the Marine. "Does CIA have any idea why it went off?"

"It's still open to conjecture at this point," Couture replied. "We do know, however, that the ICE office in Albuquerque received an eleventh-hour tip about some kind of special shipment coming across the border. The call was received a couple of hours before the blast, and it's beginning to look like the local ICE team out there may have made a late-night interdiction raid on the tunnel. The fact that thirteen ICE agents have gone missing seems to support the theory, and CIA is guessing that our Chechen friends must have detonated the bomb as a result."

The Joint Chiefs began to talk among themselves.

Couture elevated his voice. "There's no way we can sit on this, gentlemen. The president will address the nation from Air Force One within the hour. He's going to lay it on the table. He's going to announce that we suspect a nuclear weapon to be loose within the United States."

"There'll be mass exodus," someone muttered. "DC and Manhattan will be a pair of ghost towns by this time tomorrow."

"Not to mention LA," someone else remarked. "Chicago."

Couture rocked back in the chair. "Very possible. That's why the president's decided to declare martial law in each of the cities you've just mentioned. With luck and God willing, that will be the extent of it, though you can bet that all arms of local law enforcement will be stretched to the limit on a national level. This is exactly what we've been fearing, gentlemen. Our nuclear chickens have come home to roost."

15

CHICAGO

The declaration of martial law in the cities of New York, DC, and Los Angeles the week before hadn't shaken the local populations up all that much. Many citizens had, in fact, welcomed the decision. And it helped that the army hadn't marched in like jack-booted Nazis. General Couture — following the example set by Lieutenant General Russel Honoré (aka the Ragin' Cajun) in the aftermath of Hurricane Katrina — had made it crystal clear that the army's mission was to protect the citizenry and to look after them, not to treat them as the subjects of an occupation. For the most part, the soldiers did very little other than maintain a constant presence, making routine patrols into the outlying areas while leaving the duties of law enforcement to the police whenever possible. In general, there was a sense they were all in the same boat. Because if a

132

nuclear bomb did happen to go off, the shock wave, fire, and radiation would make no distinction between military and civilian personnel.

However, the same type of accord did not exist within the Windy City. For reasons that no one had so far been able to pinpoint, there had been immediate friction between Chicagoans and the 82nd Airborne Division, particularly on Chicago's South Side — the side that Jim Croce had once sung about as "the baddest part of town." Where the other four cities had lost about a third of their populations to voluntary evacuation, the vast majority of Chicagoans chose to stay put, and they simply resented a military presence in their neighborhoods.

"We Chicagoans can take care of ourselves!" the city's angry mayor declared to CNN's Anderson Cooper. "We don't need an army of occupation rumbling through our streets — this isn't Baghdad. And we'll be damned if we're going to let these terrorists scare us from our homes!"

The next night, gunfire was exchanged in southern Cook County, Illinois, between looters and soldiers. By the end of the third day of occupation, the official civilian death toll stood at thirty-two, which compelled the mayor to go back on television, this time urging his constituents to cooperate with the army. But the genie seemed to be out of the bottle by then, and some on the military side expected the violence to increase once disgruntled citizens became better organized.

For this reason, the 82nd began to circle the wagons in the southern zones outside the city, setting up FOBs (forward operating bases) from which patrols could operate. Division headquarters remained downtown. Signs sprang up at the FOBs with proverbial names such as Fort Apache and Fort Necessity, provoking General Couture to blow his stack during an early-morning inspection, ordering the signage taken down immediately.

"This is not an us-against-them paradigm, Major!" Couture growled at a veteran combat officer fresh in from Afghanistan. "And you'd better get that through your head. Nobody told you this was going to be a walk in the park — *no occupation ever is!* — but we're all Americans here, and your men *will* conduct themselves accordingly, or you *will* find yourself in a world of hurt! Do I make myself clear?"

His ass chewed out by a four-star general, the major snapped to attention, answering, "Yes, sir! Crystal, sir!"

Fifteen minutes after Couture cleared the zone, the Fort Apache sign went back up. The FOB was attacked that same night, and eight more civilians lost their lives. The next day, an actual civilian militia began to form on the north side of the city, where there was talk of marching on division headquarters. Nobody really took the talk seriously, but the threat of a nuclear bomb had obviously become a secondary concern in Chicago, and this forced the president (by this time commanding from Andrews Air Force Base) to recall General Couture for the purpose of discussing at least a partial withdrawal from the city, fearing the occupation there was doing measurably more harm than good, and that the discord might spread to the other occupied cities.

Daniel Crosswhite and Brett Tuckerman knew next to nothing about any of this. For the past week, they'd been too busy knocking over drug pushers well outside the military cordon to the south, not far from where they had returned the little girl to her home.

The little one's parents had been completely stunned to answer the door at seven in the morning and see their long-lost daughter — now almost a year older —

standing on the porch between two un-shaven white guys in dark sunglasses, clutching a truck-stop teddy bear and a big bag of McDonald's hotcakes.

"Remember . . . we were never here," Crosswhite said gravely. He handed the bag of hotcakes to the little girl's father, and then he and Tuckerman disappeared on foot down the block.

Each pusher they'd taken down over the subsequent five nights was forced to rat out the locations of his associates' hideouts, and the money had piled up fast. They were about ready to blow town the night before, but the last pusher they worked over ratted off a competitor whose house was located a half mile inside the military cordon.

"That motherfucker got half a mil easy!" the pusher had sworn, his bloody face mashed between his expensive white shag carpet and the sole of a Fort Lewis combat boot.

Now Crosswhite sat in the back of the van watching the run-down house through his night vision goggles. "What do you think?"

Tuckerman picked his teeth with a toothpick. "Looks like a shit hole to me."

"Could be intentional if they're really holding that much cash." Crosswhite reached over and jerked the black hood off the head of their battered informant, who sat against the bulkhead with his hands flex-cuffed behind his back. "If you're setting us up, asshole, I'm gonna stuff you headfirst down a sewer pipe. You got that?"

The man nodded wearily, duct tape over his mouth, nose broken, and one eye swollen nearly shut. Blood and snot oozed over the tape as he breathed.

"Let's do it then." Crosswhite put the bag back over the dealer's head and yanked the cord tight, tying it in a knot. Then they flopped him over onto his belly in the middle of the satin bedspread they had taken from his bed and roughly rolled him up in it. A sharp blow to the side of his face through the bedspread with the stock of an M4 knocked him cold.

They dismounted the van and moved swiftly toward the house, scanning the darkness through infrared as they made their way around back. A sharp burst of 9 mm gunfire from a first-floor window struck Tuckerman in his chest and shoulder armor. The two men returned fire, spraying suppressed .223 caliber fire through the window. The shooter's head disintegrated, and the body dropped with a thud inside the house. Someone else opened fire from another window, and they dove for cover behind an old brick barbeque pit that hadn't been used to cook a meal in a half century.

"It's a goat fuck," Tuckerman said, switching out the magazine on his M4. "Wanna split before the army hears this shit and rolls in?"

"No, I want my half a mil," Crosswhite said, reloading quickly.

"Dude, there ain't no money. This was a fuckin' setup."

"I don't think so. Look." Crosswhite pointed up at the eve of the house, where a small infrared camera was mounted below the rain gutter. "They've got real security here, and that means money."

"It also means we should split."

"You go if you want. I'm takin' this place down and retiring to Guate-fuckin'-mala."

Tuckerman chuckled. "When we get killed, it'll be your fault."

"Roger that."

They each pulled the pin from a high-explosive grenade and then hurled them through the windows. Even as the grenades were exploding, they were pulling the pins on two more, hurling them into the house on the tail end of the first pair of explosions. Glass blasted outward in blinding white flashes, and the entire house groaned within from the force of four nearly simultaneous detonations.

Tuckerman and Crosswhite dashed from behind the barbeque pit and blew the back door off its hinges with plastic explosives. Three busted bodies littered the kitchen floor, one of them missing most of its head, and the smell of cordite hung heavy in the air. They found two more busted bodies in the dining room and a matching number of scattered Tec-9 machine pistols, which they kicked contemptuously aside. The inside of the house was now a shambles, but there was a lot of expensive stuff in the place: leather sofas and chairs, a big-screen hi-def television, stereo . . . the works.

"Let's get the money." Crosswhite put a burst of fire through the basement door and kicked it apart with his boot. They took off their goggles and switched on the rail-mounted flashlights attached to their carbines, making their way down the stairs, careful to watch for booby traps. Procedure and all common sense dictated that they clear the entire house before cornering themselves in the basement, but both men had seen enough combat by this point in their lives that they felt safe enough trusting instinct, and instinct told them the fight was over.

In the basement, they found what they

had been told to look for: a steel gun locker in the corner with a combination dial on the front.

"Looks tough," Tuckerman said, chewing the inside of his cheek.

"It's a gun locker, not a bank vault." They put plastic explosives on the dial and all three hinges, set the timer, and ducked upstairs.

The blast shook the floor, and they scurried back down to find the locker laying over on its side with the mangled quarter-inch steel door still wedged crookedly in place. The steel locking pins had held for the most part, but banded stacks of fifty- and hundred-dollar bills were falling out through the opening. They pulled a pair of nylon gym bags from beneath their body armor and went to work filling them with cash.

Three minutes later, they were dashing out the back door with red and blue lights dancing in the trees and on the walls of the neighboring houses. They darted across the backyard, hurling the heavy bags over a fence and jumping over after them, snatching them up again and scrabbling over a pile of car tires, old asphalt shingles, and rotting drywall to make their way deeper into an increasingly deteriorated and largely desolate neighborhood.

They could see army Humvees between the houses racing up and down the streets, and it quickly became apparent the army was cordoning off the block. "I got a feeling we'd better get ready to look like a pair of harmless civilians in a hurry," Tuckerman said.

"I think you're right."

They hid the bags of cash beneath the foundation of a collapsed garage, filling in the opening with broken cinder blocks to conceal the bags and dashed down the alley.

A searchlight snapped on at the end of the lane, and a voice boomed out "Halt!"

Both men froze in their tracks, knowing the next sound they would hear would be machine gun fire — if they were lucky enough to hear anything at all.

Two paratroopers with red, white, and blue 82nd Airborne patches on their sleeves came forward into the light dressed in universal camouflaged ACUs, carbines pulled tightly into their shoulders. "Weapons on the ground!" one of them bellowed. "Now!"

"Take it easy," Crosswhite said, noting their unit insignia and muttering to Tuckerman, "Let me do the talkin'."

"This should be good," Tuckerman

mumbled, dropping the M4 and putting up his hands.

Crosswhite's weapon clattered to the asphalt half a second later. "Don't shoot," he said coolly. "We're all on the same side here." He lifted his hands casually, no higher than his shoulders. "Captain Daniel Crosswhite, Special Forces."

Tuckerman couldn't help releasing an ironic snigger that very nearly caused Crosswhite to lose his military bearing and bust up laughing.

16

CIA Director Shroyer sat in the back of an armored limousine facing White House Chief of Staff Tim Hagen as they traveled north along the interstate toward Baltimore, where the CIA had set up a temporary headquarters well away from Langley, Virginia, now considered a potential target for nuclear attack.

". . . And with the national election only two months away," Hagen was saying, "our victory is far from assured. Public sentiment is shifting against the president for the first time since before the Sandra Brux abduction, and it's shifting fast enough to cause him genuine concern. Even small-town America is frightened of being nuked, and so far we've done nothing to alleviate their fear. The declaration of martial law has backfired in a big way — as I knew it would — and pulling the 82nd out of Chicago isn't likely going to help. It's going to make the president look weak, whether or not voters agreed with the occupation in the first place. We need a resolution, George, and we need it fast. We have to find that fucking bomb."

"You think I don't know that?" Shroyer loosened his tie. "It's worse than looking for a needle in a goddamn haystack. What about the FBI? NSA? Why aren't you climbing up their asses? We're supplying them all the intel we've got, but our resources are limited with the search being inside the US. You know CIA doesn't have any official jurisdiction."

Hagen leveled his gaze. "Which is exactly why you and I are having this conversation."

This caught Shroyer off guard. "Excuse me?"

"The president feels the urgency of circumstances may call for some *behind the scenes* tactics," Hagen explained. "With FBI and NSA having so much constitutional red tape to deal with, it's very possible they just don't have the necessary flexibility to bring this crisis to the immediate resolution we all require." He took a moment to check an incoming text, and then continued. "He feels that since no one in Congress will be expecting CIA to operate independently within our borders, that no one will suspect them should anything *untoward* take place during the hunt for the bomb. Our nation is in a desperate state of flux, and, as everyone knows, desperate times often call for desperate measures."

Flexing his fingers, Shroyer glanced out the window at the passing cityscape and then allowed his gaze to shift back toward Hagen. "Is it safe for me to assume, then, that the rest of this conversation will be off the record?"

Hagen shrugged. "My entire trip out here is off the record."

"In that case, it sounds to me like you're giving me the go-ahead to resume domestic black operations. Is that what you're doing?"

"To my knowledge," Hagen replied innocently, "there has never been a domestic black operation, so I have no idea as to what you might be *resuming,* but in any event, it doesn't sound like you're catching my meaning. Maybe it would help if you took a moment to consider some of the more colorful events in recent CIA history."

"Such as?" Shroyer said dryly.

"Well, are there or are there not certain persons within the *company* who have a fairly recent history of operating far outside their authority — persons of various talents who could be rather easily disavowed, or perhaps even brought to trial, in the event that it became necessary in order to protect the White House?"

Shroyer understood that he could all too easily find himself the subject of a congressional investigation if he were to accept such a cryptic, off-the-record conversation as clearance for the resumption of domestic Black Operations. "I need assurances, Tim."

"Of course," Hagen replied. "And I'm authorized to provide them — so long as you can assure *me* that you at least have a viable place to start."

Shroyer bit his lip and nodded. "The evidence is weak, almost nonexistent," he admitted, "but we *may* have a thin lead on the Chechen insurgent we're looking for. It's complicated, though. We'll have to go through his Saudi financier to get to him — if he *is* a financier — a low-level member of the House of Saud named Muhammad Faisal. Another rub is that he happens to be a naturalized American citizen."

Hagen smiled with satisfaction, for of course he had suggested the gambit of resuming domestic Black Ops to the president himself, knowing in his bones that CIA couldn't possibly have shared 100 percent of their intel with their rival intelligence agencies — *they never did.* He took a small bottle of Evian water from the limo's built-in refrigerator, unscrewed the cap, and settled back comfortably into the seat with a casual gesture at the secure telephone in the console.

"May I suggest you start making calls, George? There's no telling how long we've got. We may be out of time already."

Shroyer picked up the phone and dialed a number from memory. "This is Shroyer," he said. "Get me Bob Pope with the Special Activities Division." He sat back in the seat and waited nearly a minute before Pope came on the line.

"Bob?" he said. "It's George. I'm sitting here with the White House chief of staff. Do you have anything more to add to what we talked about last week concerning Muhammad Faisal?"

"Nothing at all," Pope said. "You told me to stand down on that."

"Well, the weather's changed," Shroyer said, locking eyes with Hagen. "You're a go. Find the bomb." He hung up the phone and sat looking out the window.

"Will he be able to find it?" Hagen asked after a few moments.

"Christ, how do I know?" Shroyer said

tetchily. "I just hope you know what you've cleared me to do — or more precisely, what you've cleared me to clear *him* to do. Pope sees all life on earth as some kind of damn sociology experiment. I don't even know what the hell he's talking about half the time. He's liable to pull anything."

Hagen absentmindedly brushed a speck of lint from his pant leg. "Yes, well, let me worry about Pope. He's not as well insulated as he thinks he is."

"Meaning?"

"Meaning he's got a weakness for younger women," Hagen said, "and one of his little Asian protégées has been playing him for a fool, feeding intel to the Chinese. NSA caught onto her last month. Pretty soon we'll have enough on him that it won't matter who he's got files on. Not even the devil himself will be able to cover his ass."

A shadow crossed Shroyer's brow. "Why wasn't I told?"

Hagen shrugged. "You obviously don't share everything with NSA, why should they share with you? Either way, no matter how this crisis ends, Pope's days with SAD are numbered. Let's just hope he's got enough gas left in the tank to find that RA-115 before it's too late."

Shroyer felt a sudden sense of intuition.

"What does he have on you? Why do you suddenly want him out?"

"There's nothing *to* have on me, George. I play by the rules." Then Hagen smiled. "But I'll soon know what he's got on everyone else."

17

CHICAGO

Back in Chicago, Crosswhite stood with his hands high over his head while two paratroopers from the 82nd Airborne Division stripped him and Tuckerman of their combat harnesses and body armor. A second lieutenant, along with several other troopers, stood watching as a hulking staff sergeant stepped into the light, speaking into the lieutenant's ear, glancing scornfully at Crosswhite, and then doing a double-take.

"Captain?" the sergeant said. "What the hell are you doing here?"

Crosswhite grinned. "Getting felt up by the corporal. How've you been, Sergeant Nipples?" The sergeant's real name was Naples, but Nipples had been his nickname since before he and Crosswhite had taken jump training together at Fort Benning.

The lieutenant allowed the barrel of his carbine to drop slightly. "You know this man, Sergeant?"

"Yes, sir," Naples said. "He's a Medal of Honor winner; one of the men who rescued Sandra Brux."

The corporal and the other trooper both stood back, everyone now regarding Crosswhite and Tuckerman not only with increased curiosity but also a sudden hint of respect as well.

"Got any ID?" the lieutenant asked Crosswhite, now less sure of what he had on his hands.

"I don't generally carry my wallet on classified missions, Lieutenant. Do you?"

The lieutenant had never been on a classified mission, and everyone present knew it. "Dog tags, sir?"

Crosswhite put down his hands and indicated for Tuckerman to do the same, realizing they'd gained the initiative, thanks to Naples's having vouched for him. "I'm not permitted to disclose the details of my mission, Lieutenant, but you do realize there's a nuclear weapon in play, correct?"

"Yes, sir, but I wasn't made aware of any Special Forces activity in this sector, so I'm going to need —"

"You weren't made aware of it, Lieutenant, because you're a goddamn butter bar." This was a pejorative referring to the gold

151

color of a second lieutenant's rank insignia. "Now, I suggest you cut us loose and let us be on our way before your interference costs us the fucking ball game. You know Chicago is a primary target, and I don't exactly have time to lose here."

Tuckerman saw the lieutenant shift his weight and realized that Crosswhite's bullshit was working. He made a show of checking the time, pulling his sleeve up his arm to look at his watch and muttering audibly to Crosswhite that they were falling behind schedule.

"I know we're behind schedule," Crosswhite said irritably. "What do you want me to do about it? These men have a job to do too."

The lieutenant looked at Naples and jerked his head, leading him out of the beam of the spotlight and into the dark. "What do you think, Sergeant?"

Naples cradled his M4. "Sir, I've operated with Crosswhite. He's Delta Force, *exactly* the kind of guy the Pentagon would send into the field to find a loose nuke."

"But why here, Sergeant, in the middle of this run-down neighborhood? I'm not buying it."

"Sir, where better to hide a fucking atom

bomb in the US than a neighborhood like this?"

"Gentlemen!" Crosswhite called. "We're wasting time!"

Naples sized up the vacillating lieutenant, who, at just age twenty-three, was a full ten years younger than him. "Sir, I really don't want us to be the reason that goddamn bomb goes off. I advise we send them on their way ASAP."

The lieutenant considered it a moment longer then nodded. "Okay, Sergeant. We'll —"

A Chicago PD patrol car whipped around the corner with lights flashing and sped up the block, slamming on the brakes just a few feet from the line of parked Humvees. The passenger door opened and a very pissed-off police captain got out.

"What in the Jesus Christ hell is going on!" he demanded. He stabbed a finger toward Crosswhite and Tuckerman. "Why are those two men not under arrest? We just found a man beaten half to death in the back of their van. These two sons a bitches have been robbing every fucking drug den on the South Side!"

The lieutenant looked at Crosswhite. "What's he talking about?"

"The asshole in our van is an informant,"

Crosswhite said. "And you people are fucking around in a top-secret Special Forces operation."

The police captain's eyebrows soared in disbelief. "What the fuck are you talking about?" His voice was shrill and almost womanlike. "Who the fuck says so?"

Sergeant Naples took Crosswhite aside, ordering the corporal and the other trooper out of earshot. "Captain, I'm asking you soldier to soldier . . . are you really on a goddamn mission, or are you running around robbing fucking drug dealers?"

Crosswhite looked him dead in the eyes. "Sergeant, if I'm knocking the shit out of drug dealers, you'd better believe there's a good goddamn reason for it! Now remind that fucking cop that the police are subordinate to the army under martial law and get him the fuck out of here so we can be on our goddamn way. I've got family in this fucking city, and I don't intend to see them wiped out because some local flatfoot got his ass up in the air. Now get fucking rid of him!"

"Sir!" Naples turned on his heel as two more patrol cars pulled up and unloaded four more cops.

The lieutenant faced him as he approached. "Sergeant, turn the prisoners over to the police. I'll get Major Byard on the radio and have him start checking Crosswhite's story."

The police captain directed the arriving officers to take the prisoners into custody. "Put 'em in separate cars!"

"Stop!" Sergeant Naples ordered, and everyone froze in place. "Lieutenant, the prisoners are in our custody, and our authority overrules the police."

"I understand that," the lieutenant said, "but their story does sound —"

"Halt!" Naples shouted, shouldering his M4 to aim it at two cops as they started moving toward the prisoners.

Three other cops drew their pistols and aimed them at Naples, and a dozen more troopers brought their weapons to bear, creating a lethal standoff.

"Get ready to run!" Crosswhite said to Tuckerman.

"Stand down!" the lieutenant ordered. "Stand down right now!"

Naples stood firm, his finger on the trigger and ready to fire. "Sir! I know Captain Crosswhite. I've served with him in combat. And no disrespect intended, sir, but you just don't have enough time in grade to make this call on your own. So I'm asking you to reconsider. If you won't cut them loose to carry out their mission, at least hold them at the FOB until we can confirm their story. If you turn them over to these men, they're liable to end up dead before we can get word from the Pentagon."

"We're not going to kill anybody!" the police captain rejoined. "Who the hell do you think you are making that kind of accusation?"

Naples ignored him, his eyes fixed on his targets. "Lieutenant, the heat for them ending up dead will fall on your head because these cops are subordinate to your authority. Now, what are your orders, sir?"

His inexperienced mind racing, the lieutenant stood thinking it over, seeing the sergeant's point about him taking the blame if Crosswhite's story was true and anything happened to him while in police custody.

"Very well, Sergeant. I'll take your advice. We'll transport them to the FOB until we can get confirmation one way or the other. Now, lower that weapon before somebody gets killed."

"Yes, sir, but I strongly recommend we let them on their way."

"I've made my decision, Sergeant. Now, carry out my orders!"

"Yes, sir." Naples lowered his carbine, and everyone slowly stood down.

A minute later, Crosswhite and Tuckerman were put into the back of an armored Humvee, and the doors were slammed shut.

"Well, I gotta hand it to you," Tuckerman said. "You almost pulled off the most brilliant piece of bullshitting I've ever seen — almost."

Crosswhite sighed, pulling off his gloves and jacking his boot up against the back of the passenger seat. "Well, we're not in handcuffs yet, so be ready to move when the opportunity presents itself. We may have to knock a few heads together to get away."

Tuckerman let out a snicker. " 'Captain Crosswhite' . . . 'Special Forces!' Dumbass."

Crosswhite chuckled. "What'd you want me to say, dickhead? I don't think 'washed-up, has-been Green Beret' would've had quite the same effect."

18

LAS VEGAS

At thirty-eight, Muhammad Faisal was something of a Vegas playboy, preferring skinny blonde American women who were fake breasted and dim witted. Being from Saudi Arabia, where women were treated as far less than equal, he had little use for a woman of intellect. He wanted her pretty, subservient, and on her back as much as possible. He treated them well enough, in that he spent plenty of money on them and wasn't physically abusive, but he was bossy and showed them little respect, feeling free to slap their behinds in public and ordering them to fetch him food or drink no matter who was present.

He owned a three-million-dollar home just outside of Las Vegas, but he kept a suite at the Luxor hotel, spending many nights a week at the poker tables. Though gambling and drinking were against the fundamentals of Islam, Faisal was no less hypocritical within his faith than many other religious persons around the world, cherry-picking which parts of the Koran to abide by and which to ignore. He held a low status within the House of Saud, even though his maternal grandfather had been first cousin to King Faisal, who had ruled Saudi Arabia from 1964 to 1975. It was because all of his ties were on his mother's side that he had never enjoyed the same status as many of his cousins.

Having lost all interest in "family" business by his early twenties, he had elected to drop out of Oxford University and pursue the British nightlife on a full-time basis. During a trip to the United States a year after the September 11 attacks, he got his first taste of Las Vegas and was permanently hooked, immediately setting course for American citizenship.

In the ensuing months and years, Faisal enjoyed his first real advantages of being a member of the House of Saud, appealing to the family to intervene on his behalf with the US Citizenship and Immigration Services agency to request that they negate the necessity for him to leave the country every six months to renew his tourist visa. Two years later, the family intervened a second time to help procure his green card granting him permanent residency within the United States — all of this without ever having set foot inside an INS building. By the end of his fifth year, he was granted US citizenship without ever having sat for a single USCIS interview.

During Faisal's unhindered journey to citizenship, he became a consummate poker player, thriving on high-stakes tournaments and private games alike, drinking and womanizing with the best of them as the Islamic rules of his youth were quickly forgotten. It was in December 2010, however, that he received a grim reminder of his Islamic ties.

He was approached by a pair of AQAP operatives, a former Saudi marine named Akram al-Rashid and his brother Haroun, both of whom had immigrated to Canada as a way of bringing the jihad to the Western world. Word of Faisal's gambling exploits had been reported by Al Qaeda spies lurking around Vegas, and it so happened that money won in the American casinos was the hardest to trace.

"Are you Wahhabi or not, Muhammad?" Akram al-Rashid had asked him point-blank early in their first meeting. "It's a simple yes or no question."

"I am Salafi," Faisal replied. "Do not call me Wahhabi."

"Call yourself what you will, brother, but do not think there will not be a price to pay for the decadent life you lead here. Do you believe that Allah has turned a blind eye to it? He hasn't, I promise you. Now is the time for you to make your decadent life of use to him, or you risk the forfeit of your soul."

By the end of the meeting, Faisal had agreed to give money to the jihad, not because he was worried about the afterlife, but because it had been easier than arguing. He held no affection for the United States, even though he'd sought to make his home there. What he loved was the freedom to gamble, party, and enjoy sex with many different women. If handing over a few million dollars a year to the AQAP movement kept the fanatic jihadists off his back, then it was worth it, because money was not a problem, and if these donations happened to keep him in good stead with Allah, as al-Rashid had promised, then so much the better. All he wanted was to be left alone.

Then a few years later the Chechens got into the game, and the al-Rashid brothers asked for another meeting, dramatically altering Faisal's involvement with AQAP.

"We need you now more than ever, brother," al-Rashid whispered to him, his eyes glazed over with holy zeal. "Allah has miraculously granted our Chechen friends in the RSMB an opportunity to purchase an atomic weapon. With your help, we can at last strike the United States a decisive blow."

Faisal had been shocked and horrified. This was a long, long way from blowing up buses in the streets of Tel Aviv or tossing a satchel bomb into a crowded Alexandrian night club. Those types of attacks would have continued to take place with or without his money. "I'm not helping you buy an atomic weapon! Are you insane? I live here."

"The weapon will not be used against Las Vegas, brother. Do not worry."

"Las Vegas is not my concern!" Faisal retorted, already realizing there would be no dissuading AQAP from its course to help the RSMB, but he'd had no intention of being the man to fund the purchase of such a hellish weapon. "Nuclear weapons leave the world unlivable."

"It is not this world you should be concerned with, brother."

"Regardless," Faisal said, shaking his head. "Find someone else."

"We *will* find someone else," al-Rashid

replied, his eyes narrowing. "Never fear. But tell me this, brother . . . in which direction do you think the Americans will be guided when they begin their search for suspects after the attack is eventually successful? *As it will be successful!* In the direction of those who helped us . . . or in the direction of those who refused us?"

"I *have* helped you!" Faisal insisted. "I've given you millions. I refuse one time, and you threaten to feed me to the wolves?"

"You must help us achieve *this* victory," al-Rashid persisted. "There is no other victory that matters now, no other path for you to follow. Otherwise the FBI will find their way to your door within days of the attack. The House of Saud will be forced to turn its back on you forever, and you will rot inside of an infidel prison . . . but not until after you are tortured by the CIA for information that you will be unable to provide."

Al-Rashid sat back, watching Faisal twisting on the hook. Then, after he felt the man had twisted long enough, he pulled him into the boat. "Enough arguing now, Muhammad. You know it can serve no purpose. In the coming weeks you will go to Germany to meet with our Chechen brothers in the Riyad us-Saliheyn Martyrs' Brigade. It has all been arranged."

That conversation had taken place five months ago, and Faisal had been in their pocket ever since, having no choice but to provide whatever funding they required . . . drinking more than ever, gambling more than ever . . . and losing more than ever. And since the New Mexico Event, he had slipped into an even deeper depression.

He stood at the window of his hotel suite overlooking the Great Sphinx, whirling an ice cube around the bottom of an empty whisky glass.

"What's the matter, Muhammad?" asked his chief bodyguard, Ma'mun, also a minor member of the Saudi royal family. "I've never seen you this way."

"Kashkin and al-Rashid have been lying to me," Faisal said. "There have been *two* bombs since the beginning. That's why they wanted so much money so urgently."

"Should we leave the city? Are we in danger here?"

Faisal gave him an ironic smile. "To destroy Las Vegas would be more like a bad joke than an act of terror."

Ma'mun thought about that a moment. "Yes, I agree."

"We're as safe here as anywhere," Faisal assured him. "All we can do is hope the city doesn't wither on the vine after the American economy begins to collapse . . . which will surely happen after the second weapon is used. These are a panicky people. They have been spoiled by too many years of safety and isolation. Look how they act already. Martial law in their major cities? Please. Do you believe the Jews would react this way?" He wagged a bony finger. "They would not. No, the lives of the Jews would go on as normal. And when the bomb finally went off, they would mourn their dead and begin to rebuild . . . their faith in their Jew god even stronger than before."

Ma'mun nodded grimly. "For all that is bad about them, yes, the Jews are very brave. I do not deny it. But I think no braver than the Americans."

Faisal took a seat on his Italian black leather sofa and kicked off his slippers. "You forget, my friend. The PlayStation generation controls here now." He sighed then. "But we shall soon see which of us is right."

Ma'mun took out his iPhone, running his thumb over the apps. "The lease on the hotel suite is up for renewal this week."

"Renew it." Faisal lit a cigarette and sat pondering his own words about the Jews. It was true they would not be so easily panicked. They were very accustomed to living with the knowledge that every day could be their last. Perhaps it was time he took a lesson from them and began to live his own life the same way.

"Arrange a game for tomorrow evening, Ma'mun. Also, call the agency and be sure there are enough women available. I think it's time for me to resume my winning ways."

At last Ma'mun had reason to smile. *"Na'am sayyideti."* Yes, sir. He turned and left the room.

19

Crosswhite and Tuckerman sat in a holding cell in one of the local police precincts now being utilized by the 82nd Airborne as a forward operating base. On the front of the building was a sign that read Fort Apache. They had been cooling their heels there for the last eight hours, and Crosswhite was beginning to wonder what the hell was going on. It shouldn't have taken more than a few hours for the Pentagon to renounce them for the liars they were and order them turned over to the Chicago police. The division was preparing to withdraw from the city by order of the president, so it was remotely possible that he and Tuckerman would just be left behind for the police to take charge of when they reoccupied the building. Still, it was odd that the major in command of the FOB hadn't come to tell them what was going on or even just to chew their asses for having lied. He'd been a pretty big prick upon their arrival.

The guards who checked in on them from time to time claimed to know nothing.

Crosswhite let go of the bars and turned to look at Tuckerman, who sat on his bunk against the wall, clearly unhappy in the knowledge that he was destined to spend the rest of his life sleeping on such a bed. "Does this make any sense to you? We should have heard by now."

Tuckerman looked up at him. "We're not exactly a priority, Dan. We're just a couple of two-bit criminals. Be careful you don't go believing your own bullshit."

Crosswhite frowned. "That's not the point."

Tuckerman smirked. "As if there is a point. Sit down, will ya? You're making me nervous. What's your hurry, anyhow? You're gonna spend the rest of your life in a fucking cell. At least here we don't have to put up with anybody's bullshit."

"I ain't giving up that easy," Crosswhite said. "The next time they open this door, we're making our move. We may not get away, but we can at least go down fighting."

"Not me," Tuckerman said. "I didn't get into this to kill GIs. I did the crime. I'll do the time." He tilted his head back against the wall. "Wonder if anybody will ever find that money. Maybe it'll still be there if we ever get out. If I get out first, I'll leave your half."

"You're fucking dreaming," Crosswhite said. "They'll never let us out. People are dead, remember? And it doesn't matter they were shit bags. The law's the law."

"Yeah, but we also saved that little girl. We might get parole in twenty or thirty years."

Crosswhite rolled his eyes and turned to grip the bars again. "Hey!" he shouted. "We need some food back here, guys!"

A steel door opened, and the sound of boots on concrete came echoing from around the corner. Sergeant Naples appeared and stood staring at him. "Guess what," he said.

Crosswhite stared back. "Don't tell me . . . the bomb went off in some other city."

Naples shook his head. "I made some calls of my own. Turns out you're not even active duty anymore. Word is you got run out of Delta."

Crosswhite let out a heavy sigh and turned to lie down on his bunk, putting his boots up on the bars. "So what's that tell ya?"

Naples scratched his head. "Tells me the brass musta been pretty pissed about you getting the Medal of Honor for making

169

them look bad."

"None of it was as it appeared, believe me." Crosswhite laced his fingers behind his head and lay staring up at the ceiling. "Why don't you do us a solid, Nipples, and unlock that door before you guys pull out, huh? You got my word we won't make a move until after you're gone." He lifted his head. "Don't just leave us to the local yahoos."

Naples shook his head. "You'll be gone long before we pull out. We just got word your CO is on the way to pick you up."

Crosswhite stole a startled glance at Tuckerman and sat up on the bed, turning to put his boots on the floor. "Come again?"

"About an hour ago, Major Byard got a call from some guy named Pope back in Langley. I'm guessing you know him? Anyhow, Byard still can't believe you guys are actually attached to SOG." This was the Special Operations Group of the CIA. "I told him last night you were the real deal, but he didn't believe me, and now he's out there feeling stupid." He chuckled, clearly enjoying the major's embarrassment. "This Pope said to tell you your orders have changed and that you'll remain here under protective custody until a Colonel Shannon arrives."

170

At that, Tuckerman turned and put his boots on the floor. "*Colonel* Shannon."

"Right," Naples said, shaking a cigarette loose from a box of Marlboros and lighting up. "I don't know what the hell your original orders were, but it doesn't sound like SOG is too happy with you two. Byard was ordered to keep you under lock and key until the colonel gets here."

Crosswhite stared across at Tuckerman. "What do you wanna bet the asshole shows up looking like Sam Trautman from *Rambo*? Just to rub my nose it."

Tuckerman went slack in the jaw. "He wouldn't."

"Fuck he wouldn't." Crosswhite bummed a smoke from Naples and lay back on the bunk again, resting an arm across his forehead. "One thing is for sure . . . if Pope pulled him off that ranch of his and away from Marie, you can bet your jockstrap he won't show up here happy."

"What the fuck is going on anyway?" Naples wanted to know. "I put my ass on the line for you guys last night. The least you can do is cut me in."

Crosswhite sat back up, drawing deeply from the cigarette. "Nipples, I'd love to cut you in — but I have absolutely no idea what the fuck is goin' on."

Naples grinned at him, clearly believing that he was lying. "You SOG guys are all alike. Sorry I can't let you out, Captain." He turned to walk away.

"Hey, how about a couple of MREs?" Crosswhite asked. "I don't know where you've been the past eight hours, but these jamokes haven't given us anything to eat all day."

Naples chuckled. "I'll see what I can do. Sit tight."

When the door slammed, Tuckerman opened his mouth to speak, but Crosswhite sat up and put a finger to his lips. "Be careful, Conman. The gods are obviously smiling on us. Let's not risk saying anything to piss them off."

Tuckerman nodded, getting up to take a leak in the stainless steel toilet mounted to the wall between the bunks. "Roger that," he said over his shoulder. "I do feel safe saying this much . . . if you hadn't found that little girl — well, I ain't religious, but I figure some things were just meant to be. Know what I mean?"

Crosswhite nodded, exhaling smoke through his nostrils as he considered how jacked up his life had been ever since receiving the Medal. "All I know for sure is that I've felt like a runaway train ever since I got rotated back from the Sandbox — with no way to put on the brakes." He drew hard from the cigarette, wanting to alleviate his surging anxiety. "Now there's a loose nuke to worry about, we're locked up in this fucking cage, and *Colonel* Shannon is apparently coming to save our asses." He flicked an ash into the walkway. "Fuck, you must be right. How is this *not* meant to be?"

20

Trooper Trent Logan was a badge-heavy cop, no two ways about it, and Montana wasn't exactly a crime-saturated state, so he treated every traffic infraction, no matter how minor, like the Lufthansa heist of 1978. Post command received at least five complaints a month from motorists traveling the stretch of I-90 between Billings and Bozeman, and Logan had taken a lot of ribbing during his first year on the job for being such a gung-ho rookie. But after hitting the mother lode one Sunday afternoon, he received what he considered to be the ultimate vindication.

He stopped a seventy-year-old woman driving a yellow, near-mint-condition 1985 Cadillac Eldorado for a simple "lines and lanes" violation just outside of Big Timber. No other state trooper in the nation would have stopped her that day for swerving to

174

miss a chunk of splintered two-by-four on the highway, but Trooper Logan was no other state trooper. He lived by a code, and that code meant there was no room on his interstate for road raging old ladies, no matter what their excuses. So he pulled her over and cited her for the lines and lanes violation, brusquely admonishing her to abide by the traffic laws of the sovereign state of Montana. Then, as he was giving back her license, he noticed for the first time that she was supposed to be wearing corrective lenses while driving, and he asked where her glasses were.

"Oh, I broke them a few days ago," the lady said. "The new ones will be ready next week. Here, see?" She dug the LensCrafters receipt from her purse and offered it to him.

But Trooper Logan had no interest in receipts. A crime had been committed.

"Ma'am, you're driving while impaired. Please step out of the vehicle." He placed her under arrest and cuffed her hands behind her back. Then he put her into the backseat of his cruiser and called for a "hook." It was during the vehicle inventory, which he conducted during his wait for the tow truck, that he discovered a gym bag containing ten pounds of methamphetamine in the trunk.

The elderly lady was successfully indicted two weeks later on the felony-one charge of transporting with intent to distribute a "super bulk" amount of a controlled substance — a crime that would likely ensure that she spend the rest of her life in prison — and then Logan went on a tear. Convinced that every motorist in Montana was running drugs, no matter how innocent his or her appearance, he began routinely making traffic stops for infractions as petty as one mile an hour over the speed limit, never hesitating to call for the canine unit on the slightest suspicion. His fellow troopers quickly grew tired of this beyond-gung-ho approach, and the friendly ribbing turned into open and often unpleasant criticism. Trooper Logan didn't pay them much attention, though. As far as he was concerned, he was operating on a whole different level of law enforcement, and if his fellow officers couldn't appreciate that, screw 'em.

So when he clocked a green SUV traveling in the opposite direction doing seventy-two in a seventy-mile-an-hour zone, Logan didn't hesitate to hit the strobes and "shoot the median." The SUV was already pulling over when he cleared the grassy median and got the cruiser back onto the highway, but this didn't stop him from giving the siren a short burst as he pulled up. He stepped out of the cruiser and adjusted the brim of his Smokey the Bear hat to eyebrow level as he strutted up on the passenger side of the vehicle, the heel of his hand resting on the butt of his Sig Sauer P229 in .357 caliber.

"Good evening, sir," he said in an impersonal tone of voice. "Driver's license, registration, and proof of insurance, please."

The fifty-three-year-old man behind the wheel handed him a German passport, an international driver's permit, and the rental agreement for the car.

Trooper Logan had never seen a German passport, nor had he seen an IDP. "Do you know why I stopped you, Mr. Jaeger?"

Nikolai Kashkin looked at him with his pale blue eyes and smiled. "I assume I must have been speeding," he said with a German accent.

"Do you know how fast you were going, sir?"

Kashkin shook his head. "I'm sure you know better than I, officer. I'm not about to argue with you."

Logan especially distrusted the really cooperative ones, believing that most people hated cops. "You're a long way from home, Mr. Jaeger. What brings you to the United States?"

"I'm making a tour of your national parks," Kashkin said enthusiastically. "I'm on my way up to Glacier now."

"Uh-huh," Logan said, paging through the passport, attempting to make heads or tails of the many stamps and dates. "How long do you plan to be in the US, sir?"

"A couple of months," Kashkin said. "Possibly longer. Mount Rushmore was closed when I tried to see it a few days ago, and I would like very much to see that before I return home." He had actually only just heard of the monument's closing over the radio the hour before.

"Well, it might be a while," Logan said. "I'm sure you've heard that terrorists have smuggled a nuclear weapon into the country. Rushmore's been closed as a precaution."

"Yes, that's very terrible," Kashkin said sadly. He thought it insane that anyone could believe he would waste the weapon on a useless rock in the middle of nowhere, but he did enjoy hearing over the radio that thousands of American tourists were being disappointed all across the country due to the closing of so many national monuments.

"Wait here, sir." Logan returned to his cruiser and sat behind the wheel, digging out a reference manual to foreign passports and identification from the bottom of his gear bag sitting on the passenger seat. So far he had only ever used the manual to look for reasons to hassle Canadian tourists, whom he often referred to as — quite cleverly, in his opinion — "Mexicans who spoke good English."

The German passport was three years old and appeared valid when compared with the example in the manual. The IDP, however, was another matter. There were a number of different examples of these in the manual, and the example of the German-issued IDP didn't match the one that Mr. Hans Hartmann Jaeger was carrying. Most US law enforcement officers would have taken into account that the manual was three years old and therefore outdated by current anticounterfeiting technology, but, here again, very few US law enforcement officers operated at Trooper Logan's level of professionalism.

Since hitting the mother lode back in April, he'd succeeded in convincing himself that he had a sixth sense about people, and this evening he believed that sixth sense was telling him there was something wrong about this kraut tourist. He wanted to search the German's vehicle and find out what he was hiding, but he didn't have probable cause, so he decided to ask for permission, knowing from his extended experience with harassing Canadians that many tourists didn't realize — as many Americans didn't realize — they had the right to refuse a search request in the absence of probable cause or reasonable suspicion.

He left Kashkin's ersatz identification on the seat and walked up on the driver's side of the SUV. "Mr. Jaeger, do you mind if I search your vehicle? It's just routine, sir; a service we like to perform on all traffic stops after sundown."

Kashkin went on alert, seeing the veiled suspicion on the trooper's face. He knew there was nothing wrong with his passport or his IDP, both of them issued legitimately by the German government under the name of a dead German citizen whose identity he had managed to assume with the help of a fellow RSMB member working inside the Federal Ministry of the Interior. The SUV was rented with a legitimate credit card and the vehicle properly insured. So what was making this young cowboy so distrustful? Had there been a leak somewhere? Was the US government onto him specifically? Or was this something else? He would have to find out one way or another before continuing with his mission.

"I don't understand," he said with a confused smile.

"It's just a service we like to perform, sir. The same service we like to perform for everyone after sundown."

A service? That made no sense at all to Kashkin. "May I get out of the car while you perform this *service,* officer?"

"Yes. That makes it a lot safer for everyone, sir." Logan opened the door for the older man. "I'll give you a seat in the back of my cruiser, so you don't get hit by a car. It won't take long at all, sir."

They walked back toward the cruiser with its strobes flashing in the failing light, and Kashkin began to feel the tightening in his chest again over his heart. He couldn't allow himself to be locked in the back of the police car. When the trooper found the guns in the back, he would be trapped with no hope of escape.

When they reached the front of the cruiser, the trooper took him by the arm. "First, I'm going to need to pat you down, sir, for your safety as well as mine. Do you have anything sharp or otherwise dangerous anywhere on your person, sir?"

Kashkin patted the breast pocket of his shirt. "Only this mechanical pencil."

"That's fine, sir. Go ahead and place that on the hood for me."

"Certainly." Kashkin took the pencil from his pocket, and with blinding speed jabbed Logan in the eye with it.

Logan reeled away, grabbing his eye with both hands. Kashkin lunged forward, delivering him a right-hand blow to the side of the neck. Logan landed heavily on his knees, severely stunned by the abrupt interruption of blood and oxygen to his brain, and crashed over onto his side, crushing his Smokey the Bear hat.

Kashkin kicked him in the side of the head to send the hat flying and dragged him by the gun belt around the blind side of the cruiser, where he slugged him in the temple. Then he used the trooper's own handcuffs to secure his hands behind his back and took the pistol from its holster, concealing it beneath his shirt as he returned to the SUV. He snatched the keys from the ignition and opened the back, taking out a folding fighting knife and returning to where Trooper Logan was struggling to sit up, bleeding from his left eye.

"Stop right there!" Logan ordered, seeing the open black blade in Kashkin's hand, and scrabbling to get his feet beneath him. "You just stop right there! Keep the fuck away

182

from me!"

Kashkin had seen men in the trooper's situation many times before, completely helpless, completely doomed, and completely refusing to accept it. He pounced on Logan and jammed the blade deep into his inner right thigh, hitting bone and twisting the blade.

Logan shrieked and writhed around beneath Kashkin's weight, unable to throw him off.

"Tell me what you know about me!" Kashkin demanded. "Tell me everything!"

"I don't know *anything* about you!" Logan screamed. "Nothing! Get the fuck off of me!"

Kashkin ripped the blade up through the muscle toward Logan's groin, and Logan let out another horrible shriek. "Tell me what you know," Kashkin said lustily, "or I will skin you alive."

The interrogation went on for three loud and bloody minutes before Kashkin was finally satisfied that Logan was nothing more than a nosy American lawman with nothing better to do than pester people out minding their own business. He cut one of the whimpering cop's carotid arteries and left him to bleed out in the dark. Then he retrieved his passport from the cruiser, rip-

183

ping the dash cam from its mount and switching off the strobes. Within a minute, Kashkin was gone up the interstate.

In his final seconds of life, it never occurred to Logan that he'd brought this incident upon himself. It did occur to him, however, that the vicious man who had just carved up both of his legs and his groin would probably never be caught. He would never be caught because Logan had long stopped calling in most of his petty traffic stops, wanting to cut down on being ridiculed by his fellow officers. This meant the dispatch center had received no information about Kashkin or his vehicle, and without the dashboard camera, there would be no evidence as to who had committed the murder.

Logan's last thoughts were of self-pity and under appreciation.

21

CHICAGO

The steel door around the corner opened and then clanged shut. A few moments later, Crosswhite looked up from his bunk to see a "full bull" Green Beret colonel standing in front of their cell with a chest full of ribbons — including the sky blue ribbon of the Medal of Honor.

"Christ," Crosswhite muttered. "I see it and still don't believe it."

"Holy shit," whispered Tuckerman.

Gil Shannon stood in the corridor, staring at them through the bars, his blue eyes hard and cold as he took in their combat boots and the black fatigues.

He crossed his arms and looked at Tuckerman. "What the fuck are you two made up for? And you'd better not lie to me."

Crosswhite said, "It's my fault, Gil. We were —"

"I didn't ask you a goddamn thing!" Gil

said, not taking his eyes from Tuckerman. "I asked you a question, sailor."

Tuckerman sat up fast. "We were prospecting, Master Chief."

"Colonel!" Gil snapped.

"Yes, sir, Colonel," Tuckerman said, withering slightly beneath Gil's gaze. "We were prospecting, Colonel . . . knocking over drug dealers and taking their cash."

"How many civilians are dead?"

Tuckerman looked at the floor. "Counting tonight, sir . . . ten. Tonight was a goat fuck."

Gil stood glaring at the younger former Navy SEAL, his jaw muscles flexing beneath his chiseled features. He looked as though he wanted to say something vile but was thinking better of it.

Crosswhite cleared his throat. "Permission to speak, uh, Colonel?"

"Denied," Gil said, cutting him a menacing glance and refocusing on Tuckerman. "Why are you not at the VA getting treatment for your PTSD?"

Tuckerman seemed to shrink even more, shaking his head. "I got —"

"Look at me when you're talkin' to me!"

He looked up. "I got . . . I just . . . I dunno. I just couldn't take it around that place, Gil. All those fucked-up vets and their bullshit problems." He shook his head again and looked back at the floor. "Hell, half of 'em never even saw any real combat."

"So you're sayin' you were the only *real* motherfucker in the place, is that right?"

Tuckerman lifted his head. "No, that's not what —"

"What you're saying," Gil went on, "is that *this* is what real men do after they come home from combat. You're saying *real* motherfuckers go out and murder civilians — *American* civilians."

Tuckerman lowered his head in shame. "Gil, I . . . I got lost."

"You bet your fuckin' ass you got lost, boy! And you!" Gil said, turning on Crosswhite. "Winner of the Medal of Honor leading a goddamn vigilante hit squad — despicable!"

Crosswhite held his gaze. "We saved a child, Gil."

"Yeah, and then you executed her captors without a trial!" Gil retorted. "I know all about it. Detroit PD is shaking every fucking tree in that city looking for you two clowns. Now that I see you, I got half a mind to call and tell them right where to look."

Crosswhite got to his feet and grabbed the bars. "Then do it!" he hissed. "But don't you forget that I jumped into the Valley of the Shadow to save your ass when nobody else could. So either let us outta this fucking cell or call the Detroit heat. Either way, I've listened to all your shit I'm gonna! You wanna hear we did wrong? Fine. We did wrong! We fucked up! We both deserve the goddamn chair! What else you do want? You wanna hear it's my fault? Okay. It's my goddamn fault! Anything else — *Colonel*?"

Gil stared back at him. "I think that about covers it, Captain."

"Good!" Crosswhite dropped down on the bunk, resting his elbows on his knees and holding his head in his hands as he stared at the floor. "Fuckin' Green Beret. Fuckin' colonel, no less! Shit, Shannon, you don't make a pimple on a Green Beret's ass."

Gil looked at Tuckerman, who dared to crack a smile. "I gotta admit, though, Master Chief . . . the uniform, the rank — it's you."

Gil let some of the hardness out of his face. "You two both better understand something," he said quietly. "If it wasn't for that little girl you rescued, Pope would have left you both right here to rot."

Tuckerman looked over at Crosswhite. "Told you."

Crosswhite sighed, his anger spent, leaving only tired resignation in its place. "So what now, Gil?"

"We got a goddamn suitcase nuke to find." Both men perked up. "Pope needs operators he can easily disavow in case the White House needs plausible deniability. Either of you two clowns know anybody I might suggest to him?"

Tuckerman got to his feet. "I'm on board, Chief."

Crosswhite was only a half instant behind him. "So am I."

Gil's face became hard again. "I'm in command. Understood?"

"Roger that," Crosswhite said. "As a Green Beret or — or what?"

"Are you kidding? This army rag is already givin' me a fuckin' rash. Pope thought it the best way to keep this dogface major out front from making waves." He looked at Tuckerman. "ST6/B has been reactivated, but no active-duty personnel can be part of it."

"What's the *B* stand for?" Crosswhite asked, slightly mystified.

"Black," Tuckerman said. "Domestic ops."

"No shit?"

"Yeah, right up your fucking alley," Gil said grimly. "So congratulations, pogey bait. You're the first man in the history of the United States Navy to be made a SEAL without having to pass BUD/S." *Pogey bait* was typically a Marine Corps term dating back to the days of the China Marines, US Marines stationed in Shanghai prior to WWII. It could be used to describe a number of things, one of them being a non-grunt who was afraid of getting his uniform dirty. BUD/S (Basic Underwater Demolition/SEAL) was a six-month course at the Naval Special Warfare Training Center in Coronado, California.

"I got your fuckin' pogey bait right here," Crosswhite said, grabbing his groin.

"Listen," Gil said. "When we get out front, I don't want any horseshit. Maintain a strict military bearing until we get on the helo. Got it?"

Crosswhite frowned. "I can't tell that fuckin' major to kiss my ass?"

"You can if you don't mind spending the rest of your life in one of these fucking cages."

"Well, if you put it like that," Crosswhite said glumly, "I don't guess it'll be necessary."

"I didn't think so." Gil took a big brass Folger Adam cell key from his pocket and unlocked the door. "Remember, I do all the talking."

"Got it," the other two said in unison, and they followed him down the corridor.

22

CHICAGO

It was all Crosswhite could do to keep his eyes to himself as they entered the precinct booking area where Major Byard and seven other 82nd Airborne paratroopers stood waiting for the mysterious trio to emerge from the cellblock. The 82nd had been Crosswhite's unit before he was transferred to Delta Force, a Special Mission Unit of the US Army under the auspices of the CIA, an SMU not dissimilar from SEAL Team VI. He had heard rumors of a domestic ST6 unit during recent years: rumors, for example, that they'd gone into New Orleans after Hurricane Katrina to neutralize civilian gun squads that were terrorizing the police after all law and order had broken down in that city. He hadn't given these rumors much credence, of course, because there were always rumors circulating among the Special Ops community. Oddly enough, however, rumor often preceded the truth, and it seemed that tonight was no exception to that inexplicable military paradigm.

"Excuse me, Colonel," Major Byard said, stepping importantly from behind a desk to intercept him with a sheet of paper. He was a ginger with coarse red hair and a face full of freckles. "Sir, I've just received orders that seem to conflict with yours. The Pentagon has ordered me to turn these men over to our MPs."

Pope had warned Gil this could happen if he didn't get in and out fast enough.

"Let me see," he said, putting his hand out for the paper. He pretended to read the order as he pondered how best to resolve the dilemma. He glimpsed a sergeant E-5 that he had noticed on the way in: a soldier with a nonmilitary-issue patch Velcroed to his body armor. The patch read, "Want my respect? Earn it." He had seen similar patches worn by various soldiers during his last year in Afghanistan, and he had not approved of it, though it had not been his place to remark about it, because he was a navy frogman. However, he had made it known that he'd better not ever see such a patch on the uniform of anyone operating within the DEVGRU teams.

Deciding now was a good time to take issue with the patch, he glanced up from the paper. "Sergeant Barbiero, is it?"

"Yes, sir." The sergeant came to attention, startled to be singled out.

"Front and center, son."

Barbiero broke ranks to stand before the Green Beret colonel. "Yes, sir."

Gil stood eyeing the patch on his body armor long enough for it to become obvious what he was about to take issue with. "Sergeant, are you familiar with the term *silent insolence*?"

Crosswhite saw Major Byard's expression fall and understood right away what Gil was playing at.

"Yes, sir," Barbiero said quietly. "I've heard the term, sir."

Gil looked him in the eyes. "What exactly do I need to do to *earn* your respect, Sergeant? Since my rank alone doesn't seem to be enough."

Barbiero was quickly beginning to sweat. Everyone in the room saw plainly that Gil was a Medal of Honor winner, and a full bull with the Medal of Honor was not a man with whom to fuck — not even by accident. "Sir. You have my *complete* respect, sir."

"Remain at attention," Gil said, turning to Byard. "Major, I couldn't help but notice the Fort Apache sign on the front of this FOB as I was getting off the helo. I seem to remember reading an operational directive recently put out by General Couture that strictly forbade the posting of any such signage as which may be regarded as provocative in nature by the civilian population whose safety it is you have been charged with protecting."

Byard was in Deep Shit, Kentucky, and he knew it. "Sir, my apologies. I haven't seen that directive," he said lamely, which was true. He'd been too busy to read the incoming dispatches, but he and everyone else present knew this was no excuse. He thanked God this colonel was unaware of Couture's personal order to remove the sign the week before.

Gil passed the paper off to Crosswhite, who suppressed a smile as he folded the order in half. Then he removed the green beret, feigning an effort of patience as he wiped a hand across his forehead.

"Gentlemen," he said heavily. "It is bad enough that you have failed in your mission to protect this city, resulting in the disgraceful withdrawal now taking place." He took the time to eyeball every paratrooper present, each man feeling the weight of the colonel's iron will and lowering his gaze in shame. "But when a member of General Couture's personal staff cannot walk into an FOB of the vaunted 82nd Airborne Division — *the division of Sergeant York and the Argonne offensive!* — and expect to see the general's orders being carried out . . ." He shook his head, allowing his own personal anger to show. "Well, I'm afraid that I find myself at a loss for words in the face of such utter disappointment."

He reached out to gently pull the patch from Sergeant Barbiero's body armor. The *scraaatch* of the Velcro sounded very loud in the quiet room full of humbled soldiers, and Gil could see the beads of sweat rolling down Barbiero's face. He gave the patch to Tuckerman, saying, "Throw that away for me, please."

"Yes, sir," Tuckerman muttered, stepping back to drop the patch into a trash can beside a desk with a plaque resting on the corner that read: Watch Commander.

Gil stepped over to Major Byard, saying to him quietly, "Major, exactly where would you like for me to sit and wait while you further delay my mission to locate the nuclear weapon that threatens this nation?"

Byard swallowed a lump in his throat the size of a robin's egg. "Colonel, please accept my profound apologies for any and all delays — the responsibilities for which are entirely mine. I have no intention of delaying you further, sir. I just thought it my duty to notify you of the discrepancy."

"I see," Gil said, his chin jutting. "In that case, this nation thanks you for your generous consideration, Major." He turned to Crosswhite and Tuckerman. "Gentlemen, follow me. I fear we may already be too late."

Without a word, they followed Gil out the door and across the parking lot to a waiting Sikorsky UH-60 Black Hawk. They mounted up, and Tuckerman slid the door closed. Gil spoke briefly to the pilots, and they lifted off in under sixty seconds.

Gil stripped off the green army jacket and set it aside on the bench seat as he sat facing Crosswhite and Tuckerman. "From here on, all that's happened is completely forgotten. Understood?"

They nodded.

"Okay," he said. "This is what we're up against. At least one Chechen insurgent has smuggled a Russian RA-115 suitcase nuke into the country. At present, we have no clue where it is. What we do have is the name of a possible accomplice, so we're headed to Las Vegas for the purposes of abduction and interrogation. Be advised . . . this man is not only a member of the Saudi royal family, but he is also a naturalized American citizen entitled to all rights afforded him under the United States Constitution. We will very likely be violating most of those rights. Do either of you expect to experience a conflict of interest where this is concerned?"

Both men shook their heads.

Gil nodded with satisfaction. "I didn't think so."

"Are we sure about this suitcase nuke?" Crosswhite said, all business now. He was back where he belonged, and he could feel the capillaries expanding throughout his body as the blood once again began to pump with true military purpose. "I thought the RA-115 was a ghost."

"All the isotope readings from the New Mexico Event remain consistent with this scenario," Gil said. "So, yes, confidence is very high. Pope's doing what he can to get us the original schematics from his Russian counterpart, but for the time being, we will be operating mostly blind where the device itself is concerned. All we know is that it probably isn't any bigger than a footlocker and shouldn't weigh more than a hundred pounds. We can assume a two-kiloton yield."

"The damn thing could be anywhere,"

Tuckerman said.

"You don't know the half of it."

Being the only man in the helo qualified to wear the green beret, Crosswhite leaned across to pick it up. Then he put it on and smoothed it into shape. "Do we have half a chance of finding it before it goes off?"

"I have no idea, but Pope thinks 9/11 is their target date. That gives us less than three days."

"So how's this work?" Tuckerman asked. "Are we back on the payroll now, or what?"

Gil shook his head. "Pope's gonna cover your tracks and make all this Chicago shit go away. In exchange for that, you two are gonna lay it back on the line for your country. If we survive, you get to return to your lives. And you *will* get your ass back to the VA for treatment."

"Yes, Master Chief!"

"So where were you when this shit kicked off?" Crosswhite asked. "Before you became Barry Sadler, I mean." Staff Sergeant Barry Sadler, a Green Beret during the Vietnam War, was famous for cowriting and singing the ultrapatriotic hit song "The Ballad of the Green Berets."

Gil took a moment to unpin the Medal of Honor ribbon from the army jacket and slip it into his pocket. "I was in Morocco — and that's all you get to know."

Crosswhite wrinkled his brow. "After the medal ceremony at the White House, I thought you went back to Montana to stay with Marie for good."

A shadow of pain fell across Gil's face. "We're separated at the moment. And I don't wanna talk about that either."

A short time later, the helo set down at Chicago's O'Hare International Airport. They loaded into a Humvee that took them across the tarmac to a waiting Lockheed Martin C-5M Super Galaxy strategic airlifter, a giant US Air Force transport powered by four General Electric CF-80C2 turbofan engines. The nose assembly was in the up position, allowing the Humvee to drive directly into the cargo hold.

"I take it you flew in on this thing?" Crosswhite asked, clearly impressed.

"Pope's hunting a loose nuke," Gil said. "So he gets whatever the fuck he asks for. All of our kit is aboard — anything we might need — so get familiar with where everything is. And get out of those goddamn PMA clothes." PMA stood for paramilitary asshole. "The rest of the team will meet us in Vegas."

Crosswhite and Tuckerman exchanged

glances. "Who's the rest of the team?"

Gil chuckled. "All the rest of the Bank Heist misfits who got run out of the navy." Operation Bank Heist had been the unauthorized rescue mission that Crosswhite had led in an attempt to secure the release of Warrant Officer Sandra Brux from Hezb-e Islami Khalis forces in Afghanistan the year before.

"You mean you actually managed to find them all?"

"Yeah, and believe it or not, you two ass clowns are the only ones I had to break out of jail."

23

WASHINGTON, DC

Pope ordered a chai latte in the Starbucks on Connecticut Avenue in Washington, DC, and then crossed the shop to take a seat across from an elderly gentleman named Iosif Hoxha.

"Thanks for agreeing to meet, Joe. It's been a long time."

"Yes, it has. You're looking well, Robert."

Hoxha was seventy-six years old, a former KGB agent, swarthy and bald with a gray beard and dark brown eyes. His upper lip was clean shaven below a bulbous red nose — the nose of a man who drank too much vodka. He had immigrated to the United States a couple of years before the fall of the Soviet Union, having seen the writing on the wall from a distance. No one in the States other than Pope had any idea that he was former KGB because he was not Russian. He was Albanian, a former Soviet spy whom Pope had brought over from the dark side in the early eighties as a CIA field agent working in Europe.

"You're aware how cliché we both must look," Hoxha said, unscrewing the lid from a sterling silver flask to add a shot of vodka to his coffee. "Two old spies meeting here in Washington under imminent threat of nuclear destruction."

Pope chuckled. "I was hoping it would be cooler out so I'd have an excuse to wear my trench coat."

Hoxha laughed, proffering the flask.

"Why not?" Pope added a dribble to his latte.

They both lifted their paper cups. "What should we drink to?" Pope asked.

"To the women we will never know," Hoxha said with a slight smirk.

Pope smiled as they touched cups.

"So," Hoxha said with a sigh. "You have very serious troubles these days, no?"

"I'm in a tough spot, Joe. I admit it. The kind of spot a man like me knows better than to let himself get into."

Hoxha nodded grimly. "It happens to those of us who stay too long in the trenches."

"I suppose that's true," Pope said with a sense of melancholia. "The White House chief of staff is setting me up for the fall, and I have no choice but to step forward."

"You know, I've heard things about Hagen," Hoxha said thoughtfully. "But nothing of use to you, I'm afraid. No one passes me that kind of information anymore." He chortled. "No one passes me anything anymore."

The corners of Pope's mouth turned downward. "I haven't come to you for that kind of information, Joe. The kind of information I need is older than Hagen, much more valuable, and much harder to come by."

Hoxha sat watching him across the table. "I'm sure it is."

"I need to know about the RA-115."

Hoxha stiffened slightly.

Pope caught the momentary lapse of composure in the eyes and realized with relief that he'd gambled his very limited time on the right man.

"The White House thinks the Russians are stonewalling," he went on, wanting to keep Hoxha off balance for the moment, "but I don't think that's it. I think they're afraid to admit that nobody in their present administration was aware the RA program was even real before we brought it to their attention. Is that possible? Is it possible even the Russians thought the damn thing was nothing more than a rumor?"

Hoxha took a gulp from his coffee, and then set it down and laced his fingers around the cup as if to warm his hands. "I am an old man, Robert, but there are still people in Albania who would kill me if I was stripped of my citizenship here and sent back to Tirana."

Pope realized that Hoxha must know even more than he had hoped. "Rest easy, Joe. This isn't that kind of meeting. I'm not here to threaten you with ultimatums. I've come as a friend to ask you for your help. No one will ever know we spoke about this."

Hoxha drummed his fingers on the table-top. "How sure are you the device in New Mexico was an RA-115?"

"Very."

"And of the device you're searching for now?"

"Even more so." Pope was stretching the truth slightly, but he felt it necessary.

Hoxha pulled nervously at his ear. "Well, you're probably right about the Russians. I doubt there's anyone left alive at the upper levels who would know anything about the RA series. They were all old men like I am now when those debates were taking place."

"Debates? What debates?"

"On how best to wipe you all out," Hoxha said. "The Soviets were scared to death of your nuclear rockets lining the German frontier, convinced you were just waiting for the right moment to launch your surprise attack. You have to remember, Robert . . . these were old military men who had experienced Hitler's surprise attack as junior officers. They had no other frame of reference from which to view the world."

"I understand," Pope said patiently, resting his chin on his palm to appear the perfect listener.

Hoxha vacillated a while longer but then seemed to finally come to terms with the situation. He shrugged and said, "I only ever handled one of them — and it was only for a few days."

"So you've seen one with your own eyes," Pope said, some of his excitement showing. "You know what it looks like."

"I know what the RA-*100* looked like." Hoxha took a drink of his coffee. "It was a one-point-five-kiloton weapon with a plutonium core, but it was never deployed outside of Europe. They believed the implosion detonator to be flawed, because the test unit fizzled. There was talk the flaw was intentional and that the designers were executed, but I never knew if that was true. The RA-

115 was the last of the series, the most reliable, and the only one ever deployed outside of Europe. It was a two-kiloton weapon with a gun-assembly detonator and a uranium core."

"Can you sketch the device for me?" Pope pushed a brown napkin across the table, offering the pen from his shirt pocket.

Hoxha met his gaze and then took the pen, roughing out a quick cutaway sketch of the RA-100. It looked like a miniature version of the twenty-one-kiloton Fat Man bomb dropped on Nagasaki, Japan, in 1945, minus the stabilizing fins. "This would fit into a large suitcase and weigh roughly thirty-four kilograms."

Pope approximated the weight to 75 pounds. "And the RA-115?"

Hoxha stared at him some more, saying finally, "Again, I never saw one, but if I had to guess —" He flipped the napkin over and roughed out another cutaway sketch. Not surprisingly, it resembled the sixteen-kiloton Little Boy bomb dropped on Hiroshima, three days before the United States targeted Nagasaki. "It would be bigger and slightly heavier than the RA-100, longer because of the gun assembly . . . bulkier but more reliable." He took another drink of coffee and cleared his throat, sitting forward to rest his elbows on the table. "I was told that it would fit perfectly into a US Army duffel bag — 'like a glove,' they said."

Pope's scalp began to tingle. "How much heavier?"

Hoxha shrugged. "Forty-five kilos, perhaps a little more."

"So around a hundred pounds." Pope sat back, running his fingers through his thick head of white hair. "That's light enough for a strong man to carry on his back if he uses the shoulder straps."

"Yes, it is." Hoxha lifted his eyebrows and let them fall.

"Is it complex? Difficult to disarm?"

Hoxha shook his head. "Not unless it's been modified. You knew the Soviets. They weren't big on complexity."

24

CALIFORNIA,
San Diego Bay, Naval Air Station North Island
Petty Officer First Class Adam Samir was a US Naval Explosive Ordnance Disposal (EOD) specialist stationed at Naval Air Station North Island (NASNI) in San Diego Bay. He was a second-generation Iraqi American who spoke no Arabic, but that didn't prevent him from receiving suspicious glances from time to time. He handled it well enough. If he noticed anyone looking at him a little too long or a little too hard in the grocery store, Samir would smile and say, "I'm as American as apple pie and Chevrolet." His perfect English and good nature were usually enough to put the wary person at ease.

There were two fleet aircraft carriers based permanently out of San Diego Bay: USS *Carl Vinson* (CVN-70) of Carrier Strike Group One and USS *Ronald Reagan*

(CVN-76) of CSG-7. But NASNI was home to a great deal more than just a pair of carrier strike groups. The complex covered five thousand acres and encompassed more than 130 vital US Naval Commands (ashore, afloat, and airborne), including Naval Special Warfare Group One (SEAL Teams 1, 3, 5, and 7); Naval Special Warfare Group Three (SEAL Delivery Vehicle Teams, or SDVTs, 1 and 2); more than fifteen different helicopter commands, eight attack submarines, and the tenant commands of CSG-3 and CSG-11, built around the carriers USS *John C. Stennis* (CVN-74) and USS *Nimitz* (CVN-68), permanently based out of Naval Base Kitsap, Washington, and Naval Station Everett, Washington, respectively. On any given day, there could be up to two hundred aircraft of all types on the island.

All of these assets in one place meant that a tactical nuclear strike on San Diego Bay would be devastating to the combat readiness of the US Pacific Fleet as a whole. This was not at all a comforting prospect in the face of intensifying nuclear ambitions on the part of North Korea, particularly if one paused to consider the North's increasingly aggressive rhetoric toward South Korea and Japan.

Near the end of his shift, Samir walked into his CO's office and came to attention. "You wanted to see me, Lieutenant?"

Lieutenant Roy Potts looked up from his desk. "At ease, Adam. I'm afraid I've got shitty news for you."

Though Samir had been expecting this, his heart still sank. "Yes, sir?"

"I'm afraid I have to cancel your honeymoon plans."

Samir was getting married the next day, and the honeymoon was set for Jamaica.

"It's not just you," Potter continued. "All leaves are being canceled, and everybody's being recalled because of the nuke. The wedding's tomorrow, correct?"

"Yes, sir."

"Why don't you two stay at the Hotel del Coronado for a few days? I'll clear you to stay off the base, if you promise to remain on the island and report in once a day."

Samir smiled. "Thank you, sir. That'll make things a lot better, sir."

"I'm sure it will," Potter said with a chuckle. "If you have any trouble getting a room over there, let me know. The hotel manager owes me a pretty big favor."

"I will, sir. Thank you again, sir."

"You're welcome. Dismissed."

25

LAS VEGAS

A US government hangar at the Las Vegas airport had been turned over to SEAL Team VI/Black for the duration, and all civilian personnel were ordered to stay away. Air Force MPs ringed the perimeter at one hundred meters. The rest of the eleven-man SEAL team was there waiting for the C-5 upon landing and set about at once unloading the kit, which included all weapons and equipment Gil thought it might conceivably need during the search for the RA-115. He had left virtually nothing to chance, as was made evident when a SEAL everyone called Alpha pried the lid from a crate containing two deflated CRRCs. These were Combat Rubber Raiding Craft manufactured by Zodiac Marine & Pool.

Alpha stood looking at them. "Know something we don't, Master Chief?"

"I'd better," Gil remarked offhandedly.

"Make sure the men know we've got stand-to immediately after the cargo is unloaded. I want everything assembled, loaded, and ready to go to war immediately that it's needed. Understood?"

"Aye, Chief."

"Once that's done, I want everything practical loaded back aboard the aircraft and stowed for immediate access."

"Aye-aye."

Gil went forward and up the ladder into the cockpit to speak with the pilots.

"You'll taxi for refuel yon side of the tarmac between a pair of yellow strobes," he told them. "You'll be able to see them when you put the nose assembly back down. When that's completed, you'll taxi directly back here to remain on standby for the duration of my mission." He took a sheaf of folded papers from his back pocket and handed them to the pilot, an air force major who was patiently waiting for Gil to finish so he could remind the navy man exactly who was in command of the aircraft. "These are your orders, Major, signed by the president and giving me tactical command of your aircraft. This supersedes your rank and puts you at my indefinite disposal. Simply stated, Major, this aircraft and its entire crew will go where I say, when I say, and *do* exactly as I say."

The major glanced at his copilot and unfolded the orders, flipping to the last page to verify they had been signed by the president. He looked up at Gil and nodded. "I guess this pretty well designates where the bear shits in the woods."

Gil smiled. "Now that the formalities are out of the way, Major, let's hope those orders are worth the paper they're printed on and that this isn't just a big waste of avgas."

The pilot decided he liked Gil and returned the smile. "Any idea what our chances are?"

Gil shook his head. "None, but we go until the president says quit."

"Roger that," the pilot said. "We'll be ready when you need us."

Gil gave him a salute and disappeared back down the ladder.

Two hours later, the equipment was ready and much of it stowed back aboard the Galaxy. The men were assembled in the ready room for mission brief when Gil entered and stood before them dressed in blue jeans, cowboy boots, and a black Under Armour compression shirt.

"Gentlemen," he said grimly. "It's good to

see you again. I'm sorry the circumstances are what they are."

"We're just glad to be back aboard," Alpha said. He was twenty-nine years old and built like an outside linebacker.

Gil nodded. "About that . . . I don't know how this is going to play out. Right now we're obviously very important, but none of us in this room is exactly popular with the present administration, so I want it understood there are no guarantees about the future."

"Fuck the present administration," growled a SEAL named Trigg. "We're here to do what we were trained to do."

"Hooyah," said Gil. "Now let's establish the pecking order. Anybody got a problem with having a green beanie as second in command?"

Crosswhite cleared his throat. "Uh, Gil, I'd just as soon be a member of the rank and file on this one, if that's —"

"I didn't put that question to you, Captain."

Crosswhite shut up, and Gil stood waiting to see whether any of his SEALs were set to complain. As expected, they were all fine with Crosswhite filling the role of second in command. They had all served under him during Operation Bank Heist, and he had fallen on his sword for them when the mission failed to liberate Warrant Officer Brux, taking the blame along with Master Chief Halligan Steelyard, who was killed weeks later during Brux's eventual rescue.

"Excellent." Gil snatched a cigarette from Crosswhite as he was about to light it and stuck it between his own lips, bumming Crosswhite's lighter at the same time. "Alpha, you're the ranking petty officer after me, so you'll play third fiddle." He drew from the cigarette and exhaled through his nose. "I don't anticipate a leprosy pandemic, so you should do just fine."

The room broke up with laughter, and Alpha lowered his head, his face flushing. The joke was left over from Operation Bank Heist, during which the team had encountered an old woman infected with leprosy. She had lost most of her fingers to the disease, and her eyes had turned completely white due to an untreated trachoma infection. Upon seeing her up close and realizing with horror that he was in the company of a leper, Alpha had wigged out completely, forcing Trigg, his best friend on the team, to subdue him with a rear naked choke.

"Take heart, Alphabet," Gil said with a smile. "We all have our weak spot — you just happen to be the only man among us to have found his."

There was more laughter, and Alpha shook his head, crossing his arms and looking off across the room to see a tall, white-haired man he had never seen before standing in the doorway dressed in civilian clothes. He pointed at the man. "Gil."

The laughter dropped off as Gil turned his head to see Bob Pope standing in the doorway with a red backpack over one shoulder.

"I hope I'm not interrupting," Pope said, pushing his glasses up onto his nose.

"Not at all, Bob. This is your show. I'm just warming up the crowd." Gil turned to the team. "Gentlemen, this is your boss, SAD director Robert Pope, whom you already know by reputation."

All the team members had worked under Pope throughout their time as SOG operators, but this was the first time any of them had seen him.

"Hey, guys," Pope said with a boyish smile, giving them a short wave. "How are you?"

None of the SEALs knew quite what to think. The man they saw standing before them in baggy khakis and a flannel shirt did not at all resemble the mysterious CIA spook they had previously imagined.

"Well, I suppose we'll get to it," he said, unzipping his pack and removing a stack of files, which he handed off to Gil. "If you'll pass those around for me."

Gil gave the stack to Crosswhite, who took one and passed the rest on.

"Okay," Pope said, taking a seat on the edge of the table. "Open your files, and you will see a photo of a man named Muhammad Faisal. He's the man you're going to bring me. He is not only an American citizen but also a member of the House of Saud." He went on to tell them the rest of what he knew about Faisal, ending with the disclosure of what little evidence there was linking him to the Chechen terrorist group RSMB.

The briefing took less than three minutes, and as Pope stood up and zipped his backpack closed, the SEALs sat looking at one another in open disappointment, scarcely able to believe the president had moved heaven and earth to bring them all together on such a paltry amount of actionable intel.

"Any questions?" Pope asked.

Trigg put up his hand. "Sir, if we know where to find this guy, why doesn't the FBI just bring him in?"

"Because where's the fun in that for us, Petty Officer Trigg?"

Pope smiled. "Kidding aside, the FBI has a list of rules they have to follow, and we can't afford the risk of Mr. Faisal refusing to cooperate. If he's detained and demands a lawyer — which he would be stupid not to do — the FBI will have to comply, and the time lost could cost us everything. We're looking for a live nuclear weapon; that means all rules go out the window."

Another SEAL named Speed, the team's only black member, put up his hand. "What about NDAA?" This was the National Defense Authorization Act. "It doesn't matter if you're a citizen anymore. Anybody suspected of terrorism can be held without due process, right?"

Pope crossed his arms. "That's a common argument these days, Petty Officer Hall, yes. One that many constitutional lawyers are still debating. But let us suppose for the sake of argument that it's true; do you think the Saudi royal family would stand for us denying one of their own access to a family lawyer? And even if they did, suppose Faisal still chose not to talk. What then?"

"So you all see the dilemma," Gil said. "Faisal is the one and only lead we have on the nuke, and that means we can't afford to take any chances. This guy has to be taken and interrogated — by whatever means necessary — and nobody can know the US government had anything to do with it. We are going to make him vanish into thin air.

"And anyone who gets in our way is going wake up in the halls of Valhalla."

"What kind of time do we have?" Crosswhite asked. "Couldn't this nuke go off any minute?"

"It could," Pope said. "However, September 11 is only two days away. I believe that's our date. Now, flip to the last page." He directed them to a photocopy of Iosif Hoxha's cutaway sketch of the RA-115. "This is not an exact schematic, but it's the closest approximation we have to a Soviet-made RA-115 two-kiloton suitcase nuke. As you can see, the weapon is of the gun-detonator design. Our most reliable intelligence indicates that it should weigh approximately one hundred pounds and fit snugly into a navy seabag."

"That's pretty small," Tuckerman said.

"You begin to see what we're up against," Gil remarked.

"And no leads at all as to where it is?" asked Crosswhite.

"None," Pope answered. "For all I know, it could be right here in this hangar — perhaps in one of your own seabags."

Everyone glanced around, collectively

focusing on Tuckerman seated at the back. They all knew him as the shadiest character on the team, and he hadn't been given the nickname Conman without good reason.

"Don't look at me," he said with a smirk. "I don't have the fuckin' thing."

Everyone laughed.

"Ah, yes," Pope said. "Mr. Tuckerman, petty officer first class. It's curious your teammates would choose to single you out at this moment. How are your poker skills these days, Mr. Tuckerman?"

Tuckerman sat up straight in the chair. "Just fine, sir. Why do you ask?"

Pope smiled. "Because why else would I liberate a pair of vigilantes from the brig if not to utilize the exceptional skills of one or the other? The renegade Captain Crosswhite here is talented, but he's not exactly indispensable with that arthritic hip of his."

Everyone faced the front again, looking wide eyed at Crosswhite; none of them knew anything about his and Tuckerman's brief incarceration by the 82nd Airborne.

Crosswhite shrank a bit in his chair.

"Take good care of the company you keep, Captain." Pope shouldered the pack to leave. "It seems to keep saving your life."

26

LAS VEGAS

Pope slipped into his hotel room to find Li-juan Chow asleep in bed. Her name meant "beautiful and graceful," and she was definitely both, with a mind to match: a brilliant intelligence analyst and computer technician whom he'd recruited right out of MIT ten years earlier. She was thirty-four, exactly half his age, and over the past decade, he had come to love her with all of his soul, despite the folly of it. He stood watching her sleep — his peaceful Chinese princess — and was overcome by a profound sense of melancholia. Exactly when their relationship would come to an end, he did not know, but he knew that it must be soon.

He opened his laptop and went online to check in with the system back in Langley, making sure that all of his surveillance programs were still running nominally. Some of the programs were of his own design, and the intelligence they gathered went into his own personal database: everything from satellite photos to banking transactions. He was a very, very curious man about a great many goings-on around the globe, and he wanted to learn as much about the world as possible before he was finally forced into retirement. Some of his most secret programs would, of course, remain accessible to him even after his retirement, but he would have to be careful to limit his time in the cloud, because technology was constantly evolving, and his personal programs — many of which ran parallel to the CIA programs and accessed all of the same intelligence — wouldn't likely remain secret forever.

Satisfied that all was as it should be, he turned off the computer and went to take a shower. When he came back from the bathroom, Lijuan was sitting propped in the pillows wearing a nightgown made of blue silk that extended to her knees.

"How did it go?" she asked, her English as perfect as her body.

"Good," he said, shouldering into a hotel robe and pulling the towel from his waist. He sat down on the bed and gathered her into his arms. "They're the best at what they do, so it should go well. My biggest concern is that Faisal won't know enough to help us."

"And if he doesn't want to talk?"

"Oh, he's going to talk. He won't have any choice about that. The trouble will be in knowing when to quit extracting information. A man begins to make up lies once he runs out of truth."

"What sort of torture will they use?" she asked softly, slipping her hand inside his robe to touch his chest.

"Whichever I tell them. They're reliable men."

"They must be barbarians," she said sadly. "To be able to cause such pain without remorse."

"Am I any less barbaric for giving the order?"

She rested her head against his chest. "Can't you just retire? Can't we leave and go to Singapore like we've talked about?" She lifted her head to gaze soulfully into his eyes. "What does it matter what happens here now? This country doesn't care about all that you've done for it; all that you've sacrificed. The president and his men will betray you in the end — you know they must. We have enough money, Robert. Let us go away . . . tonight. Right now."

He caressed her hair, wanting very much

to go with her to Singapore, to live out the rest of his life and to die in her arms. Christ in heaven, what man wouldn't? But Singapore was another world and beyond their destiny.

"You won't allow them to betray me," he said with a smile. "You're my protection against them."

She shook her head, a tear falling. "You put too much faith in me, Robert."

He petted her and kissed her hair. "Do you trust me?"

"Of course," she said.

"In that case, you should have nothing to worry you. I tell you that you are my talisman against them, and you can believe it." He smiled and touched the tip of her nose with his finger. "Now, no more tears for me. I'm as safe in your arms as anywhere on earth."

She hugged him tight, allowing the cloth of his robe to soak up her tears. She was not afraid for herself, only for him, and she knew that they would crucify him after she fled.

"When will they take Faisal?" she asked.

"Tomorrow night. Once I leave here in the morning, you can take your time about getting back to Langley. Midori has everything under control there."

"Are you sure Langley is safe?"

He opened her nightgown with a long index finger and smiled. "If we could be so lucky that they'd waste such a weapon on Langley, Virginia."

27

MONTANA

Since killing the trooper, Nikolai Kashkin
had been camped in the foothills above Gil
Shannon's horse ranch, and so far he'd seen
neither hide nor hair of the former Navy
SEAL he had come to assassinate. Each
morning, he awoke in the wee hours before
sunrise, slowly emerging from his tent like a
lazy bear coming out of hibernation. He
would stretch and yawn and leisurely set
about preparing his backpacker breakfast
over an MSR pocket stove. Then, after
breakfast, he would sit beneath the trees,
listening to the birds while enjoying his
morning coffee and watching the sunrise. It
was a pleasant time for him, perhaps the
most pleasant he had experienced since he
was a boy.

Upon finishing his coffee, Kashkin would
say his morning prayers and then pick up
the German Mauser Karabiner 98k rifle

with Zeiss optics and make his way to the ridge overlooking the ranch, where he had carefully prepared himself a sniper's nest among the rocks.

Throughout his boyhood, he had enjoyed hunting with his father's father in the great forests near his home. His grandfather had been a sniper in the Red Army during the Second World War, and he had taught Kashkin the art of shooting game at long distance with an old Soviet Mosin-Nagant, but Kashkin had long since grown attached to the German Mauser, which he considered a more elegant weapon. There were more modern sniper rifles on the market with higher calibers and greater ranges, but he had never desired to bother with them. Besides, he was too old to be learning new tricks at this stage of the game. With an effective range of a thousand meters, the Mauser was more than enough rifle for the job at hand, and its 7.92×57 mm round was more than enough bullet to put a man down and keep him down. His one-shot kill ratio during the First and Second Chechen Wars was evidence enough of that.

Kashkin felt no personal rancor toward Shannon, though he was aware that the SEAL had executed a Muslim cleric with a garrote in Afghanistan. In Kashkin's experience, most clerics were pushy, arrogant men seeking to burnish their egos while claiming to do the work of Allah. He understood that to assassinate one of them was a horrible insult against Islam, but he doubted very much whether the late Aasif Kohistani had been any different from the others he had known, so he doubted equally that there had been any great loss.

Akram al-Rashid and his people in AQAP had held up their end of the bargain by helping to purchase the RA-115s, so Kashkin would hold up his end by shooting Navy SEAL Gil Shannon dead in his very own backyard. He supposed this would send a definite message to the American Special Forces community, particularly if it served as a prelude to a devastating nuclear strike, but to Kashkin, killing Shannon would be little more than a justifiable act of vengeance — "an equal wound for a wound," as it said in the Koran.

For the fourth morning in a row now, he lay prone in his hide eight hundred meters above the ranch, watching the woman with long, dark hair as she went about her morning routine of loosing the horses into the various paddocks outside the stable. He assumed she was Shannon's wife, and he enjoyed watching her despite himself. He had never been one to covet another man's woman, be he friend or foe, Muslim or not, but the woman was undeniably pretty, and her beauty, when combined with the heady experience of living so closely with nature, was enough to make him stir.

Keeping her in the crosshairs throughout most of the morning, he wondered idly if blowing off one of her arms might draw Shannon out of the house. By this point in the stalk, however, he was growing confident that his prey was not bedding down in its usual lair. So he began to think in terms of going down to the ranch and putting a knife to the woman as a means of finding out where Shannon was and when he would return. She might even get him on the phone to expedite that return.

Marie Shannon had been married to a professional sniper for almost ten years, so when she saw the glint of Kashkin's scope high on the ridge, she knew that something was god-awful wrong because she'd seen a glint the morning before in precisely the same spot. She hadn't thought much of it the day before, however; the Fergusons crossed the ridge from time to time between the ranches while hunting coyotes, and it was only human nature to scope things out from above.

She continued currycombing Gil's Appaloosa, Tico, maintaining an easy smile in case the shooter's optics were strong enough to make out her facial features. A Chesapeake Bay retriever named Oso Cazador (Bear Hunter) came trotting across the yard and paused to take a leak on a post. He was a big dog, one hundred pounds, with a devilish canine smile and a reddish brown coat.

"Oso," she said, without looking at him. "Get inside, baby."

The dog looked at her, as if unsure if he'd heard her correctly.

"Go check on Grandma!"

The dog turned and ran back to the house, jumping onto the deck and ducking inside through the dog door.

Marie guessed there was a price on Gil's head and that the shooter wasn't up there for her, but even knowing there was a rifle pointed in her general direction was more than enough to make her want to run for the house. She was just able to suck in her fear and finish combing the horse before finally dropping the comb into the green bucket at her feet and walking the short but hellish few feet into the stable.

Once inside, she sat down on a bale of

hay and at last allowed herself to tremble. She wrapped her arms around her shoulders, swearing quietly at her husband for bringing an assassin to their gate. Part of her knew she was nuts to believe there was a sniper in the foothills above the ranch, but another part of her realized that thousands of people the world over lived with snipers all around them all the time, never knowing when someone might be shot dead in front of them. Now that reality had come to Montana.

She got up and walked to the far end of the stable, pausing at the door to draw a breath, and then set off casually across the yard toward the house — knowing she would be within the shooter's line of sight for better than a hundred feet. It was the longest hundred feet of her life, but she made it to cover and hurried up onto the front porch, jerking open the screen door, and ducking inside.

"Mama!" she called. "Where are you?"

Oso came running over to her.

"Right here," her mother said, poking her head around the kitchen doorway. "Why? What's the matter?" Her name was Janet. She was seventy-six years old and just over five feet three inches tall, with long gray hair she wore in the braid of a horsewoman.

"Stay away from the windows on the west side of the house." Marie trotted up the staircase. "And don't go outside!"

Janet stood in the kitchen drying her hands, then set down the towel and went upstairs. She found Marie in the spare bedroom taking Gil's Browning .300 Winchester Magnum with a 3 to 24 Nightforce scope from the gun safe in the corner.

"Marie, what in hell's half acre are you about?"

"We'll find out in a minute." Marie lay the rifle down on the bed and gathered her long brown hair behind her head, weaving it quickly into a loose braid. Then she picked the rifle back up, popped off the lens caps fore and aft, and slipped past her mother into the hall, making her way to the master bedroom on the west side of the house.

Oso followed her excitedly, thinking they must be going hunting.

Janet followed too, a discerning frown creasing her face.

"Stay away from the windows, Mama." Marie knelt beside the bed opposite the windows, extending the legs of the bipod on the hunting rifle and resting it on the mattress. She put her eye to the scope and trained it on the ridge overlooking the house. When she spotted Kashkin, wearing

232

an olive drab ball cap, hunkered down in the rocks behind the scoped Mauser, the urine in her bladder turned to ice water. The house was not built parallel to the ridge line, so she was looking at him angle-on and angle-off to Kashkin's right at about 30 degrees. From the look of him, he seemed to be glassing the house, but she knew there was no way he could see deeply enough into the room to spot her because the room was too dim.

She pulled back the bolt and rammed one of the torpedo-nosed .30 caliber rounds into battery.

"Marie, what are you doing?"

She safed the weapon and got to her feet. "Have a look," she said. "Up in the rocks above the ranch."

Janet knelt beside the bed and pulled the stock into her shoulder. She was not a stranger to shooting, and she didn't have to adjust the aim much in order to spot Kashkin in his nest.

"Lord A'Mighty!" She sat back from the rifle. "What's he doin' up there?"

Marie got down beside her. "Al Qaeda put a price on Gil's head. He must be some kind of damn bounty hunter." Janet got up, and her daughter retook her position behind the rifle, pulling the stock back into her shoulder and making the weapon hot. "Bring me a sofa cushion from downstairs, and fill Gil's CamelBak with water for me," she said intently. "I can't see enough of this guy for a shot, so I'll have to wait until he gets up. And lock the dog door, so Oso can't get out."

Janet watched her, grim faced. "Are you sure you want to do this? What if you're wrong? What if he's just some ignorant fool up there bein' silly?"

"Mama, you don't believe that any more than I do." She continued to study Kashkin through the scope. He didn't look like an Arab in the eyes, which was about all she could see, but if he was a bounty hunter, he could be anybody — even an American. "Now please bring me a cushion for my knees. I won't last long on this hardwood floor, and I don't dare take my eyes off this man. There's no tellin' when he'll let out, and I can't afford to let him get away."

Janet went below and returned with the sofa cushion, slipping it under Marie's knees one at a time. Oso jumped onto the bed, whining because he still thought they were going hunting.

"Get down."

"But what about your conscience?" Janet said. "If you shoot that man, you'll have to

234

live with it the rest of your life."

"Gil lives with it, so I reckon I can too. That man's up there lookin' to kill him, and I can't abide it — I *won't* abide it!"

Janet stood nodding for a moment and then went to fill Gil's CamelBak with water. When she returned, Marie was naked from the waist down with the bedspread bunched up beneath her on top of the sofa cushion.

"Marie Anne! What on earth!"

"I might have to pee later. This way, I can pee on the blanket and not have to worry."

Janet set the CamelBak down on the mattress and took a seat on the cane-back chair in the corner, resting her hand on Oso's big head. The dog was getting frustrated with all the waiting. "We could call the police, ya know."

"They'd just make a circus of it, especially when the media found out. And suppose he got away?" She took her eye from the scope for just a moment. "This is business between Al Qaeda and the McGuthrys, Mama."

"Oh, so now you're a McGuthry again."

"This is McGuthry land," Marie said, repositioning herself behind the scope. "Daddy wouldn't have done any different."

Janet sat back in the chair with a sigh. "Well, your daddy wasn't always the smartest man in the world."

"Mama, you know I'm right; otherwise you'd be downstairs on the phone right now callin' the sheriff — in spite of anything I had to say about it."

Janet clicked her tongue. "Maybe so. And then again, maybe I'm still tryin' to make up my mind."

"Well, until you do, I'll be right here behind this rifle."

By the time the sun began to set, Kashkin's back had grown stiff, just as it had during the past three days. He thought it odd that the woman hadn't come back out to bring the horses into the stable as she normally did, but there was no telling with people.

A coyote yammered somewhere off behind him, and his eyes shifted immediately to the colt down in the paddock. Surely she wasn't going to leave the colt outside overnight with predators roaming the land. A single coyote would be foolish to attempt getting past the colt's mother, but a pack of coyotes might be another story.

He thought back over the day, only now completely conscious of the fact the woman had definitely changed her routine. For three days running, she had cleaned out the horses' stalls, but not today. And after combing the Appaloosa, she hadn't taken

236

the green bucket back into the stable. He recalled her route back to the house that morning and realized she'd taken the shortest route possible instead of entering through the back door the way she normally did, always leaving her dirty cowboy boots on the back porch.

He scanned the tree line beyond the ranch to the east, briefly imagining policemen staring back at him through multiple pairs of binoculars. Then he scanned the dirt road far beyond the ranch to the south. He saw no sign of law enforcement anywhere, but somehow he was sure he'd been compromised. He could feel it. Paranoia began to creep its way into his mind, and over the next ten minutes, he talked himself into believing that Gil might be stalking him. The painful tightness in his chest returned, and he decided he'd waited long enough. He would go down into the house and take the woman alive, forcing Shannon to show himself.

He took a satellite phone from the bugout bag beside him and called the al-Rashids. "This is Kashkin," he said. "Let me speak to Akram."

"He's not with me right now," said Haroun al-Rashid, the younger of the two brothers. "Is it done?"

"No, it is not done," Kashkin said. "It's possible I've been compromised; that the target is stalking me. If you do not hear from me by tomorrow morning, you should proceed with plan B."

"What? *How* are you compromised? Are we *all* compromised?"

"No, only me. You are safe. So good luck, my friend. I must go now. May the blessings of Allah be upon you."

"No, Kashkin, wait —"

Kashkin switched off the phone and smashed it against a rock.

He then drew his knees beneath him and began to pray, stretching the muscles of his lower back at the same time. When he was finished, he stood up and had a good look around, drawing a breath before taking that first step downhill toward the ranch.

He didn't hear the shot because it was muffled by the house, but when the .30 caliber round struck him, it tore out his right floating rib and a good deal of flesh along with it. Kashkin wasn't aware of any pain, just the queer sensation of having instantly had all the air sucked from his lungs.

Marie knew she'd hit him from the way he'd grabbed his side. Her shoulders were aching from sitting hunched over the mat-

238

tress all day, but she shrugged it off and worked the bolt to ram another round into battery before placing the reticule of the scope right below Kashkin's chin.

She drew a breath, held it . . . and squeezed the trigger a second time.

The round hit Kashkin dead center in the sternum and slammed him onto his back. He landed with his arms splayed out at his sides, and though all that Marie could see of him now was the sole of his right boot propped up on a rock, she knew she'd taken him out.

She sat back from the bed and looked up as Janet hurried into the room.

"He's down," she said, getting stiffly to her feet and taking her jeans from the edge of the bed. She stepped into them and gathered up the pee-stained bedspread, stuffing it down the laundry chute in the hallway. "I'll wait til dark, then rig the travois to Tico and go up and get him. We'll bury him on the ranch."

28

MONTANA

Marie sat in the saddle atop the ridge in the light of the moon, looking down from the back of Gil's Appaloosa mare. Kashkin was flat on his back with his eyes wide open, staring up at the glowing crescent in the sky, his arms splayed as if to embrace the heavens. The ground beneath him was stained black with his blood, and there were two cruel-looking bullet holes in his khaki Swiss Army shirt. The Mauser lay near a small rucksack water pouch, and pieces of a shattered satellite phone were scattered at his feet.

Oso sniffed at the body and growled low in his throat.

Marie pulled a Winchester model 94 in .45 caliber from the saddle scabbard and stepped down from the horse.

"Back," she said to Oso, and he obeyed, sitting on his haunches.

Walking over to the body, she stood on the left arm and prodded Kashkin in the neck with the muzzle of the rifle to make certain he was dead before returning the Winchester to the scabbard. She gathered up the Mauser and rucksack, shouldering the ruck and pulling back the bolt on the rifle to eject the 7.92 mm round. It landed on the ground, and she crouched to pick it up, holding it in front of her discerning brown eyes.

The "boar's tooth," Gil called it . . . the round that might have killed her had she missed. She put the round into the pocket of her Carhartt jacket and gripped the Mauser with both hands, pivoting on her right foot to gaze out over her father's ranch. It was hard reality to accept, but war had once again come to this land, and she was now no less a combatant than her husband was. She had killed another human being in a sniper duel, and this was a claim that even few Navy SEALs could make.

"Damn you, Gil," she whispered.

She hung the Mauser from the saddle horn by the shoulder strap and did the same with the ruck. Then Marie went to stand over the body once again, her hands on her hips as she nervously chewed her lower lip.

She didn't want to touch the corpse, but there was no other way to get it down the hill. She pulled on her leather roping gloves and crouched to take hold of Kashkin's left wrist, pushing the arm down against his side. He had been dead for six hours, so he was only about three hours into rigor mortis. Full rigor occurred at twelve hours, when the muscles were at full contraction, so he wasn't yet stiff as a board, but he wasn't entirely limber, either.

Within a half hour, she had him wrapped in a game bag and strapped to the travois attached to Tico's saddle. She was mounted up and ready to start down the hill when it occurred to her she hadn't seen Oso for the past five or ten minutes.

She called to him, and he barked twice from a distance. It was the same bark he used whenever he had treed a raccoon, and she knew that he wouldn't come unless she went and got him. He was very hardheaded that way. So she shucked the Winchester out of the scabbard and dismounted.

"We don't really have time for this, Cazador," she muttered, taking a flashlight from the saddlebag and starting off through the juniper pines in the direction of the barking. She called out again to get a better fix on the dog's location, and he answered as he had the first time. A minute later, she saw him sitting on his haunches in the beam of the flashlight beside a green Timberline tent some two hundred feet back from the ridge. The tent was pitched in a copse of junipers, and there was nothing outside it save for a small pile of coals that Marie found cold to the touch and a pair of white boxer briefs draped over a branch.

The sight of the camp was enough to make her sick to her stomach. The idea that someone had been camping up here without a care in the world, waiting patiently to blow her husband's brains out, both frightened and infuriated her. She unzipped the tent and shined the light inside to see a large green backpack, a blue sleeping bag, and a pile of cooking equipment. There was also the lingering odor of an unwashed human being. Quickly rifling through the pack, she found the usual incidentals, numerous bags of backpacking food, and a small laptop computer. She crammed everything into the backpack then hurriedly struck the campsite, making sure to scatter the charcoal from the fire.

Forty minutes later, she stood beside her mother in the well-lighted stable looking down at the dead man lying in the center of the gray plastic tarp.

Oso sat across from them whining.

"He doesn't look much like a Muslim to me," Janet remarked.

"Me neither." Marie knelt beside him and went through the cargo pockets of his olive drab trousers. She found his German passport, driver's permit, and the key to a rental car.

Janet knew they were both way out of their depth. "We should call somebody, honey."

"Like who?"

"Like you *know* who. I understand ya don't wanna hear it, but we gotta tell Gil sooner or later, and there ain't no point to waiting."

Marie folded the tarp back over Kashkin's stiffening body. Then she went to the wall and picked up the phone, calling Gil's number and being sent straight to voice mail. She swore under her breath and left a message for him to call her right away.

29

CANADA,
Ontario, Windsor

Haroun al-Rashid knocked on the door of his brother's house, shouldering past his sister-in-law as she opened it. "Akram!"

"In here," said Akram al-Rashid, seated in the kitchen and eating breakfast. He stood up from the table, recognizing the distress in his younger brother's voice. He was thirty-five, light skinned, and athletic looking, with short black hair. Akram was handsome when clean shaven, but this morning he had a dark five o'clock shadow, and he was dressed sloppily in a white tank top and gray sweatpants. "What's wrong?"

"Kashkin is dead."

If Akram found this news overly disturbing, it didn't show. "How do you know?"

Haroun explained about the phone call the evening before and that Kashkin had never called back. "So the American must have killed him," he went on, clearly agitated. "Now you'll have to go to Detroit and gather our men. We assured our people back home that we could deliver the American's head, and if we fail to do it . . ."

Akram nodded, crossing his arms and leaning against the kitchen counter. "Yes," he said thoughtfully. "It would be bad if we failed to deliver."

"Very bad," Haroun agreed. "We gave that stupid Chechen a lot of money, and now that he's dead . . ." He looked around nervously and then held out his hands in a gesture of helplessness. "I have no idea who has control of the bomb, Akram. That idiot disconnected before I could even ask. The entire operation could be in jeopardy, for all we know."

Akram had spent six years as a Royal Saudi Marine, and at times like this, he still emanated an aura of military confidence. He was not a man to be shaken easily, but his brother Haroun, a bookworm, was very excitable and dependent upon Akram for moral support and encouragement.

Akram gave his shoulder a reassuring squeeze. "Kashkin was an experienced strategist. A very intelligent and capable man. He would never have gone after the American until the bomb was safely delivered to his people. Don't worry."

He glanced at his twenty-four-year-old wife, who stood in the living room looking worried, saying something to her in Greek that Haroun did not understand. She answered him timidly and went into the bedroom and closed the door.

"She is pregnant," Akram told his brother. "We just found out."

Haroun's eyes lit up. "Congratulations, brother!"

Akram seemed not to hear it. "Listen. If I do not return from killing the American, it will be your responsibility to marry Melonie and raise my son — as it *will* be a son. Allah has told us so."

"But . . . but I don't speak Greek. How could I even — ?"

"You will learn," Akram said heavily. "She is obedient and loyal, but she is not very smart and could never learn our language. So it will be up to you — your responsibility. You're my brother, and I will be counting on you in the event that Allah summons me into the void."

Haroun lowered his head. "I will learn Greek. I promise." He knew that for Akram to travel so far into the United States on such an intrepid mission, with American law enforcement on such high alert, would be near suicide. He looked up. "She will accept me?"

Akram shrugged. "What choice will she have? But do not worry. We have discussed it, and she understands her duty." He sat down to finish his breakfast, bidding his brother to take the chair across from him. "Now, enough doomsaying."

Haroun was still frustrated that Kashkin had provided so little information. "He said the American was stalking him, but he was very calm about it, very accepting."

"As we should all be at such a time." Akram tore off a piece of unleavened bread and put it into his mouth. "I have vetted this American. He is a man who does things his own way. This makes him unpredictable and dangerous — as Kashkin has apparently learned — but it also makes him vulnerable."

"Our people in Detroit will follow you?"

"Of course," Akram said, pushing runny egg yolk around on his plate with a piece of bread.

The uncertainty was apparent on Haroun's face. "And you trust that stinking pig mercenary we hired? Duke?"

Akram shook his head. "I trust his greed. His greed is very reliable." He chuckled and reached out to muss his brother's hair.

"Relax. It's taken a long time for us to become established on this continent, but soon the American military will begin to understand with great clarity that the war has finally come to their homeland — that we are now in their rear among their families and supply."

"The bomb will teach them that in very certain terms," Haroun said gravely.

"Yes, but it's unfortunate the first bomb was detonated prematurely. We're going to need another, so be sure to squeeze Faisal for more. Tell him that soon we're going to need money from his personal account."

"Do you already know where to find another weapon?"

Akram shook his head. "No, but once the second bomb goes off, and our friends abroad see how successful we were, how vulnerable the US really is, doors are going to open. Everyone is always afraid of the largest wolf in the pack — until he stumbles."

"And then others fall upon him?"

"They fall upon him quickly, before he can get back up."

30

LAS VEGAS

The Las Vegas Metropolitan Police Department was somewhat different from other metropolitan police departments in that the LVMPD was a joint city-county police department for both the city of Las Vegas and Clark County, Nevada. The department was not headed by a chief of police appointed by city officials but rather by a sheriff elected by the citizens of Clark County. This meant the LVMPD was not under the direct control of either the city or the county. It was under the direct control of Sheriff Jack Moleska, and Jack Moleska didn't appreciate being bothered at home during breakfast by a bunch of G-men in dark suits.

"Exactly who are all you people?" Moleska said, standing on his front porch in his pajamas looking at a veritable crowd of Secret Service agents on his lawn. He was tall, with thinning dark hair and a narrow face.

"We're with the Secret Service, Sheriff."

"All of you, huh?" Moleska handed back the agent's identification. "And you say you have some kind of warrant?"

"Yes, sir." The agent produced a single-page warrant, offering it to Moleska. "This warrant is issued by the United States Foreign Intelligence Surveillance Court in Washington, DC."

"Uh-huh." Moleska took the time to read the entire warrant. It directed him to provide a "secure perimeter" outside the Luxor hotel and casino while "federal agents" entered the hotel for the purposes of taking into custody a "subject wanted for questioning."

He looked at the agent. "So who the hell's the subject?"

"I don't know, sir. I haven't been given that information."

"Well, where's the warrant for him?"

"I don't have that information either, sir."

Moleska stood looking at the Secret Service man. "So is this an FBI operation? Secret Service? Marshal Service? Ninja Turtles? Who?"

"There again, Sheriff, I haven't been made privy to that information."

Moleska gestured with the warrant. "Do you serve this kind of warrant often, Agent Rivers? I ask because I've never seen anything like it in thirty-five years of law enforcement. With the exception of" — he had to read the letters directly off the warrant — "the USFISC letterhead, this so-called warrant doesn't actually *name* anyone at all."

"It names *you,* sir."

Moleska narrowed his gaze. "Okay, you listen . . . this is *my* city. *My* county. So you go back to wherever you came from, and you tell the federal government that I'm not an idiot. I can read between the lines as well as anyone, and this warrant directs me to stand by and watch what amounts to some kind of *federal abduction.* Not only will I not be a party to it, but I won't allow it to take place inside my jurisdiction. Understood?"

"Understood, sir." The agent lifted his hand and spoke into his sleeve.

A few moments later, the back door to one of the government sedans opened up, and a tall, white-haired gentleman came strolling up the concrete drive smiling.

"Hello, Sheriff," the man said, offering his hand. "My name is Pope. May we have a word in private?"

Like most people, Moleska couldn't help being disarmed by Pope's boyish smile. "Sure, step inside."

He turned and opened the door, allowing Pope to precede him into the house. Moleska shut the door, and the two of them crossed into the living room. "Now, what's this all about?"

"Sheriff, I'm with the Central Intelligence Agency."

Moleska held up the warrant. "*That's* why nobody's mentioned on this piece of paper. The CIA has no authority inside the US."

"That's correct," Pope said. "Unfortunately, however, there's a live nuclear weapon loose inside the country, and we're the agency with the best chance of finding it before it goes off — which we expect to be in about thirty-six hours. That leaves us very little time for following the rules, as I'm sure you can understand. So I tell you this in all candor, Sheriff . . . if you refuse to look the other way on this . . . if you force the book on us . . . our one and only suspect is going to lawyer up and laugh while the clock on a Russian suitcase nuke ticks down to zero."

The sheriff lowered his gaze, folding the warrant in half. "Let me get dressed. I'll be right out."

31

SOUTHERN CALIFORNIA,
Edwards Air Force Base

The president stood smoking his pipe on the tarmac at the foot of the stairs below Air Force One. There were a number of troops and Secret Service men about, all of them very alert and focused on the landscape surrounding the plane in the early-morning sunlight. He was very presidential looking in his Air Force One jacket: a man in his midfifties, gray at the temples, with expressive blue eyes and a perpetual tan. Even though he now led the nation from Edwards Air Force Base, located twenty-two miles northeast of Lancaster, California, he slept aboard the blue and white Boeing 747, which was kept ready for takeoff at a moment's notice. He slept aboard the plane for two reasons: one, the First Lady preferred the Posturepedic mattress aboard the plane to the cheap military mattress in their base quarters, and two, if something cata-strophic happened in the middle of the night, requiring a fast getaway, he would already be aboard.

General Couture had only just learned of the resurrection of SEAL Team VI/Black, and he was less than thrilled by the news. "You are aware, Mr. President, that we're violating the United States Constitution?"

"I am, General, but I was thinking about President Truman last night — thinking about his struggle over whether or not to use the atomic bomb against the Japanese. He was troubled by the idea of killing thousands of civilians. But in the end, he did it because he wanted to save American lives. That's the same way I came to my decision last night, and I have to say it wasn't that difficult. It's one man we're talk-ing about. One's man's rights. One man's life against thousands."

"And if he doesn't know anything, Mr. President? If he's innocent?"

The president shrugged, turning to rap the spent tobacco from his pipe against the stairway railing. "That's what presidents are elected for, General, to make the tough calls and to live with the results."

Couture conceded the point, knowing that the issue of SEAL Team VI/Black was well out of his hands.

"Tim Hagen tells me the two of you had something of a disagreement outside the Oval Office the other day." The president chuckled as he drew a pouch of fresh tobacco from his jacket pocket. "You don't really care for him, do you?"

The general straightened his shoulders. "I think he's a worm, Mr. President; that you could do a great deal better."

"He is a worm," the president said, dipping the pipe into the pouch. "He's a sycophantic little prick, as a matter of fact, but he's also the single most intelligent man that I know — present company excluded, of course," he added with a friendly grin.

Couture offered the driest of dutiful smiles.

"What do you think of Bob Pope?" the president said. "I ask because NSA has recently found a mole on his staff. He's been sleeping with one of his Asian protégés, and she's been giving information to the Chinese."

Couture felt his hackles raise up. "Does Pope know? Is he party to it?"

The president shook his head. "NSA doesn't think so. They think he's allowed *love* to cloud his judgment, and that he's trusted her with a higher security clearance than he should have." He flicked a butane lighter to life, breathing the blue flame into the bowl of the pipe and puffing it to life. "She's scheduled a flight to Australia for tomorrow night. NSA's going to wait and arrest her at the airport to keep Pope from knowing."

"Mr. President, do you feel certain we can trust Pope with tonight's operation?"

"Yes," the president said. "George Shroyer and Cletus Webb at CIA both believe he's a solid patriot. That's good enough for me. Nonetheless, once the bomb is found, whether by Pope's people or by someone else, he's out of SOG for good." The president chortled quietly. "Then I guess we'll get to see who he's got files on."

Couture hated this aspect of government, resenting most of the civilians he had no choice but to work with. The entire cast reminded him of a bunch of school kids playing out a childish high school drama.

"I suppose so. Well, Mr. President, I should let you go up to breakfast, sir."

"Do you think we're going to find that nuke, Bill?" The president was looking him dead in the eyes.

Couture didn't waste a moment answering. "No, I don't. I'm sorry, but I think they've got us by the balls this time."

The president nodded, putting the stem of the pipe between his teeth. "So do I. That's also part of why I'm prepared to let Pope run with ST6/B. We've got nothing to lose."

The president, still smoking his pipe, ascended the stairs and stepped onto the plane. Tim Hagen was eating breakfast with a laptop computer sitting off to the side.

"I've got good news," Hagen said with a smile.

The president took the pipe from his teeth, feeling a sudden surge of adrenaline. "They found it?"

"Well, no," Hagen said. "It's about the latest poll results . . . you're leading by almost thirty points now, Mr. President."

The president narrowed his gaze, allowing Hagen to feel the weight of it before saying, "Tim, I sometimes wonder if you have an ounce of human compassion in your entire body."

32

LAS VEGAS

"Okay, listen up!" Gil said, taking a seat on the edge of the table. "Tonight we execute the illegal abduction of an American citizen. We will be breaking the law. This means we have zero room for error. Is that understood?"

Every one of the team members nodded his head, all of them steely eyed and focused.

"The plan is simple and straightforward. Four of us will enter the Luxor casino. We will be escorted by a CIA plant working as a hotel concierge to Muhammad Faisal's suite's elevator, which opens up just outside his door on the twentieth floor. When we arrive, we will blow the door and sweep the room, killing his entire five-man security team. Once Faisal is secured — *alive* — we will bring him directly back here for interrogation."

Crosswhite cleared his throat. "Sorry, but do we plan on shooting our way out of there? Because that casino is wall to wall with security."

Gil grinned. "Did I not say, *simple*?"

"Yeah, and that doesn't sound too simple to me. Then again, I'm not a navy man."

Gil got up and put out his hand for a cigarette. "The sheriff and the head of casino security have been advised that we have a FISA warrant for this guy — which isn't exactly true — and they have both agreed to help. So there won't be any trouble with security on the way in or out, neither with the cops or hotel security."

"Who explains the bodies we leave behind?"

"Can any of you think of a better cover story than to blame it on the bastards who hit us in Benghazi? The State Department's going to blame Faisal's abduction on AQAP . . . Al Qaeda in the Arabian Peninsula . . . the sworn enemy of the Saudi royal family."

"Wow!" someone said. "Threaten us with a nuke, and our moral ethics go right out the fuckin' window."

Everyone laughed.

"Lying to the Saudis," the SEAL went on, shaking his head in disappointment. "Tell

260

me it isn't so." His name was Clancy, the team prankster.

Gil drew from the cigarette. "I think you'll get over it." He waited a moment for the men to regain their focus before continuing. "We'll wear *shemaghs* and carry AK-47s, using hand signals to communicate, jabbering in gutter Arabic to make sure any witnesses we leave behind will corroborate our terrorist cover story."

"What about the five million security cameras?"

"Pope's hacked into their system. He's going to make sure nothing is recorded. Once we've got Faisal, we stuff his ass in a laundry cart, and the CIA man brings us back down in a service elevator. Then we bring him back here and find out what he knows . . . by whatever means necessary."

"And the president knows about all this?" Alpha asked dubiously.

"Given the briefing I received from Pope, I'm left with that assumption, yes. However, do not forget that every man in this room has a well-documented history of acting against orders. This means we could all be disavowed very easily without the president taking any damage if he chooses to double-cross us. Regardless, once the op jumps off, we're in it to the last man. Nothing and no one *can* or *will* be allowed to prevent us from completing this mission."

Tuckerman put up his hand.

"Yeah, Conman?"

"I don't like to be the guy to point out the fly in the honey jar here, but how do we know the target will be in the room when the entry team makes the breach?"

"Actually, that's where you come in. Like Pope said, he sprung your ass for a particular reason. It's going to be *your* job to make *sure* Faisal's in the room."

"Excuse me?"

"Pope has secured you a one-million-dollar line of credit with the Luxor casino. He's also secured you a seat at tonight's high-stakes poker game. Muhammad Faisal will be at the same table."

"No fuckin' way," Tuckerman said, laughing with nervous tension as everyone turned to look at him again.

"The son of a bitch never leaves the hotel these days," Gil said. "Pope considers that an encouraging sign of his guilt."

"Okay, so what am I supposed to do after I whip his ass at poker?"

"Con your way into his hotel suite and be ready to take his ass to the floor the second we blow the door. If he gets clipped, it's game over."

"Piss," Tuckerman mumbled to himself. "It's all gotta ride on me."

"Hey, what about after the interrogation?" Trigg asked. "Suppose Faisal doesn't know anything? I mean, we don't have jack shit for evidence on the dude. It's entirely possible he's innocent. What happens to him then?"

Gil shrugged. "He can't ever be allowed to tell the Saudi royal family that we took him — or what we did to him afterward. No matter what he knows . . . or doesn't know . . . the royal family will be told that he was killed in a terrorist attack executed by AQAP. So if he is innocent — well, that's just something we'll have to live with."

33

After three and a half hours of Texas Hold'em on the floor of the Luxor casino, there were only three of the original ten players left at the table: Conman Tucker- man, Muhammad Faisal, and Big Ray, a professional gambler out of San Antonio, Texas. Big Ray wore a black cowboy hat, dark sunglasses, and gaudy, diamond- studded gold rings on the thumb and middle finger of each hand. The dealer had just flipped open the turn card, and Tucker- man could see from the way that Ray now seemed to ignore his hole cards that he'd be gone before the flip of the river — the river card being the last of five community cards to be flipped open before the end of the hand.

Faceup in the center of the table were the three flop cards: the queen of diamonds, the queen of spades, and the four of hearts. The turn card, also faceup, was the king of spades.

Faisal eyed his hole cards for a moment and then laid them flat, suppressing a smile as he made a ten-thousand-dollar bet.

Tuckerman immediately raised it to twenty, letting out an obnoxious snigger toward Big Ray sitting to his left.

"Think you're pretty fuckin' funny, don't ya?" This was the first Big Ray had spoken the entire game, and Tuckerman knew he was finally finished.

Tuckerman turned over both of his hole cards for Big Ray to see: the two of clubs and the queen of hearts. Combined with the two flop-card queens, this gave him a very strong three of a kind.

He sat grinning ear to ear, looking right at Big Ray. "We call those three natural queens where I come from." Then he laughed out loud, and Big Ray tossed his cards into the muck, shoving back from the table and swearing a blue streak as he stormed off through the crowd surrounding the table.

Tuckerman, to his great satisfaction, watched him go and then glanced across the table at Faisal. "How about you, Muhammad? Whatcha got over there, buddy?"

Faisal smiled. Tuckerman had been cleaning his clock all night, and to lose this hand would put him out of the game, but he flipped over his own hole cards to expose the king of hearts and the king of diamonds. Combined with the turn card king, these cards gave him an even stronger three of a kind than Tuckerman's.

"Would you like to surrender now?" Faisal asked good-naturedly, coolly enjoying the thrill of victory.

Tuckerman was hard pressed to hide his sudden unease. He was up against the clock, and if he didn't force Faisal from the game very soon, he was going to blow the mission's timetable. Big Ray had given him fits all night, stretching the game out longer than he had planned for, so he didn't have time for Faisal to die a slow death. He needed to finish him.

He sucked his teeth. "Why don't we just see where the river takes us, huh?"

"Why not?" Faisal replied, his eyes glowing in triumph.

The dealer burned the top card by placing it facedown in the center of the table and flipped open the river card . . . the two of spades.

A collective gasp swept through the crowd.

"Fuck!" Faisal hissed acidly, tossing his

cards into the muck at the center of the table.

Tuckerman pumped his fists and cheered, "Full house, *bay-bee*!"

Faisal sat back from the table with a bemused smirk as the jabbering crowd began to disperse. "How many times did you bluff tonight?" he demanded to know. "I know you bluffed at least twice, you son of a bitch. No one is that lucky — no one!"

Tuckerman laughed. "I've got a shamrock tattooed to my ass, partner."

"This was supposed to be *my* night!" Faisal protested. "The night to break my losing streak, and I would have done it, if not for you. You owe me a drink — no, make it two!"

"Yeah, yeah, okay, fine," Tuckerman said, stacking his chips. "But up in your suite, huh? I'm tired of sitting down here with the common people."

Faisal wavered a moment, glancing briefly at Ma'mun, his bodyguard, standing near the wall.

"Oh, come on," Tuckerman said, pretending not to even notice Ma'mun. "Don't tell me you don't have a suite here in the hotel, you rich bastard. Hell, if I had your money, I could probably afford to burn mine."

Faisal was easily flattered when it came to

his money, and he couldn't help liking Tuckerman, admiring the way he had succeeded in getting inside of Big Ray's head early in the game. Big Ray was normally a monster at the table, and Faisal had lost to him many times, but tonight Ray had made two critical miscalculations in a row, and those errors were entirely because of Tuckerman's constant niggling.

Fuck it, he thought and grinned. "Yeah, okay. But tomorrow night you're giving me a chance to win some of my money back!"

Tuckerman sighed as they stood up from the table. "I can't promise I'll be available tomorrow night." He knew Faisal was on the hook now and wanted to keep him there. "But if I am, I don't plan to lose. That's entirely against my creed."

"Of course, you'll be available." Faisal put a hand on Tuckerman's shoulder. "Don't talk nonsense. I can see you're not a man to walk away from a challenge. Hey, where are you from, my friend?"

"Right here in Vegas," Tuckerman said proudly. "Born and bred."

"Well, that explains it!" Faisal said. "And what do you do — when you're not cheating at poker, I mean?"

Tuckerman chortled, keenly aware that Faisal's bodyguard did not approve of this budding new friendship. "I lead a high-wire act with Cirque du Soleil over at the Bellagio. You should come see us."

Faisal laughed and clapped him on the back, saying to Ma'mun, "Call up to the suite and make sure there are enough girls."

Ma'mun began to protest.

"Just do it, Ma'mun. I'm not in the mood to argue this evening. I've decided I'm going to get this man drunk, get him properly laid" — he stabbed his finger into Tuckerman's chest — "and then tomorrow night I'm going to take all of his fucking money!"

They both broke up laughing, and to look at them, one would have thought they'd been friends for years.

"Like I said," Tuckerman warned him, enjoying being back on the con, "I may have another obligation tomorrow night."

"Your obligation is to *me* tomorrow night," Faisal insisted, some of the spoiled child in him showing through. "And I won't take *no* for an answer, my friend."

"Well, okay." Tuckerman chuckled. "Since you insist."

34

The president could smell the ozone in the darkened operations center the moment he stepped through the door, the static electricity in the air making the hair on his arms stand on end. He saw General Couture on the far side of the room talking to Colonel Eugene Bradshaw with the 432nd Air Expeditionary Wing, attached to ACC (Air Combat Command). Bradshaw was the air force liaison officer whose job it was to coordinate communications with Creech AFB, located forty-some miles northwest of Las Vegas.

The president looked at the giant hi-definition monitor on the wall, seeing the overhead infrared video feed of the Luxor hotel and casino provided by a loitering reconnaissance UAV (Unmanned Aerial Vehicle) based out of Creech. The op center was alive with the murmured communications of a half dozen men and women wearing headsets, rapidly running their fingers over keyboards to collate minute-by-minute information coming in from various intelligence sources and military commands. This was the president's first experience in such an environment, and only with some difficulty did he manage to keep the sense of wonderment from his face.

"Mr. President," Couture said as he approached with the colonel. "Allow me to present Colonel Bradshaw with the 432nd Wing."

Bradshaw was dressed in his air force camouflage ABU (airman battle uniform). He was in his midforties, tall and slender, with a plain face and dirty blond hair cut in a sharp flattop. "How do you do, Mr. President?" He extended his hand. "It's an honor, sir."

"Likewise," the president said, wiping the perspiration from his palm before shaking the colonel's hand. "Are we about ready here, gentlemen?"

"Yes, sir," Bradshaw said. "As you can see, the UAV is already over the target."

The target, the president repeated softly. "My God, I never expected to hear our own military use that word in reference to an

American city."

"I can use a different word if you prefer, Mr. President."

"You mean a euphemism?" the president asked. "No, Colonel, thank you. I'm a big boy — or at least so my mother tells me."

Both field grade officers smiled dutifully.

"And how is she?" Couture asked, knowing that the president's mother had been in and out of the hospital numerous times during the past few months.

"She's holding her own," the president said. He gestured at the video feed. "What exactly do we expect to see?"

"Not a great deal, really," Couture replied. "We'll see the entry team enter through the main doors, and then nothing until they come back out."

"I'm worried the security video from the hotel will conflict with our AQAP cover story," the president said. "How are we going to deal with that?"

"Pope's people have already hacked into hotel security, sir." The whole operation was distasteful to Couture, but he'd had no better plan to offer in the limited time available to them. "So there won't be any video."

"Okay," the president said with a sigh. "I guess that's one less thing to worry about."

Bradshaw stole a glance at his immediate

superior then looked at the commander in chief. "Mr. President, if I may speak out of turn, sir?"

Couture's eyebrows lifted slightly.

"Sure," the president said easily. "That might be a refreshing change."

Bradshaw smiled. "It may be somewhat of a bold assertion on my part, sir, but we have an entirely unprecedented situation on our hands. There is no standard procedure for protecting this nation from an imminent nuclear attack within our borders. All of this is pure OJT, every bit of it. So if we're found out in the long run, so be it. No one is going to be able to blame us for what we do tonight because we're acting one hundred percent in the interest of the American people. Win, lose, or draw, we're looking for a *live nuclear weapon,* and I'll be proud to stand shoulder to shoulder with you in front of Congress — should it ever get that far."

The president would never admit it to anyone, but the colonel's remark actually made him feel better. "Thank you, Colonel. Let's hope I never have to hold you to that."

35

Luxor Hotel

Arabic music played on the stereo while Conman Tuckerman sat on the sofa in Faisal's suite with a gorgeous, dark, and leggy twenty-three-year-old black girl on his lap. She sipped from a glass of Armand de Brignac "Ace of Spades" Rosé champagne — the second most expensive champagne in the world. Her name was Missy, and she smelled like heaven, with big brown eyes and short, curly black hair, and Tuckerman could tell she was enjoying his company; he'd been with enough Vegas call girls to know when they were just going through the motions. Within moments of his entering the suite, she'd gravitated toward him.

Tuckerman knew that Faisal was scheming to keep him in the casino until the next night so he could win back his two hundred thousand dollars. It was a common gambit in the casino world, but it didn't matter. By sunrise, Faisal would be either dead or wishing for it. What made Tuckerman worried was the presence of Missy and the other girls. He hadn't expected there to be seven of them in the room. He hadn't anticipated any girls, in fact, though he probably should have. This was Vegas, after all, and Faisal was a known "matador."

"Join me in the other room?" he whispered into Missy's ear.

She looked at him and smiled. "Sure." She set down the glass and stood up from his lap, taking his hand.

"Muhammad, do you mind if we uh . . ."

"Not at all," Faisal said, looking up from the opposite sofa, his hand up a young blonde's skirt. "Enjoy yourself my friend."

Tuckerman led Missy into the far room and closed the door.

"I'm glad you're here," she said, peeling out of her black body dress. "Those other guys give me the creeps." She slid her arms around his neck and kissed him affectionately.

He drank her in as long as he dared before holding her out at arm's length. "Look, you're not going to believe this, but I need you to put that dress back on."

"What? Why? What's wrong? You're not a

cop, are you?"

"No." He took his wallet from his jacket and pulled out three thousand dollars' worth of crisp hundred-dollar bills, all of his CIA flash-around money. He picked her purse up and stuffed the money into it.

"What's going on?" she asked, more intrigued than alarmed.

He took his cellular from inside his jacket. "Listen to me very carefully," he said, typing out the text message: "Seven hookers in the room!" He sent the message and put away the phone. "I'm with the CIA."

She laughed. "Baby, I already like you, and I'm a sure thing."

He snatched her dress off the floor and held it out to her. "Listen! I want you to put this back on and get the fuck out, because in about five minutes, federal agents are coming through that fucking door, and you *don't* want to be here."

She saw that he was serious and took the dress. "Is this guy a terrorist or something?"

"Yes," he said, fully aware that he was breaking every fucking rule in the Black Ops handbook.

The phone vibrated in his pocket, and he read the message. "See?" He held the phone out for her to read: "Keep your head in the game! Six minutes and counting!"

She stepped quickly into the dress, pulling the straps up over her shoulders and slipping into her heels. "Am I gonna be in trouble?"

He gave her a quick kiss. "Whatever you do, don't ever tell anyone you were here tonight."

"Okay," she said, nodding her head in earnest. "I promise."

"Look embarrassed when we go back out there." He reached for the doorknob. "I'm gonna tell them you started your period and walk you straight to the door."

"Okay."

He took her by the hand and led her from the room.

"Wow, so fast!" Faisal exclaimed, looking up from the blonde's exposed breasts. "Are you ready for another, my friend?"

A few of the other girls laughed, and so did a couple of Faisal's people.

Ma'mun just stared. The only man in the room not paired off, he sat glumly on a stool over by the bar.

Tuckerman kept Missy moving toward the door. "This broad's on her period and didn't even fucking tell me."

"Okay," Faisal said. "There are plenty to go around." He didn't personally see the big deal about a girl on her period, but he took being a host seriously, and if the girl had displeased his guest in some way, then it was time for her to leave.

Tuckerman opened the door and stepped out into the hall with Missy. "Take the stairs." He stepped back into the room and closed the door.

"You don't think you were kind of rude?" asked the girl on Faisal's lap.

Tuckerman frowned at her. "Champagne and blood do not mix."

The mood in the room changed from one of lustful camaraderie to one of collective embarrassment.

"I'm sorry, my friend," Faisal said solemnly. "It is my fault."

"Don't be silly," Tuckerman said, waving him off. "I don't think the girl even knew, to be honest." He shrugged and sat back on the love seat. "Maybe I overreacted. I'm the one who should apologize."

"I'm sure she didn't know," the blonde said. "We live together, so our cycles are the same, and she's a whole week early."

"Hey!" Faisal said. "Enough now! No more talk about bloody vaginas — please!"

Everyone laughed, including Faisal's security men, and the mood improved over the next couple of minutes, but Tuckerman was worried. He'd seen women shot and killed many times before, and it didn't sit well with him. He checked his watch again . . . ninety seconds left.

36

The CIA plant/concierge was of Arabic descent. He'd been working at the Luxor for the past eighteen months, spying on Arabic gamblers, and though he had gotten to know Faisal pretty well during that time, he had never once suspected the man might be funding terrorists. He stopped the elevator on the nineteenth floor. "I sure hope you guys are right about this."

"Makes two of us," Gil replied, wrapping a green and black *shemagh* around his head. The other three operators were Alpha, Trigg, and Speed. Once all their faces were concealed behind *shemaghs,* making them look like Shiite raiders, they unzipped the valises they had brought along and armed themselves with suppressed AK-47 rifles.

"You're sure there's no guard outside the room?" Gil asked.

"If there is," said the concierge, "he'll be the first one I've seen."

"Okay," Gil said to the others. "Remember, only gutter Arabic." This was a shorthand form of communication they had developed during their time in the Middle East that they could use in the dark without immediately giving themselves away as Americans. It was barely rudimentary Arabic, but to the untrained American ear, they would sound enough like Arabs to convince any witnesses they were terrorists. "And try like hell not to hit the women."

He checked his watch. "Okay," he said to the concierge. "Ninety seconds. Let's go."

The concierge turned the key, and the inclinator rose to the twentieth floor. The doors opened with fifty seconds to go, revealing an Arabic security man sitting on a chair against the wall. He looked up just in time to catch a 7.62 mm round right between the eyes. His head snapped back as blood, brain, and bone spattered the wall, and he fell out of the chair. The bullet had continued on through the wall, but didn't seem to have alerted anyone.

No one said a word to the CIA man about getting it wrong as they dismounted the inclinator and attached the breaching charges to the door; combat was an ever-evolving set of circumstances, where nothing ever remained the same.

With ten seconds left on the clock, Tuckerman sat forward on the love seat to line himself up with his target. The door imploded with a bang, and he launched himself at Faisal, delivering a flying elbow to the bridge of his nose and taking the couch over backward, dumping both Faisal and the girl onto the carpet.

The girls screamed, and Faisal's security men struggled to gain their feet even as they were being shot down with perfectly placed bursts of heavy-caliber fire. Blood flew as the men went down without ever managing to draw their weapons. Only Ma'mun succeeded in drawing a pistol before he took a three-round burst to the face, exploding his head. His pistol went off as he flew back against the bar and crashed to the floor.

With all secondary targets down, Gil ran forward and pulled Tuckerman off of Faisal, making sure they were both still alive, and quickly secured Faisal's hands with flex cuffs. The women were sobbing and lying on the floor covering their heads, two of them wounded by flying door fragments. Only Faisal's blonde was silent. Speed and Trigg began dragging the others one by one into a bedroom, shouting violently at them in gutter Arabic, to keep up the charade.

Tuckerman got to his knees beside the blonde and saw the bullet hole just above her left eye. He grabbed her up into his arms, realizing that Ma'mun had inadvertently shot her as a result of a motor reflex spasm in his arm.

Gil kicked the dead girl out of Tuckerman's arms and hauled him to his feet, shoving a silenced USP .45 into his hands and growling at him to get moving. Speed slammed the door to the bedroom where the other five girls were now flex-cuffed on the bed, all of them still sobbing loud enough to be heard through the door.

Tuckerman moved to cover the hall where the CIA man was pulling the laundry cart from the elevator. Alpha gave Faisal a shot of sodium pentothal to knock him out, and Trigg tossed him over his shoulder, carrying him into the hall and dumping him into the cart. They covered him with bed linens and began wheeling him down the hall toward the service elevator, with the CIA man leading the way.

Missy was still standing in the stairwell debating whether to leave her roommate behind when she'd heard the explosion that took out the door to Faisal's suite. She grabbed the door handle and opened it a crack, just in time to see what looked to her like an Arab terrorist charging into the room with a machine gun. She was still peering through the crack in terror when the Arabs came back out of the room pushing the laundry cart in front of them, an Arabic concierge leading the way.

The door to the nineteenth floor burst open one flight down, and six men with pistols in their hands poured into the stairwell. One of them wore a white T-shirt with LAPD — Los Angeles Police Department — on the front. They were in town for their shift sergeant's bachelor party in the room directly beneath Faisal's suite. They'd heard the blast and were on their way up to check it out.

"What the hell's going on up there?" the sergeant demanded. He was the one in the T-shirt, a barrel-chested fellow with a thick mustache, and, being in his midthirties, the oldest. The others looked like they were probably in their mid- to early twenties, rookies mostly.

"Terrorists!" Missy blurted, jumping back from the door.

The sergeant mounted the stairs with the rookies right on his tail. They stopped at the door to the twentieth, and Sergeant Mustache opened it a crack to see men in Arab headgear shoving a laundry cart down the far hall.

"Fucking towel-heads with machine guns!" he said in a harsh whisper. "Definitely *tangos*! We'll hit 'em hard and fast!"

Tuckerman was looking back over his shoulder toward Faisal's suite when the door to the stairwell opened and the cops poured into the hallway. Shots rang out, and he was knocked off his feet. He opened fire with the .45 at the bodies coming toward him, downing a big man with a mustache wearing an LAPD T-shirt.

The rookies panicked and began pouring fire down the hall.

The SEALs whipped around with their AK-47s and shot down the remaining five out-of-town cops without having time to think about what they were doing. The CIA man was dead with a bullet through his head and throat, and Tuckerman was bleeding out fast through a hole in his gut.

"It's the abdominal aorta," Trigg muttered in a low voice, grabbing a hotel towel from the laundry cart and jamming it against Tuckerman's belly. "He's gonna bleed out."

A guest dared to poke his head from his

room. Gil whipped around with his AK-47, and the guest ducked back inside, slamming the door.

"We need a fuckin' AAT!" Trigg hissed, referring to an abdominal aortic tourniquet, a pneumatic Velcro tourniquet that wrapped around a wounded soldier's abdomen, functioning a lot like a pneumatic pressure cuff used for taking blood pressure.

"Put 'im in the goddamn laundry cart!" Gil ordered.

"He'll fucking bleed out!" Trigg grabbed a sheet from the cart and started to wrap it around Tuckerman's body. The towel was already completely soaked with blood. "We can twist this tight over the towel. Call for an ambulance!"

"Get him on the elevator!" Gil took his iPhone from his harness and turned it on. He did not notice that Marie had left him a voice mail and would not have paid it any attention if he had. They got Tuckerman onto the service elevator, and Speed ran back for the laundry cart containing the unconscious Muhammad Faisal. The dead CIA man was left behind in the hall.

Gil had seen enough men die in combat to know that Tuckerman would be dead before they made it to the ground floor, but he got Crosswhite on the phone and made sure the paramedics would be ready to meet them at the service entrance below.

"Who were those fuckin' assholes?" Speed asked ripping the *shemagh* from his head.

"Beats the fuck outta me." Gil knelt down beside Tuckerman, putting his hand beneath his head. "How ya doin', partner? You gonna hang on for us?"

Tuckerman reached for Gil's free hand. "Thanks for not letting me rot in prison," he said softly. "I'm sorry I disappointed you." He glanced at Trigg. "You can let go, dude. The pressure's killin' me."

Trigg's face contorted with emotion, and he released his grip on the twisted sheet tourniquet.

Gil squeezed his hand, feeling the dying man's grip fading fast. "Anybody you want me to talk to when this is over? Anybody you want me to go see?"

Tuckerman shook his head, his face pallid. "I'm good to go, Chief. You guys are my family."

Gil bent down to kiss his forehead. "You rest easy, brother. We'll catch up to you on the other side. You wait for us there! Hear me?"

Tuckerman winked. "You know I do . . ." A few moments later he was gone, leaving behind only the faintest of smiles.

37

LAS VEGAS,
Luxor Hotel

With word of the shooting on the twentieth floor quickly spreading throughout the hotel and casino, Sheriff Moleska's men were already flooding inside by the time the service elevator reached the ground floor. He stood beside Pope directly outside the service entrance, where the SEALs were now loading the mysterious laundry cart into the back of a white van with US Government plates. They climbed in after it, and Gil slammed the door. Beside the van, two Vegas paramedics loaded Tuckerman's body into the back of an ambulance.

Moleska looked at Crosswhite. "How big of a mess did they leave up there? I'm already getting reports of a bloodbath."

"Gil?"

Gil turned to the sheriff. "Five or six unknown gunmen rushed us from the stairwell and killed my man. They're all dead. A hooker took an errant round to the head. She's dead too. Also, the hotel concierge. All on the twentieth floor." He looked at Crosswhite. "We gotta roll."

"Hold on a minute," Moleska said. "What about the gunmen? Were they Faisal's people or somebody else?" Pope had shared Faisal's identity, since the sheriff would have learned it soon anyhow. "I need to know whatever you people can tell me right now, because once you disappear, I'll be on my own to sort this mess out."

"I'm sorry, sir, but those concerns don't fall within my mission profile."

Gil went around the driver's side and got in behind the wheel. Crosswhite climbed into the passenger seat, and the van pulled out.

Pope offered the sheriff his hand. "Sheriff Moleska, thank you. If we find the nuke in time, you'll be the man this nation has to thank for it — though I'm afraid that's going to have to remain a perpetual secret."

The sheriff only half shook his hand, realizing he was being treated like a schmuck but not really knowing what to do about it. "This is pure bullshit, you know that?"

Pope walked off, but not before promising

that the president would personally be helping clean up the mess.

38

LAS VEGAS,
Airport

Pope arrived at the hangar only a few minutes behind Gil and the others. He had just received word through one of his informants inside the NSA that Lijuan had been taken into custody at Los Angeles International Airport, and his guilt was almost more than he could bear. He had not only allowed the NSA to discover that she was a mole, but he had known she was a spy for the Chinese before he had ever even recruited her. Over the past ten years, he had used her as a conduit into the Chinese intelligence network, making her an unwitting accomplice in his grand caper. And though she had performed exactly as planned over the years, he had not. He had allowed himself to fall in love with her, and for a man to allow a woman he loved to hang herself with her own rope was a fiend-

291

ish act of betrayal — irrespective of his responsibility to his country.

"So who's doing the interrogation?" Crosswhite asked.

"Gil and I," Pope answered.

"I'd like to be present."

"No."

"May I ask why?"

Pope leveled his gaze, his blue eyes gentle. "Because you lost a friend tonight, and you're known to fly off the handle."

"We all lost a friend tonight," Crosswhite said, taking exception to what he considered a slight. "These men have known Tuckerman longer than I have."

Pope's expression did not change. "The fact you've taken offense only confirms the appropriateness of my decision — which is final."

Crosswhite felt Gil staring at him and took a step back, remembering all too well that Pope was the reason he was not on his way to prison. "In that case, I'd better see about making sure we're ready to move on whatever intel Faisal is willing to share."

"Good idea," Gil said, giving him a wink.

As Crosswhite walked off across the hangar, Gil could see that Pope was deeply troubled. "I accept full responsibility for everything that went wrong tonight."

Pope shook his head. "The mission was a success. Faisal is here."

"Civilians are dead and wounded," Gil said. "Tuckerman's body will be identified, and he may even be linked with the Chicago killings. I should have insisted we bring his body back with us."

"Neither Tuckerman nor Crosswhite were ever in Chicago," Pope said. "That's been taken care of. As for the killings at the Luxor, that's the president's mess, and his people will have to clean it up. Our job is to find the RA-115." He took a Red Sox baseball cap from his back pocket and pulled it on. "Now let's go see what Mr. Faisal has to tell us."

The first rule of enhanced interrogation was never be afraid to lie to the subject. It was important early in the process for him (or her) to believe there was hope of returning to his or her life. It wasn't always effective, but this gave the interrogator his best shot at getting the information fast.

This was why the first thing Gil said to Faisal was, "If you ever want to get near that American pussy again, I suggest you tell us everything you know about the RA-115."

Faisal was sitting on a bench in the pilots'

locker room with his hands still flex-cuffed behind him. The surgeon had given him a shot of adrenaline to wake him up and declared him to be in good health, save for the broken nose he'd received from Tuckerman's flying elbow. But a clean bill of health wasn't exactly good news for Faisal; it cleared Gil to treat him as brutally as he needed to.

"I don't know what that is," Faisal said with a shrug. "I swear to you."

"It's a Russian suitcase nuke." Gil tore the top from a box of common garbage bags. "We need to know where the fuck it is, and you're going to tell us — one way or another." He pulled a bag from the roll and dropped the box onto the bench beside a roll of duct tape.

"I'm a member of the Saudi royal family." Faisal's voice was shaking. "I demand to speak to our lawyer."

"The family's already given you up," Pope lied. "How do you think we found out about you?"

For Faisal, that was the worst piece of news he could have received. Not only had the family somehow discovered his ties to AQAP, they had completely disinherited him.

Gil saw the crushed look in Faisal's eyes.

"Do you think we'd torture a member of the royal family without King Abdullah's consent?"

Faisal's eyes filled with tears. "What do you need to know?"

Gil smacked him hard across the face. "I already told you, numb nuts! Where's the fucking bomb?"

Faisal shook his head, feeling his bladder letting go. "I swear to you, I don't know! I only provided the money. It's Kashkin you want — the Chechen! You need to find Kashkin. He brought the bomb from Mexico."

Pope recognized the name Kashkin but couldn't remember from where. He took a satellite phone from his pocket and stepped to the back of the room.

"So where do I find Kashkin?" Gil pressed.

"I have no idea."

"Listen, fuck stick. This little Q&A is about to get real unpleasant for you." He opened the black garbage bag and shook it out to fill it with air.

"Please!" Faisal said. "I don't know where to find Kashkin or the bomb. If I did, I would tell you! Do you think I want to be here? He was in Vegas on the day of the accident, but I don't know where he is now."

Pope put away the phone and came forward. "Did you *speak* with Kashkin on the day of the New Mexico Event?"

"Yes!" Faisal answered. "That was the last time."

This told Pope they had a recording of Kashkin's voice.

"Names," Gil said. "Give us the names of everybody you know who was involved."

Faisal knew that to admit to helping AQAP would doom him forever with the family. He had to at least try to save himself. "Kashkin was my only contact."

Pope stepped forward, producing an ice pick from what seemed like thin air, stabbing it deep into Faisal's face alongside his busted nose and leaving it there.

Faisal shrieked in terror, his eyes crossing as he tried to see what had been stabbed into his face.

Gil took a step back, shocked to see such a vicious act coming from an otherwise very mild-mannered man. They let Faisal scream himself out, which took about thirty seconds before he fell to sobbing like a child.

Pope took hold of the ice pick handle, and Faisal screamed again.

"Shhhh!" Pope looked down into Faisal's horrified eyes. "Listen to me now. Listen to me, Muhammad. I'm going to do that over and over again until your face looks like a tomato unless you stop lying to me. Okay?" He was thinking of Lijuan sitting in a government holding cell, alone and afraid.

Faisal blinked once, afraid to move because of Pope's grip on the wooden handle sticking out of his face. "The al-Rashid brothers," he whined. "Akram and Haroun. Wahhabi fanatics with Al Qaeda in the Arabian Peninsula. They came to me for money four years ago. I didn't want to help them buy the bomb, but they threatened me."

Pope knew of the al-Rashid brothers, and to hear their names made him nauseous. "Are they still living in Canada?"

"Yes."

"Where in Canada?"

"Windsor!" Faisal sobbed.

"Very good," Pope said softly. "Now, what other names can you give me?"

Faisal was sobbing openly now, his upturned face awash in his tears. "I swear to you I don't know anyone else."

"But you've already lied to me so many times, Muhammad. How can I possibly believe that?"

"I'm not lying now!" Faisal wailed. "Please believe me!" He choked painfully on the blood and mucus draining down the back of his throat from his pierced sinus cavity, each convulsion causing the sharp steel probe to contort the musculature of his face. "Pull it out!"

"Look into my eyes, Muhammad. I'm going to stab you in the face again because I believe you're lying to me."

"No!" Faisal shrieked. "I'm telling you the truth!"

Pope pulled the ice pick from Faisal's face. "Hold his head, Gil."

Gil reluctantly grabbed hold of Faisal's head to steady it.

"No!" Faisal shrieked with such force that it sounded like his vocal cords might snap. "I don't know anything more! *For the love God! I don't know anything!*"

Pope stood back and looked at Gil. "What do you think?"

Gil had seen enough, both of the ice pick and of Faisal's testimony. "I'm pretty sure he's tapped out."

They left Faisal sobbing uncontrollably on the floor of the locker room.

Gil had some difficulty concealing his discomfort as he stood in the hall watching Pope think things over. He would have personally preferred the bloodless method of torture by suffocation, but he had to admit that Pope had gotten results very quickly after that stab to the face.

"Should we call the president?" he asked. "We're going to need to get the Canadians on board to help us find —"

"No," Pope said, half lost in thought. "We don't need their help. I already know where the al-Rashid brothers live. They're across the Detroit River from Detroit." He stood staring at the floor.

"What's wrong?"

Pope looked up. "I classified the al-Rashid brothers as low risk six months ago." He shook his head. "The ultimate failure on my part — absolutely unforgivable."

"What are you going to recommend to the president?"

"Nothing at all. It's our mission to find the bomb, and that's what we're going to do."

"Right," Gil said, "but the president needs to get the Canadians on board."

"And risk the Canadians screwing things up?" Pope shook his head. "No way. You and your team are going to cross the river and bring the al-Rashids back to American soil, where we can deal with them however we need to."

"Bob, that could be considered an act of war against an ally."

"Yes, it could, and that's precisely why the

president has chosen a team that he can easily disavow. Don't forget what you signed on for. We're all expendable assets."

Gil nodded. "Okay. You gather the intel, and I'll brief the men." He gestured at the locker room door. "What about him?"

"Forget him," Pope said absentmindedly. "He's my problem now."

39

LAS VEGAS,
Airport

Gil took Crosswhite aside after briefing the team on a probable incursion into Canada. "This stays between us."

"Okay."

"Pope took an ice pick to Faisal's face."

Crosswhite pulled back his shoulders. "How, exactly?"

"I mean he stabbed the fucker in the face with an ice pick."

"Jesus! I guess it worked, huh?"

"You could say that." Gil put out his hand. "Gimme a smoke."

"When you gonna buy your own?"

"After I smoke all yours." Gil lit the cigarette. "Something's up with him."

"Pope? Or Faisal?"

"Pope. He's on edge about something. First he snaps and stabs a guy in the face, and now he's ordering us into Canada without consulting the president."

"Gonna go over his head?"

"We just have to make sure we don't get caught on the wrong side of the river, that's all."

A few minutes later, he was sorting his gear and decided to check his iPhone on the off-chance that Marie had called.

He listened to her voice mail and called her right back.

She answered on the first ring. "Gil?"

"Are you okay?"

"Yeah," she said. "Where are you?"

"I'm in Nevada."

"How fast can you get here?"

"I can't," he said. "What's wrong, baby?"

She didn't reply immediately.

"Marie, what's wrong?"

"I can't tell you over the phone. Why can't you come home?"

"Because I'm — I'm working."

"Jesus!" she said. "Can't you tell me what the hell you're doin' just once? You're not even workin' for the goddamn navy anymore."

He knew instantly that something was gravely wrong. "Is it Mom? Did something happen?"

"Gil, tell me what the *fuck* you're doin' that's so important!" Her voice was shrill, and it scared him deep in the pit of his stomach.

"I'm looking for the goddamn nuke!" he blurted. "There, ya happy? I just gave out classified information over a fuckin' cell phone! Now what's wrong, honey? I don't have time for this."

She fell silent, and he could just imagine her sitting at the kitchen table with her head in her hand; Oso sitting next to the chair, whining. "Marie, please tell me what's wrong."

She sniffled hard, and he knew she was crying.

"Baby, please tell me."

"There was a man here," she said finally. "Up on the ridge — with a rifle."

Gil's heart skipped a beat, but he remained composed. "Is he still there?"

"I shot him, Gil. I shot 'im from the bedroom window and hid his body in the stable."

His eyes filled with tears, knowing that his wife would never again be the same woman. Now there would always be a hardness to her, a hardness where once there had been only innocence.

"I love you," he said softly. "Tell me what happened."

When they finished talking some twenty

minutes later, Gil got off the phone and called an old friend of the family named Buck Ferguson, who owned the ranch on the other side of the valley from his own. He told Buck what was going on and asked him if he wouldn't mind keeping an eye on Marie and his mother-in-law until he could get there himself.

"Hell, no, I don't mind!" Buck said. "The boys and I are leaving right now."

With that taken care of, Gil crossed the hangar to where Pope was on his satellite phone with a high muckety-muck in the DOD. "We need to talk right now."

Pope saw the look in his eye and cut the call short. "What's wrong?"

"I gotta get to Montana."

"You gotta what?"

"Get to Montana."

Pope looked around as if there might be a clue to this unexpected intrigue elsewhere in the hangar. "Gil, I don't understand. We're airborne for Detroit in less than an hour. I just got us clearance to land on Grosse Ile."

Gil told Pope what had happened on the ranch and that Marie was in possession of the dead assassin's laptop computer.

"Can she access the hard drive?"

"It's password protected. Look, the assassin's not an Arab. Marie says he's a Caucasian with a German passport. So he's probably Chechen. If he is —"

"He could be connected with the bomb," Pope said, finishing the thought for him. "Okay, listen, there's no way I can let you go to Montana. What I'll do is have an Air Guard helo pick the computer up from the ranch and fly it back to the air base at Great Falls. From there an F-15 from the 186th can rendezvous with us in Detroit. That's the fastest way for us to get our hands on it. Tell Marie to have the computer and passport ready and waiting when the helo gets there."

Aside from her emotional well-being, Gil was also concerned for Marie in a legal sense. "What are you going to tell the president about Marie shooting the guy? She hasn't called the police."

"The truth," Pope said with a shrug. "What else?"

"And if he decides to sic the attorney general after her?"

Pope adjusted his cap with a smile. "He'd never even consider such a thing. In fact, he'll probably invite her to the White House for a Medal of Freedom ceremony. We already know how much he loves bestowing our nation's highest honors upon members of the heroic Shannon family."

Gil smiled dryly. "When ya get a minute, kiss my ass, will ya?"

Pope laughed. "You remind me of your father."

40

DETROIT

Akram al-Rashid entered a warehouse in Detroit toting a black rifle case and placed it on a table in the center of the room in front of eighteen American-born Al Qaeda recruits, most of whom he had recruited from Detroit's large urban Muslim population. They were all of Arab descent, and half of them had served in the United States military. The youngest of them, Tahir, was eighteen, a former agnostic whom Akram had personally converted to Salafism. This made Tahir Akram's most trusted because there was no fanatic like a converted fanatic, and Tahir had already volunteered to wear a suicide vest.

There was a nineteenth man among the recruits, but he was not Arabic. He was not even Muslim. He had green eyes, reddish hair, and went by the name of Duke. He was an American mercenary, motivated by profit alone. This made him the least trusted of the group, but what made him valuable were his credentials as a former Marine and SWAT team sergeant with the Detroit Police Department.

Duke had gotten himself fired shortly after the city had gone into receivership. Disgusted over the city's abolition of public employee rights to arbitration, cutting their benefits and pay, he had taken a weekend job as an informal nightclub bodyguard for a local pimp who called himself Fabulous Jay. It had been a lucrative gig, too, until someone had decided to take a shot at Fabulous Jay in the club's VIP section. The shooter had nicked Jay in the shoulder with his first shot, and Duke had blown him away with a .40 caliber double tap to the sternum.

After a thorough investigation into the shooting, it was discovered that Duke had lied about what he was doing in the club that night, and he was eventually fired after nineteen years on the job, with complete loss of pension and benefits.

Akram heard about Duke from a spy within the police department and approached him at the junkyard where he'd taken a job driving a forklift. The promise of a quarter million dollars for work as a hired gun had sounded great to Duke, and he'd accepted on the spot, walking off the job without even telling his boss.

Now the ruddy ex-cop sat rocked back in a folding chair with his fingers laced behind his head, dressed in black trousers, tactical boots, and a black Under Armour T-shirt. The other team members gave him a wide birth, not because they feared him but rather because they didn't like having an infidel in their midst. Another suspicious thing was that Duke openly believed they were all connected to the atomic bomb, yet he didn't seem to resent them for it. He even cracked jokes about it.

"Hey, Akram," Duke asked, "which city gets turned into glass, huh? Inquiring minds want to know."

Akram gave him a dry smile as he unbuckled the rifle case. "I've told you before the Chechens are responsible for the bomb. We have nothing to do with it."

"Yeah? Then how the hell do you know Detroit ain't the target?"

Akram's eyes appeared flat and reptilian. "We don't."

Duke sobered for a moment and then laughed it off. "I can't wait to find out who gets it. It's better than a fucking movie."

One of the other former Marines on the

team still had enough grunt left in him to resent mercenaries. His name was Abad. He had a hatchet face, very dark eyes, and still kept his hair cut in military fashion. "You expect us to believe you really don't care?" he asked in perfect American English.

Duke turned his head. "Only fucking thing I care about, son, is getting paid and moving to Brazil, where they got all that hot poontang. After that, this whole country can burn to a crackly crisp, for all I care. I put in nineteen goddamn years, and what did I get when those rich bastards finally bank-rupted the city? Shit-canned! So I ain't about to —"

"Enough," Akram said quietly. "Duke is a soldier of Allah like the rest of us — even if he doesn't realize it. Nothing happens that is not God's will." He spoke predominantly in English because not all of the recruits spoke fluent Arabic.

Akram took the rifle from the case and extended the legs of the bipod, resting it on the table.

Duke let out a whistle. "Now, that's a fine piece of artillery."

Akram smiled. "You know this weapon?"

"You bet your ass I know it. That's a McMillan TAC-50." The TAC-50 was a .50 caliber sniper rifle manufactured in the

United States, though used predominantly by Canadian forces. Duke dropped his feet to the floor and leaned in closer for a better look. "And I'm guessing that's the A1R2 with the hydraulic stock. Am I right?"

Akram was impressed. "You've fired one?"

"Not the R2," Duke said, "but I've fired the A1 a number of times. Who're you planning to blow away with that shoulder cannon, the president?"

"What would you say if I said yes?"

"I'd say, 'Windage and elevation, Mrs. Langdon! Windage and elevation!' " He laughed out loud, expecting the others to join him, but he saw only blank faces staring back at him. "Oh, yeah, that's right," he said sadly. "You fuckers are too young to remember the Duke."

"Who's he?" asked Tahir.

"John Wayne, knucklehead. *The Undefeated.* Jesus Christ! Wipe your mama's milk off your fuckin' chin!"

The youth stood up, his eyes full of fire.

"Sit down!" Akram ordered.

Tahir sat back down instantly, dropping his gaze to the floor between his feet.

Akram cut Duke a fatherly look of disapproval.

Duke rolled his eyes, rocking back and putting his feet back up on a crate. "Windage and elevation," he muttered with a chuckle.

"I want you all to listen carefully," Akram said, once again the Saudi Royal Marine. "Our target is very dangerous. We've already sent one highly skilled operative in after him, and that operative has failed to report back."

Duke put his feet back on the floor, suddenly all business. "Is the target a military man?"

"Yes, he is," Akram said, deciding to see just how solid *the Duke* was. "He's an ex-Navy SEAL, as a matter of fact — one of your country's best. His name is Gil Shannon."

"No shit. The frogman who won the Medal of Honor?"

"Does that create a conflict for you?"

Duke's eyes glassed over. The thought of taking on the great Gil Shannon was like mainlining a syringe full of adrenaline. "You put that TAC-50 in my hands, buster, and I'll show you how *conflicted* I am."

"Good," Akram said, satisfied. "I'll be manning this weapon, but I want everyone to be familiar with it in case something happens to me. Duke, you brought your own rifle, correct?"

Duke sat up straight. "An M40A3 bolt action. Same weapon I carried in the Corps."

Abad leaned forward to see him better. "You were a Marine?"

"Yeah, what's it to you?"

"Which division?"

"The Second."

"I was with the First."

"And you don't know John Wayne, for Christ sake?"

"I never said I didn't know John Wayne — and stop with the blasphemy."

"Fuck do you care? I thought you were Muslim."

"Blasphemy is blasphemy."

"Enough!" Akram said, annoyed by Duke's uncouthness but realizing there was nothing to be done about it. "I want military discipline from this point, and there are enough of you who know what that is. We board a private jet for Montana in the morning." He looked at Duke. "Your pilot friend has received the first half of his payment, correct?"

Duke nodded.

"Good. Perhaps you should tell the men what you told me."

Duke turned in his chair to face the others. "Listen up. This pilot's an Australian — a merc like me. He ain't from here, and he ain't stayin' here after he gets paid. But keep your mouths shut about what we're up to because you never know with these Aussies. They like to get all tanked up and blab their business to whoever's around. So the less he knows, the better for us all. Just keep your traps shut and focus on the mission."

"That's good advice," Akram said. "Be sure to follow it." Then he decided to give Duke something else constructive to do. "Duke, why don't you come up here and show the men how to operate this weapon? I'm sure you're more qualified than I am."

Duke grinned and got to his feet. "You're finally talkin' my language, son."

As Akram sat in the back of the room watching Duke break down the weapon and explain how to operate it, his mind began to drift. The people of the Middle East had been hiring Western mercenaries to help them fight their wars against other Western powers since the days of antiquity, starting with Greeks during the early Greco-Persian wars. It disgusted Akram to have to admit they needed help, but he consoled himself with thoughts of Kashkin's bomb.

The bomb will create parity, he promised himself. *The first domino to fall against the Western economy — followed by another and then another. I will not live to see the final victory, but that doesn't matter. I lead a platoon in the first skirmish of* the *battle.*

After the weapon tutorial, Akram took Tahir into another room, ostensibly for a private prayer session, but he smacked the youth the moment the door closed.

"What were you thinking, allowing yourself to be so easily baited by that infidel?"

Tahir looked at the floor. "I *didn't* think. I'm sorry, teacher."

"A thoughtless fanatic is useless to me — even less useful to Allah. Do you understand?"

"Yes, teacher."

"You want to be a martyr? So pride filled that you can't even ignore childish insults from a complete fool?" Akram shook his head in disappointment, but he was secretly happy for the boy's harmless error. It had given him an excuse to shame him, to make him even more determined to carry out a bombing mission if and when the time came.

41

Somewhere in the air over Iowa, Gil and Pope went up the ladder into the cockpit of the C-5 Galaxy to talk with the pilot. The air force major climbed out of his seat and stepped to the back of the flight deck.

"What can I do for you, gentlemen?"

Gil showed him a map of Detroit, pointing to Grosse Ile in the middle of the Detroit River. The island was over six miles long and roughly two wide. "When we get to Detroit, Major, I need you to land here at Naval Air Station Grosse Ile."

The pilot looked at him. "NAS Grosse has been closed for more than forty years."

"It's still a municipal airport," Pope said. "I've already gotten us clearance to land."

"But, Mr. Pope, the runway there isn't long enough. Selfridge Air Base is only just up the river. I suggest we land there, sir."

"Selfridge is fifty miles north of the target

316

area. Grosse Ile is less than three." Pope smiled his boyish smile. "You do the math, Major."

"But, sir, I'm telling you there isn't enough runway."

Pope set down the map on the navigator's console and produced an iPad from a black satchel hanging over his shoulder. "I have the entire operator's manual for the C-5 Galaxy right here at my fingertips. We need less than thirty-six hundred feet of runway to land, and the runway at Grosse Ile is more than forty-eight hundred feet long."

"That's true, but I need eighty-four hundred feet to take off again."

"Taking off again isn't our problem," Gil said. "We've got a loose nuke to find."

The pilot stood looking at him. "My orders don't include jeopardizing this aircraft."

Pope took the sat phone from his back pocket. "Major, I press one button, and we'll be talking to the president of the United States. I've met him personally, and he's not a very reasonable man when he's upset. In my youth, I flew C-130s for Air America, so you and I *both* know that you can safely land this plane on Grosse Ile. Colonel Bradshaw is with the president, and I'm reasonably certain he knows it too."

The major put his hands on hips. "You do realize I'll be stranding a two-hundred-million-dollar aircraft on an island not much bigger than a used car lot."

"For what it's worth," Pope said, "I don't think I landed on a jungle runway of the proper length more than once or twice. If your people strip this plane down and red-line the engines, I'm pretty sure she'll clear the end of the runway."

"Not with me in the cockpit, she won't."

Pope held out the phone. "What's it going to be, Major?"

The pilot shrugged. "Orders are orders, Mr. Pope. NAS Grosse it is."

42

SOUTHERN CALIFORNIA,
Edwards Air Force Base

"Where in Detroit?" the president was asking Tim Hagen. "Aren't these al-Rashid brothers someone we can send the FBI after? Is it necessary to risk another fiasco like the one we just had in Las Vegas?"

General Couture hung up the phone. "Mr. President, NSA has just informed me the al-Rashids are not in Detroit. They're in Amherstburg, Ontario, directly across the Detroit River from Grosse Ile. NSA pulled their names off a list of people to watch, and, apparently, Pope evaluated these two yahoos earlier this year — classifying them as *low risk.*"

"So Pope does make mistakes." The president sat forward in his chair, feeling his acid reflux beginning to act up. "Okay, so where's the plane now?"

"Just touching down on Grosse Ile, sir."

The president looked at Colonel Bradshaw. "Get Pope on the phone."

"Yes, sir."

Sixty seconds later, Bradshaw had him on the line, and the president put the receiver to his ear. "Pope?"

"Yes, Mr. President?"

"You are not — I repeat *not* — to enter Canada. Is that clear?"

There was a slight pause. "Yes, Mr. President."

"I'm going to call the Canadian prime minister right now. You will wait for the Canadians to pick up the al-Rashids and deliver them to you there on Grosse Ile. Is that understood?"

"Yes, Mr. President."

"I'm serious," the president said. "This isn't Afghanistan we're talking about this time. It's Canada!"

"We'll stand by here, Mr. President."

"You'd better." The president hung up the phone and looked at Couture. "What are the odds he's going to listen to me?"

Couture was thinking, *You got in bed with these maniacs. I should leave you to them.*

"Sir, I don't think there's any reason at all to assume he'll obey that order. I recommend you send the FBI to Grosse Ile immediately with orders to take the entire team into custody. This has gone far enough, Mr. President."

The president stood from the chair and hitched up his pants. "Do it."

He looked at Tim Hagen and nodded toward the door. The two of them stepped into the hall.

"This will be the FBI's operation from here on," the president said. "So get in touch with Shroyer at CIA and see to it that all of Pope's clearances are revoked. That man is unemployed as of right now. Also, make sure the FBI knows that he's to be held for questioning in regards to the Lijuan Chow affair. My *God,* Tim!" He lowered his voice. "He was actually going to invade another fucking country!"

"What if the Canadians screw it up, Mr. President?"

"What?"

"Sir, we're wasting time. For all we know, the RA-115 could be set to go off any minute. Pope is directly across the river from the al-Rashids. He can probably have his hands on them within the hour."

"You're not actually suggesting —"

"Mr. President, I'm suggesting that you *allow* Pope to disobey your direct order to stand down. We can have an observation drone over the target area within the hour.

That will allow us to wait until the last moment before calling the prime minister to tell him that one of our special operations teams has gone off the reservation. By the time the RCMP can respond to the target area, Shannon's people will already be back on Grosse Ile with the al-Rashids." Hagen was referring to the Royal Canadian Mounted Police. "Then we'll not only have the brothers and whatever information they can provide about the nuke, but we'll also have enough to put both Pope and Shannon where they belong." Hagen smiled. "Unless, of course, we choose to turn them over to the Canadians, in which case they'll be *completely* out of our hair for the next twenty or thirty years."

"Christ, you're a devious bastard." The president held a hand to his abdomen, the burning sensation creeping up his throat. "Okay. Suppose Pope *doesn't* disobey me? Then what?"

"We'll know that within the hour, sir. If he does stand down, then we simply call the prime minister and hope for the best."

The president thought over the plan, and he could find no flaw in it. "Couture isn't going to like it."

"With respect, Mr. President, there's no reason for you to give a shit what the general does or does not like. He's a soldier, and it's his job to do what you tell him to do."

43

MONTANA

Buck Ferguson was a sixty-seven-year-old rancher who lived across the valley from the McGuthry ranch with his three sons. They were a Marine Corps family, dating back to Buck's father, who had fought on Guadalcanal during the Second World War, all of them serving with the First Marine Division. Buck had served in Vietnam in the province of Quang Tin. His oldest son, Hal, had served in Desert Storm, and his two youngest sons, Roger and Glen, had served in both of the recent Iraq and Afghan Wars.

They arrived at the McGuthry ranch in a red king cab pickup truck just as the Air National Guard Kiowa helo was lifting into the air to take Kashkin's computer and passport back to Great Falls Air Guard Base. Dressed in their ranchers' duds and holding AR-15s, they stood watching it fly away. The Ferguson men were avid sportsmen and gun enthusiasts who enjoyed hunting and fishing more than just about anything else.

Oso left Marie's side and ran down from the porch to greet them, barking and jumping around, entirely unaccustomed to so much excitement late at night.

Buck walked up the steps and gave Marie a hug. "How are ya, darlin'?"

"I'm okay," she said. "So good to you see. Thank you for coming. I told Gil it wasn't necessary, but he insisted on calling."

"It's a good thing he did," Buck said. "I'd've been madder'n a rattle snake if he hadn't."

She smiled and took him by the arm, leading him inside. Janet greeted Buck with a hug and a kiss to the cheek. The two of them had dated briefly many years earlier as juniors in high school.

She patted him briskly on the back. "You're looking fit, cowboy."

He chuckled. "Looks can be deceiving, Jan. I feel older than dirt — but not tonight. Tonight I feel forty years younger."

"I'll put some coffee on."

"Sounds good." Buck looked at Marie, lowering his voice. "Reckon we can see the heathen you gave what for?"

"Yeah," she said solemnly. "Mama, we're

goin' out back a minute."

"That's fine!" Janet called from the kitchen.

Marie led Buck out the back and across the ranch to the giant brush pile. His sons walked over, and Buck pulled back the sheet, shining his light on Kashkin's face. He put back the sheet and switched off the light.

"Odd they'd send a fella my age," he muttered. "I wonder was that the best they could do?"

"A bullet don't care who pulls the trigger," remarked Hal Ferguson. "What kind of rifle did he have, Marie?"

"I described it to Gil, and he said it's a Mauser."

Hal nodded, spitting tobacco juice. "That's a good'n. Old fart likely knew his business." He smiled in the light of the crescent moon. "Too bad for him you knew yours better."

Marie felt no pride or sense of accomplishment, only that she'd done what was necessary to protect what she held dear. "Does either of you have a lighter?"

Buck took one from his pocket, and she used it to ignite the nest of tinder and kindling she had built in the center of the brush pile. The juniper branches were dry

326

and sappy, and the pyre began to blaze quickly.

"Want me to say a few words?" Buck asked.

Marie shook her head, her face showing brightly against the rising flames. "He came to kill my husband — and for that, I hope he went straight to hell."

44

Pope stood in the cargo bay of the C-5, staring thoughtfully at the sat phone in his hand.

"What did he say?" Gil asked.

"They figured out what we're up to. We've been ordered to stand down while the president calls the Canadian prime minister."

"Shit," Crosswhite muttered. "We can have our hands on the al-Rashids in less than an hour. Hell, it'll take that long just to get the Canadians up to speed. Doesn't the president realize the clock is ticking?"

"Of course he does. That's why I think it's a trap."

Gil stole glances with Crosswhite. "What kind of trap?"

"After what we pulled in Afghanistan," Pope said, "they have to think we're as likely

328

to disobey an order as we are to follow it. That's why we're the ones chasing the bomb: the more unstable the aircraft, the more maneuverable it is. Same principle." He took off his baseball cap and stood scratching his head, beginning to see Tim Hagen's fingers in the pie. "What do you think, Gil? Want to sneak over and grab them anyhow? I honestly think that's what the president's counting on, knowing he can't order us to do it. And this way, he can disavow us all if something goes wrong."

"I'll take two men across in a Zodiac."

"Actually, I'd rather you sent Crosswhite in your place," Pope said. The implications of this were obvious.

Crosswhite flashed Gil a devil-may-care grin. "Me being the most disavowable of us all."

"You'll take Trigg and Speed with you," Gil said. "They're the best boatmen on the squad. Do you swim, or don't they teach that in snake eater school?" "Snake eater" was a term used for Green Berets.

Crosswhite gave him the finger and called to Alpha, "How fast can you get that Zodiac inflated and into the water?"

"Fifteen minutes."

"Get Trigg and Speed ready to go!"

"Aye, aye!"

Crosswhite turned back toward Gil and Pope. "How's that for delegation of authority?"

"No weapons," Gil said. "You'll work your way inland and recon the al-Rashid place. If it looks like you can snatch one of the bastards, drag his ass back. If not, no harm, no foul. Don't take any risks. If you come back empty-handed, no big deal. We'll just pretend like the mission never took place and wait to see what the president can work out with the PM." He turned to Pope. "How much longer until that F-15 gets here?"

"Pretty soon now," Pope said. "By the time it arrives, we'll either have one of the al-Rashids or we won't. If we don't, that laptop's liable to be our last and only possible lead. I believe we're fast running out of time, gentlemen."

45

DETROIT RIVER

Three SEALs set off into the night in a black Zodiac F470 CRRC. Crosswhite was forward on the port side in the team leader's position, with Trigg on the prow as the forward observer. Speed manned the coxswain's position at the stern, running the fifty-five-horsepower engine. They were dressed all in black, wearing Under Armour compression shirts and pants in case they needed to dive into the water to evade capture. On their feet, they wore Core77 Abyss boots, specifically designed for SEALs, with drainage holes along the sides and in the soles. They wore night vision goggles but carried no weapons.

They motored across a narrow inlet, making very little wake, as Crosswhite monitored a handheld GPS programmed with the exact address of the al-Rashid residence. The far shore was two miles away, but once they made landfall, they would be less than a half mile from the house. The plan was simple: snatch one of the brothers — by whatever means necessary — secure his hands and feet with flex cuffs, cover his mouth with duct tape, and carry him like a rolled-up carpet back to the boat.

Speed navigated the Zodiac through an underpass beneath Eastern River Road and gunned the engine out into the open water of the Detroit River. The far shore was not a straight shot across. They had to detour three-quarters of a mile northward around the tip of Boblo Island and then bear south again to reach their insertion point along a residential section of the shoreline. They tied up the Zodiac at a private dock behind a small cabin cruiser, where it would not be visible.

Silent as cats, they moved swiftly through the shadows, with Crosswhite leading the way, hopping the occasional backyard fence and skirting three different swimming pools to finally arrive at the backyard of the al-Rashid residence. The house was dark, and there were no visible security cameras — not so much as a privacy fence for even minimal security.

Speed knelt beside Crosswhite near a garden shed. "Either we got the wrong fuckin' house, or these dudes feel totally secure."

"We're about to find out," Crosswhite said. "You guys wait here."

He moved forward across the back lawn and up onto a spacious wooden deck, and then peered in through a window. His night vision revealed a neat and tidy kitchen. A small silver coffee pot called a *Rakwah Qahwah* rested on the stove; it had a long spout and a straight, elongated handle. The pot was used specifically for brewing Arabic coffee, and Crosswhite had seen many of them during his time in the Middle East.

He signaled the other two men forward.

"Let's find the alarm system."

After nearly five minutes of searching, they found nothing to indicate the house had an alarm.

"I don't buy that," Crosswhite whispered. "This is a wealthy neighborhood. All these houses have to be wired."

"If you were a terrorist," Trigg said, "would you want the cops showing up at your house every time there was a false alarm? Or would you figure that since you were the biggest criminal in the neighborhood, you didn't need one?"

Crosswhite peered in through the back door, seeing no keypad on the wall. He tried the knob, but the door was locked.

Speed stepped back from the house to examine the upper level more closely. It was a Cape Cod–style home with two gabled windows on the second floor. One of the windows was partly open. The autumn night was cool, and there were no flying insects this time of year. Trigg gave Speed a boost onto the roof, and Speed carefully made his way over to the window, looking inside to see a woman with dark hair asleep in bed. He signaled the others to follow him up.

Trigg boosted Crosswhite onto the roof, but the grade was too steep for Crosswhite to pull Trigg up after him.

"I'll go down and let you in ASAP."

The two commandos slowly opened the window and slipped inside to stand over the woman. Crosswhite gripped his own throat with one hand, signaling Speed to take her under control.

Speed gripped her throat and straddled her, squeezing with two hands. She immediately came awake, flailing about on the bed in horror, but Speed was easily twice her size and ten times as strong. She tried to scream, but couldn't suck any air. With no oxygen getting to her brain, she blacked out in just a few seconds. They taped her mouth and secured her hands and feet with flex cuffs from a black pouch around Cross-white's waist.

Crosswhite went to the door and opened it a crack. Seeing a short, empty hallway in his greenish-black field of vision, he could hear a man peeing in the bathroom at the end of the hall, its door ajar. The toilet flushed, and Crosswhite closed the bedroom door, stepping to the side.

"He's coming back to bed," he whispered. "I'll grab him in a choke. You slug him."

They stood in the dark waiting, but no one came into the room. Instead, a door opened and closed across the hall.

The two SEALs looked at each other for a couple of moments, giving the man time to settle back into bed.

The woman came awake and began screaming in the back of her throat, generating a hell of a lot of sound in the darkened room.

Speed whipped around, knocking her senseless with the back of his hand, but it was too late.

The door opened across the hall, and a dark figure burst into the room.

Crosswhite grabbed him in a rear naked choke, and Speed leapt forward.

A pistol shot rang out and Speed dropped to the floor. Crosswhite twisted at the torso to prevent the man from getting another shot off in Speed's direction, at the same time sweeping his feet. They landed on the floor, with Crosswhite on top of the man's back, flattening him out and sinking his arm deep beneath the chin to quickly choke him unconscious.

Speed got up holding his belly and grabbed the pistol, moving into the hall as Trigg appeared at the top of the stairs. They both moved quickly to clear the rest of the house. When they returned to the bedroom, Crosswhite had the gunman secured and ready to go.

He jerked the drapes closed and peeled off his goggles. "Trigg, hit the lights."

Trigg flipped the light switch, and they saw that Speed was bleeding badly from the abdomen.

"I'll make it back to the boat," said the wounded SEAL. "Let's go."

Trigg shook his head. "No way can you run bleeding like that, dude. You'll bleed out before we make it halfway. You need a fucking hospital."

"Check the garage for a car." Crosswhite grabbed a handful of white T-shirts from a dresser drawer and turned to Speed. "Sit the fuck down so I can dress that wound. We're not losing another man!"

Speed held the folded T-shirts against his belly as Crosswhite wrapped him tightly around with the duct tape to hold them in place.

"It's not the aorta. I'll make it."

"We're dropping you off at a hospital," Crosswhite said.

"Like hell. I ain't doin' time in Canada. I ain't doin' time *no* place. You all are takin' me back to the fuckin' boat."

"Dude, you won't fucking make it! We're half an hour from NAS Grosse, and there ain't even a goddamn hospital over there."

"Doc's over there."

"Doc's a fucking medic. You need a surgeon."

Speed shrugged. "He's gonna have to learn, cuz I *ain't* doin' time."

Crosswhite got to his feet. "Stubborn motherfucker, we already lost Conman."

Speed glanced down at the Arab on the floor, lying on his belly and looking back at him, wild eyed. "What part of 'I ain't doin' time' didja not understand?"

Trigg came into the room, jingling a key ring. "There's a black Lexus with tinted windows in the garage."

"Excellent! Let's go." Crosswhite lifted the terrified woman from the bed and tossed her over his shoulder. "Little Miss

Screams a Lot is coming with us. They can both ride in the trunk."

A few minutes later, they were backing down the drive, and Crosswhite took a sat phone from the pouch, calling Gil over on Grosse Ile and giving a grim situation report. "Yeah," he said. "Another goddamn belly wound. So make sure Doc is ready with the whole blood."

46

SOUTHERN CALIFORNIA,
Edwards Air Force Base

General Couture leaned back in his chair in Operations, where everyone was in limbo waiting for the UAV to arrive at Grosse Ile so they could determine whether Pope had obeyed the president's order to stand down. He secretly wanted to kill the White House chief of staff for talking the president into delaying his call to the Canadian prime minister. He could see by the smug look on the deviant little fucker's face that Hagen had cooked up some kind of scheme, and he suspected it probably had something to do with sticking it to Shannon and Pope.

He checked his watch. The UAV was due over Grosse Ile in ten minutes.

Colonel Bradshaw came into the room and looked at Couture, arching his eyebrows for only him to see, and then moved toward the back of the room. The general watched him for a moment, the gears slow to mesh, as Bradshaw gave him another look, stepping around to the far side of the computer console.

"Excuse me a moment, Mr. President?"

"Certainly," the president said.

Couture crossed to the far side of the room, standing with his back to the president as he looked over the top of the console where an air force major sat monitoring one of the data streams. "What is it, Gene?"

Bradshaw stood behind the major and placed his hands over the major's ears; if the major even noticed this, you wouldn't have known it to see his face. "Bob Pope's on the line in my office. He's asking to speak with you out of earshot of the president." Bradshaw took his hands from the major's ears and patted his shoulders.

Couture felt his hackles rise. A glance over his own shoulder, and he saw Hagen leaning close to the president, the two of them talking in hushed voices. "Be right back," he said, and slipped from the room.

He picked up the phone on Bradshaw's desk. "This is General Couture."

"Bill? Bop Pope."

"What can I do for you, Robert?"

"Bill, I need you to locate the nearest Life

Flight helo and get it to Grosse Ile Municipal Airport as soon as humanly possible. Make sure they bring plenty of O-negative blood."

"What's happened?"

"I'll wait on the line while you arrange the helo, Bill. There won't be a moment to spare."

Couture released an annoyed sigh, setting down the phone as Bradshaw was stepping into the office. "Gene, Pope needs a Life Flight with plenty of O-negative blood to rendezvous with him on Grosse Ile. Please make that happen ASAP — *without* POTUS hearing you."

"Yes, sir." Bradshaw disappeared and Couture picked the phone back up.

"Okay, Robert. What have you gotten us all into?"

Pope told him about the incursion into Amherstburg, Ontario, and that the Zodiac was due back at NAS Grosse within twenty minutes.

Couture bit back the obscene comment that came to his lips, instead going with "Robert, are you insane?"

"Bill, I know the president is set to double-cross me, but I need you to change his mind — to convince him to let us continue with our mission."

"Robert, I'm not even about to try to do that."

"I know you've been against ST6/B from its inception, Bill — conceptually, so have I — but you're an old enough soldier to know that you don't change horses midstream. Especially if the second horse can't swim."

Couture knew the reasons for Pope's bias against the FBI were mostly hyperbole, but he also knew the CIA man was right about switching horses midstream. It would take the FBI hours to get caught up and organized if it was suddenly put in charge of an operation it so far knew nothing about — and those hours could prove to make all the difference.

"How do you know POTUS is set to double-cross you?"

"Has he called the Canadian PM yet?"

"No."

"And is the FBI en route to take us into custody?"

"Yes." The general did not volunteer that involving the FBI had been his idea.

"And why do you think that is, Bill?"

"You're playing a dangerous game, Robert." *Why do we keep calling each other by name? Mutual respect? Or contempt?*

"Of course it's dangerous," Pope retorted. "We're looking for a loose nuke in the hands

342

of madmen."

"Suppose I talk the president into it. What's your next move?"

"I won't know until after I've had time to interrogate al-Rashid."

"Interrogate him? Muhammad Faisal claims you stabbed him in the face with an ice pick! The surgeon says you could have killed him."

"I don't even begin to understand the relevancy of that," Pope replied. "Faisal told us about the al-Rashids. They may know where to find the bomb. We're following a very definite trail here, with no time to spare."

"Never mind," Couture said. "How do you plan to get off Grosse Ile and continue the mission? It'll take an entire day to JATO equip the C-5 for short runway takeoff . . . if it can even be done." JATO stood for jet-assisted takeoff.

"I'm finished with the C-5," Pope said. "My Gulfstream is due to land here in half an hour. We'll use that. Which reminds me . . . I'll need you to authorize a refuel for it ASAP. This is a civilian airfield, and I don't carry that kind of cash."

Couture shook his head. "Anything else, Robert?"

"Yes. Call off the FBI, and tell the president there's no need to contact the PM. Our people left no witnesses or bodies behind — just some blood from our wounded man."

"I'll see what I can do. No promises."

"Thanks, Bill. I'll wait to hear from you."

Couture put down the phone and returned to Operations, where he retook his seat across from the president. "Mr. President, sir . . . I've just been informed that ST6/B has already taken one of the al-Rashid brothers into custody. He'll be ashore on Grosse Ile within thirty minutes, so there won't be a need to contact the prime minister after all. In light of this new development, it is now my professional opinion, Mr. President, that — purely in the interest of time — our wisest course of action might be to allow ST6/B to continue their mission."

The president blinked once and sat gaping at him.

47

MICHIGAN,
Grosse Ile

The Montana Air Guard F-15 landed on Grosse Ile a few minutes before sun-up, just as Speed was being loaded aboard the Life Flight helo. Doc, the team's Mexican American corpsman, was more concerned over the fact that Speed had gone into shock than he was by the loss of blood.

"It's gonna be close," he said to Gil. "Shock can be a bitch."

Gil had seen men in worse condition pull through many times, and Speed was as tough as they came. He looked at Pope. "I think you probably saved his life, Bob. Thank you."

"It's Couture we need to thank," Pope said. "He expedited the helo."

"Be right back," Gil said. He trotted out to the F-15, where the pilot stood waiting on the wing beside the cockpit.

The pilot handed down the laptop. "The passport's under the lid."

Gil opened the laptop and stuck the passport into his back pocket. "Much obliged."

"You bet," the pilot said, gesturing at the mammoth C-5 Galaxy. "How the hell they gonna get that thing back into the air?"

Gil shrugged. "Beats the hell outta me, Captain. Safe flight back!"

"You bet," the pilot said again, climbing back into the cockpit of the F-15.

Pope met Gil at the edge of the tarmac, and Gil gave him the passport. Pope examined the passport photo for a long moment, searching his memory to place the face. "Jesus . . . this is Nikolai Kashkin."

"That's the guy Faisal told us to look for."

"Damn," Pope muttered, still studying the face. "It's too bad your wife had to kill him. He's very likely the mastermind of this entire operation." He looked up at Gil. "Kashkin's father was a colonel in the Soviet tank corps. He fought under his father in the Panjshir Valley, where he was taken prisoner by Mujahedeen. He was rumored to be connected to the KGB through an old-school Georgian assassin. His name was . . . Mulinkov. Daniel Mulinkov."

Gil shook his head. "How do you remember all that shit?"

"Partial photographic memory — inherited from my father. He worked in the Magic intelligence program during the Second World War; personally deciphered the Japanese code that lead to the shootdown of Admiral Yamamoto. Anyhow, my memory's not like his, but it's similar."

A Gulfstream V with USAF stenciled on the fuselage touched down on the runway and rolled past them.

Pope smiled. "It's a fine, well-oiled machine, the US military. Gather your men and their personal weapons. We won't have room aboard for much else. We're leaving for Langley immediately. I need to execute a brute-force attack on the laptop."

A brute-force attack on a computer was an exhaustive key search used against encrypted data that could — in theory, depending on the size of the bit encryption — require a supercomputer capable of generating an amount of energy equivalent to thirty gigawatts of electricity for an entire year.

Gil put the laptop under his arm. "Shouldn't we have a go at interrogating al-Rashid first?"

"We'll get to him," Pope said. "But now

I'm sure he doesn't have the slightest idea where to find the bomb." He gestured with the passport. "Kashkin masterminded this operation. He was the linchpin, and we needed him alive. If his laptop's been encrypted with a two-hundred-fifty-six-bit encryption key, we'll never crack it. So get your team to bring the prisoners aboard the plane. We're leaving."

Langley was the last place Gil thought they should be. "Hold up a second."

Pope stopped midstride. "What's wrong?"

"Are you telling me this was a waste of time? The al-Rashids are a dead end?"

"The al-Rashids were the money, Gil. That's what Kashkin was doing at your ranch — returning their favor." He pointed at the laptop. "That thing's our last chance. So if we manage to crack it, Marie really will deserve the Medal of Freedom."

Gil rolled his eyes. "She'll be thrilled."

48

By noon, Pope had established that Kashkin's computer was encrypted with a 180-bit encryption key. He looked across the lab, where Gil sat on a desk waiting with Crosswhite. The rest of the team was still aboard the plane in a CIA hangar watching over Haroun al-Rashid and his sister-in-law Melonie.

"I won't be able to break into this computer," he said. "It could take a year or more. You'd better have a go at al-Rashid."

Gil got up from the table, the frustration evident on his face. "I wish you'd cleared me to do that before."

"He doesn't know where the bomb is, Gil. I'm clearing you now only because there's no other hope."

Midori Kagawa, a Japanese American woman of thirty-five with short black hair, pushed back from her desk on the far side of the lab. "What about asking Lijuan?" she suggested in perfect English, having been born in Sacramento, California. "Encryption *is* her field of expertise, after all."

Pope had told Midori of Lijuan's arrest by the NSA shortly after his arrival. "You know that's not possible."

"It's possible if the president orders it," Midori replied. "And given the circumstances, he doesn't have any other choice. It's worth a call, Robert. She might think of something you haven't."

"There's nothing to think of. A one-hundred-eighty-bit encryption is virtually uncrackable."

"Virtually," Midori said, turning back to her desk. "And under normal circumstances, you'd take that as a challenge. I think you're just afraid to talk to her after what you did to her."

Gil knew nothing about Lijuan or what Pope had *done* to her — nor did he care. "I'll go have a talk with al-Rashid. I'll call you if we learn anything useful."

When he was gone, Pope got on the phone to Edwards AFB. "I need to speak with the president."

The president was on the line a few moments later. This would be Pope's second conversation with the commander in chief

since ST6/B's incursion into Canada —
though the first conversation had actually
been more of a presidential ass chewing.

"Have you broken into the computer,
Robert?" The president sounded very worried.

"No, Mr. President. I'm afraid we've
reached a dead end. Unless there's something I've missed, I won't be able to beat its
security. Shannon is questioning al-Rashid
now, but I'm certain he has no idea where
to find the bomb."

"So that's it then," the president said
wearily. "All that's left to do is sit and wait
for the damn thing to go off."

"Neither the FBI or NSA have come up
with anything, sir?"

"They claim to be chasing leads."

"There is one last thing I should check,
Mr. President — just to be absolutely sure."

"Which is?"

"By now, sir, I'm sure NSA has informed
you that my assistant Lijuan Chow has been
arrested for espionage. Code encryption is
her specialty, Mr. President. I would like for
you to arrange for me to speak with her by
phone. It's a long shot, but she may be able
to think of something I haven't."

There was a long enough pause at the
other end that Pope thought he may have

lost the connection. "Mr. President?"

"Why would she help us?"

"She wouldn't be helping *us,* Mr. President. She would be helping me."

"Hold on a minute."

The president put Pope on hold, looking at Couture, Bradshaw, and Hagen. The four of them were eating lunch in the officers' lounge. "He says he can't break the encryption. He wants to talk to his girlfriend the spy; claims she might be able to think of something he hasn't. Is there a reason I should refuse?"

Hagen cleared his throat. "Mr. President, it may be a ruse, sir. An attempt to pass her some kind of code phrase."

"Telling her to do what?" General Couture said testily.

"How do I know?" Hagen said. "The man's a genius — so is the girl! There's no telling what they might have preplanned."

Couture didn't honor Hagen with a direct response. "Mr. President, it's my recommendation you allow the call. If Chow tunnels under the wall, I'll accept full responsibility."

The president failed to stifle a sardonic snort. He reached and pressed the speaker button. "Stand by, Robert. I'll arrange for her to call you there. And since we're talking about her, how do you know NSA has taken into her custody?"

"I've been planning her arrest for a number of years now, Mr. President."

The president's gaze shot immediately in Hagen's direction.

Hagen looked back at him like a deer in the headlights.

"Would you mind explaining that, Robert?"

"Over the phone, sir?"

"This is a secure line."

"Well, Mr. President, to make a long story short . . . I've used her to gain access to the Guojia Anquan Bu database."

The president gave Couture a searching look.

"The Chinese Ministry of State Security," Couture said softly, noting the vapid look on Hagen's face. *Well, whattaya know? The whiz kid's weak on China.* "China's version of the CIA."

"How the hell did you manage that, Robert?"

"I think we'd better save that conversation for another time, Mr. President. There are still one or two stones left to look under for the RA-115. I'll wait in my office for the call from Lijuan."

"Very well. Stand by." The president broke

the connection and turned to Hagen. "Go make that call happen, Tim."

"Yes, sir."

When he was gone, the president leaned back in his chair. "What the hell am I going to do with that son of a bitch?"

"Pope or Hagen?"

Colonel Bradshaw chortled softly, and the president was hard pressed to hide his own amusement.

"You know, General, I didn't think so much of you at first. I thought you were a self-promoting showboat, parading around with that damn bodyguard of yours: the major and his dual pistols."

Couture grinned, the jagged scar on the left side of face standing out. "I've been a show-off all my life, Mr. President — and so far it's served me well."

49

Pope was at his desk, waiting in the dark, when the phone rang. "This is Bob Pope."

"Hello, Robert." Lijuan's voice was soft and sounded very sad.

"Are you okay?" he asked gently.

"I haven't been mistreated, if that's what you mean."

"Yes, that's what I mean."

"How long have you known?" she asked. "From the beginning?"

"Yes." He gripped the receiver. "I'm sorry."

"Don't be," she said. "I'm not angry with you. I was trying to run off and leave you holding the bag when I was arrested. Did they tell you that? Or was it you who sent them after me?"

"You know me so well," he said. "How did you not see through me?"

"Your love blinded me. I didn't think a

man like you could ever love a woman if you knew she was planning to betray you. But you're shrewder than I thought — more cold."

"I gave you so many opportunities to tell me."

"Yes, and like a fool, I let them all pass, didn't I?"

They sat in silence for a moment.

"I need to ask you a favor," he said finally.

"I won't betray my people, Robert."

"No," he said. "I know better than to ask that. I need your help with a one-hundred-eighty-bit encryption. It's on a laptop belonging to the Chechen who smuggled the bomb into the country. He's dead, and there are no other leads. We're running out of time."

"*That's* the reason they put me through to you. I knew it must be something more than love."

"This is very painful for me, Lijuan."

"I wonder if you feel pain the way others do," she said thoughtfully. "I don't think so."

"Will you help me?"

She remained quiet for a long moment. "A one-hundred-eighty-bit key is uncrackable inside of a year, Robert. You know that. I created an algorithm that *might* have managed it in eight months, but it was only theoretical. Please get out of Langley, Robert. There's no chance of finding that bomb. There never was."

"Li, please give me something."

"Do you promise to come and visit me in whatever dungeon they send me to?"

"If they'll allow it, yes. Of course I will." But he knew they would never allow it.

"Then tell me about the Chechen."

Over the next few minutes, he told her all he knew about Nikolai Kashkin. Then he waited quietly as she thought things over.

"You may be in luck," she said finally.

He sat up straight in his chair in the dark office, reaching to turn on the desk lamp and grab a pen. "What is it?"

"Well, he was your age . . . a simple old-soldier type — not a technical wizard. So if he used a commercial AES 180-key generator and installed it on the computer himself, he *may* have used the default settings to generate the key, which, theoretically, *might* give you a chance to replicate it."

The default settings! Pope thought. *My God! How did I not think of that? I'll tell you how: common sense has eluded you all your life. How are you going to manage without this woman?*

"You're already off in your own little

357

world now, aren't you?" she said.

"You know me," he replied. "I have to hurry, Li, but thank you very much. I'll come to see you as soon as they'll permit it. I promise."

"You know that wisdom tooth I told you about?" she asked. "The one that came in crooked?"

She had never told him about a crooked wisdom tooth. "What about it?"

"It's beginning to bother me. I wonder if they'll let me see a dentist here."

"I'm sure they will." His voice sounded thin and reedy to him.

"I love you," she said. "I look forward to seeing you again, Robert — someday."

"I love you too," he said hoarsely, knowing now that she was carrying a cyanide capsule in a false molar.

"Good luck to you, Robert." The phone clunked in the cradle at her end, and the connection was severed a moment later.

He stood immediately up from the desk and made his way back to the lab without even hanging up the phone.

50

LANGLEY

Haroun al-Rashid was strapped to a seat at the back of the plane, still dressed in his pajamas. His sister-in-law sat toward the front, facing the tail, also in her pajamas, with her hands still secured behind her back.

"Don't bother pretending you don't speak English," Gil said, pulling a black trash bag from the roll and giving the box to Cross-white. "You and your brother Akram have been living in Canada for the past eight years, and you've been under surveillance for much of that time. So tell us where to find the nuclear weapon that Kashkin smuggled into the country, and this won't have to get ugly."

Haroun smirked, recognizing Gil's face from the dossier he and his brother had received from the AQAP network. "You are going to die soon."

Gil frowned. "Kashkin is dead."

Haroun didn't seem surprised to hear the news. "Do you think Kashkin will be the last? Do you think you can fight all of Islam?" He shook his head. "Sooner or later, you will be killed — and your wife will be killed too."

Gil glanced at Crosswhite. "I reckon that covers the formalities."

Crosswhite put out his hand for the bag. "May I?"

Gil gave him the garbage bag, and Crosswhite slipped it over al-Rashid's head, smoothing the plastic over his face to dispel most of the air. Haroun tried to bite his finger through the bag, and Gil delivered him a straight punch to the face, breaking his nose. Crosswhite sealed the bag at al-Rashid's neck with a strip of duct tape.

"Catch you on the flip side, dick head." Crosswhite smacked him across the back of the head.

Haroun did not panic the way most prisoners did when the air quickly began to run out. He drew shallow breaths, keeping calm as he rationed the tiny bit of air remaining in the bag.

"Looks like somebody's had some training," Crosswhite observed.

Gil gave Haroun a stiff jab to the solar plexus. Haroun gasped and then began to

360

struggle against the restraints, sucking the plastic in and out of his mouth.

"That got things rolling," Crosswhite said happily.

"Where is the bomb?" Gil asked in a calm voice. "Tell us the truth, Haroun, and this stops."

Haroun began to thrash his head around, trying to locate an air pocket within the bag that did not exist. His breathing became increasingly rapid, the plastic sucking in and out of his mouth. A short time later, his head slumped to his chest, and he was out.

Crosswhite tore the bag open and pulled it down over his head. Blood ran from al-Rashid's busted nose over his lips and chin.

Haroun's sister-in-law moaned aloud at the sight, knowing she was next.

After sixty minutes without results, Gil and Crosswhite stepped off the plane for a smoke break, leaving a few other SEALs to watch the prisoners.

"What do you think?" Gil asked.

Crosswhite shrugged, lighting a cigarette. "I go until you say quit."

"That's not what I asked you."

Crosswhite exhaled. "I don't think he knows a thing about that damn bomb. We just put the fucker through an hour of hell, and he didn't say a single word. But what the fuck do I know, Gil?"

"What about Akram's wife?" Gil said, the idea of torturing a woman beyond repugnant to him.

"She only speaks Greek." Pope had told them Akram found her living on the streets of Athens, converting her to Islam before he married her.

"I'll see what Pope thinks."

A half hour later, they marched Melonie al-Rashid into an office there in the hangar and sat her down at a desk, freeing her hands and giving her a bottle of water. A few minutes later, the phone on the desk rang, and Gil picked up the receiver, handing it to Melonie.

She looked at him suspiciously, taking the receiver and putting it to her ear. "Hello?" she said in her own language.

"Is this Melonie al-Rashid?" asked Iosif Hoxha in slightly accented Greek.

"Yes," she answered. "Who is this?"

"My name Iosif Hoxha. I'm Albanian, but I grew up in Kakavija on the border with your country."

"I recognize the accent," she said.

"Have you been harmed?"

"They hit me once, but I haven't been seriously harmed — not yet."

"That is good," he said, keeping his voice friendly. "The Americans do not want to harm you, but you must tell me everything you know about the atomic bomb that your husband and his friends have brought into the United States. That is the only way I can guarantee your safety."

"What atomic bomb?"

"Melonie, you must not play stupid. They will hurt you like they did Haroun."

"I do not doubt that," she said shakily, "but there is no bomb. Akram goes to kill the American assassin — the sniper."

"Where is Akram now?"

"Somewhere in America. Please, will you tell these people I know *nothing* about a bomb! If I did, I would tell them. I want to return to Athens. Will you help me get home?"

They went round like this for another three minutes before Hoxha was satisfied that Akram had kept her in the dark about most of his business. "Okay, Melonie. I will call the American commander and explain what you have told me. Good luck to you."

"Thank you," she said. Hoxha broke the connection, and she put the phone down in the cradle, finally opening the bottle of water and drinking it all gone.

"I'm guessing she didn't tell him a damn

thing we can use," Gil said to Crosswhite.

"She told him something," Crosswhite said, seeing it in the young woman's eyes. "I don't know how useful it'll be, but she told him something."

51

As it began to grow dark, Marie Shannon stood on the house's back porch, looking up at the ridge where Buck Ferguson's two youngest sons, Roger and Glen, had pitched camp to keep watch over the ranch. A storm was coming in from the west, and she was growing concerned about the distant rumbling of thunder.

Buck came out the back door and stood beside her, a Colt .45 on his hip.

"It's fixin' to blow," she said. "You should probably call the boys down for the night. I don't want 'em struck by lightning."

"They'll be fine. They've been camping in these mountains all their lives. If Iraq and Afghanistan didn't kill 'em, these mountains sure as hell won't."

She smiled. "Thank you again for coming, Buck."

"Gil would do the same for us if it was

the other way around. We take care of our own out here, always have. You're too young to remember, but when I was over in Vietnam, your daddy used to look in on Liddy and the boys for me. He was a good man, your daddy."

"And Liddy was a good woman. I remember she used to bring me warm chocolate chip cookies."

"Yeah, she was a dandy," he said with a chuckle. "It's a shame they're both long gone. But then again, ain't nothin' meant to last, is it?"

"No, I reckon not," she said sadly.

They sat on the porch talking until the wind began to blow and the rain began to drive.

"I'd really feel better if you called 'em down, Buck."

He smiled at her in the porch light. "Honey, they're grown men. You don't think they know enough to come down on their own if they start gettin' wet?"

"At least call 'em for me?"

Buck took the cell phone from his pocket and looked at the screen. "As usual," he said. "No signal. That tower they put on my land ain't worth a holey shirt."

"Maybe it's the storm."

"That ain't helping, but service around

here is always spotty, even in good weather."

Up on the ridge, Roger and Glen were nice and dry in their tent, both of them lying on the same sleeping bags they'd used during the war. Each of them had an AR-15 carbine, and they'd brought Kashkin's scoped Mauser along as well. They lay in the dark listening to the thunder, the wind buffeting the tent. There was sporadic lightning, but it didn't seem dangerously close.

Roger, the youngest at twenty-two, had killed three Taliban during his first tour in Iraq, but Glen, twenty-five, was not yet blooded, at least not that he knew of. He'd fired a few thousand rounds in combat but never knew if he'd hit anyone. He kind of hoped not.

"Think it'll blow all night?" Roger wondered.

"Weather Channel said it will."

"Weather Channel don't know shit about mountain weather."

Glen lit a cigarette with a First Marines Zippo lighter and tossed the pack at his brother. "Think anybody could see the glow of the cherry through the tent wall?"

"Who the hell would be out in this?"

Glen rolled onto his elbow, his face faintly visible in the glow. "We're out in it."

Roger lay on his back, tapping an ash from his cigarette onto the front of his Carhartt jacket and rubbing it in. "If it's gonna blow all night, we might as well make our way back down to the house. We can't see shit from in here anyhow."

"Let's give it an hour," Glen said. "It might ease off."

"The old man's right," Roger said. "Bastards won't make another try at Gil anytime soon. If they were super committed, they'd have sent more than one dude the first time. I think they probably shot their wad for now. Their priority is the nuke."

"Sons a bitches," Glen muttered. "Where you think it's at? I bet it's in New York. Those fuckers love shittin' on New York."

"That's why I think it's DC. They won't bother LA on any account. Even Chechens aren't stupid enough to blow up Hollywood. Everybody likes our movies too much."

"Buncha hypocrites." Glen exhaled smoke through his nostrils.

They bullshitted awhile longer and smoked another couple cigarettes before deciding it was likely to rain all night. "If it quits, we can always come back up."

They crawled out of the tent, slinging their weapons barrel-down over their shoulders as they walked the ridge line in the down-pour.

It was Roger who saw the red laser dot appear on the back of his brother's head in the driving rain. At first he thought his eyes were playing him tricks, but his instincts were fast to set him in motion.

"Get down!" He shoved Glen forward, spinning to unshoulder his carbine.

He did not hear the 5.56 mm NATO round that struck him in the forehead, drop-ping him in his tracks. Just as Glen did not hear the rounds that struck him in the back. He hit the ground without ever grabbing for his weapon.

Duke rose soaking wet from a copse of junipers fifty feet away, strolling forward to stand over the bodies that lay crumpled on the muddy horse trail, slinging his sup-pressed M4 and raising the infrared binocu-lar up onto his forehead.

Akram stood from his place among the rocks and came forward.

"See, it's like I told you," Duke said over the sound of the storm. "Even these idiots knew ya gotta hold the high ground . . . but then, you desert folk probably don't see much high ground where you're from. Am I right?" He laughed and turned around, ordering two other men to drag the bodies from the trail into the junipers. "Likely gonna be a long, wet night. You all better get used to the idea right now and stop standin' around with your hands in your pockets." Then he walked off, mumbling beneath his breath, "Ya haji pricks."

52

MONTANA

The power to the house went out, and Buck stood up from the couch where he'd been reading the latest internet news about the intensifying search for the nuke. Lightning flashed, and Janet saw him clearly for a brief instant, his hand on his pistol.

"Probably just the storm," she said. "It happens out here a lot."

"My place too, but this ain't a good night to be in the dark."

Marie came hurrying down the stairs with Oso growling, gripping Gil's Springfield Armory .45. "Something's wrong," she whispered. "Oso's upset."

Oso went straight to the back door and began to scratch at the locked dog door.

"Wake Hal up!" Buck said, drawing the pistol. "Janet, you and Marie get upstairs. Take Oso with you."

Hal was already coming down, a carbine

in each hand. He crossed the room and gave one to his father. "We got movement outside by the stable, and it's not the boys."

After cutting the power and phone lines, Akram gathered his team of twenty men in the stable and stripped off his soaking jacket. The odor of horse manure was offensive to him, and it made him feel unclean. He ordered Abad and the rest of the men to cover the entrances. The Muslims were equipped with civilian-grade, first-generation night vision goggles, but Duke had brought along his third-generation military-grade binocular, which allowed him to see in infrared in addition to utilizing ambient light.

"If anyone comes out of the house," Akram said, "shoot them immediately."

Duke sat down on a bale of hay. "So what's our next move gonna be?"

"I'm not sure," Akram said glumly. "I hadn't planned on it raining." Where he came from, rain had never been a problem. "I'll take the TAC-50 up into the loft. You set up down here, and we'll wait for Shannon to show himself."

"We could assault the house," Duke said. "We've got the manpower."

"We'll wait to see. If Shannon's in there

ready for us, it could be a disaster. We don't know how many more men he has inside with him."

"Listen, you want to end this duck hunt before morning, or you wanna fuck around out here all night in the goddamn rain?"

"You need to stop with the blasphemy."

Duke chortled. "I'm talkin' about the Jew God."

"It's as Abad told you before . . . blasphemy is blasphemy."

"You want to kill this prick or not?"

Akram narrowed his eyes, wishing it was time to put the American to death. "I'm listening."

"You need to send in that kid with the bomb vest. Even if the blast doesn't get Shannon, it's gonna fuck up whatever defense they've organized in there and set the house on fire. Then we shoot whoever comes running out."

"Tahir!" Akram called in the darkness, his face illuminated briefly by a flash of lightning. "Come here." It was a brilliant idea to send a bomber into the house. But Akram was irked with himself for not having thought of it on his own.

Tahir appeared with a pair of night vision goggles on his face, an AK-47 hanging from his shoulder. "Yes, teacher."

"Your moment has arrived." Akram put his hands on the youth's shoulders and squeezed. "I need you to go into the house and detonate the bomb. You will arrive in heaven instantly, bathed in the affections of Allah."

Tahir shivered, and then felt the warmth of his urine running down the inside of his leg into his boot. "Yes, teacher." His voice felt raw, and he suddenly realized that he did not want to die. But there was no turning back.

Akram unzipped Tahir's jacket and readied the dead-man switch, putting it into the youth's fist. "It is very easy," he promised. "All you have to do is let go of the handle, and Allah will take care of the rest."

"Will there be pain?"

"None," Akram promised. "And your name will live forever."

Weak in the knees, Tahir leaned back against the stall door where a horse stood eating from a bucket of oats. "Should I sneak across or run?"

"Be stealthy," Akram said. "Work your way to the red truck, and from there you can run full speed to the back of the house. If you cannot force the door, break in through a window. Whatever you do, you must stay alive long enough to get inside, where the pressure wave will do the most damage. If you see our target, get as close as you can before releasing the detonator."

"I will not fail," Tahir said numbly, feeling utterly empty inside his skin.

Akram broke open a hay bale and spread it on the ground, getting to his knees and beckoning the youth to do the same beside him. "Now let us pray. This straw will serve as our *musallah* and protect us from the dung of these animals."

A few feet away, Duke sat watching them in infrared as they knelt in the hay, bowing their foreheads to the ground. He felt nothing but contempt for them.

It's too bad I don't have all my money yet, he thought, *because I'd waste every one of you crazy fuckers and be on my way.*

53

MONTANA

Glen Ferguson came to in the rain, face-down in a patch of brambles beneath the weight of his brother Roger's body, the sharp tip of a dead juniper branch jagging deep into the flesh below his left eye. He had never been so cold in his life, and for nearly a minute he was completely unable to move. At first he thought one of the bullets had nicked his spine and left him paralyzed, but then he realized he could still move his fingers and toes. He became conscious of the dead weight pressing down on his back, and drew his arms up beside him, pushing against the earth to roll himself over. The branch tore a chunk of flesh from his face as it pulled free, but he was cold enough that he hardly felt it.

He lay there a moment, feeling the icy rain beating on his face, and then groped inquiringly at Roger's body. "Oh, no!" he gasped, suddenly lucid and struggling to sit up. He was aware that he'd been shot multiple times, and he was becoming cognizant of the damage to his skeleton and musculature.

He felt Roger's carotid artery, but there was too much rain pelting down, his fingers too cold to detect a pulse. His thumb slipped into the exit wound at the back of the skull, and he jerked his hands back in horror, wiping them on his soaking Carhartt jacket.

The bastards had killed his little brother. At first he couldn't believe it and simply sat there dumbly in the driving thunderstorm with Roger lying across his lap. Finally it dawned on him that the killers were still out there somewhere, trying to kill his father and older brother. He checked his watch, seeing that an hour had passed since he and Roger had decided to head down to the house.

He hefted Roger's bulk aside, trying not to look at him, fearful of seeing his brother's death mask. When he tried to stand, he grew so dizzy that he nearly pitched over into the brambles, so he sat back down, probing about in the dark for his AR-15. It didn't seem to be anywhere around, so he began crawling back toward the trail. Lightning flashed, revealing the tent fifty feet away, and he crawled over to it, pulling himself in out of the rain.

Glen stripped his soaked cotton clothing, which was rapidly driving him into the advanced stages of hypothermia, feeling his body temperature rise as soon as he was naked. He checked himself over in the inky blackness to locate three exit wounds in his upper chest. The holes were small, about as big around as a pencil, and the bleeding was not profuse. He could feel the bone of both clavicles creaking as he moved his shoulders, and the fingers of his left hand didn't respond with as much dexterity as they should have, but he could still use both arms and hands, and that was all that mattered.

His Gore-Tex boots had kept his socks dry, so he pulled the boots back on over them, and rolled up his three-layered ECW (extreme cold weather) sleeping bag. Then Glen took the scoped Mauser from beneath Roger's bag and loaded in the five-round stripper clip by feel. He tucked the remaining four rounds into his brother's Camel-Bak rucksack and rolled the ruck up inside the sleeping bag. Slipping from the tent a few moments later, he found that he still couldn't stand.

He set off crawling toward the ridge naked

and dragging the Mauser with his right arm and the sleeping bag with his left. The rain drove down on his back, and muddy droplets spattered his eyes, but he was only vaguely aware of the cold, which he knew must have slowed his bleeding so far. When he got to the ridge, he pulled himself into Kashkin's sniper nest and unrolled the sleeping bag, zipping himself up inside its waterproof Gore-Tex shell.

The increase in body temperature would increase the bleeding, but he was dying of hypothermia even faster. Glen aimed the Mauser down the hill at the ranch and peered through the scope to see no signs of life. Three separate lightning flashes revealed nothing. He grew alarmed and unzipped the bag with the intention of crawling downhill to the ranch, but the instant the icy wind and rain hit his exposed flesh, his body was wracked with an intense pain ten times worse than any fever chill he had ever experienced. He jerked the zipper back up and decided to stay put.

Groping around inside the sleeping bag, he took a folding knife from the CamelBak and cut two armholes in the bag so he could operate the rifle without exposing his shoulders to the cold. Then he took Roger's wool watch cap from the ruck and pulled that onto his head. After eating a Snickers bar and sucking down a quart of water, he felt a great deal better and settled in behind the rifle. There were no broken windows on the back side of the house (except for Marie's boarded-up bedroom window), and that told him the fight down there was probably yet to begin.

"You've still got overwatch, Dad."

Lighting flashed, and he saw a figure dart from the stable, running for cover behind a steel water trough.

Glen quickly worked the bolt and pulled the stock into his shoulder. "Lord God," he whispered beneath the rolling thunder. "I beseech you in the name of all that's holy . . . send me another flash of lightning and let me blow this motherfucker's head off."

54

MONTANA

Hal stood back from the upstairs window beside Marie, both of them studying the stable with every flash of lightning. They caught glimpses of men with AK-47s moving about inside, but for the most part, the enemy was keeping out of sight, so they had no idea how many they were up against.

Marie had taken Gil's Browning from the gun safe and lain it across the guest bed for Hal to use. "Are we waiting for them to make the first move or what?"

"Right now we have the advantage," he said. "Every minute closer to daylight works in our favor. If they move to surround the house, we've got trouble because we won't be able to see them."

"What do you think is going on with your brothers?"

"I don't know," he said. "We underestimated the enemy, and I got a bad feeling the boys might have been taken by surprise up there."

"God, I hope you're wrong. Your father will never forgive — Look!" She pointed out the window. "Somebody just ran from the barn and ducked down beside the water trough."

Hal wrapped a poncho liner around his upper body and head to reduce his heat signature, stealing a peak around the window frame. Lightning flashed, and he saw a perfect snapshot of Tahir crouching beside the corrugated water trough. "I didn't see a weapon. Did you?"

"No, but he was clutching something in both hands. Like he was really afraid of dropping it."

"A grenade, maybe?"

"I don't know."

Hal went to the top of the stairs. "Dad, be ready for a grenade!"

"He's running toward the house!" Marie shouted.

Akram lay on his belly in the loft with the stock of the TAC-50 pulled into his shoulder, watching through the nightscope as Tahir jumped up from the water trough and took off in a headlong dash for the house, not bothering to maneuver from cover to cover as he'd been told. He cursed the youth for his stupidity and cowardice, for it was now obvious the boy's heart was not in the mission; that he was merely going through the motions to get it over with as quickly as possible.

There was a flash of lightning, and a rifle shot rang out. The boy fell in the mud and lay there gripping his leg with his free hand, his mouth open in a scream of pain that was carried off on the wind.

Akram got to his knees, cupping his hands around his mouth and shouting, "Get up and run!"

Though Tahir could not hear him, he managed to get his feet beneath him and to gallop off toward the house again, still gripping his wounded leg as he approached the deck on the back of the house.

The entire ranch was lit up by a brief moment of daylight. Another shot rang out, and the boy exploded in a blinding flash.

The shock wave blew out the windows on that side, peeling back the two-by-sixes on the deck and blasting the house with a hailstorm of debris, but the structure remained intact, and nothing caught fire.

Enraged, Akram began to back away from the loft door, but Duke arrived and dropped down next to him, training his M40 sniper rifle up the slope.

"Shannon's not in the house. He's up there on the ridge. Keep your eyes peeled for muzzle flashes, because we probably won't live to see more than one."

Akram got back down behind the TAC-50, believing he could almost feel the omniscient eyeball of the Navy SEAL sniper watching him through the scope of his own rifle from up on high, leering down on them like Black Death. He struggled to dominate his flinching reflex — as if one could flinch away from an incoming round — and swept the bulky rifle in twitchy movements from point to point along the crest as he searched for their target.

"You'd better relax," Duke cautioned, able to feel Akram's herky-jerky movement through the straw. "You'll never spot him that way. Keep your sweep smooth. He probably displaced after shooting that dumb-fuck kid on the chance we saw his muzzle flash. So we got a minute or two before he's resettled. Just keep calm, and we'll get him."

Akram resented the American's composure, but he knew Duke was the better shooter, so he shoved the .50 cal in his direction. "We'd better trade."

Duke grinned. "Hell, you speak my language better every day." They swapped, and he put his eye to the expensive night scope. "Watch what a man of talent can do with this fine piece of artillery — and keep your finger off the trigger over there. You're my spotter now. If you shoot and miss, that'll be our ass, so just help me find the squid fucker and let me blow his ass in half."

They studied the rocks above for the next four minutes.

"I've got something!" Akram said. "A rifle."

"Where?"

It took another minute for Akram to help Duke locate the target.

"Ah, there he is," Duke said. "And do you know what, my camel-jockeying friend?"

By now Akram was past taking Duke's invectives personally. "What?"

"The reason we're still alive is that he can't fucking see us. He's got no night vision up there. He's blind as a fucking bat without the lightning."

"So kill him already!"

The Duke chuckled. "Patience, Kimosabe. This ain't a shot you want me to rush. If I miss, and he sees the flash, he'll fire this way on pure reflex — and who the fuck knows which one of us he'll hit, eh?"

Akram reached nonchalantly down his leg

to unsnap his pistol, planning to kill the Duke the second Shannon was dead.

"And before you get the wise of idea of putting a bullet through my head," Duke said, taking his eye from the scope, their faces faintly visible in the glow of distant lightning, "we'll need to walk up there to be sure he's dead. You don't wanna kill your best marksman until you know that goose up there is cooked, do you?"

Akram smiled. "The thought never crossed my mind."

Duke put his eye back to the scope. "Don't piss down my back and tell me it's rainin'."

He placed the reticle on the nose of the face he was looking at. He couldn't make out the features because the shooter had a wool watch stander's cap pulled down tight to his eyebrows, and the rest of the face was obscured by the scope.

"It's too bad this can't be a fair fight," he muttered. "I almost feel bad about it." He squeezed the trigger, and the rifle kicked against his shoulder. It wasn't the mule kick he was expecting, however, because the hydraulic piston in the rifle's stock had greatly absorbed the recoil.

When he recovered the sight picture a second later, the shooter's rifle was still sticking out from the rocks — but the head behind the scope had disappeared.

"Bull's-eye!"

"Did you get him?" Akram was unable to see for himself because the optics on Duke's M40 weren't as good as those on the .50 cal. "I can still see the rifle."

"I wasn't aiming at his fucking rifle, jerk-weed." Duke got to his knees, swinging the TAC-50 around to point it at Akram. "Now, here's how we're gonna play this, Zatoichi. We're goin' up there to check the body . . . just me and you. If he's dead, we're walking down the backside of the ridge to the trucks and leaving all those dumb fucks downstairs behind. You're gonna transfer the rest of my cash as soon as we get back to the hotel, and if you don't like that idea, I can just blow you the fuck away right now."

Akram backed away from the M40 and got up on his knees. "I'm guessing I leave my guns here?"

"You guess correctly, Buster Brown. So drop the pistol, and let's move it out."

55

MONTANA

Buck carried Janet upstairs and laid her on her bed. She'd been hit in the forehead by a chunk of two-by-six in the explosion and was only half conscious. Marie sat beside her in the dark, holding an icepack against the contusion.

Oso shadowed Marie everywhere she went, able to smell the adrenaline in the air and knowing something was wrong.

"What happened out there?" she said to Buck. "Could you see?"

He grunted in frustration. "The guy running at the house was a suicide bomber."

Hal was listening from across the hall in the guest room, where he kept an eye on the stable, Gil's Winchester .300 in hand. "Why didn't he get closer before blowing himself up?"

Buck crawled across the hall to take up firing position beside him. "Because I think one of your brothers shot him. I'm pretty sure I heard a rifle shot."

Then they heard the booming report of the TAC-50 in the direction of the stable, and both men ducked down.

"Anybody hit?" Buck said.

"We're fine over here," Marie answered.

"They're not shooting at the house," Hal said. "They're shooting up at the ridge."

"That means they're shooting at your brothers!" Buck stole a quick peek out the window.

For the first time, Hal was beginning to think his brothers might still be alive. "If they're still on overwatch, that's gonna make the bastards think twice about sticking their heads out of the stable."

Buck took the Winchester .300 and crawled down the hall into Marie's bedroom, where the wind and rain were blowing in through the shattered windows. He used the powerful scope to seek out Kashkin's sniper nest that Marie had shown him during the day. When the lighting flashed again, he saw clearly the fore stock and muzzle of the Mauser protruding from the rocks.

"It's them!" he called. "I can see the Mauser."

"Who's behind it?" Hal called back.

"I can only see the rifle."

Marie left her mother's side and slipped into the guestroom. "Hal, you have to go for help before they decide to surround the house. They won't let this rain discourage them for long."

"Is your mom bad off?"

"I think she'll be okay, but once the shooting starts, this house isn't going to stop AK-47 bullets. Even I know they'll cut clean through one side and out the other."

Buck crawled into the room and stood the Winchester against the wall. "You're right. But it's you who should go for help, honey. If you're quick, you can make it to Chatham's place on foot in less than an hour."

"I don't like the idea of going to Dusty for help. I haven't talked to him in years."

"That doesn't matter now," Buck said. "We all gotta set our differences aside."

Over the next ten minutes, Marie very reluctantly prepared herself to go, dressing in hiking boots and Gore-Tex rain gear. She filled a CamelBak with water and strapped the Springfield .45 to her hip.

"Oso's gonna carry on like a spoiled kid when I go, so keep him close."

"Be sure and skirt well south before you turn east," Buck said. "You don't want those sons a bitches to see you, and you don't want the boys up on the ridge mistaking you for the enemy. We'll hold out here until you get back with the cavalry."

She crossed the living room to a ground-level window on the far side of the house and knelt down to give Oso a hug. "You look after Grandma now," she told him, rubbing his head.

She stood to open the window, and the Chesapeake Bay retriever began to whine, knowing she was about to leave without him. "Hold 'im, Buck, or he'll jump right out after me."

Buck took the dog by the collar. "You're good to go, honey. Be careful!"

She slipped out into the rainy night, and Buck pulled down the sash. Oso ran directly to the front door and began to bark.

"She'll be fine," the big man said, going over and taking him by the collar. "Let's go upstairs and look after Jan."

Oso fought him the entire way, and with the big animal twisting around and around, it was like trying to drag the Tasmanian devil up the stairs.

"Sumbitch, you're stubborn!" Buck stumbled on the last step.

Sensing Buck's loss of balance, Oso jerked hard to break his grip and scrabbled down

391

the stairs. He raced through the living room toward the back of the house and leapt out through one of the broken windows, disappearing into the night before Buck could even make it to the bottom of the steps.

Marie wasted no time putting distance between herself and the house. Knowing where all the obstacles and pitfalls were, she had little trouble making her way in the dark, but she was completely unaware of the humanoid figure slithering from beneath the horse trailer on the far side of the yard, drawing a knife and moving out after her.

The American-born Al Qaeda shadowed her through the dark, his footfalls every bit as muffled by the rain as hers, dogging her far out into the night and almost losing her as she broke left to the east, but catching up to her as she arrived at the barbed wire fence marking the southern property limit.

Marie was in the process of climbing over when someone grabbed the hood of her jacket and pulled her violently off the fence. She landed hard on her back, knocking enough wind from her lungs to stifle a scream. The dark figure began kicking her in the ribs, forcing her to roll onto her belly. Then he pounced on her back, straddling her and sinking his fingers deep into her now soaking hair, yanking her head back to expose her throat. She felt the cold steel of the blade press into the jugular.

The angry Muslim had spent the entire night freezing in the mud beneath the trailer, but now his miseries were about to be rewarded. He hissed into her ear, "I'm going to cut your fucking head off, and show it to your husband!"

"No, wait!" she gasped, her arms pinioned at her sides by his legs.

He redoubled his grip on her hair, jerking her head back as far as it would come and crying out in triumph, *"Allahu Akbar!"*

Marie screamed, and one hundred pounds of snarling, soaking-wet *canis lupus familiaris* slammed into the Muslim from behind, knocking him forward over her head onto his hands and knees. Oso Cazador sank his teeth into the back of the man's neck, snarling wildly as he jerked the man about like a rag doll.

The interloper flailed helplessly beneath the dog, unable to roll onto his back or to shake off the animal. He made a desperate attempt to flip himself over but felt a sharp pinch between his C4 and C5 vertebra, and his body suddenly stopped responding to his commands.

Oso was an experienced killer, having

killed many varmints — and even a coyote — in just this same manner, and he knew what it meant when a prey's body went limp. He released his grip on the man's neck and sat back on his haunches, wagging his tail and looking at Marie for approval. When she didn't immediately sit up, he went to her, licking her face and beginning to whine.

Exhausted by the adrenaline dump, Marie lay with her face in the mud, almost too weak to move. "Good boy," she mumbled, forcing herself to reach out and stroke the dog. "Good boy, Cazador."

The dog went back to licking her face, and the warmness of his tongue ignited within her an internal heat source that spread a faint glow of warmth through her body. After a few moments, she found the strength to sit up against the fence post, pulling the hood up over her head to keep the rain from running down her back. She made a halfhearted attempt to stand and was jarred by a stabbing pain in her left side. The pain was not unfamiliar to her; she had broken ribs twice before: once by falling from a horse and once by getting kicked by one.

"It's gonna be a long walk," she said to the dog.

The man lying facedown in the mud

began to moan, and she pulled the .45 from the holster beneath her jacket, crawling over onto his back and pressing the muzzled to his side.

"How many are you?" she demanded.

"I can't move," he whimpered. "I need a medic."

"You need a helluva lot more than that," she said, resting with her face against his back. He was much warmer than the ground, and she thought it odd that she could be comforted by the heat of a man who had almost murdered her. "How many are you?"

"Twenty. I need a hospital . . . please."

"You need a coroner." She canted the muzzle slightly downward toward the earth and squeezed the trigger. The pistol report was muffled by his body, and she felt him recoil against the jolt of the Federal hollow point ripping through his internal organs. He died almost instantly from the hydro-static shock. She felt the air rush out of him and rolled off, sitting up against the string-ers of barbed wire and reaching out to her dog.

"Come here, boy," she said. "Help Mama get to her feet."

56

Akram radioed to Abad that they were going up the hill to make sure that Shannon was dead and to shoot anyone coming out of the house. He and Duke climbed down from the loft at the back of the stable and made their way up the hill.

No one had heard Marie's scream over the driving rain.

After the climb, they came to stand over the more or less headless corpse of Glen Ferguson, still zipped up in the ECW sleeping bag with his arms sticking out through the improvised holes.

Duke kicked the Mauser downhill and raised the infrared binocular up onto his head, shining a Tactical Touch flashlight onto the bloody mess at their feet with a derisive chuckle. "Nice of him to provide his own body bag like that. Whattaya say there, Akram? Think he's dead?"

Akram couldn't help smiling. Now, no matter what happened to him, the fiend murderer Gil Shannon was dead, destined to fuel the fires of *Jahannam* for all eternity. "I think he's burning in hell."

"Good. Now let's get the fuck outta this rain and head back to the hotel to square up."

"How do I know you won't kill me the moment I transfer the rest of your money?"

"Because I ain't no fourteen-carat son of a bitch like you — *that's* how."

"Forgive my bluntness, Duke, but you are a traitor to your own people."

"That's between them and me. I put in nineteen goddamn years of loyal service, and they kicked me to the curb. Now what's it gonna be, tough guy: do or die?"

Akram felt something hot and wet spatter his face, followed by the distant echo of a rifle shot.

Duke dropped his flashlight, and the strap of the TAC-50 slipped from his shoulder. He put a hand to his stomach, where his fingers found a gaping exit wound the size of a baseball. "Fuck," he muttered, and dropped dead to the ground.

Akram dove between the rocks as another round ricocheted off a boulder. He grabbed the strap of the TAC-50 and pulled it to

397

him while radioing Abad that Shannon was firing from inside the house.

Automatic weapons fire broke out down below, and Akram pulled the infrared binocular from Duke's head, snatching the dog tags from what was left of the body, before scrambling back down the trail on the eastern side of the slope. He radioed for the men to cease fire, and ten minutes later linked back up with them in the stable, where they all stood around in a heated frenzy.

"Where's Duke?" Abad asked.

"Shannon shot him," Akram said, throwing the dog tags at him. "He tricked us!"

Abad shined a red penlight on one of the tags, reading Glen's name and seeing the "USMC." The idea of killing Marines was distasteful to him, and he was ready to be done with the entire mess. "Uday is missing."

"What do you mean he's missing?"

"Just what I said. He's missing. He was under the horse trailer covering the front of the house. Now he's not there, and we can't find him. I told you we needed more radios."

"Have you tried his phone?" Akram asked testily.

"There's no damn signal out here."

Akram combed his fingers through his wet

hair. "So what are you saying? That someone came out of the house and dragged him inside?"

Abad may have been a devout Muslim, but he'd been raised in America, and the American in him didn't have the patience for Akram's condescending Arabian bullshit. "I'm saying he's *missing*! Open your ears!"

"Who do you think you're talking to?"

"I'm talking to you," Abad said, stepping forward. "And I'm telling you one of our men is missing. We need to end this, Akram, and we need to end it soon."

When the firing had died off, Buck crawled down the hall with the Winchester into the bathroom, checking on Janet, who was curled up beneath a blanket in the cast-iron bathtub. "You okay in here, Jan?" Lighting flashed, and he saw a big chip in the porcelain where a bullet fragment had struck the side of the tub.

"Fit as a fiddle," she answered. "How are you men doing?"

"We're okay," he said, pulling himself up against the tub. "I got one of 'em up there on the ridge."

"Good for you!"

"Jan, I think Glen and Roger might be dead."

She peaked over the edge of the tub. "You can't know that."

"Two of them godless sons a bitches were just standin' up there with a flashlight, like they didn't have a care in the world. They were lookin' down at somethin'. I think it was one of my boys."

She reached out, touching his face in the darkness. "If it was, Buck, he's in a better place now. But don't give up hope."

57

When Pope at last broke through the firewall on Kashkin's hard drive, gaining full access to the encrypted data, it wasn't necessary for him to translate the Chechen text in order to know which city had been targeted. The myriad photographs of Washington, DC, were obvious in any language.

He grabbed for the phone. His call to Edwards was answered on the first ring. "White House Chief of Staff Tim Hagen speaking."

"This is Pope. Get the president."

The president of the United States came on the line. "What do you have, Robert?"

"Mr. President, you need to order an immediate evacuation of Washington, DC. I still have to translate the Chechen text to English" — he was rapidly paging through a series of JPEG files — "but I'm looking at dozens of photos taken in and around the capital. All of our most important buildings have been photographed in detail; multiple telescopic photos of security points around the White House and the Capitol building."

"How fast can you remit those files for evaluation at our end?"

"I'll translate them immediately and send them within the half hour, Mr. President, but in the meantime, sir, I strongly recommend you order the evacuation."

"I'll do it immediately. Now, forward those files as soon as you can."

"Yes, sir. There's something else, Mr. President."

"What is it?"

"Our interrogation of Haroun al-Rashid revealed nothing," Pope said, "but his sister-in-law told us that her husband, Akram al-Rashid, is on his way to Gil Shannon's place in Montana to assassinate him."

"Okay," the president said. "Then it's lucky that Shannon is with you. I assume his wife is moving to a safe location?"

"Not exactly, sir. She's still on the ranch, and she's not answering the phone. I've cleared Shannon to fly to Montana in the Gulfstream V."

There was another typically long pause at the president's end before he made his reply. "To be frank with you, Robert, I'm getting tired of losing my temper — especially with you. So let me make something perfectly clear without shouting . . . Shannon and his team are not your personal army. Is that understood?"

"Yes, Mr. President."

"Are they in the air now?"

"They are, sir. I've already alerted the Montana Highway Patrol and the local FBI office in Helena."

"Excellent," the president said. "In that case, we're going to allow the local authorities to do their jobs. You do realize that Shannon's team gunned down six off-duty police officers and a young woman during the Vegas operation."

"Mr. President, the young woman was shot by one of Faisal's men, and there was no way we could have anticipated out-of-town law enforcement getting involved. It's the fog of war, sir."

The president grunted. "Well, fog or no fog, Shannon and his team have served their purpose. I'm going to order them back on the ground and fully debriefed."

58

MONTANA

Marie and Oso arrived at the Chatham ranch looking like a couple of drowned rats. A bed-headed Dusty Chatham answered the door in his bare feet, naked to the waist in a pair of blue jeans. He was forty-five with a black beard trimmed close to his face. The Chathams and the McGuthrys had a long history of bad blood dating back to the late forties, all of it over land disputes. There had never been any rancor between Marie and Dusty, however, the trouble having always been between their fathers and grandfathers.

"Marie?" Dusty's face was a mask of disbelief.

"Dusty, I'm really sorry to bother you so late, but I've got big trouble. Can I use your phone?"

"Yeah," he said, stepping back to let them inside. "Hey, that's a big dog."

404

"He just saved my life."

He shut the door. "How'd he do that? What's going on?"

"You won't believe it, but Al Qaeda just tried to blow up my house." Her cracked rib was making it painful to breathe, and she was using both hands to apply pressure to it. "They came for Gil, but he's not there, and we think they've already killed Glen and Roger Ferguson."

He gaped at her. "What? Marie, slow down and tell me what's really going on."

"I swear it's the truth."

"Al Qaeda? Here? How many?"

"About twenty, I think. I snuck off to find a phone, and Buck stayed behind with Hal to protect my mother. She's hurt. I gotta call Gil so he can get us some help out there before it's too late."

"Sure, there's the phone over there on the wall, but how do you know it's Al Qaeda?"

"I don't have time to explain, but I swear to God it's the truth. They put a price on Gil's head right after he won the Medal of Honor."

There was almost no one in the state of Montana who didn't know about Gil being a war hero. "Make your call. I'm gonna get dressed and grab my rifle."

She moved toward the phone. "Dusty, I

405

can't ask you to get involved in this."

"Don't be silly, Marie. I never had nothin' against you. It was our dads who didn't wanna get along."

She took the receiver from the hook on the old push-button phone. "Gettin' along is one thing, Dusty, but gettin' shot at is another."

"Just call your old man," he said, trotting upstairs. "I'll be right down."

Gil answered a minute later. "Hello?"

"Gil, it's me!"

"Thank God!" he said. "I've been calling the house, but no one answers. Are you guys all right?"

"No. Al Qaeda's back, and there's about twenty of 'em. I think they've already killed Glen and Roger. I'm at Chatham's place now with Oso. Buck and Hal are still back at the ranch lookin' after Mama. She got hurt when they tried to blow up the house, Gil."

"How bad are *you* hurt?" Gil's tone was hard and deep, very soldierly. "And don't tell me you're fine. I can hear it in your voice."

"I got a cracked rib, but I'm okay. One of them caught me trying to escape in the storm, but Oso saved me."

Gil dominated his terror. "Are you safe now?"

"Yes."

"Okay. I'm already in the air with my team and headed that way. You stay put."

"Dusty's getting his rifle. I think he means to go help Buck."

"You're kidding! He hates Buck." Dusty and Buck had gotten into huge festering arguments at nearly every cattle auction for the last ten years, each regularly accusing the other of intentionally driving up the bid just to piss off the other. "Talk 'im out of it if you can. He'll only get himself killed. Either way, you stay put. Hear me?"

"But Mama's —"

"Mama's in good hands, Marie. I mean it! You stay put!"

"Okay."

"I gotta go forward and talk with the pilot. I love you."

"Love you too."

She was hanging up as Dusty was coming down the stairs dressed in his Carhartt rain gear, toting a scoped .30-06 bolt-action hunting rifle.

"Dusty, Gil doesn't think you should go over there. He's on the way with his team now."

"What team?"

She pulled her wet hair back from her face. "Navy SEALs. They're on a plane headed this way."

"Well, I ain't no SEAL, but I can shoot, and if two of Buck's boys are already dead, he's gonna need help holdin' the fort until the cavalry shows up." He took a black cowboy hat from a peg on the wall and put it on. "Ya know, your mama picked me up at school once when I was little. My step-mom flipped her car over in the blizzard, and with everybody busy trying to find her, they all sorta forgot about me. But not your mama. I remember her tellin' me on the way home that cattle folk gotta look after one another, even if they don't always get along. I reckon she was right."

"Dusty, she wouldn't ask you to risk your neck because she gave you a ride home in the snow."

"I know it." He took a box of cartridges from a drawer. "I'm gonna get saddled up. You make yourself at home."

He pulled the door open.

"Dusty, wait!"

He looked at her.

"You got an elastic bandage?"

"All horse people got elastic bandages. Why?"

"Help me wrap this cracked rib, and I'll

go with you. You'll need me to point out who was where when I left."

"I don't think that's a good idea, Marie. No offense, but you're a woman, and you're hurt."

"How many Al Qaeda have you killed, Dusty?"

"None, but that's not what I'm talkin' —"

"Well, I've killed two already, so round me up a goddamn bandage, will ya? I'd like to get back in this thing before it's over."

59

IN THE SKY OVER WYOMING

"Master Chief, I'm sorry as hell," the pilot of the Gulfstream V was saying. "I really am, but I've been ordered to divert to Creech AFB, and that's what I've got to do."

"My hearth and home are under attack," Gil said. "Do you understand what that means? Al Qaeda is on the ground trying to kill my family."

"I understand," said the pilot, an air force captain. "But my orders come straight from Colonel Bradshaw, and his orders are straight from the president himself. What can I do?"

"You can stay on course!"

"No, I can't. I'd be flying straight into a court martial. *You* may not have a problem disobeying orders, but I'm not wired that way. Besides, the FBI and the Montana State Police are both en route to your ranch. I'm sure everything's going to be okay."

Gil knew he had to get to Montana. The Helena office of the FBI didn't even have a helicopter at its immediate disposal, much less any kind of hostage rescue team. And as for the Montana State Police, they were good guys, but most of their training was traffic related, and Gil knew they'd be no match for a trained Al Qaeda hit squad — especially if they were AQAP operators.

He shifted his gaze to the copilot. "How about it, Lieutenant?"

The copilot pointed at the pilot. "My orders come from him."

Gil left the cockpit mad enough to shoot somebody, pulling the door closed after him.

Crosswhite was waiting there. "What did they say?"

He shook his head. "They aren't *wired* like me."

"What about John Brux?" Crosswhite suggested. "Think he could help?"

Gil cocked his eyebrow. "You got 'im in your fuckin' pocket?"

"Look, these fuckin' planes will damn near land themselves," Crosswhite said. "We'll just get Brux on the phone, and he'll tell us how to program the computer."

"That's a pretty good idea." Gil chuckled. "Once in a while, you're almost worth having around."

A few minutes later, they had John Brux on the sat phone, and Gil broke the situation down for him. Brux was the former air force pilot who had flown topcover for Gil's unauthorized mission to rescue Sandra Brux, Brux's wife.

"We owe you everything," Brux told him over the phone. "So, yeah. *Hell,* yeah. If you can get in the pilot's seat, I'll tell you how to program the computer."

"Stand by." Gil looked at the rest of the team. "Any of you guys have a problem taking the cockpit if the pilots won't give it up?"

The SEALs all popped out of their seats.

Crosswhite put his hand on the cockpit door. "Just give us the order, Chief."

Gil nodded reluctantly. "Take the plane."

Crosswhite opened the door and stepped into the cockpit. "Excuse me, Captain."

The pilot looked back at him. "What now?"

Crosswhite placed a gentle hand on his shoulder. "Well, you can put this plane on autopilot and vacate the cockpit. Or you can try to resist us and probably end up crashing the goddamn thing. Which is it gonna be?"

"Bullshit! You'll kill us all if you try landing this thing yourselves."

"We've got a G-V pilot on the phone who says he can talk us through the landing. So get outta the goddamn seat."

The pilot looked at his copilot. "See? I told you these crazy fuckers would pull something."

The copilot shrugged. "I don't recommend a fight, sir."

"No shit!" the captain said bitterly, turning to Crosswhite. "I'll land in Bozeman, but every fucking one of you is gonna swing for this."

Crosswhite grinned. "If I had a quarter for every time somebody said that to me." He kept Brux on the phone so he could tell him how to verify if they were flying in the right direction.

Ten minutes later the radio came to life . . . "Air Force Flight One Sixty-Eight. This is Nellis AFB. Please advise as to why you have not corrected course."

Crosswhite put his hand on the pilot's shoulder. "Don't give them a reason to shoot us down, eh?"

The pilot gave him a look. "This is Air Force One Sixty-Eight. Nellis, we are continuing to Bozeman Yellowstone International."

"Standby, One Sixty-Eight." There was a ninety-second pause. "One Sixty-Eight,

413

that's a negative. You are ordered to divert to Creech AFB."

"Tell them we've got engine trouble," Crosswhite said.

The pilot advised they were having hydraulic trouble and that Nellis was too far.

"Um, stand by, One Sixty-Eight."

Three minutes later . . . "One Sixty-Eight, you are clear to proceed to Bozeman Yellowstone. Be advised you'll be catching the tail end of a cold front coming down from the northwest, so expect chop."

"Roger that, Nellis. Thank you." The pilot looked back at Crosswhite and smirked. "You think you've won, but they're gonna have every cop in Montana waiting there to greet us. You wait and see."

Gil cleared his throat from where he leaned in the doorway. "Which is why we'll be landing ten miles away at a private airfield." Gil handed him a slip of paper. "Those are the exact GPS coordinates."

The pilot took the paper and passed it to his copilot. "Enter the coordinates, Lieutenant."

60

The pilots stared out the windshield as they taxied the G-V toward a waiting midnight blue Douglas DC-3 twin-prop transport plane waiting at the end of the runway. Stenciled on the fuselage in bright yellow was the slogan "Dive the Sky!" One of the DC-3 pilots stood beside the aircraft next to a pile of parachutes and jump harnesses. The night was still heavily overcast, but the rain had ceased, leaving the air cold and damp.

Gil gave the pilot on the ground a thumbs-up. A few seconds later, the DC-3's engines coughed and the propellers began to turn.

"Whose C-47?" the lieutenant asked. This was the military designation for the twin-prop transport.

"Belongs to a buddy of mine," Gil said. "A retired airborne Marine. He gives skydiving lessons now." He looked into the back. "Gear up, men! He's got our chutes laid out on the deck beside the plane."

The air force captain applied the brake and killed the jet engines, and then turned around in his seat. "I seriously doubt anybody anticipated this move. I guess it helps having home field advantage."

"We'll see," Gil said grimly.

He left the cockpit, accepting his .308 Remington MSR (Modular Sniper Rifle) from one of his SEALs and trotting down the stairs to greet the DC-3 pilot on the ground. Crosswhite and the other eight SEALs were quickly shrugging into their jump gear.

"Jack," he said, offering his hand. "I can't tell you how fucking much I appreciate this."

"Bull butter," replied fifty-year-old Sergeant Major Johnathan Frost. He had gray hair and a mustache, and he spoke with a Missouri accent. "Got an extra M4? I'm jumping with you guys. Bart can bring the plane back himself."

"I can't let you do that, Jack. You've got a wife waiting at home."

"Then it's a good thing I brought my AR along." Frost grinned. "You can't keep me from jumping outta my own plane, Gil."

"Fuck," Gil muttered. "Clancy! Get Jack an M4 outta the kit!" He turned back to Frost. "You're an irresponsible husband, Jack Frost."

Frost clapped him on the back. "I guess it takes the pot to call the kettle black."

"Eat me, jarhead."

Six minutes later, they were loaded onto the DC-3 and roaring down the runway.

61

MONTANA,
Five Miles South of Gil's Ranch

Special Agent Carson Porter had been with the Bureau for five years, chasing bad checks all across the Big Sky State, and though he had arrested one or two tough hombres in his limited tenure, this was his first time leading an operation where gunplay was *expected,* and he was finding the pucker factor to be greater than he had previously anticipated.

The Highway Patrol's local post commander, Lieutenant Quentin Miller, was just pulling up with four other cruisers in tow, and so far no one from the Gallatin County Sheriff's Department had arrived.

Porter got out of the unmarked Ford Crown Victoria and stepped across the road. The rain had recently abated, and a chilly fog was quickly setting in. "Quentin, how are you?"

The post commander sat behind the wheel of his marked Highway Patrol car. "Tired as hell. How many bad guys are supposed to be up there? We haven't been told shit."

"As many as twenty with automatic weapons. Where's everybody else?"

"Who everybody else?"

"The rest of your men? The Sheriff's Department?"

"I don't know. Your people didn't contact the sheriff?"

Porter threw up his hands. "Christ, Quentin, you work hand in hand with those guys. You're telling me you didn't even give them a call?"

"Hey, goddamnit! I was asleep in bed when Colonel Reed called from Missoula telling me to hightail it out here with a security detail, and that's what I did. He said the operation was under federal jurisdiction. Call me stupid, but I assumed that meant the FBI would be handling the logistics."

Porter glanced at Agent Spencer Starks as he came across the road. Starks was an African American who had served as a loader in an M1 Abrams during the early days of the Iraq War. His tank had been hit by an RPG fired from a rooftop, and he had taken enough shrapnel in the left shoulder to send him home for the duration.

"It's already fucked up, Spence."

Starks shook his head. "Doesn't surprise me."

"Okay," Agent Porter said. "I guess we're it then. What did you guys bring for fire-power?"

Miller thumbed over his shoulder toward the trunk. "We each got an AR in the back, standard issue. Four mags apiece."

"No body armor?"

"Just our vests. We're not SWATs."

"What do you think?" Porter asked Starks.

Starks rubbed a hand over his bald head. "I think if we don't get our butts up there pretty soon, there won't be any reason to bother."

"Hey, has anybody thought to call up there to the ranch?" Miller ventured. "You know, just to make sure this ain't a snipe hunt? I know Shannon's this big war hero and all, but it does sound pretty far-fetched. Al Qaeda here in Montana? Come on."

"That's no harder to believe than a nuke in DC," Starks said.

"Did they find it yet?" Miller asked.

"No, but they're evacuating the city as we speak."

"Calling up to the ranch would be a good idea," Porter said. "But I don't have the number."

Miller chuckled. "That's the FBI for ya . . . Forgetful Bureau of Intimidation."

"Hey, I'm doing the best I can. The DC bureau dropped this shit in my lap an hour ago with almost no intel. They were busy scrambling their asses off to evacuate the city like everybody else."

Porter and Miller looked at each other, neither man willing to admit he didn't want to go up that foggy country road undermanned and ill equipped.

"I've been up there once before," Miller remarked. "It's open country all the way. If we go with headlights, they'll see us coming. We might end up gunned down in our cruisers."

"Yeah, and without lights," Porter added, "we might run off the road. I think we'd better call and wait for the sheriff to get his SWAT team out here. I don't want a Dade County repeat." He was referring to the 1986 fiasco in Miami in which two FBI agents had been killed in a Wild West–type shootout with a pair of very determined desperados.

Miller sat back in the seat, adjusting his creaking leather gun belt. "Well, it's your call. Like I said, I was told this operation was under federal jurisdiction."

With Starks at the wheel, the FBI's black Crown Victoria peeled out and tore off up the dirt road.

Porter whipped around to see the taillights of the unit disappearing into the fog.

"Where the fuck is that idiot going?" Miller said.

"Shit!" Porter spit in the road and stood with his hands on his hips. "He's gonna get himself killed up there."

"Yeah, well, it ain't your fault," Miller said. "You know how those people are."

Porter turned his head. "Quentin, what the fuck is that supposed to mean?"

The highway patrolman shrugged. "Nothin'. You'd better give the sheriff a call."

Porter patted his pockets for his cellular. "Perfect! I left my phone on the seat."

Miller pressed the number for the sheriff on his own phone and offered it out the window. "Hey," he said with a grin. "Be sure and tell them to bring a body bag for the Fearless Black Infiltrator." He sat behind the wheel, laughing at his own joke.

Porter put the phone to his ear and stood looking at the chortling cop. "Anybody ever tell you you're a jackass?"

62

SOUTHERN CALIFORNIA,
Edwards Air Force Base

The president and National Security Advisor Jeremy Lewkowicz were speaking privately in the briefing room at Edwards, awaiting the arrival of the cabinet, when General Couture entered the room.

"Sir, President Patrushev is on line one."

More than a little surprised, the president took the phone from the cradle. "Let's hope this isn't more bad news."

He pressed the button and said, "This is the president of the United States."

"Mr. President, how are you?" Russian president Patrushev asked in a somber voice. His English was quite good.

"Very, very busy, President Patrushev. How may I help you, sir?" It had already been made crystal clear to the Russian ambassador that the United States was extremely displeased with the Russian government for allowing not just one but two of its nuclear weapons to be stolen and smuggled onto US soil.

"I'm afraid I have bad news," Patrushev said, "and I wanted to call you about it myself."

The president stared at Couture. "I'm listening, Mr. President."

"One of our intelligence people in North Korea has verified that the North will execute a surprise attack against the South the moment it is reported there has been a nuclear detonation in Washington, DC."

The president sat down, grabbing a pen and scribbling "North K to attack S after detonation."

"How certain are you, Mr. President?"

"The source is very reliable," Patrushev said. "Your troops on the Korean Peninsula should ready themselves for war. I am calling because I want to personally assure you that we will not attempt to take advantage of the situation in any way. Nor will we condone such a move by Pyongyang."

"I appreciate that, Mr. President. Is there any chance you can talk Pyongyang out of making this move?"

"The Chinese are attempting to do so now, but I would not hold much hope. Kim Jong-un is not a stable man — as you know."

"President Patrushev, I'm sure you're already aware of this, but in case you are not, sir, our military now stands at DEF-CON One."

"Yes, I have been told."

"Then with that in mind, Mr. President, considering the grave news which you have just shared with me, are you willing to keep your navy at a safe distance in the waters around the Korean Peninsula? I ask you this, Mr. President, because there exists the very great possibility that our capital city is about to be destroyed by a nuclear weapon of Russian manufacture. The last thing I want — the last thing *either* of us wants — is for war to break out between our two nations."

Couture glanced at Lewkowicz, his eyebrows soaring. The president of the United States had — in so many words — just threatened a Russian president with nuclear war for the first time since the 1962 Cuban Missile Crisis.

There was a long moment of silence before Patrushev made his reply. "I will order all surface vessels withdrawn from the Sea of Japan until this crisis is resolved. Will that be satisfactory, Mr. President?"

"Yes, it will, sir. I am grateful for your consideration in this matter."

"Very well," said Patrushev. "I wish to you good luck in finding the device — wherever it was manufactured."

"Thank you, sir. Is there anything more I can do for you at this time, Mr. President?"

"It is *I* who will remain at *your* service, Mr. President. Please do not hesitate to call if I can be of any further assistance to you."

"Thank you, sir."

"You are welcome," Patrushev said. "Good-bye."

The president of the United States hung up the phone and looked at General Couture. "He's agreed to pull the Russian surface fleet from the Sea of Japan. What's that tell you?"

Couture didn't hesitate. "It tells me he *knows* the nukes are Russian — and he's worried a second detonation could lead to war. What about Korea?"

"The North plans to attack South Korea the minute they hear there's been a detonation in DC. Patrushev said the Chinese are trying to talk them out of it, but he doesn't expect success."

Tim Hagen came into the room. "I have news from Montana, Mr. President."

"Is Shannon's family safe?"

"Nobody knows yet, sir, but the Gulf-stream didn't divert to Creech as ordered.

It landed at a private airfield in Montana, and Shannon's team took off in a private plane."

The president was too rattled by the prospect of war on the Korean Peninsula to get worked up over Gil Shannon's whereabouts. Going to war with North Korea within minutes or hours of losing Washington, DC, would make for a logistical nightmare. Kim Jong-un may have been unstable, but his military advisors were clever. North Korea would never get a better opportunity to try to reunite the peninsula.

"Fine. Leave it alone. We'll worry about Shannon later."

"But, Mr. President —"

Couture cut him off. "I believe the president of the United States just gave you an order, Mr. Hagen. I suggest you obey it."

Hagen looked at the president, expecting support.

"Go and greet the cabinet for me when they arrive, Tim." The president sat back with a sigh and began to massage his temples. "We're very busy here at the moment."

63

MONTANA

With Oso Cazador locked in the Chatham house, Marie and Dusty saddled up a pair of horses and set out for the ranch in a thickening fog. Marie's breathing was less painful with the elastic bandage wound tightly around her rib cage, but the jouncing of the horse caused the occasional stabbing pain.

"I'd sure feel better if you headed back," Dusty said.

Marie held the reins with one hand as they rode, the other inside her jacket over her cracked rib. "I think maybe we should skirt north."

"Is the old Indian trail still there?"

"Yeah. You know about that?"

"That's how I used to get to the Fergusons when we were kids. I was a trespassin' little son of a bitch, Marie."

She laughed in spite of her pain and fear.

You never knew where you might find a friend in this world.

"I was always worried I might run across your daddy up there," he went on. "I was scared to death of that guy."

"He was a grump, but he was harmless."

They rode along through the fog, the horses puffing steam from their flaring nostrils. Marie was shivering with cold, and she was grateful for the heat of the animal between her legs.

Dusty dismounted at the northwestern border of the Chatham ranch and used a pair of side cutters to snip the barbed wire fence. "I can still remember when this fence line used to run another couple hundred yards over that-a-way." He pointed in the direction of the McGuthry ranch.

Marie smiled. "If we survive, I'll let you move it back to where it was."

He laughed and pulled the wire back out of the way so it wouldn't snare the horses' legs, and they crossed over to pick up the old Indian trail, following it through the rocks just below the foothills toward Marie's ranch.

Back at the Chatham residence, Oso quickly concluded that Marie wasn't coming back for him anytime soon. The scent of the house and the man who lived in it were foreign to him, and he was growing increasingly anxious about being alone in the foreign environment. Already missing the familiar comfort of his leather chair, he decided that it was time to leave and got up from the floor near the back door to hunt for a way out.

He caught the scent of fresh air coming from the back hall and followed it to the source at the end of the corridor, where the door to the laundry room stood ajar. He nosed his way inside and stood in the dark, listening. A distant flash of lightning illuminated a half-open window above the washing machine. The screen was down, but that didn't concern him. He had learned young there wasn't a screen window or door on earth that could keep him in if he really wanted out. It hadn't taken Marie or Gil very long to learn that frustrating little fact of life either.

He jumped onto the washing machine and, with his head, pressed against the screen until it bowed outward. Then he gave it a shove, and the screen tore away from the old wooden frame. After that, it was just a matter of shouldering up the sash and leaping out into the fog. He put his nose into the air, but Marie's scent was undetectable in the mist. That didn't matter. He knew his way home.

64

Special Agent Spencer Starks was not looking to become a hero. Far from it. To begin with, most heroes wound up dead, and he had no intention of concluding his FBI career as the thirty-seventh Service Martyr in the Hall of Honor. On the other hand, he believed fully in the old dogface axiom that had been drilled into his head during basic training: "Do *something* — even if it's wrong!"

And those dudes back at the crossroads didn't have the slightest clue. That didn't make them bad guys, it just made them the wrong guys for the job, and it was probably a good thing they knew it. The problem for Starks was that even if he wasn't exactly the *right* guy for the job, he wasn't exactly the *wrong* guy, either, and he couldn't just stand around back there listening to their hemming and hawing while people were fighting for their lives five miles up the road.

Sure, he might get there too late to do any good, but somebody had to try, and since he was the only combat vet on the scene, the responsibility fell to him.

At least, that's how he saw it.

Starks was making pretty good time driving through the fog with the parking lights on, and according to the odometer, he was almost at the ranch. He was glad for the fog, thinking it might allow him to approach the scene without drawing fire. The main gate appeared out of the mist, and he pulled the car to the side of the road, killing the lights and the engine. He dismounted with a pair of Heckler & Koch MP5 submachine guns, one slung around his back, and the other in his hands with the stock extended.

The night was dead quiet, and he couldn't see more than five feet in any direction. Missing the protection of an Abrams tank and its Chobham armor, he knew that to continue directly up the dirt road would be unwise, so he took the iPhone from his pocket and checked to make sure that the compass app was functioning correctly. The agent took a bearing and left the road moving east, hoping the house would be more or less directly north of the main gate.

His load-out consisted of six magazines for the machine guns and three mags for his laser-sighted Sig Sauer .40 caliber pistol. He promised himself that he would withdraw if he lived long enough to run out of machine gun ammo. If he couldn't get the job done with ninety machine gun rounds, he wasn't likely going to turn the tide of battle with a pistol.

He came to a barbed wire fence and followed it north. Suddenly Starks stumbled over a dead body. Crouching down to examine it in the dim blue glow of his iPhone screen, the first thing he noticed was a vicious bite wound to the back of the neck.

"Looks like a Montana werewolf got your ass." He rolled the body onto its back and noted immediately the Arab features of the face. "Welcome to America, asshole." Starks peeled the night vision goggles off the dead man's head and was about to move out, when he heard someone trotting toward him in the fog.

He slid to his belly, resting his thumb on the laser button of the MP5.

A figure appeared out of the fog gripping an AK-47. Starks's laser sight appeared green in the night vision. He fired a six-round burst, and the man flew backward off his feet.

Starks jumped up and pounced on the body, bashing in the face with the stock of the MP5, as he had been trained to do as a soldier. Quickly stripping the body of the rifle and ammo pouch, he slung the MP5 and moved forward with the AK-47, feeling suddenly invincible as he muttered his uncle Steve's old catchphrase from an all but forgotten war: "Charlie owns the night — but we're taking it away from him."

65

Flanked by a pair of security officers, CIA Director of Operations George Shroyer and Deputy Director Cletus Webb walked into the computer lab, where Pope was still sifting through the data he had pulled from Kashkin's hard drive.

Pope looked up from his computer and smiled. "Have you come to revoke my clearances, George?"

Shroyer shook his head. "No, not yet." He signaled the two security men to wait outside in the hallway. "But that's coming. I just spoke with the president. He's grateful for what you've done to help us track the bomb to DC, but he's decided the time has come for you to think about retiring from government service. The reason we're here is to begin your debrief."

Pope glanced at the clock on the wall. "Debrief at two o'clock in the morning,

George?"

"Well, frankly, Bob, we're all a little nervous about what else you might be up to."

Pope looked at Webb and smiled. "Are you nervous, Cletus?"

Webb shook his head, returning the smile. "No, Bob. I'm your biggest fan, but the president is right. You've taken things too far; you've become a loose cannon."

"The loose-cannon metaphor implies that I'm equally dangerous to both sides, and that's not true."

"You're right. Poor choice of words."

Shroyer cleared his throat. "DOD is moving the ISIS machine into downtown DC as we speak. It'll begin sweeping the city within the hour. So we're very confident."

The ISIS was the Integrated Standoff Inspection System specifically designed to detect SNM (special nuclear material, such as plutonium and certain types of uranium) at a distance. The multimillion-dollar machine was enclosed within a fifty-three-foot trailer towed behind a semi-tractor. It worked by aiming gamma rays at containers suspected of holding SNM. These rays of high-energy photons penetrated the suspect container and excited the radioactive particles within the nuclear material by inducing a reaction called photofission. The result was a burst of high-energy particles that could be detected by the ISIS up to a hundred meters away. However, the machine's primary application was scanning shipping containers from overseas.

"The ISIS is a good machine," Pope said, "but it's untested in this type of application. It wasn't designed to search a cityscape for shielded weapons."

"DTRA says it can do the job," Shroyer said. DTRA was the Defense Threat Reduction Agency, under the egis of the Department of Defense.

Pope crossed his arms. "I guess we'll see. It is all we've got."

"The president wants you to explain to me exactly what you meant when you told him you'd gained access to the Chinese Ministry of State Security."

Pope rocked back. "That information is for the president's ear."

"In this instance, he and I are the same person. We can call him if you think I'm making that up."

Pope knew the time had come to play his final ace. "Over the last few years, I've allowed Lijuan to share sensitive material with the Chinese; nothing that would give them a technical advantage but enough to make them confident in the material and to keep them coming back to her for more."

"What *kind* of sensitive material?"

"Communications software, passcodes, access to a CIA mainframe here and there."

"Are you out of your fucking mind?" Shroyer flared. "That's high treason!"

Pope looked back and forth between them and smiled. "Try proving that, George."

"What?"

"I said try proving it. You'll never even figure out what information was shared, much less how it was done."

"Oh, no? We'll just see what Lijuan Chow has to say about that. She's being held as a terrorist. Did you know that? Her life in prison can be particularly miserable."

Pope felt sick to his stomach. "When was the last time anyone spoke with Lijuan? Is she under constant observation? Or is she alone in a cell?"

"What does that mean?"

Pope shrugged. "It's just a question."

Shroyer looked at Webb. "Call the detention center and make sure she's being kept under observation."

Webb left the room.

Shroyer turned on Pope, pointing a finger. "You're going to wind up in prison right alongside her if you don't watch your step.

Do you realize that?"

Pope shook his head. "No, George. I'm going stay right where I am, and I'm going to keep right on helping defend this country — just as I have for the last ten years."

Shroyer shook his head. "You've lost your damn mind. Do you really think that box of secret files you have is going to save you?"

Pope stared at him for a long, unnerving moment. "Have you ever seen any secret files, George? Have you ever even heard of me threatening anybody with one? Or have you heard all of the same innuendos as everyone else?"

Shroyer blinked.

"I'm going to stay right where I am because I've given this agency access to the Chinese Guojia Anquan Bu mainframe. That means we can read their mail now, George, and we can read it in real time. Hell, I'm more likely to end up with *your* job than I am to end up in prison."

Shroyer knew that if Pope was telling the truth, the president would have no choice but to keep him around. The country couldn't afford to lose his knowledge of the Chinese intelligence network. "How in hell did you manage it?"

"I allowed the Chinese to *steal* a communications program they thought was designed for one of our own defense systems. Lijuan passed it on to them, having no idea that I'd written the program specifically for the Chinese — or that I'd written in a very complicated series of back doors."

"They'll eventually find them and take them out — or discard the program altogether."

Pope shook his head. "They didn't even examine the programming; they put it directly into service. They stopped being suspicious of Lijuan's material a long time ago because I kept it so pristine. I had to give up some very valuable information to gain that kind of confidence, but in the end it's going to be worth it."

Shroyer gaped at him. "It's you! *You're* the one who's been leaking intel to the Chinese these past ten years."

"Again," Pope said, "try proving it."

Webb returned. "Lijuan was found dead in her bunk half an hour ago. The doctor at the detention center thinks it was cyanide."

Appearing suddenly ill, Pope removed his glasses and leaned forward to rest his elbows on the desk.

Webb look at him with more empathy than anger. "Did you know, Bob?"

Pope massaged the bridge of his nose. "I had a very strong suspicion."

"And you didn't think to warn us?" Shroyer asked accusatorily.

Pope ignored him.

"I asked you a question, Robert."

Pope's response was eerily soft. "It was necessary for her to die . . . this way, she can't ever be interrogated, and the Chinese will remain confident in the integrity of the information she passed on to them — all in accordance with my original plan."

"Jesus, you're a ruthless bastard," Shroyer muttered.

Pope looked at him. "Do you know China's greatest advantage over the rest of the world? Aside from their massive population."

Shroyer stared.

"It's their patience, George. They are an infinitely patient people. And patience is the very bedrock of wisdom. They're looking to take over the world, and it doesn't matter to them if it takes another hundred years. Their sole weakness is their intellectual arrogance, and that's what I took advantage of. I took advantage of it by making a deal with the devil in exchange for my soul, and I did it because something had to be done to buy this nation time."

"Time for what?"

"Time to realize that we've grown lazy . . .

that laziness is a prelude to weakness . . . and that we need to make some fundamental changes to the way things are run."

66

MONTANA,
Gil's Ranch

Hal was peering out the upstairs window when a group of armed men suddenly materialized out of the fog, rushing the house with AK-47s. "Here they come!"

He opened fire through the window, and they scattered in the mist.

"They're flanking the house!"

"Got 'em!" Buck opened fire from the master bedroom.

A hail of 7.62 mm bullets tore through the house like micrometeorites, shattering windows, lamps, dishes, and mirrors.

Janet covered her head with her arms, pulling herself into the tub as tightly as she could while chunks of plaster and tile rained down, the occasional round ricocheting off the cast iron surrounding her.

A short while before, they'd heard the burst from Agent Starks's MP5 and been left to assume that Marie had been caught out and killed, their hopes of rescue crushed and Janet left without a great deal to live for.

Hal dove to the floor as a hail of automatic fire tore apart the wall, belly crawling down the hall to meet Buck in the doorway to the master bedroom.

"They'll be in the house any second," the older man said.

Hal offered his hand to his father. "It's been an honor, Dad."

Buck grabbed his hand. "I couldn't be prouder of any of you. We'll stay shoulder to shoulder. Take as many of these godless sons a bitches with us as we can."

They crawled toward the top of the stairs to arrive at the landing just as the front door was kicked in. They opened fire and killed a gunman in the doorway. The rest pulled back.

From his hiding place behind the horse trailer fifty yards from the front porch, Agent Starks could see and hear the muzzle flashes from numerous automatic rifles. He couldn't see anyone clear enough to be sure if it was friend or foe, but he knew the chatter of an AK-47 and decided that it was better to do *something* rather than nothing.

He opened fire on one of the muzzle flashes near the porch with the captured AK-47, and the gunner went down screaming, his legs shot apart. One of the others returned Starks's fire, and bullets struck the horse trailer near enough to his head that bits of spall tore into his face. He displaced rapidly, falling back to an old stone well to the west of the house. The night vision goggles he'd taken from the dead guy weren't doing him much good in the fog, so he assumed that the enemy probably couldn't see him any better than he could see them.

The horse trailer continued to take fire for a short time, and the man he'd shot began screaming in a mixture of Arabic and English for the others to help him. The firing trailed off, and the enemy fell back from the house into the mist, shouting back and forth, obviously confused to have taken fire from outside the house.

Taking a chance, Starks broke cover around the far west side of the house. He put his back to a large propane tank and lowered himself into a crouch. The stone well came under fire a few seconds later, and he rose up to peek in through the window, noticing a three-inch gap below the sash. He stuck the muzzle of the AK-47 beneath it and pushed it up, calling inside, "FBI! Anybody alive in there?"

"Whattaya make of that?" Buck whispered.

"Somebody shot that haji out there on the porch, and it wasn't us," Hal said.

"Yeah!" Buck shouted down. "We're alive!"

"Am I clear to come inside?" Starks shouted.

"Come ahead! We're upstairs!"

They listened as Starks clamored in through the window and bounded across the living room, having no trouble finding his way to the staircase with the night vision goggles. He trotted up the stairs and took a knee between the two prone men.

"Agent Spencer Starks." He offered his hand. "FBI."

"Buck Ferguson, First Marines. This is my oldest son, Hal. How many are you?"

"Just me." Starks got down on his belly between them. "It's a cluster fuck down at the crossroads. There'll be more cops, but probably not until first light."

"Don't they know we're takin' fire up here?"

"They might by now, but that Highway Patrol commander won't budge before it gets light."

Buck groaned. "Gotta be Quentin Miller."

"One in the same," Starks said with chuckle.

"My boys went to school with that jackass. He's worthless as tits on a boar hog."

"And about as smart!" Janet called from the bathtub.

Everyone laughed.

"What's it look like out there?" Hal asked.

"Right now, I think they're pretty confused." Starks shrugged the MP5s from his back. "They're trying to figure out who was shooting at them from outside."

"Did you see any other Americans out there?" Buck said. "A woman or a couple of men in their twenties?"

Starks shook his head. "All I saw up close was a dead haji down near the gate with his neck torn out — looked like he'd been killed by a werewolf."

"Had to be Oso. Maybe Marie made it after all."

"Marie Shannon?"

"Yeah, she made a break for the Chatham place about an hour and a half ago. We stayed behind to look after her mama. Janet got herself a pretty bad concussion when those Jeezless bastards tried blowin' up the house."

"I don't know if you heard," Starks said, "but they've tracked the nuke to DC. It's caused a hell of a lot of confusion in the Bureau's command structure."

A window shattered downstairs, and a few seconds later, they could see flames spreading across the living room floor.

"Fucking hajis!" Hal hissed, jumping to his feet and starting down the stairs.

"Hal, get your ass back up here!"

"Dad, we gotta fight that fire!"

"And get your ass shot off, boy? That's exactly what the hell they want. Now, get up here. I already lost two sons!"

Hal came back up, and Buck slipped into the bathroom. "I'm sorry, Jan, but you're gonna have to get outta the tub. They lit the house, honey."

"Fine by me," she grumbled, gripping the edge of the tub to pull herself up. "I've kindly had enough of this layin' around. Where's my Winchester?"

"Right here by the sink," he said, helping her out. "But stay down on the floor. We got smoke comin' up the steps."

Buck grabbed the edge of the claw-footed bathtub, jerking it away from the plumbing coming up from the floor, and water began spraying into the room. He smashed the commode away from the wall, and water gushed from the line onto the wood floor. Lastly, he jerked the sink from the wall, and within a minute, a steady flow of water was running from the bathroom into the hall and down the stairs.

"Good thinking," Starks said.

Another hail of gunfire showered through the walls, driving everyone belly down on the wet floor.

"I don't think they can afford to keep that up," Starks said. "The haji I took this rifle from only had two extra magazines."

"Assassins on a budget," Janet said bitterly.

Buck chortled.

"Are we gonna make a break for it or not?" she asked. "I don't much fancy layin' here in the water until that fire works its way up the wall and steams us to death." She took Starks by the hand, saying in a low voice, "God bless you for comin' to help us."

"It's my job, ma'am."

"All the same, son. Welcome to the family. You're a McGuthry now."

67

Akram stood with Abad and a number of other men watching the house catch fire.

"They'll be coming out soon," Abad said. "Do you want them alive? We can shoot them in the legs if they won't surrender." They could still hear the man calling out from the front porch where Agent Starks had shot him down. "He's going to burn up if we leave him there. He's too close to the house."

"Go and get him if you like."

Abad wasn't about to risk his neck. "You know, I don't think Shannon is here," he heard himself say.

Akram looked at him askance. "What are you talking about?"

"Too many of us are still alive. I think we've been tricked somehow."

Akram dismissed this out of hand. "That

451

makes no sense."

Abad shrugged. "You're the expert."

Marie and Dusty reined their horses to a halt on the easternmost side of the ranch, seeing the orange glow of the house fire through the fog.

"My God!" she said. "They lit the house!" She dug her heels into the flanks of the horse and took off through the mist.

Dusty quickly caught her up, diving from his saddle to grab her horse by the bridle and bring it to an abrupt stop. "We can't go ridin' in there like a pair of wild Indians, Marie! You wanna get killed?"

"My mother's in there!"

"You don't know that. Anything coulda happened by now. We gotta do this smart, or we could end up dead."

She reached beneath her jacket and drew the Springfield .45. "You're right," she said. "I didn't think. We'll do it smart."

"Okay then." He released his grip on the bridle, and when he turned for his horse, she dug her heels in again and galloped off.

"Son of a bitch!" he hissed, jumping into the saddle and shucking the .30-06 from the saddle scabbard. "Why can't women ever listen to reason?"

He took off after her, galloping the horse

carefully through the dark, waiting for it to stumble or break a leg. Marie quickly drew out of sight, and when he couldn't hear the galloping of her horse over his own, he reined to a stop and sat in the saddle, as unsure of himself as he had ever been.

Wild gunfire broke out in the direction of the house, and though it was too far off for it to have anything to do with Marie, it was more than enough to emphasize the gravity of the situation.

"Damn," Dusty whispered, feeling the fear well up in his gut. He flicked the reins to start the horse walking. "Come on, Shiloh. I don't reckon we can turn back now."

Akram and three other men stood covering Buck Ferguson and Agent Starks as the two stepped out onto the front porch with their hands in the air.

"Don't shoot!" Buck shouted. Glancing down at the man on the porch who had recently bled out, he stood just behind and to the left of Starks. "We give up!"

Akram watched them through Duke's infrared binocular. "Where is Shannon?"

"He's upstairs with a bullet in his head," Buck said. "You killed him in that last salvo of yours. We're all that's left."

"Go in and check it out," Akram said to

one of his men.

The man looked at him in alarm. "But the house is on fire!"

"Check it out!" Akram screamed.

Buck dropped his hands, jerking the Sig Sauer pistol from the small of Starks's back. At the same time, Starks brought up one of the MP5s, and they both opened fire as they danced away down the length of the porch.

One of Akram's men went down. As for the others, half of them fired wildly at Buck and Starks, while half ducked for cover. The two men jumped off the far end of the porch and disappeared from sight.

"After them!" Akram screamed, and five men chased them into the fog.

Around the back of the house, Abad heard the firing, but he ordered his group to hold their positions. The house wasn't fully engulfed yet, and he couldn't risk anyone escaping out the back. The heat from the fire on the west side had driven the fog back some twenty feet from the house, so they could see pretty well.

He heard a rumbling sound behind him and whipped around just in time to be trampled beneath a charging quarter horse. He fumbled to get up, but a hoof whacked him in the side of the head to sprawl him out.

His men were still jumping for space as Marie reined the horse hard around and shot one of them in the back with the .45, expertly backing the animal to trample Abad a second time, crushing his chest. She fired two more shots, hitting another man before someone cut loose with a burst of automatic fire, killing the horse beneath her.

She rolled clear as the horse crumpled to the ground, causing her to lose her grip on the pistol.

A giant of a man grabbed her by the hair and jerked her to her feet. He was drawing back his arm to punch her in the face when Hal burst out the back door to blow him away.

Marie snatched up the pistol and ran onto the deck, grabbing Janet as she came stumbling out the door, her hair and clothing badly singed and smoking. Hal leapt off the end of the deck, caving in a man's skull with the barrel of the MP5. A burst of fire from his left dropped Janet to her knees, a single bullet through both buttocks. Hal wheeled and shot the man through his guts, charging forward to sprawl him out with the stock of the submachine gun. He took a bullet through the back, however, and spun to return fire, downing his attacker before going down himself.

Marie saw him collapse and disappeared with Janet around the western end of the house.

Out front, Buck and Starks had taken cover behind the stone well, where they were now pinned down and exchanging fire with the enemy.

"This doesn't look too good," Starks said. "Is there any place behind us we can fall back to?"

"Nope." Buck popped up to squeeze off a shot in the direction of the last muzzle flash. "Nothing but open country for two hundred yards until you reach the tree line. Why don't you try getting away in the fog? I gotta stay here and keep these bastards busy to buy time for Hal and Janet."

Starks squeezed off a few more rounds. "We don't know if they even made it out of the house."

Buck fired again. "Ain't that the bitch of it?"

"How deep is this well?"

"About ten feet — been dry for years. Why?"

"Oh, I dunno," Starks said. "I figure we can jump down it when we run outta ammo; save everybody the trouble of diggin' us a grave."

They heard Marie behind them in the fog, urging her mother not to give up.

"Marie, over here!" Buck hissed. "At the well!"

The women came out of the fog, and both of them collapsed to the ground. "Oh, thank God!" Marie said.

"Where's Hal?" Buck asked.

Marie put her hand on his arm. "I'm sorry, Buck. I'm so sorry."

He put a hand to her face, dying a thousand deaths inside. "It's not your fault," he said starkly. "Come on now. We're gonna lower you girls down the well. Then me and Starks here are gonna draw these sons a bitches away."

Marie looked at Agent Starks. "Who are you?"

"FBI, Mrs. Shannon."

"Thank you for coming." She took his hand.

"He's a fine man," Janet mumbled, struggling to remain conscious.

The enemy opened fire, and Starks answered it with a burst from the MP5. "Not much time left. We'd best get you two down the well."

"No." Marie shook her head.

"Marie, don't argue." Buck's voice was peremptory as he fought to control his emotions. "If you girls don't survive this, then my boys died for nothin'. Now you're goin' down the well so we can lead these bastards the hell outta here." He set the pistol down on the ground. "Okay, you first, honey, so you can catch your mama. Hurry up, now!"

That's when the propane cylinder on the western side of the house exploded in a giant fireball, burning back the fog to bathe them all in a brilliant flash of light and driving them flat against the earth with their arms shielding their heads.

68

IN THE SKY OVER GIL'S RANCH
Trussed up in his jump gear, Jack Frost
ambled down the aisle to the back of the
plane, where Gil stood poised to be the first
man out the open door. "We're approach-
ing the DZ!" he shouted into Gil's ear. "The
fog down there makes it tough to see, but it
looks like the house is on fire."

"On fire?"

"You wanna do a flyby before we jump?"

"Fuck no!" Gil shouted, glancing up to
make sure the jump light was still red. "I
gotta get down there!"

"Roger that! I'll let them know up front.
I'm the last man out the door, so I'll see
you on the ground!"

A minute later, the plane banked gently to
the northwest, giving Gil a heart-stopping
view of his home, which was now completely
engulfed in flames. Ten seconds after that,
the green light came on, and he threw

himself out the door, with the rest of the team following right behind. They couldn't wait more than a few seconds apiece to deploy their chutes because they were already jumping below five thousand feet. And there was too much fog below to visually time their descent even with the infrared goggles, which provided almost no depth perception even under the best of circumstances.

69

With the house a roaring inferno, Buck found himself staring straight up the muzzle of an AK-47. Agent Starks was flat on his back, out cold with a huge goose egg on his forehead where he'd been struck with a rifle butt. Janet lay unconscious in the lee of the well, and Marie was on her knees with Akram's knife to her throat.

"Where is Gil Shannon?" Akram shouted at Buck. "I'll cut off her head!"

"He's not here!" Buck was enraged and ready to hurl himself at the man covering him with the rifle. "He's with the government, looking for your goddamn bomb! Now let her go before I rip off your head and shit down your neck!" He got to his feet, and the Al Qaeda fighter screamed for him to get back on his knees.

"Go fuck yourself, heathen!"

461

"Buck, don't!" pled Marie. "Don't give them a reason to kill you!"

"I'm sorry, honey, but we're as good as dead." He looked at Akram. "Ain't that right, you filthy cocksucker?"

Akram recognized the rabid look in Buck's eyes. They were the eyes of a man unhinged. "Shoot him," he said in Arabic.

The gunman fired his AK-47 directly into Buck's chest, and the old Marine flew backward, dead before he hit the ground.

Marie screamed, and Akram hauled her to her feet by her hair, pressing the blade of the knife into the flesh alongside her nose. "Now tell me where your husband is."

"I don't know," she wept. "You cut the phone lines; I couldn't reach him."

"Who killed Kashkin . . . the first man to come here?"

"I did."

He jerked her hair, twisting her head around and hurting her. "You're lying!"

"I'm not!" she spat in defiance, her anger suddenly overtaking her fear. "I shot the bastard twice from the bedroom window. Then I burned his body right over there!" She pointed toward the pyre.

Akram saw by the blazing fury in her eyes that she spoke the truth and slapped her to the ground. "You're going to be very sorry your husband was not here."

"Go to hell!" She crawled around the well to check her mother.

Akram conferred with the man who had taken Abad's place as second in command. "How many men are left?"

"There are thirteen of us."

"Get them ready to go. We're leaving the same way we came in — and we're taking these three with us."

The man turned, shouting orders for an organized departure.

Then Akram heard an airplane engine overhead and pulled on Duke's infrared binocular for a look up through the foggy overcast. He saw what he recognized as an old C-47 and scanned the binocular back along its line of flight to see parachutes opening in the sky over the northeastern corner of the ranch.

"Paratroops!" he shouted in Arabic, pointing up. "Kill them before they get to the ground — *move!*"

The men rallied quickly, gathering up any extra ammo they could find and running out to meet the enemy without really knowing exactly where he was going to land.

Akram waited until they were well away before slinging the TAC-50 around his back and snatching Marie up by her hair again.

She fought him, so he shoved her back to the ground and unslung the rifle, putting the muzzle of the TAC-50 to her mother's head.

"No!"

"Then do exactly as I say!"

She submitted, and Akram used one of Starks's bootlaces to bind her hands tightly behind her back. Then he shoved her out in front of him toward the west, and the two of them moved away briskly, with Marie none the wiser about the parachutes descending over the ranch.

Once they were clear of the light from the fire, he spun her around and gave her a short jab to the abdomen, dropping her to her knees. He pushed her over onto the ground and jerked her pants down, cutting off her underwear with the knife and stuffing them into her mouth. He then tore a sleeve from her shirt and tied it tightly around her head to keep them in place.

"Now get up!" He pulled her pants back up and kicked her in the butt to get her moving again. "Remember . . . I stab you in the stomach the first time you make a sound."

70

MONTANA,
Gil's Ranch

The SEALs were taking fire before they even made it to the ground. Gil felt rounds ripping into his armor as he landed firmly with both feet together, hitting the release on the jump harness, and then hitting the deck to lay down a horizontal arc fire from his M4, forcing the heat signatures across his field of vision to stop firing and seek cover. This bought the rest of his team members valuable time in the moments before they touched down. The sight of a lifeless body impacting the ground to Gil's left, however, told him that one of his men was already dead.

He switched out the magazine and began trading fire with the enemy as they were taking cover behind water troughs, wood piles, horse trailers, and corral posts. The SEALs were shouting back and forth, sorting themselves out and preparing to move forward.

Jack Frost crawled up beside Gil. "Take any lead on the way in?"

"Don't think so. You?"

"Lost most of my foot." Frost fired the rest of the magazine and pulled another magazine from his harness.

A quick glance, and Gil saw that, indeed, much of Frost's left foot was gone from the instep forward. "The only easy day was yesterday," he said, firing a burst and putting a man down as he broke from the stable toward the water trough. "One of my men is dead yonder."

"I saw him hit," Frost said. "Couldn't tell who it was."

Crosswhite scrambled up on Gil's left and hit the dirt. "Gil, why don't you make a break and flank these sorry cocksuckers to the west? Go find Marie and let us reduce these guys. It's obvious they don't have infrared."

The team was formed up now and laying down lethal grazing fire, pinning the enemy and maneuvering forward aggressively for the kill.

Gil detached from the M4 and unslung the Remington MSR, peering through the nightscope to place the reticule on the face

466

of a man firing at their muzzle flashes from the loft above the stable. He squeezed the trigger, and the .308 Lapua Naturalis round struck the man to the left of the nose, mushrooming perfectly within the brain box to blow the head almost completely apart. An instant later, Gil was up and sprinting for the house over open terrain. It was during this sprint that he realized he was missing the little toe from his right foot along with part of the metatarsal bone, requiring him to roll the foot inward as he ran and giving him a slight limp.

Even with his damaged foot, he managed to quickly cover the hundred yards to the house, emerging from the fog to see that it was fully engulfed. The eastern half of the roof collapsed inward, and thousands of sparks shot skyward. A dead horse and a number of bodies littered the back lawn. No one inside the house could possibly be alive, so he ran around front, where he nearly shot Dusty Chatham standing beside his horse with a Browning hunting rifle slung over his shoulder. Dusty's face was gleaming with sweat.

"Jesus! Is that you, Gil?"

"Dusty! Where's Marie?"

Dusty shrugged, looking slightly ashamed. "I dunno. I just got here. Buck Ferguson's dead, and Janet's been shot in her hiney." He pointed toward where they lay, just beyond the firelight. "She's over there with some FBI guy; he's pretty bad off too."

Gil found his mother-in-law unconscious, her pulse weak. The sight of Buck Ferguson's body filled him with a nauseating sensation of dread. Agent Starks was semiconscious, but he was so badly concussed that he could only mumble confused responses to Gil's urgent questions.

"Who's doin' all the shooting yonder?" Dusty asked. "That the cavalry?"

"Yeah, a day late and a dollar short," Gil muttered, disgusted with himself and terrified for his wife. "Is it possible Marie's in the house, Dusty?"

Dusty looked at the house and then back at Gil. "I don't know, Gil. I don't think so, but I don't know. The house was already burning when we crested the rise."

"Marie!" Gil shouted, looking helplessly around. "Marie! . . . *Marieee!*" He turned on Dusty. "Where was the last place you saw her?"

"Just over the rise." Dusty pointed back toward his ranch. "She bolted on ahead of me. I'm sorry, Gil, I froze up . . . I was afraid to follow her with all the shooting."

"Did she ride in on the dead horse out back?"

Dusty nodded.

Gil ran back around the house to double-check the bodies, finding Hal Ferguson struggling to get to his feet, coughing blood and bleeding from a hole through the left side of his chest.

"Hal!"

Hal saw him and fell back to the ground. "Christ, am I glad to see you."

Gil took a knee and rolled the wounded man onto his bad side to keep the blood from draining into the good lung. "Have you seen Marie?"

"Not since I got hit," Hal grunted. "You shoulda seen her, Gil. Christ, she was blazing away with a .45 like a cavalryman."

"Hal, I can't find her. Was she hit?"

"I dunno. Last I saw her, she was running off with Janet."

This gave Gil hope. "Okay, Marine. Hold on." He took Hal by the arm and hefted him up over his shoulder.

"My dad's dead, ain't he?"

"Yeah," Gil grunted, his foot hurting like hell under the added weight.

He carried the wounded Marine around to the front of the house, putting him down beside Buck's body. "I'm sorry I got your family involved in this, Hal."

Hal pulled himself up alongside his father, seeing the bullet holes in his chest, the calmness of his death mask. He looked up at Gil with tears rolling down his cheeks. "We're Marines, Gil. My family's been involved in this shit since Guadalcanal." He wiped his face with bloody fingers and shook off the dread, knowing that Gil didn't yet realize his younger brothers were very likely dead as well. "Better go find your wife now. Don't let all this be for nothin'."

Gil lifted Janet's legs, resting her feet on the edge of the well to help keep the blood flowing to her vital organs, where she needed it most. Then he looked at Dusty. "My team will be here soon. Keep Hal on his wounded side so he doesn't bleed into the good lung."

Dusty nodded. "Gil, I'm sorry about —"

"Don't apologize." Gil put a hand on his shoulder. "You showed up, and that means a lot." With that, he moved out toward the stable where his men were dragging an enemy survivor out of the main door by his heels.

The survivor was shot in the hip and couldn't walk. "Just shoot me," he said in American English. "I've said my prayers."

Gil ignored him for the moment, turning

470

to Alpha. "Who bought it on the way down?"

"Clancy," Alpha said. "Took one in the head."

Gil turned back around to step on the Al Qaeda man's fractured pelvis, causing him to howl. "Why is your English so fuckin' good?" He took his foot off the wound so the man could answer.

"Because I'm an American!" the Al Qaeda man gasped. "And you're a —"

Gil stepped on him again. "Where's my wife?"

The man gritted his teeth in agony, sneering. "Go fuck yourself!"

Gil stomped on the hip, breaking the fractured pelvis apart with a sickening crunch. "I said, *Where the fuck is my wife?*"

The Al Qaeda man screamed in furious agony. "Go fuck your mother!"

Gil lifted his bloody foot and stepped back. "He's not gonna talk."

Crosswhite drew his knife. "I'll make the man talk."

Gil shook his head. "Not this one."

"Then he's dead."

"No. We'll let the FBI have him. Did you clear the stable?"

"We did. She's not in there, Gil."

One of the SEALs pointed toward the

471

well, where Oso was sniffing the unconscious Janet. "That your dog, Chief?"

Gil turned. "Sure as hell is." He cupped his hands around his mouth and whistled. The dog froze and looked toward the stable, spotted Gil, and came running.

Gil ducked inside and reemerged with one of Marie's Carhartts. He held the jacket to the dog's snout. "Where's Mama? Find your mama now!"

The dog ran back to the well, with Gil hot on his heels. He put his nose to the ground and began moving in a zigzag pattern toward the northwest. After forty or fifty seconds of sniffing, he stopped and looked back at Gil, barking once to let him know he'd picked up the scent.

Gil turned to Dusty. "Can I borrow your horse?"

Dusty handed him the reins. "He's all yours."

Gil mounted up, looking down at Crosswhite. "Secure the area as best you can, then pull yourselves into a defensive perimeter. Get Pope on the horn and bring him up to speed on everything that's happened. Tell him it's safe to get the FBI in here. I'm going after Marie."

"Sure you want to do that alone?"

"Got no choice. You boys can't ride, and

you'll never keep up on foot." He looked down at all of them, saying, "I can't ever repay what you men have done." Then he reined the stallion around and dug in his heels. "Oso, find your mama!"

The dog took off, and Gil galloped after him.

Crosswhite and the others watched them go.

"What's he gonna find out there?" Alpha wondered aloud.

Crosswhite shook his head and shouted, "Doc!" at the corpsman who was busy tending to the wounded Al Qaeda fighter near the entrance to the stable. "Leave that fucker alone for now. There's three of our people over here who need help!"

71

MONTANA

Holding another human being dead to rights in the crosshairs can fill a sniper with an undeniable sense of invincibility. Akram had never before experienced that feeling of power, and as he watched the thermal image of Gil making his way up the slope on the back of the horse, the Remington sniper rifle resting butt down on his thigh, his face cracked into a smirk. For almost a year now, he had planned for Shannon's death, and Allah had at last seen fit to grant him the privilege of killing the American at his own game.

He knocked Marie to the ground with the butt of the TAC-50 and took a knee behind a granite boulder, placing the reticule on Gil's chest at one hundred yards. He fingered the heavy trigger, drawing a shallow breath as he began to gently squeeze, awaiting the surprise of the rifle's report.

Marie had listened to the gunfight back at the ranch as Akram dragged her up the slope through the rocks, wondering who had arrived to help and where they had come from. She knew that her mother would soon die without medical attention, and she was hard pressed to fight off an encroaching feeling of despair as Akram took her farther and farther away. The firing had died off fifteen minutes ago, leaving her to guess at the outcome of the battle below, but whatever the situation was back on the ranch, one thing was obvious: her captor was about to blow somebody out of his socks — and she was damned if she was going to just lie there on the ground like a half-wit and watch him do it.

She kicked out with both feet, catching Akram on the hip with the heels of her boots. The big rifle went off, and he whipped around angrily, snarling, "Stupid bitch!" and stomping her shin with a combat boot. He swung the rifle back down the slope, quickly working the bolt and squeezing off another shot.

"Yes!" he hissed in English, working the bolt again to squeeze off a third a shot. Then he jumped to his feet, holding the rifle high over his head in triumph.

"*Allahu Akbaaaaaar!*" he shouted at the

heavens. *"Allahu Akbaaaar!"* God is great!"

He turned and stepped on the side of Marie's face. "Your murdering husband's brains are in the dirt, and his soul is burning in hell!" He ejected the spent casing and rammed another round into the battery. "Allah is indeed merciful! His greatness cannot be questioned!"

Marie felt the life running out of her, her will to fight slipping away. How could Gil be dead? It didn't seem possible.

With what felt like the strength of ten men, Akram snatched her up by the hair again, putting his face close enough to hers that she could smell the stink of his coffee breath. "I have defeated your husband." He shoved her forward contemptuously. "When we reach the truck, I will take you as a man takes the woman of his enemy, and my victory will be complete. If we were in my homeland, you would become one of my wives, and you would bear my children to the glory of God."

She struggled to breathe with her panties stuffed in her mouth, stumbling numbly forward through the dark, her wrists bound so tightly behind her back that she no longer had feeling in her hands.

Akram chuckled, unable to suppress his overwhelming happiness. To be victorious

476

— to enslave the women of your enemies — was a glorious prize granted by Allah in exchange for doing his will on earth. He had read of such glory and had dreamt of it many times as a boy, but he had never truly believed it possible. The West had kept the East in a stranglehold for centuries with its superior technologies, but now times were rapidly changing — for the everlasting glory of Allah.

"I would take you here and now," he said, feeling his ardor beginning to build, "but it's too dark to see what I'm doing." He chuckled again, obnoxiously.

Marie whipped around and kicked him, burying the toe of her cowboy boot firmly in his groin.

Every star in the universe seemed to explode before Akram's eyes. He dropped the TAC-50 to grab himself between the legs with both hands, letting out a veritable squeal of pain as he collapsed to the ground.

Unable to see how badly he was hurt, Marie turned and ran as fast as she could through the fog, her cracked rib making it impossible to draw more than the shallowest of breaths through her nose as she careened down the dark slope, her feet quickly getting away from her. She tripped over a nub of granite in the narrow trail, pitching forward off her feet with no way to break her fall and struck the side of her head against a rock, knocking herself unconscious.

Back up the trail, Akram lay writhing on the ground, crying like a child, never having known such pain in his whole life. His entire essence was consumed by the throbbing agony, every labored breath felt like a desperate gasp for life. He vomited and shivered, sucking the vomitus back into his throat, choking and gagging as he attempted to expel the burning bile from his chest.

After what felt like an eternity, the pain at last began to subside, and he gathered his knees beneath him, hacking up the phlegm and bile lodged at the back of his throat. As his mind began to clear, he realized with much shame that this agonizing, humiliating experience was entirely his own fault. Allah had found him prideful in his victory and seen fit to punish him for indulging in physical arousal over the infidel woman at a time when he should have been focused on completing the mission. There would be time enough for earthly pleasures, but for now the enemy was almost certainly still searching for him, and his first responsibility was to escape and to evade, to ensure his further service to Allah.

Groping about, he found the rifle and used it to steady himself as he got back to his feet, the lingering ache in his testicles a grim reminder that he had been dealt more than a glancing blow. He slipped the infrared monocular back on over his head and hobbled off down the trail in search of the woman. He found her about fifty yards down the slope, sprawled pathetically among the brambles with her hair a tangled mess of twigs and leaves, the side of her face split and bleeding.

He smacked her awake, and then grabbed yet another handful of her hair and pulled her to her feet, shoving her forward down the trail and giving her a kick in the rump to get her going. She had made her obligatory play at freedom, and he could respect that. But she had failed — and failure was stupid.

72

Oso kept his nose to the ground as he led Gil quickly away from the burning house to the northwest, and Gil soon realized that Marie had gone up the rocky slope west of the ridgeline overlooking the ranch. There were more than four hundred yards of open terrain between the house and the base of the foothills, and he couldn't see anyone in his infrared NVGs. He didn't entertain any fantasies that she had let out on her own; she never would have abandoned her mother by choice, not even to save her own skin. This meant she'd been taken as a hostage, or worse, and he didn't kid himself about his chances of getting her back alive. The men who had taken her would be more than willing to give their own lives in exchange for hers, and quick, painless death wasn't exactly part of their creed. They specialized in revenge, and quality vengeance called for the infliction of as much human suffering as possible.

Gil felt like a man riding out to meet the end of the world, and the Remington gave him little comfort. He'd have sooner faced down an atomic explosion with a squirt gun than what he was expecting to face up in the foothills, and for the first time in his life, he understood what true fear really was: true fear was not being able to protect those you loved. He didn't dare pray or to even hope for the best. He'd dealt out enough death and misery in his time to know better. Eventually the bell tolled for everyone, and to ask for an exception in your own case was cowardly and pointless.

He did chance to make himself one promise: no matter what else happened up there in the dark, he was going to kill every last son of a bitch on the mountain who had so much as looked cross-eyed at his wife, and if that meant God got his ass whipped in the process, so be it. He wasn't asking any quarter, and he sure as hell wasn't giving any.

He followed Oso up the slope with the Remington resting butt down on his thigh, finger on the trigger, and the reins in his left hand. He was putting a lot of faith in his body armor giving him an edge, but what the hell, he was up on a horse, practically daring the enemy to pick him off. What else was he going to put faith in?

About halfway up, Oso began to whine, smelling the excess adrenaline in the microdroplets of Marie's perspiration and knowing that she was in danger. Gil knew by the dog's rising anxiety that the scent was getting stronger and decided to dismount, knowing it would be safer to continue the pursuit on foot.

The Remington exploded in his hand, shot completely in half. A piece of the synthetic stock embedded itself deep in the side of his neck. The stallion started and reared up. Gil fought to stay in the saddle, knowing that a second shot would be on the way any second. Then the stallion dropped like a dead buffalo, its heart blown apart by a .50 caliber round. The shot echoed through the valley as Gil rolled clear of the dead horse. A third shot penetrated his Kevlar IBH helmet at an oblique angle on the left side of his head, tearing a half-inch furrow along his scalp front to back an inch above his ear. It grazed his skull, scorching the bone and knocking him cold.

He came to a minute later, with Oso licking and pawing at his bloody face. Gil stood up and tore the fractured helmet from his head. The NVGs were totaled, and one look at the Remington told him that the night-scope was equally fucked. He took a step, and the world began to spin. He lost his balance and toppled over. Clawing back to his feet, he forced himself to take another couple of steps, but he toppled over once more.

He groped to his knees. Fighting to stay conscious, Gil grabbed Oso and unbuckled his collar, tossing it aside so the enemy above would have nothing to grab onto.

"Go get your mama!" he said, knowing he was sending the dog to his death. "Get your mama, Cazador! Kill the motherfuckers!"

He smacked the big Chesapeake Bay retriever on the rump, and Oso took off up the slope. "I'm right behind you!"

The world began to spin again, and he fell over.

A short time later, a man screamed somewhere up over the rise. A few seconds after that, Oso let out a horrible cry of pain, and Gil experienced an adrenaline surge strong enough to bypass the scrambled circuitry in his brain. He shoved himself to his feet and drew his .45, scrambling clumsily up the trail.

73

MONTANA

Marie knew that Akram would eventually rape and kill her, so if she was going to survive, her only hope was to stall for time and pray that someone caught up to them.

She pretended to pass out and fell to the ground.

Akram didn't waste any time playing her game. He delivered her another swift kick in the butt. "Get up!"

The blow hurt like hell, but she continued to feign unconsciousness.

"If you don't get up," he said calmly, "I'll piss on your face."

Marie certainly didn't want that, but it was better than getting killed, so she continued to play opossum.

"Stupid bitch," he muttered, reaching down to unzip his fly.

A dog snarled in the fog, and he turned just in time for Oso to slam into him full

484

tilt, sinking his teeth into Akram's groin and taking him to the ground, thrashing his head from side to side like a frenzied mako shark.

Akram screamed and stabbed at the furious animal's head. The blade glanced off the dog's skull, partially severing the ear, but Oso continued to thrash. Akram felt something pull free inside his scrotum, and he panicked, stabbing the dog again. This time the blade sank deep into the dog's shoulder. Oso howled in pain and reeled away with the blade embedded to the hilt.

Akram rolled to his knees and reached to grab the TAC-50.

Too late, he saw Marie's foot coming at his face. The toe of her boot caught him under the chin, and his head snapped back. He rolled over and caught her leg as she tried to kick him again, twisting her knee to bring her down and jumping up. He drew a Beretta from the holster at his side.

"Now I'm going to kill your fucking dog!"

"Machine gun — left flank!" a voice boomed through the fog at the top of the rise. "Kill anything that fuckin' moves!"

Akram wheeled around, unable to see where the infrared binocular had fallen during his fight with the dog. Believing he might already be surrounded, he aimed the Berretta at Marie, but in the split second before pulling the trigger, he realized the report of the pistol would bring the enemy right down on his head, and he suddenly realized that he wasn't yet ready to die for Allah. He holstered the weapon and grabbed up the TAC-50, taking off down the hill with one thought in mind: saving his hide. He gripped his groin as he ran to keep his injured testicles from jouncing around inside his trousers.

With the first signs of twilight now visible in the east, Gil appeared out of the fog gripping his 1911 pistol. He saw Marie sitting against a rock bound, gagged, and bleeding. He rushed to her side, pulling down the strip of cloth that held the gag in place and tossing her panties into the brush.

"Are you okay?"

"Thank God, you're alive!" she sobbed, seeing the horrific wound to his head.

"Where are they, baby?"

"It's just one. He took off down the trail. Cut me loose!"

Holding a small penlight in his teeth, he took a folding knife from his harness and carefully cut the bootlace from around her wrists. Her hands were purple and swollen.

"I can't feel a thing," she said, flexing her fingers. "I can barely move them."

"They're gonna hurt bad once the blood

gets flowing." He smoothed her hair back from her bloody, grime-covered face and kissed her.

"I'll be back."

"Forget him," she said, grabbing his arm. "Help Oso. He's over there in the scrub."

Gil found Oso in the brush, lying on his side with the knife protruding from his shoulder. The dog was panting heavily, his heart was racing. Gil pulled the knife out slowly, and the dog whimpered, but once the blade was free, he rolled to his belly and got to his feet, holding the injured foreleg off the ground, licking Gil's face, with his left ear hanging crookedly from the side of his head.

The sight of his battered wife and carved-up dog was enough to mitigate completely any and all ill effects the bullet had caused. Angrier than he'd been in his life, Gil stood and took an emergency flare from his harness, firing it into the air back toward the ranch. Then he pulled a strobe light from the same pouch and switched it on, setting it down on a rock.

"The team will be here soon. I'm goin' after the cocksucker."

"Don't. He's got that rifle."

"I'll shove it up his ass."

"Where are the men you were shouting to?"

"There aren't any." He shrugged and smiled. "That was just an old Davy Crockett trick." He crouched down to touch her face. "You gotta let me go kill this guy. He's headed for the logging road, isn't he?"

She nodded, touching his head wound, where she could see the white of his skull. "He said something about a truck."

He got to his feet. "He's takin' the long way. I'll get there ahead of him."

She glanced down to see that a sizable chunk was missing from his boot. "What happened to your foot, baby?"

He grinned. "That little piggy went to market."

74

MONTANA

By the time Akram stumbled from the trail and onto the logging road, he looked and felt like he'd just fought a running battle with a mountain lion. His face was torn and bleeding from crashing headlong through juniper thickets, and his injured testicles were throbbing. He ripped open the back door of a green Ford Excursion and tossed the TAC-50 onto the seat. He was reaching for the driver's door a moment later when he realized that both tires were flat on that side of the vehicle. In disbelief, he looked over at the second truck to see that it had been disabled in the same fashion.

"Ain't that a bitch?" Gil said, standing at the edge of the road twenty feet in front of the truck.

Akram looked up, shocked to see his enemy standing there in the dawning light bleeding from a head wound. He flexed the fingers of his gun hand, considering whether to go for the pistol, but he could see that Gil's holster flap was loose, so he chose to wait, allowing the arrogant American time to make a mistake.

"I like seeing you bleed," he said. "Your wife, she bleeds too. So does her mother."

Gil stepped fully into the road. "Ever seen a Gary Cooper movie?"

Akram smirked and stood up straight, squaring himself to face Gil directly. "Even if you kill me, there will be another and another — always another until you and your wife are both dead."

"Dog's ass."

Akram went for his pistol.

Gil jerked the 1911 and shot a hole through Akram's wrist before he could even touch the Berretta.

Akram held his arm in shock, scarcely able to believe a human being could move so fast with such accuracy. He stood gaping at his left hand now dangling uselessly at the end of the radius bone, the end of the ulna shot completely away. His knees gave out, and he slumped against the fender of the Ford.

Gil came forward to take the Berretta from his hip, tossing it over his shoulder into the brush. He holstered the 1911 and stood looking at Akram, the heel of his hand resting on the butt. "I reckon you can guess what happens now."

Akram spit in his face. "The bomb goes off. That's what happens . . . and there's nothing you can do about it."

Gil reached to take hold of Akram's nearly severed hand, twisting it around.

Akram screamed, sinking to his knees beside the wheel of the truck. "Allah will punish you! He will punish all of you!"

Keeping a grip on the hand, Gil stood looking around. "Well, in the meantime, you can tell me where to find the bomb."

"Fuck you!"

Gil nodded. "I figured you'd say that." He gave the hand a powerful jerk, and the ligament popped as the appendage broke off the end of the bone.

Akram screamed, clutching the bleeding stump to his chest.

Gil crouched down, holding the hand as if it were nothing more significant than an empty glove. "Here's the deal, partner. You're gonna do the right thing and tell me where to find that bomb, or I'm gonna do some horrible shit to you — the kind of horrible shit *you* people do. Is that what you want? You want to look out there in the road and see your body parts layin' in the dirt?

Because that's what you're gonna see. Just as sure as God makes little green crocodiles, that's what you're gonna see." He tossed the hand out into the road, where it landed palm down and flopped over. "See there? That's the beginning."

Akram stared back at him, his eyes burning with defiance.

Gil jabbed a thumb into his eye, and Akram jerked his head back, whacking it against the fender of the truck.

"See how silly it gets? How fast a man loses his dignity? This is why you don't let yourself be taken alive." Gil shook his head. "Just tell me where to find the goddamn bomb." He jammed a thumb deep into Akram's other eye, and the man's head bounced off the fender again as if they were playing out a macabre Three Stooges parody.

Half blind, Akram swatted at Gil's eyes, but Gil grabbed the hand, twisting it hard around until the wrist snapped. Akram screamed, and Gil adjusted his grip, getting to his feet as he continued to twist the arm, popping the elbow and jamming his bloody boot hard into Akram's armpit to dislocate the shoulder. Akram sprawled with his face in the dirt, bawling out loud, and Gil let the ruined arm drop to the ground.

"And these are just the prelims." Gil crouched back down, picking up a stone and tossing it down the road. "You gotta understand me when I tell ya this *ain't* Guantanamo. Hell, this ain't even Afghanistan. This is downtown hell, and you're on the corner of Main and Broadway with the devil's boot on your neck." He took hold of the now-quaking Akram to help him sit up against the tire, drawing his Ka-Bar and placing the blade alongside Akram's nose. "Now, you tell me where to find that fuckin' bomb — right *fuckin'* now — or you're gonna get the VIP tour! And I absolutely do *not* mean maybe."

Akram's eyes were too badly injured to keep them open, but he could feel the cold steel against his face, and he knew what it meant. With shock setting in, he shivered uncontrollably, swallowing hard before mumbling, "San Diego."

Gil cut off his nose and Akram screamed.

"Don't lie to me!" Gil grabbed one of his ears and laid the blade alongside of his head. "We know it's in DC! Tell me where!"

Akram clutched his face, screaming in pain and horror. "Washington was the primary target, but the bomb never got there!"

Gil cut off the ear and Akram went berserk

with impotent rage, beating ineffectually on Gil's leg with his one good arm as Gil grabbed a handful of his hair and began to slowly scalp him. "Where's the fucking bomb, asshole?"

"San Diego!" Akram shrieked. "San Diego! *San Diego!*"

Gil let go of his scalp and crouched down in front of him. "Where in San Diego?"

Akram began babbling prayers to Allah, his blood pouring down over his face. "I don't know," he stammered, shivering like he was attempting to shit a peach pit. "Kashkin. Kashkin's people have it. The Chechens. The bombs were Kashkin's plan . . . Kashkin's plan."

Gil stood up and drew the 1911. "Shovin' my wife's panties in her mouth was the single dumbest thing you *ever* fuckin' did." He put the muzzle to the top of Akram's head.

Crosswhite and a pair of SEALs burst through the brush, ready to throw down with their M4s.

"Wait!" Crosswhite shouted.

Gil pulled the trigger, and Akram fell forward onto his face. "Wait for what?"

"What the fuck do you call that?" Crosswhite said, his chest heaving from the near-legendary run up one side of the mountain and down the other.

Gil holstered the pistol. "Due process. Did you find Marie?"

"Yeah, she's fine. The dog too." Crosswhite kicked the hand from the road and came forward. "Alpha and Shearer are carrying them down to the ranch." He pointed at the body. "He have anything to say before you blew his brains out?"

"Yeah. Gimme the sat phone. I gotta call Pope."

Crosswhite gave him the phone, and he got Pope on the line.

"Bob, it's Gil. Listen, the bomb is *not* in DC. It's somewhere in San Diego. The DC bomb went off in New Mexico."

"How do you know?"

"Because Akram al-Rashid just told me."

"Gil, we have to be sure. Are you *sure* he's telling the truth?"

Gil looked down Akram's battered body. "I'd bet my life on it, Bob."

75

LANGLEY

Pope hung up from talking to Gil and immediately called the president.

"What do you mean it's in San Diego?" the president asked, his aggravation clearly evident. "How the hell could Shannon possibly know that?"

Pope told him what little he knew.

"And al-Rashid just volunteered that information?"

"I doubt it was that simple, Mr. President."

"Look," the president said, "NSA and FBI have both looked at the Kashkin files, and they concur with your DC assessment. All of our resources are moving toward the East Coast, and now you're changing your mind because of a forced confession?"

"Mr. President, we know there were two bombs. It makes sense the enemy would choose targets on opposite coasts, and the

Pacific Fleet *is* based out of San Diego Bay. We have two nuclear aircraft carriers in port there right now — priceless targets in the eyes of the enemy."

"Look, we've already got everything moving toward DC. If we pull back now, and you're wrong . . . Christ, I don't even want to think about it! How do we know it wasn't the other way around? How do we know it wasn't the San Diego bomb that went off in New Mexico? Al-Rashid could very easily have lied about that."

Because of the carriers, Pope believed in his bones that the target was San Diego . . . specifically, San Diego Bay. "Please trust me on this, Mr. President."

"I'll have NSA and FBI look at the files again," the president said. "Right now I've got my hands full trying to figure out how we're going to deal with the possible invasion of South Korea."

Pope was off the phone a short time later, scanning back through Kashkin's files. An hour passed without him finding a single piece of evidence to even hint at San Diego.

Midori, his assistant, sat across the table scanning through Kashkin's browser history but could find nothing related to the West Coast. "Maybe he used a separate computer for each target," she suggested.

Pope glanced over. "It's possible." He reopened Kashkin's email account, since those files wouldn't be specific to either computer. A half hour later, after skimming dozens of innocuous emails for the second time, he clicked on an email marked "no subject" that Kashkin had sent to someone in Chechnya the month before. He had opened it earlier but hadn't seen anything about DC, so he had quickly moved on to the next email.

Opening the note, he paged down to find a list of ten real estate addresses . . . all of them on Coronado in San Diego Bay.

He grabbed immediately for the phone, starting to dial the president, but then he thought better of it and called Gil instead.

"Gil, it's Pope. I've got a question for you: If the chips were down, and you had to call on one of the West Coast SEALs to save your butt, who would it be?"

76

SAN DIEGO BAY,
Coronado Island, a Half Mile from the USS
Ronald Reagan *(CVN-76)*

Kashkin's nephew Bworz sat in a recliner in the corner of the tiny living room, watching television as he listened to two of his men squabbling in the kitchen over who had eaten whose food out of the refrigerator. With eight men living in the small two-bedroom house, unable to go outside except for at night for fear of raising the suspicions of the neighbors, it was becoming rather cramped, and the men were growing increasingly edgy.

He went into the bathroom and closed the door, looking into the mirror and lifting his upper lip to check his gums, which had begun bleeding the day before. At first it had scared him, realizing he was suffering from radiation poisoning, but then he decided it didn't matter. The idea of dying didn't frighten him. He welcomed it. He'd lost his wife and son to the Russians years earlier, leaving him with nothing to live for but the jihad.

In addition, his uncle Kashkin had not yet returned from Montana, and there had been nothing in the news about Gil Shannon's death, so Bworz had come to the conclusion that Kashkin was either dead or captured. If that was the case, he and the men would have to stay with the bomb right up until the moment of detonation. His uncle was a brave and dedicated man, but no one was immune to torture, and the Americans would surely torture him to find an atomic weapon.

His only worry was that the men might see the blood on his teeth and realize that radiation was leaking from the bomb. If that happened, they might desert him, so Bworz was careful to take a drink of water before talking.

He urinated and then went into the kitchen, where the two men were still arguing, refilling his glass at the tap and turning to watch them. He took a drink and then set down the glass.

"Shut up. The both of you. I'm tired of listening to it."

They stopped and looked at him.

"When is Kashkin coming back?" one of them asked irritably. His name was Tomas.

"He's not."

"How do you know?" said the other. "Has he called?"

Bworz shook his head. "He would never risk exposing our location to the NSA."

"Then we should leave," Tomas said. "We've planted the bomb, so our job is done."

"Our job is *not* done," Bworz said. "We must now remain with the bomb until the end — in case Kashkin was captured and forced to talk."

Overhearing this, the five men sitting in the living room quickly came crowding into the kitchen.

"What's this now?" one of them asked.

"If Kashkin doesn't return," Bworz said, meeting their gazes individually, "then we must all remain here with the bomb until *the* day. Until *the* moment. My uncle is a devout man, but no one can stand up to torture for very long — as some of you know from personal experience. It's a risk we cannot take."

"So change the timer," Tomas said. "Set it for five hours and let's go."

Tasting blood, Bworz took another drink of water. "Only Kashkin knows how to change the timer."

"Oh, well, that's bloody convenient!" Tomas said in British English. He had studied in London. Only half the men understood what he'd said.

Bworz stared at him. "Are you afraid, Tomas?"

"I fear only Allah," Tomas said. "His judgment. If we have to die, we have to die. But *do* we have to die? That's the real question. What will be the point in staying if we can't self-detonate the bomb in the event the house has been compromised?"

"To defend the bomb," Bworz said, "or to move it."

"I don't like it," one of the men said. "We could never defend this house from a military attack, and they *will* attack if they think there's a bomb here."

"It doesn't matter," Bworz said, deciding to gamble. "There's no point to leaving. We're all dead anyhow."

"What's that mean?" Tomas said.

Bworz bared his teeth to show them the blood. "We've all been poisoned. The bomb is leaking radiation. I've been around it longer than any of you, but not by much. So you all have a personal choice to make. You can die here with me, painlessly and for the glory of Allah, or you can run away like cowards to die a coward's death. Because I tell you this, brothers . . . cancer stalks us all. And the only cure is to die."

One of the men dropped his gaze to the floor, muttering, "It is God's will."

Bworz set the water glass down on the counter and slipped through them toward the living room. "The choice is yours. I'm going to pray."

77

SAN DIEGO

Lieutenant Commander Jedidiah Brighton of SEAL Team III was eating breakfast with his wife and son in their home just north of San Diego when his iPhone chirped on the table. He sat chewing as he thumbed at the screen to check the message.

His wife, Lea, saw him make a face as he pushed the phone aside. "What is it?"

"A list of addresses over on Coronado. Some real estate idiot must be spamming the shit out of everybody in the county."

"Dad, you just said a cuss word," said his six-year-old son, Tony. He had the same blond hair and bright blue eyes as both of his parents.

Brighton winked at the lad. "Daddy's allowed."

"Yes, Daddy's allowed," Lea said, "but that doesn't mean he should do it, does it?"

"He said *shit*!" Tony declared proudly.

Brighton laughed.

His wife frowned. "Quit encouraging him."

"It's not a big deal."

"No? Then *you* talk to his teacher the next time she calls." She got up from the table and went to the refrigerator. "He's been in kindergarten only a couple weeks, and she's already called twice about him swearing at the other kids."

Brighton suppressed a smile and looked at his son. "No more cussing in school. Got it?"

The boy nodded, scooping Cheerios into his mouth.

"What did he say, anyhow?" There was the twinkle of mischief in the SEAL team leader's eye.

Lea frowned. "We'll discuss it later."

The iPhone rang, and Brighton glanced down at the name of the caller. "What the hell does *he* want?"

"Who?"

"Gil Shannon."

"Oh, the hero?" She cut into her pancakes with her fork. "Better answer it before you miss your big chance."

"Dad said *hell*!"

She glared at the boy. "Enough! Eat your cereal."

Brighton picked up the phone, deepening his voice. "Commander Brighton."

"Jed, it's Gil Shannon. Are you in San Diego?"

"I'm eating breakfast. What do you need?" There was no great love lost between the two SEALs. Gil had served under Brighton with SEAL Team III before his transfer to DEVGRU/ST6 on the East Coast, and even before the East Coast–West Coast rivalry became an issue, the two equally strong-minded men had never gotten along. To make it worse, Brighton knew most of the details of Gil's unauthorized mission to rescue Sandra Brux, and the fact that Gil had been awarded the Medal of Honor for it annoyed him to no end.

"Jed, the loose nuke's somewhere on Coronado Island. Bob Pope is emailing you a list of suspected addresses as we speak. You need to put together a crew and check them out ASAP. Today's September eleventh."

"What are you talking about?" Brighton set down his fork. "They've been evacuating DC for the past twelve hours."

"I know, but DC's not the target. It's NASNI." The Naval Air Station North Island.

"There's been no intel to that effect that

506

I'm aware of." Brighton sat back from the table. "You're not even with the teams anymore. What the hell's going on?"

"What's he talking about?" Lea whispered.

Brighton held up his hand to quiet her.

"I'm with ST6/Black now," Gil went on.

"Fuck, why doesn't that surprise me? I thought they were disbanded."

"Dad just said *fuck!*"

Lea pointed a slender finger across the table. "You're cruisin', buster!"

"Jed, look . . . they want to fry the base and take out the carriers. You and I don't have to like each other, but I called you because you're the go-to SEAL on the West Coast. And you know me. You know I wouldn't break it down like this if I thought there was another way. In a couple hours, a two-kiloton Russian nuke is gonna level that island."

"What about FBI? DHS? Why aren't they moving on this supposed intel?"

"I don't have the details, but I suspect they're tangled up in a pissing contest with Pope. It's typical G2 bullshit, Jed, and Pacific Command is gonna pay the price." He let out an exhausted sigh. "Jed, listen . . . I'm at my ranch in Montana, where I just debriefed one of the AQAP insurgents who burned down my fucking house and beat

507

the hell out of my wife."

"You're shitting me! What the fuck happened?"

"There's no time to explain anything. What matters is that I gave this asshole the VIP treatment, and he gave me San Diego as the target. So are you gonna trust me on this, or are you gonna let the idiots in G2 fuck the West Coast teams right out of existence? I know you're all a bunch of candy asses out there, but I like to think even a West Coast frog is smarter than that."

Brighton would have preferred to think that Gil had lost his mind, but he knew in his gut that he hadn't. "This coming from the SEAL who was awarded the Medal of Honor as a device for political propaganda."

Gil chuckled. "Now, there's a point we *do* agree on."

"Fuck," Brighton muttered, running a hand over his closely cropped head, agreeing it was probably time to bury the hatchet between them. "Is Marie gonna be okay?"

"Yeah. She got the shit kicked out of her, but she's gonna be all right. So did I call the right frog or what?"

Brighton got to his feet. "I'm moving now. Call me back with any additional intel."

"Roger that. Good luck, Commander." Gil broke the connection.

Brighton put down the phone and took his wallet from his back pocket, pulling out five hundred dollars in cash and giving it to his wife.

"What the hell is this for?"

He picked up his son from the chair and kissed his face. "I want you two to get in the car and drive east. Don't stop until dark or until you hear from me. Keep the radio on. If you hear anything bad, you turn south for Texas and head for my parents' place."

"Bad like what? Bad like what, Jed?"

"The nuke is here — here in town — and I gotta go find it. There's no time to go through channels."

"God *damn* Gil Shannon!" Lea pushed away from the table as her eyes began to fill with tears. "Why'd he have to call you? Of all the SEALs in San Diego, why'd that prick have to call you?"

Brighton held his son tight against him, his words catching in his throat . . . "Because I'm the best, baby."

78

SAN DIEGO BAY,
Coronado Island, Hotel del Coronado

Senior Chiefs Eddy Cox and Billy Caraway were both passed out on a pair of beach loungers in front of the Hotel del Coronado when Cox's iPhone began to chime. With standing orders not to leave the island now that the military stood at DEFCON 1, a number of SEALs from Team III had taken rooms at the hotel, and with the announcement the night before that DC was being evacuated, Cox and Caraway had spent the night drinking hard.

Cox didn't even look at his phone; he just pitched it out into the sand. But then Caraway's phone began to ring, and the two of them sat up looking at each other, bleary eyed.

"What the fuck?" Cox mumbled. "Better check who it is."

Caraway dug the phone from the pocket

of his surfer shorts. "Fuck, it's Brighton."

"Senior Chief Caraway," he answered, sounding surprisingly spry considering the volume of tequila he'd imbibed the night before. "What can I do for you, Commander?"

"Are you and Cox still at the Del?"

"Aye, sir."

"Listen very carefully, Senior Chief — and this is *not* for publication . . . the loose nuke is somewhere on Coronado, and we have to find it before 08:45. So gather your squad and meet me in the parking lot in front of the hotel. I'm crossing the bridge now."

"Aye, sir!"

"Do *not* draw attention to yourselves. We are *black*. Understood?"

"Aye, sir!"

Caraway sprang up from the lounger, glancing at the time before tucking away his phone. "Fuck me! It's already 07:00! Get up, dude! We gotta roll!"

Cox swung a leg over the lounger, putting a foot in the sand. "Fuck was that about?"

"The fuckin' bomb's here on the island! We're mobilized black!"

Cox looked up at him, suspicious as hell. "You takin' a shit?"

"No! Get the fuck up! He'll be here in five, and we gotta gather the squad."

A minute later, they were moving briskly through the hotel, which was crowded with international tourists flowing to and from the elaborate breakfast buffet. Constructed almost entirely of wood, the 680-room beachfront luxury inn had been the largest resort hotel in the world when it first opened to the public in 1888. The Del had since been the centerpiece for a number of feature films, including *Some Like It Hot,* starring Marilyn Monroe.

Topping the stairs to the second floor, Caraway turned left down the hall, and Cox turned right.

Caraway burst through the door of a room where two team members were bedded down with a pair of French girls they'd picked up the night before. "Stand to!"

The women quickly covered up as one of the SEALs came out of the john gripping a .45. "What the fuck, Senior Chief? I almost blew your shit away!"

"We've been activated, Santiago! You two be out front in three minutes!" Caraway disappeared down the hall.

Five minutes later, seven disheveled SEALs stood in a huddle in front of the Hotel Del dressed in flip-flops, shorts, and T-shirts.

"Okay, here's the skinny," Caraway said,

keeping his voice low. "There's a nuke loose on the island, and we got almost no time to find it. Brighton's on his way to dope us in on the details. But be advised we are black, so don't call anybody and don't say anything to give away our mission to the locals."

"I thought the bomb was in DC," one of them said.

"I don't know the backstory," Caraway admitted. "Maybe the CIA got it wrong. Maybe we're looking for a second weapon. All I know is that Brighton said we gotta find it by 08:45."

"Today's 9/11," remarked another SEAL, checking his watch. "First plane hit the tower at 08:46 eastern time, and it's already after ten o'clock back in DC. Hell, boys, I'll bet they got it wrong."

Cox spotted Chief Petty Officer Adam Samir coming out of the hotel with a gorgeous brunette on his arm. He smacked Caraway on the back. "Look over there: Ain't that Samir from EOD?" Explosive Ordnance Disposal.

"Yeah, get 'im!" Caraway said. "We might need him."

Cox slipped through the crowd to catch Samir by the elbow as he was stepping up to the valet booth. "Samir, I need to talk to you a minute."

Samir looked at him as he handed the man inside the booth the ticket for his car. "What's up?"

"It's private," Cox said, offering the woman a strained smile.

"Just a second," Samir said to his new bride. He led Cox up the sidewalk, spotting the other SEALs on the far side of the carport. "Make this quick. I'm on my honeymoon."

Cox felt his stomach fall. "The nuke's here on the island, and we're going after it. Commander Brighton's gonna be here any second. We might need you."

"What are you talking about? The nuke's in DC."

Cox shook his head. "Somebody fucked up. It's here."

Brighton pulled up in a black 2012 Ford Bronco, and the SEALs began loading in.

"That's him," Cox said. "Look, this ain't a fuckin' drill, dude. It's the real deal, and if we don't find the damn thing by 08:45, your honeymoon is over anyway."

"Shit!" Samir hissed, knowing that SEALs wouldn't joke about this kind of thing. "Gimme a minute." He went over to his wife. "Baby, you gotta get off the island."

"Why?" she said, her face tightening with fear. "What's wrong?"

"The bomb is here on Coronado. When the valet brings the car around, get in and go to your mom's up in LA. Don't stop for gas — don't stop for nothing. I'll be there as soon as I can."

"Adam, it's our honeymoon! Let somebody else go!"

"Who?" he asked. "Who else are they gonna find to do my job, baby? They're rolling right now, and I'm the only EOD guy here." He took her by the arms and kissed her. "I love you!"

The valet pulled up and got out, holding the door open for her.

"I'll call you soon as I can," he promised.

She was too angry and hurt to say anything. She just got into the car and pulled the door shut.

Samir had never felt like a bigger piece of shit in his life as he trotted over to Brighton's Bronco. Cox was holding the seat forward for him to cram himself in the back with the others.

"It's a stroke of luck you being here," Brighton said, shifting into drive and pulling out.

"With respect, sir, I don't feel lucky at all. What the hell is going on?"

"I was just briefed over the phone by SOG's chief spook back in Langley," Brighton said. "There's an RA-115 suitcase nuke here on Coronado . . . two-kiloton yield, gun-barrel detonator. Built with 1970s technology, but possibly modified."

"Conspiracy buffs have been talking about the RA-115 for years, sir."

"So you've heard of it. That's good. You know something about it, then."

"What I know, sir, is that it's a myth."

"Try telling that to the refugees living in those big white tents outside of Albuquerque, sailor. The isotopes from the New Mexico Event are from Russian uranium — and that's confirmed top secret." He took a sheet of paper from the dash and gave it to Caraway, who sat beside him in the middle. "We got ten addresses to check out. Now, which one of you maniacs runs around with the illicit weaponry in his rig? And don't tell me nobody!"

The five SEALs crammed into the back all looked at Senior Chief Cox.

"Uh, sir, that would probably be me," Cox admitted. "But I can explain. Most of it fell off an army deuce and a half that I was following back from —"

"Stow it," Brighton said. "I pardon you for your sins. Where are you parked?"

"That's my Blazer over there in the hotel lot, sir. The red one."

"A Chevy," one of the others muttered. "Good ol' Government Motors."

"Hey, fuck you, Mopar!"

Samir snickered.

They stopped behind Cox's Blazer, and he jumped out, opening the back door and unlocking a steel Knaack jobsite storage box.

Brighton looked inside. "Christ, Chief. Leave anything on base for the navy?"

"I like to think we're ready for anything, sir."

"I can see that." Brighton reached into the box and removed one of two Benelli 12-gauge entry weapons, giving it to Caraway. "Put that in my rig."

There were also a pair of M4s, an Mk 48 squad automatic weapon (SAW), a semi-auto SR-25 in 7.62 mm, and a pair of semi-auto US Navy Mk 12 Special Purpose Rifles (SPRs) in 5.56 mm. They divided up the weapons into two groups, loading half into Brighton's Bronco.

"Cox, you take four men and the SAW." Brighton tore the paper with the addresses in half, handing him the bottom of the page and checking his watch. The time was almost 07:30. "You take the five addresses here on the south end. I'll take Caraway and three other men north — the EOD man

517

comes with me.

"Now remember," he said. "Keep it casual. Don't go looking for a fight. Just knock at the door and have a quick look around. We're probably looking for Chechens, so if you see anything suspicious, hear anybody speaking with a Chechen accent, call us. SOG is working to get an FBI team in here on the quiet, but those gears are slow to mesh, so don't count on backup from law enforcement. For now, we're it. Any questions?"

"Yeah, what do we do if we actually happen to find the bomb?" Cox asked.

Brighton looked at Samir.

"Don't touch it," Samir said. "Secure the perimeter and call me. If there's a timer, be sure to sync it with one of your watches, but get the hell away from it. There's no telling what they've done to it or if it's even properly shielded. If it's really an RA-115, then it's old enough that the shielding may have corroded by now, and you don't want to be exposed." He looked at Brighton and shook his head. "Hell, sir, we don't have a goddamn Geiger counter."

Brighton put a hand on his shoulder. "If it makes you feel any better, son, I'll be right there beside you — no matter what."

79

SAN DIEGO BAY,
Coronado Island

Caraway studied the addresses as Brighton drove northeast up Orange Avenue. "Let's gamble and head straight up to Second and Alameda," he said. "That's practically right outside the main gate to the base — only about three thousand feet from where the *Reagan*'s docked."

"First, we'll hit the one on Sixth." Brighton hung a right past Spreckels Park. "We're right here anyhow." He pulled to the curb in front of a white split-level home with a Sold sign in front.

Caraway got out and sauntered up onto the brick porch, knocking at the door. He waited a minute, and then knocked again, harder this time. He heard a thump and stepped aside, wishing he had a pistol. A minute later, he knocked again. After three full minutes, he went back to the Bronco and spoke to Brighton through the open window. "No one's answering, but somebody's gotta be in there. I heard a thump."

"What kind of a thump?" asked one of the SEALs in back.

Caraway shrugged. "I don't know . . . a thump."

"What's your gut tell you?" Brighton asked, his head on a swivel, watching for trouble. "We're racing the clock here."

Caraway stood up, glancing back at the house. Then he reached into the truck and took out the Benelli 12-gauge with a fourteen-inch barrel. "I'm gonna have a look around back. If you hear this thing go off, you know we're at the right place."

The SEALs in the backseat primed their weapons.

Caraway disappeared behind the head-high shrubbery lining the walk leading around to the back of the house. All of the shades were drawn, and the house appeared to be deserted. He tried the knob on the back door. It was locked, so he took a step back and kicked it open. If the place had a burglar alarm, it was silent.

Caraway shouldered the shotgun and moved inside, his finger on the trigger as he crossed the empty kitchen. He smelled a faint odor of spoiled food coming from the fridge. He slipped through the dim of the empty living room and made his way to the foot of the stairs. On the floor by the front door was a small wooden knickknack sign that read "Home is where the heart is" in tacky red lettering. He picked it up and turned it over to see the tiny loop of wire on the back. He hooked it over the trim nail sticking out of the door and returned quickly to the Bronco, concealing the shotgun behind his leg from passing traffic.

He got in and took his sunglasses from the dash. "We can go. This ain't the place."

"What was the thump?" asked Samir.

"A friggin' tchotchke fell off the wall." He looked out the passenger window and shook his head, muttering, "Son of a bitch."

Brighton paused with his hand on the shifter lever. "What's wrong?"

Caraway lifted his foot. "I blew out my flip-flop kicking the door in."

One of the SEALs in back chuckled as Brighton pulled away from the curb. "You didn't bring your tactical flap-jacks, Senior Chief?"

Caraway took off both flip-flops and threw them out the window in disgust.

A short time later, they parked across the street from a single-story house on the corner of Second Street and Alameda Boulevard. It was a simple, boring-looking home with half-brick siding. The curtains were drawn, and an American flag flew from a pole mounted beside the house. Pope's email listed the place as having been up for rent, but there was no sign in the yard now, and there was a late-nineties Jeep Cherokee parked in the drive with Texas plates.

"Anybody else think this is the place?" Brighton said.

Caraway looked over the seat at the SEAL who'd almost shot him back at the hotel. "Santiago, gimme your piece. I'm going to the door."

Santiago handed over the Sig Sauer .45.

"Hold on a second," Brighton said. A pair of Coronado police cruisers pulled to a stop on the NASNI side of Alameda Blvd. "What the hell is this shit?" A faint smile flickered across his face a moment later as he imagined his son saying, "Daddy said *shit!*"

"Cat's out of the bag," Samir said. "SOG must have put word out over the wire."

"No," Caraway said, "SOG doesn't do that. This is something else. Somebody with the FBI must have sent word to the local fuzz." He checked the pistol to make sure there was a round in the chamber. "This is gonna get fucked up in a hurry, Commander. Whattaya wanna do?"

"Beats me," Brighton muttered, opening the door. "Everybody stay put."

Caraway gave the piece back to Santiago. "Somebody get Cox on the phone and tell him to roll this way."

They watched as Brighton made his way across the street toward the lead cruiser.

One of the SEALs kept an eye on the house. The curtains parted briefly and then closed. "I got movement inside."

"Everybody get ready to dismount the vehicle," Caraway ordered.

Brighton went around the front of the cruiser to the driver's door, keeping a smile on his face. "Good morning, Sergeant. I'm Lieutenant Commander Brighton, SEAL Team Three."

The cop glanced over at the Bronco, but with the sun glinting off the dark-tinted window, he couldn't see into the vehicle. Judging by the "bone frog" tattoo on Brighton's upper arm — along with his military bearing, the sergeant trusted that he was probably who he said he was. "What can I do for you, Commander?"

"I absolutely know how this is gonna sound, Sergeant, but I came over to find out what you guys are doing here."

The cop stared at him, sensing that the SEAL knew more about what was going on inside the home than he did. "We were sent over here to keep an eye on that house on the corner. What can you tell me about it?"

Brighton kept the smile on his face, feeling they were being watched by unseen eyes. "Sergeant, the Special Operations Group back in Langley has intelligence to indicate there may be a live nuclear weapon inside that house. To make matters worse, it could well be set to go off in less than an hour."

The cop glanced over. "You mean it's here? On Coronado?"

"Makes sense, doesn't it, with two nuclear aircraft carriers docked less than half a mile away?"

The sergeant got on the radio to the car behind him. "Mike, pull on past me down the block and park out of sight of the house."

The cruiser behind him pulled away to the east, and the sergeant looked up at Brighton. "You got more SEALs in your rig over there?"

"I do," Brighton said. "We were about to move on the place when you guys pulled up. Do you mind if I ask where your intel came from?"

The cop shook his head. "Mine came from dispatch; don't ask me where dispatch got theirs. Listen, I'm gonna pull over there behind my man and get on the phone to my captain. As far as I'm concerned, this just became a military operation — hell, we're thirty feet from the base. I'll let my people know the navy already has men on the scene in plain clothes so this doesn't turn into a big mess."

"Thanks, Sarge. Tell 'em we have an EOD man on the scene as well, will ya?"

The cop nodded. "What are you guys gonna do?"

Brighton smiled. "We're gonna get inside that house and disarm the weapon."

"Semper Fi." The cop winked and stepped on the gas, pulling away from the curb.

Brighton went back to the Bronco and got in. "The jig's up. This corner's gonna be swarming with local heat any minute, so it's now or never. Anybody got any doubts?"

"None," Caraway said. "They're in there peeking out the goddamn windows at us."

"We'll pull around the corner and double back on foot."

As they were pulling around the corner, three black SUVs came racing up the street toward the house from the south. The front door to the house opened, and two Caucasian men came running out with AK-47s, firing on the SUVs from the sidewalk before the drivers even had time to stop. The

SEALs opened up through the back window of the Bronco as Brighton made a right around the corner. He hit the brakes just out of sight, and the team dismounted in flip-flops and bare feet.

Caraway grabbed Samir. "Stay here. If you get hit, we won't have anybody to work the bomb."

The SEALs ran between the houses, making their way back to Second Street, where they spotted four bloody FBI agents crouched behind the wheels of their SUVs. Several agents were dead in the vehicles. One of the panicked survivors spotted the SEALs and fired his M4, hitting Santiago in the chest and killing him instantly.

"Cease fire!" Brighton screamed, knocking away the barrel of Caraway's Mk 12 before he could shoot the FBI man. "US Navy! Cease fire!"

"What the fuck are you doing here?" demanded the agent who had pulled the trigger.

"He's dead!" one of the SEALs shouted, his fingers on Santiago's carotid artery. "You motherfucker!"

Caraway grabbed his shirt and jerked him close, shouting, "Enemy front — eyes on!"

The SEAL forgot the FBI man for the moment and maneuvered for cover as a high volume of AK-47 fire from the house raked the line of SUVs. The sergeant and the other Coronado cop appeared at the corner gripping M4s as they maneuvered through the yard. They were both hit by grazing fire and immediately fell back under cover.

"The bottom of that house is brick," Caraway said. "It's gonna be tough reducing these guys in a hurry."

"We got tear gas in the last truck," the FBI man said. "But getting to it is gonna be a bitch. Those two guys who shot us up are still running around loose over there."

Brighton raised up to fire a few rounds from the SR-25, calling down the line to Caraway. "Chief, we still got two tangos loose outside the house. Call Cox and tell him to get his ass up here!"

"He's on the way!"

A Chechen dressed in jeans and a black T-shirt stepped from the shrubbery two houses down on the same side of the street and opened fire with an AK-47, killing all four remaining FBI agents and wounding another SEAL before Brighton dropped him.

Now only Brighton and Caraway remained combat effective.

"Fall back through the houses!" Brighton shouted, grabbing the wounded SEAL by the wrist and dragging him. "There's still another one loose in our rear!"

Caraway ran down the walk, grabbing the SEAL's other arm, and together they dragged him back through the neighboring yards to the police cars where the two wounded cops lay bleeding in one of the cruisers.

"Backup's on the way," the sergeant groaned, holding his gut.

"Where the hell is Samir?" Brighton said.

"The Arab lookin' guy?" The other cop pointed down the block. "One of those bastards took a shot at us from over there, and he took off after him with my M4."

Cox's red Blazer came screaming down Alameda from the northeast, screeching to a halt when Caraway ran out to flag him down. The naval air station across the street had gone on alert, and Marines were gathering at the gates along with armored Humvees bristling with .50 caliber machine guns.

Cox sat gripping the wheel. "We saw what happened to the FBI from the other end of the street and came around this way."

"We have to move on that house and take it now," Brighton said. "If the feds show up in force, they'll shut us down, and there's no telling how much time they'll waste putting together their master plan." He looked at his watch. "It's 08:15."

"Why haven't they just blown up the damn thing?"

"They probably don't know how," Samir said.

Brighton turned around to see the EOD man standing there with a long gash in his forehead, holding an M4. "Fuck you been, sailor?"

"Killing a Chechen," Samir said, wiping the blood from his face with his hand. "At least I think he's dead. I hit him pretty fucking hard with the barrel of this rifle."

Caraway grinned. "It's a carbine."

"Whatever," Samir said. "They haven't blown the bomb because they don't how to reset the timer, and it doesn't have a dead-man switch."

"How do you know all that?"

Samir looked around. "Because we're still here."

"Maybe they're just dedicated to their schedule," Brighton ventured. "Waiting till the last possible second."

"Sure, maybe, but would *you* be that stupid?"

Cox yanked the SAW from the front seat. "Hear all those sirens? We'd better move."

The six SEALs moved off past the houses, with the EOD man bringing up the rear.

The house on the corner came into view, and the Chechens inside began taking potshots at them.

Cox propped the SAW's bipod on a brick wall. "I'll pin 'em down. You guys flank left and right!" He opened fire on the front of the house, raking it back and forth in steady bursts of suppressing fire. The enemy was forced to take cover under the hail of fully jacketed 5.56 mm rounds. Brighton took Samir and one other SEAL across the street toward the north side of the house. Caraway and three others ducked between the FBI vehicles with M4s to flank south.

Sirens were screaming in from every direction now, police cruisers, ambulances, and fire trucks alike.

Caraway and his people ran around to the back door, firing directly into the house on full auto. Men inside began shouting to one another in panicked Chechen, realizing they were about to be sieged out.

Brighton and his men stopped at the side door on the north side, holding fire to await Caraway's imminent breach.

Cox's combat instinct told him the moment was ripe, so he bolted across the street and kicked in the front door, spraying automatic fire into a pair of wounded men laying on the floor.

Three Chechens came shouting from the kitchen at the back of the house. Cox summersaulted beneath their arc of fire, twisting around with bullets ripping into his legs as he let loose another murderous hail of fire, cutting through the wall and killing all three men as they became tangled together in their attempt to get clear. He ran out of ammo and tossed the SAW aside, grabbing an AK-47 from the dead man beside him.

"I'm in!" he screamed. "I'm in!"

He got unsteadily to his feet, bleeding from his legs as he stomped pugnaciously through the tiny house. Someone was shuffling around in the back bedroom as Caraway brought his men in through the back door. Cox limped down the hall to find a man shoving something into a crawl space at the back of the closet. He shot him with the AK-47 and dragged him out by the feet.

Caraway came into the room, seeing that Cox was badly wounded. "Whattaya got?"

"Get Samir," Cox said, sinking painfully to his knees. "The bomb's in the closet."

80

SAN DIEGO BAY,
Coronado Island, Inside the House

Bworz and Tomas stood peering out through a crack in the drapes as Commander Brighton got out of the Bronco and strolled casually up the block toward where the cruisers were parked on the north side of the house.

"He has to be here for us," Tomas said. "His truck is full of commandos."

"They're not commandos!" Bworz said sarcastically, slinging his AK-47. "Look how he's dressed. Use your head. They wouldn't send a man in sandals, they'd send the Marines. There are hundreds of them right across the street."

"Then who are those other men in the truck? They look like Marines to me."

"Yes, well, this island is full of military men. Rest easy."

Brighton began to pass out of sight around the corner, but they couldn't open the drapes to watch him for fear of being seen. "Someone check the other side of the house and see where he's going."

One of the men stepped into the bedroom on the north side of the house and came right back out. "There are two policemen parked right across the street. He's talking to them."

Everyone unslung and primed his weapon as he moved to take a firing position.

"Admit it!" Tomas said to Bworz. "They forced your uncle to talk. They know we're in here."

In his heart, Bworz knew it was true, but he didn't understand why the Americans were moving so casually. "Why would they send police instead of Marines?"

Tomas shrugged. "Does it matter?"

"Yes, you fool, it does matter! You don't send two policemen and men in sandals to retrieve an atomic bomb. You send Marines! And there are hundreds of them right across the street. Something is wrong here. Maybe Kashkin did talk, but if he did, they obviously don't completely trust his information. So keep your wits about you — all of you!"

He closed the gap in the drapes and glanced at his watch. They wouldn't have to hold out for long before it would be too late for the Americans to disarm the bomb. Kashkin had wired a series of booby traps and false leads into the detonator that would make it impossible for even an expert explosives technician to decipher the nest of wiring in under a half hour. Once there was less than twenty minutes or so left on the clock, it wouldn't matter whether Bworz and his men were still alive or not.

"He's going back to his truck!" called a man from the other room. "And the police are leaving."

Bworz smiled at Tomas. "See? They're unsure of themselves, and they're wasting time. We'll let them continue to waste time. In half an hour, we'll be in the presence of Allah, and these infidels will be burning in hell."

"Hey!" someone shouted from the bedroom on the south side of the house. "Three black trucks are racing up the street! They're coming right at the house!"

Tomas glared at Bworz and threw open the door to see three black SUVs screeching to a halt in front of the house. He tore off across the lawn firing from the shoulder, followed by another Chechen gunner, and Bworz kicked the door closed after them.

Running out to meet the lead SUV, Tomas fired point-blank into the FBI SWAT team as they attempted to dismount. His compatriot raked the other two trucks until his magazine ran dry, and both men disappeared down the sidewalk to reload, leaving more than half of the SWAT team dead or dying.

81

SOUTHERN CALIFORNIA,
Edwards Air Force Base

The president of the United States stood in the command center at Edwards Air Force Base watching a live UAV feed coming in from five thousand feet over Coronado Island. Most of his cabinet was present, along with the Joint Chiefs, FBI Director Don Lassiter, and Andrew Sloan, the acting director of the Department of Homeland Security.

General Couture stood off to the side, his arms crossed. He and the rest of the Joint Chiefs had urged the president to dispatch squads of Marines — already stationed on Coronado Island — to investigate the suspect addresses, causing both the FBI and DHS directors to pounce, insisting that direct action by the United States military was unconstitutional and that the FBI was prepared to deal with the situation.

The president had vacillated for an entire minute before giving the nod to the FBI and setting their agents in motion.

Now everyone stood watching as three black FBI vehicles drove up Second Street toward the house on the corner.

Couture checked his watch. At least a half hour had been wasted waiting on the FBI to arrive, and now they were racing boldly up the street like they were about to serve a warrant on a methamphetamine lab.

Moments earlier, there had been some confusion over who was in the black SUV that had already pulled up in front of the house, but when a man in sandals got out and sent the police cruisers up the street, the FBI director announced that it must be someone from the FBI's lead element.

This had made no sense to General Couture or to Colonel Bradshaw, who exchanged skeptical glances. What kind of an FBI agent showed up to a raid in flip-flops?

A collective gasp swept through the room as two men burst out of the house firing AK-47s into the FBI vehicles. Meanwhile, thin wisps of smoke could be seen coming from the front of the house as the Chechens inside opened fire on the survivors of the onslaught, who fell out onto the pavement on the opposite sides of the vehicles.

Watching the fiasco was too much for General Couture, and he lost his temper. "*This* is why you send in the goddamn Marines!" he announced in an unprecedented display of disrespect for the commander in chief.

Everyone turned around in surprise.

He looked directly at the FBI director. "What did those men think they were rolling up to out there, Don, a goddamn barbecue?"

"Hey, I don't have to listen to that! This is a highly —"

"The hell you don't!" Couture retorted, his menacing glare passing over everyone in the room, including the president himself, before coming back to the FBI man. "This is a goddamn *war*! And if you people aren't prepared to fight it, then you'd goddamn well better step aside! It's a simple concept, gentlemen . . . lead, follow, or get the hell out of the way!"

The president cleared his throat, and everyone gave him their immediate attention. "General," he said, pointing up at the screen, "do you have any idea who those men are?"

Couture's eyes widened as he saw Brighton and his SEALs maneuvering against the house where all the firing was coming from.

He knew instantly by the way they moved that they were spec ops troops. "My guess would be Navy SEALs, Mr. President."

"Which means Pope?"

Couture shook his head. "Sir, I have no idea. This operation is such a mess, I don't know how anyone possibly could."

There came another collective gasp from the cabinet as the Chechen in the black T-shirt stepped out from the bushes and gunned down what was left of the FBI contingent before one of the SEALs shot him dead.

Sickened by what he saw, the president turned to the national security director. "Get every available civilian asset to converge on that location immediately. Make sure the police understand we have undercover Special Forces men on the scene."

The security director nodded and disappeared from the room.

They watched as the SEALs stormed the house a short time later, with squad cars speeding toward the site.

"If they've got their finger on the button in there," Couture said, "now's when they'll blow it."

Within two minutes, the SEALs came running back out, waving the police away from the house, and a sense of urgency swept through the command center.

"My God, it's gonna blow," muttered the secretary of the interior, taking a step back as if there might be some danger in being too close to the screen.

The president looked at Couture, surprisingly calm. "Will we be able to see afterward? Or will it take out the drone?"

Couture looked at Bradshaw. "What's our altitude, Colonel?"

Bradshaw answered, "Five thousand feet, sir. The cloud of a two-kiloton explosion can be expected to reach an altitude of fifteen to twenty thousand feet, but that's not going to matter. The electromagnetic pulse from the blast will very likely fry the UAV's circuitry. I doubt we'll have a picture after detonation."

The president looked across at the acting director of Homeland Security. "Forget, DC, Andrew. Get your assets moving toward San Diego. It looks like we're in for a real nightmare."

82

SAN DIEGO BAY,
Coronado Island

Samir shouldered into the room, moving Caraway aside as he reached into the closet and grabbed the seabag by the strap to drag it out.

Caraway snapped open a Benchmade fighting knife and gave it to the EOD man.

Samir cut the seabag open lengthwise, took one look at the corrosion around the bottom edge of the bomb casing, and said, "Everybody out, now!"

The SEALs fled the house like rats from a sinking ship, dragging the wounded Cox along with them. Only Brighton stayed behind with Samir. "How bad is it?"

Samir knelt down to examine the dead man who'd been trying to hide the bomb when Cox shot him. He thumbed back the Chechen's lips, seeing he'd been bleeding from the gums for at least the past few days.

"This is radiation sickness, sir. You'd better wait outside. He's probably been getting sick for a while, but this room is hot."

"Lethal hot?"

The EOD man shrugged. "There's no way to know without instruments."

Brighton stood beside him, taking a Swiss Army knife from his pocket and opening the screwdriver blade. "Can you open that access panel with this?"

"Yes, sir," Samir said glumly, taking the tool. "I'll come out and let you know what I find."

They could hear vehicles pulling up out front, and they could hear Caraway hollering for everyone to stay out of the house, to get back, that the bomb's core was exposed — and to get a corpsman for the wounded Cox and his other SEAL.

The weapon itself was slightly smaller than a footlocker and almost as long. Samir unscrewed the six screws securing the access panel to the battered green bomb housing and carefully lifted it up, checking for booby-trap wires attached to the underside of it before setting it aside. The modern digital clock inside read 00:22:14:03 and counting in green numerals.

Samir looked up at Brighton. "Sir, there's no way I can disarm this thing in twenty-two minutes. Even if I had the necessary equipment, it's been rewired by an expert who almost certainly booby-trapped it. I'm sorry, but we're out of time. We have to get it off the island and out to sea."

"Which means a helo."

"Yes, sir. A helo with a kamikaze pilot. Can you fly a helo, sir?"

"No," Brighton said quietly.

"Well, we can't send him out there alone. I guess we'll be a three-man crew."

Brighton shook his head. "There won't be any point in you coming along, sailor."

"Sir, I've been kneeling beside this son of a bitch long enough already that I can probably guarantee myself a case of ball cancer within the year, and there ain't no fuckin' way I'm cursing my wife with that — not before she's had a chance to get pregnant with a healthy baby. Just get us a helo, sir . . . a fast one."

Brighton knew if he went outside and tried asking for a helo in all of that craziness, the bomb would go off before anyone could even make a decision, so he took his iPhone from his pocket and made a call.

Pope answered immediately. "I've been watching from above, Commander. I'm hacked into the overhead UAV feed. Do you have the weapon?"

"Roger that," Brighton said. "It's set to detonate in twenty-one minutes, and my EOD man says he can't disarm it in that amount of time. We need a helo, and we need it now."

"To get it off the island?"

"Right."

"That's almost no time," Pope said, "but I'll do my best. Stand by."

Brighton set the phone aside and looked at Samir, giving the bomb a kick. "I think it's got us. What do you think?"

Samir stood up and put out his hand. "Can I borrow your phone, sir?" He swallowed hard. "I need to call my wife . . ."

83

SAN DIEGO BAY,
Coronado Island, Naval Air Station North
Island

Ensign Joseph Fivecoat was an SH-60 Sea-
hawk pilot who specialized in search and
rescue (SAR). He was attached to the
maritime helicopter strike squadron HSM
71. They called themselves the Raptors, and
when they were not stationed at NASNI,
they were deployed with Carrier Strike
Group Three aboard the USS *John C. Sten-*
nis (CVN-74). Fivecoat was twenty-four
years old and three-quarters Cherokee on
his father's side. He'd grown up near the
reservation in western North Carolina as
the youngest of five children, entering the
navy through the ROTC program.

The moment the base went on alert, he
scrambled to his helo and warmed up the
engines in preparation for emergency takeoff. His CO had been taken off of flight

status the day before due to an ear infection, and so far no one had been assigned to replace him. He had no idea why the base had been put on alert, but he knew the national defense condition was set at Cocked Pistol, and he wasn't about to let his helo be caught on the ground in the event of an attack, so he kept the rotors turning slowly. He was still sitting in the cockpit awaiting orders when his squadron commander pulled up in a Marine Humvee and got out.

Fivecoat opened his door. "What can I do for you, sir?"

"Do you know where Second Street dead ends into Alameda?" the commander asked.

"You mean right outside the base, sir?"

"That's right. I just received a call from the secretary of defense ordering me to send the first helo smoking to that intersection. You're the helo with the rotors turning, so you get the nod. I don't know what the hell's going on, Ensign, but it's goddamn serious, whatever it is, so get this bird in the air and get over there." He clapped Fivecoat on the shoulder and shut the door.

Fivecoat didn't have time to even guess at what the helo was needed for. He was airborne within sixty seconds and flying southeast across the base less than two hundred feet off the deck. Within a few seconds, he could see the intersection of Second Street and Alameda Boulevard. There was a large circle in the street made of road flares, and dozens of cops and firemen standing around waving their arms like madmen.

"Christ," he muttered to himself. "Somebody real important must be dyin' down there."

He didn't like the looks of the power lines, so he chose to set down on base property right across the street inside the eight-foot perimeter wall where a pair of Marines were already opening a maintenance gate, apparently having anticipated his desire to avoid the power lines.

Before he had the wheels on the ground, the young ensign could see two men rushing toward the helo pushing a medical gurney. There was a green lump on the gurney about the size of the footlocker back in his billet. He noticed everyone cutting the gurney a wide birth while rushing past. Even the Marines moved quickly aside as the two men — one of whom was dressed in shorts and flip-flops — rolled the gurney through the gate onto base property and right up to the helo.

They each grabbed an end of the lump

and heaved it aboard the aircraft. The guy in flip-flops climbed in on the copilot's side, and the younger-looking Arabic fellow got into the back with the green lump.

Fivecoat saw the bone-frog tattoo on Flip-flops's arm and realized he was a Navy SEAL.

"Get us out to sea as fast and as far as you can!" the SEAL said over the whir of the rotors. "And keep it on the deck. We only got five minutes until the damn thing goes off."

Fivecoat stole a startled look in the back, where the younger man sat against the bulkhead staring at what he now saw was a green metal box. "Until *what* thing goes off?"

"That!" Brighton said, pointing into the back. "The nuke. They didn't tell you?"

Fivecoat shook his head, feeling cruelly betrayed. "Nobody told me shit — just to get the hell over here!"

"Fuck! You were supposed to be a volunteer!"

"I didn't volunteer for a goddamn thing!"

"Four minutes!" Samir shouted from the back.

Brighton looked Fivecoat in the eyes. "The choice is yours, son. You can take off and die a hero by saving San Diego Bay, or you can sit here on the ground and die with half a million other people. I'm sorry those are your only options, but we're outta fuckin' time here."

Fivecoat's mind went numb as his training kicked in, and he put his feet on the antitorque pedals. He twisted the collective lever to lift the helo back into the air and eased the cyclic forward, nosing the aircraft toward the Pacific Ocean. "If you're gonna jump out," he heard himself say, "now's the time."

Brighton smiled. "We're coming with you."

Fivecoat nodded, minding the power lines as the helo picked up speed and left the base behind, flying barely 150 feet off the deck toward the southwest. "If we fly due west," he said, grabbing a headset and handing it to Brighton, "we might still be too close to Point Loma when it goes off."

"Understood." Brighton pulled on the headset and adjusted the mike. "We go wherever you take us."

"Three minutes!" Samir called out.

"Does he gotta call out the time like that?" Fivecoat asked over the mike.

Brighton glanced into the back, where Samir's eyes were glued to the timer. "Yeah, I think he does. He's hoping it won't go off because of the corrosion."

Fivecoat nodded. "Okay, we're at a hundred forty-six knots. Maxed out at a hundred seventy miles an hour."

Brighton returned his gaze to the northeast, still able to see Point Loma. "Can you squeeze a little more out of it?"

Fivecoat frowned at him. "Who's flying this thing?"

Brighton could see the conflicting emotions in the young ensign's eyes: mixed feelings of betrayal and determination. "Look, for what it's worth, I'm sorry as hell about this."

"It's not all bad," Fivecoat said, looking forward at the horizon, wondering if he would feel anything when it happened. "I'll be the twenty-ninth Indian to win the Medal of Honor. That'll make my mother proud."

"I'm sure she's proud already."

"Two minutes!"

"Barely time enough to sing a song," Brighton muttered, thinking about his son. He hadn't called his wife because he was too afraid, too afraid of making her cry, something he'd been putting off for months now.

He chuckled ironically, befuddled by how much easier it was to die than to break the heart of a woman who did not deserve it.

He heard Fivecoat's voice asking him in the headset, "What's funny?"

"Nothing really. Just pondering my cowardice."

Fivecoat gave him a look. "You're willingly riding a fuckin' nuke into the wild blue yonder."

"Yes, I am," Brighton said. Then he laughed. "You bet your ass I am."

"One minute!"

Brighton looked into the back, the mirth still visible in his eyes. "Any last confessions?"

Samir looked at him for a sorrowful moment, but then his face finally cracked into a grin. "I used to jerk off to my aunt Rida when I was kid! She doesn't speak any English, but she's got great tits."

Brighton laughed. "Mine's worse. I was going to leave my wife for another woman." He smacked Fivecoat on the helmet. "What about you?"

Fivecoat looked at him with a melancholy smile. "One time I was —" He spotted the silhouette of a trimaran-hulled warship a thousand yards to starboard steaming due north at flank speed. "Oh, shit . . . we've killed the *Coronado.*"

Brighton whipped his head around, seeing

"The Crown of the Fleet," the USS *Coronado* (LCS-4), an independence-class littoral war ship designed with stealth technology to combat potential asymmetric threats in the littoral zones close to shore.

Brighton touched the glass with his fingertips. "Sorry, guys."

The RA-115 detonated just under seven miles southwest of Point Loma with a blast of 1.8 kilotons, vaporizing the helo and everyone aboard in a microsecond. The shock wave shot out to a radius of two kilometers, wiping out not only the *Coronado* but also three trawlers and a handful of sailboats. Hundreds of tons of sea water flash-boiled, and the mushroom cloud zoomed to almost twenty-thousand feet over the next few minutes, visible for miles inland.

84

The UAV did not follow the helo out to sea. It remained on station over San Diego Bay, with its powerful lens keeping the SAR helo in view as it picked up speed over the ocean less than two hundred feet off the surface.

"I don't understand," Hagen said, staring at the screen. "Why did those EOD men get on the chopper if there's nothing they can do?"

General Couture gave him a cutting glance, holding his elbow in one hand and resting his chin on his fist as he watched the helo drawing out across the ocean. He turned to the naval liaison, asking in a low voice, "It's a little late for me to be asking this, Ken, but have your coastal vessels been alerted?"

"Yes, sir," the navy captain replied, "but it looks like we may lose the *Coronado.* We don't know what happened, but she didn't get the message to leave the area until a few minutes ago."

The president turned around. "We're going to lose a war ship?"

"Unfortunately, Mr. President, it looks that way. We don't know if she misinterpreted the initial message to evacuate the area or if it was something else, but she was steaming directly toward the bay until a few minutes ago. If I had to speculate, sir, I'd guess she misinterpreted the initial message as a request for evac assistance back at NASNI. She does have a pair of Sea Stallions on deck."

"How many crew?"

"Seventy, Mr. President — give or take."

The president turned back around just in time to see a brilliant flash of light on the screen. Most everyone in the room let out a startled "Oh, my God!" The video feed briefly broke apart into fragmented pixels, but the interference quickly passed, and the growing mushroom cloud drew into focus just shy of the horizon from the UAV's elevated point of view.

From sea level, the explosion had taken place four miles beyond the visible horizon, which was approximately three miles out to sea.

The president turned to the acting director of Homeland Security. "Are your people converging on San Diego?"

"As we speak, Mr. President. Every single available plane, helicopter, truck, and rail car. We won't arrive organized, but we'll arrive more quickly than we did for Katrina. We're going to sort it out on the scene, just like they did at Normandy, Mr. President."

"Well, goddamnit, it's about time somebody gets it!" the president declared. He turned to Couture. "Please kill the feed, General. I don't want any distractions while I'm talking."

Couture signaled for the air force lieutenant to turn off the monitor.

"Listen up now," the president announced, more to his cabinet than to anyone else. "By the grace of God and through the self-sacrifice of some very brave men, we have managed to save a city from devastation, but the people of San Diego are going to be terrified of nuclear fallout. They are going to need our hands-on assistance and moral support. So get on the phones to your respective offices and make sure your people are ready to move on this in every way possible. If your particular office doesn't have a prescribed way of assisting in a crisis of this nature, I want you to invent one! Also . . .

be advised you will all be joining me in San Diego just as soon as it's deemed safe by the NRC." Nuclear Regulatory Commission.

He turned to Couture. "A word in private, General."

The two men stepped off to the side, with Hagen tagging along to stand just off the president's elbow.

"Mr. President," Couture said, "allow me to apologize for my outburst before. There's no excuse. I'll tender my resignation forthwith."

The president shook his head. "That's forgotten." He put his hand on the general's shoulder, obviously deep in thought about something. "General, I want you to draw up plans for another SMU as soon as possible, a Special Mission Unit purpose-built for domestic operations . . . something like ST6/Black, but more specialized. You'll work out the details with your people, but the unit's sole purpose will be dealing with nuclear weapons smuggled onto US soil. They should all be spec ops people, and there should be multiple teams on both coasts, able to respond to multiple threats at once. Also, they should be a classified unit — at least in theory. Understood?"

Couture hid his surprise well. "Yes, Mr.

President."

"Now for the crazy part," the president continued. "Bob Pope will run the SMU, and he will answer directly to the Office of the President. As far as I'm concerned, if there's no gap between the president and the launching of a nuclear weapon, there shouldn't be any gap between him and the team that hunts them down. I know Pope's a pain in the ass, but he's obviously the most qualified man we've got for the job right now."

Tim Hagen stepped close to the president. "Sir, now may not be the best time to start invoking new policies. Perhaps we should talk about this after —"

The president looked at him with an expression of annoyance. "Tim, I'd like *your* resignation by the end of the week."

Hagen's mouth fell open as the president led Couture away, continuing to verbalize his train of thought.

"This isn't the last nuke we're going to have to deal with, General. These people are going to try and try and try until they *get* us. I'm convinced of it now. Do you agree?"

"Yes, sir, I'm afraid I do," Couture replied. "It's the emerging threat of our time. What about Master Chief Shannon? Should I suggest to Pope that he be placed in charge of training this new SMU?"

The president nodded. "Yes. If you think Shannon will agree to it. Though, by now I believe he's likely to say to hell with us all."

Couture smiled. "Despite what we'd like to believe, Mr. President, men like Shannon and Pope don't work for us. They serve a higher power — an ideal. It's just our job to keep them in check. They're valuable assets, no doubt about it. But we're lucky they're as rare as they are."

EPILOGUE

A month after the detonation of the RA-115 off the San Diego coast, Master Chief Gil Shannon sat between his wife, Marie, and Senior Chief Terry Leskavonski (aka Alpha) among a large but intimate crowd of family and interested US Navy observers at Arlington National Cemetery, where four wooden caskets were displayed beside photos of Navy SEAL Lieutenant Commander Jedidiah Brighton, Ensign Joseph Fivecoat, Petty Officer First Class Adam Samir, and Navy SEAL Petty Officer Second Class Christian Santiago. Only Santiago's casket contained a body.

Back in San Diego, hospitals were still heavily burdened with people seeking treatment for radiation sickness both real and imagined. But the Federal Emergency Management Agency (FEMA), under the egis of the Department of Homeland Security (DHS), had arrived in force within twelve hours of the detonation event, and, despite a great deal of confusion, redundant actions, and rolling blackouts, they had succeeded in averting a citywide breakdown of emergency services like the one experienced in the wake of Hurricane Katrina.

As usual, the news networks were busy making famous numerous heroic and indefatigable Americans who stood out against the backdrop of the disaster . . . doctors who'd refused to abandon their patients in zones where fallout was the worst; police officers and firefighters who had remained in contaminated areas without adequate Hazmat protection until the last of the residents had been evacuated; and everyday Americans, for rescuing perfect strangers from assorted perils during the terror and mass panic that had gripped the city in those first twenty-four hours of contamination and darkness.

Parts of the city would remain deserted or quarantined for months, possibly years to come, and only time would tell how long before the dreaded signs of cancer would begin to appear, though some preliminary estimates were forecasting as many as thirty thousand deaths over the next ten years due to thyroid cancer resulting from exposure to the radioactive isotope iodine 131.

Al Qaeda and Chechen terrorist factions worldwide had been strangely silent in the days following the event, with no one claiming immediate responsibility for the attack. The talking heads on television had offered every explanation for this, from shock, to fear, to a "false flag" attack. By the tenth day, however, factions of both Al Qaeda in the Arabian Peninsula and the Riyad us-Saliheyn Martyrs' Brigade in Chechnya had not only claimed responsibility for the nuclear attacks but also had gone so far as to threaten a third attack within the year, which had immediately caused a brief panic among a very jumpy American populace; a nuclear threat was no longer just a threat, it had become an effective form of terrorism all its own.

For now, however, the nation was beginning to calm itself, though the "San Diego Event" was still just about all anybody talked about. The detonation may have occurred on 9/11, but the practice of referring to a disaster by its date had quickly become passé. It seemed the term "Second 9/11" just hadn't played all that well among early media focus groups, and the term "New Mexico Event" had already sort of set the standard for naming the nation's future nuclear attacks.

The president of the United States stepped up to the podium without notes of any kind, and there were no TelePrompTers or television cameras. The national memorial service for the four heroes was to be held the following day, and all the news networks were eager to cover it.

"It is an honor to speak here this morning," the president said, looking very solemn and presidential in the warm glow of the rising sun. "First, I'd like to ask that you excuse the informal nature of my address to you. Since we're gathered so privately here in this beautiful, most reverent of places, I'd like to speak to you with a bit more familiarity than would normally be possible for a man of my position." He cleared his throat and allowed his eyes to glide over the four deceased heroes' immediate families, who were seated in the front row. "We've gathered here for the purpose of remembering four brave men to whom this nation owes a debt we can never begin to repay. Men who willingly laid down their lives so that thousands of others might live. This type of sacrifice is not unheard of. It happens all too often.

"But seldom has such a sacrifice had such an acute impact on the human race. In fact, I'm not sure there's ever been a sacrifice in all of human history that compares — with the possible exception of the Crucifixion, for those of us who believe in it." He gestured toward the caskets and photos positioned to his right. "Because of these four selfless Americans, there are still, quite literally, tens of thousands of generations waiting to be born, and that's an incredible thing when you stop to think about it. It truly is. And this fact alone is reason enough to immortalize these brave men for the rest of human history."

The president spoke for another ten minutes, and when he was finished, he stepped aside, allowing Lea Brighton a few tearful minutes at the podium, followed by the elderly and well-composed Cheryl Five-coat. After Mrs. Fivecoat finished telling everyone how proud her son Joseph had been of being a helicopter pilot, a devastated Sheila Samir went to the podium. She broke down completely before finishing half of what she'd planned to say, and spent an entire minute sobbing in the arms of the president, who was unable to prevent his own tears from spilling as he attempted to comfort her.

There was not a dry eye in the crowd by this point. Even Gil had to wipe his eyes, turning to whisper to Marie, "I have to give the man credit. He didn't have to do this today, but he wanted the widows to have a chance to be themselves before going to the national ceremony tomorrow. Kind of like a dress rehearsal."

Marie nodded, tears rolling down her own cheeks.

The day before had been their day of personal trial, attending a large funeral on the far side of that same national cemetery in which two SEALs from Gil's team, along with Buck Ferguson and his two youngest sons, all three of them former US Marines, had been lain to rest. Of the five, four of them had given their lives defending Marie and her mother, Janet, who was still in the hospital but due for release in the near future. (Both Special Agent Spencer Starks of the FBI and Oso Cazador were recovering nicely as well.)

Once Sheila Samir regained her composure, the president walked her back to her chair and helped her sit down beside Nancy Santiago, who was too shy to take the podium.

A US Navy rifle party standing fifty feet away and consisting of seven sailors dressed in the service dress blue "crackerjack" uniform, complete with the white "dixie-cup" cover, then executed a three-volley military salute with M14 rifles. A few moments after that, a US Navy bugler, dressed in the same uniform and standing out among the headstones a hundred feet away, began to play the bugler's cry of "Taps."

There were no flags on the caskets because everyone had agreed to save the flag folding and presentation ceremony for the cameras the following morning.

When the formalities were concluded, forty SEALs from SEAL Team III stood up from their seats and divided into two groups, with twenty men lining up in front of Lieutenant Commander Brighton's casket, and twenty lining up in front of Petty Officer Santiago's casket. Each SEAL removed the trident pin from his uniform as he filed past the respective casket, pausing to slap the trident down hard into the lacquered wood surface of the lid, being careful to keep the pins evenly spaced and perfectly straight. The slaps were audible at a distance, and when the SEALs completed the ceremonial display of respect for their fallen comrades, each of the two caskets looked as though it had been adorned with a single strip of solid gold inlay.

Gil turned to Alpha, speaking quietly into his ear. Then the two of them rose from their chairs, removing the tridents from their own uniforms, and walked up the center row toward the caskets. To everyone's surprise, they filed past the caskets of Brighton and Santiago, Gil stopping at the casket of Ensign Joseph Fivecoat, and Alpha stopping at the casket of Chief Petty Officer Adam Samir. Each man rose his hand above his head. Then Gil gave a nod, and they slapped down their tridents into the caskets at the same time.

ABOUT THE AUTHORS

Scott McEwen is the #1 *New York Times* bestselling coauthor of *American Sniper.* He is a trial attorney in San Diego, California, and has taught at Thomas Jefferson School of Law. He grew up in the mountains of eastern Oregon, where he became an Eagle Scout, hiking, fishing, and hunting at every opportunity. He obtained his undergraduate degree at Oregon State University and thereafter studied and worked extensively in London. Scott works with and provides support for several military charitable organizations, including The Navy SEAL Foundation.

Thomas Koloniar is the author of the post-apocalyptic novel *Cannibal Reign* and the coauthor of the national bestseller *Sniper Elite: One-Way Trip.* He holds a Bachelor of Arts degree in English Literature from the University of Akron. A retired police officer from Akron, Ohio, he currently lives in Mexico.